# ERIK THE RED

Tilman Roehrig

# ERIK THE RED

## A VIKING'S QUEST FOR A NEW WORLD

Translation by Oliver Latsch

Arctis

This is a work of fiction. Names, characters, places, and incidents
are from the author's imagination or are used fictitiously.

Arctis US

W1-Media, Inc.
Arctis
Stamford, CT, USA

*Erik der Rote oder die Suche nach dem Glück* first published in Germany
by Dressler Verlag, 1999
First English language edition published by W1-Media Inc./Arctis, 2020

Visit our website at www.arctis-books.com
Author website at www.tilman-roehrig.de

1   3   5   7   9   8   6   4   2

Library of Congress Control Number: 2020943692

ISBN 978-1-64690-003-9
eBook ISBN 978-1-64690-603-1
Translation by Oliver Latsch
Jacket design by Alexander Kopainski

Printed in Germany, the European Union

# CONTENTS

# SHARPCLIFF

He hadn't counted how often he'd walked the stony path from the meadow up to the farmstead and back, nor how often he'd passed the other servants and Erik. They'd all been exchanging jokes in the morning, but soon everyone had fallen quiet, silently battling sweat and weariness. *We're two-legged hay-creatures*, he thought, *and I will soon choke on this smell.*

He carried the hay-filled sailcloth on his neck and shoulders. It was his last load for the day, and having reached the barn, Tyrkir dropped his burden with a sigh. He folded the cloth and shuffled back across the yard, scratching at the fleas. The new biters were everywhere, under his tunic, on his neck and arms. The two vertical jambs, the crossbeam, and the driftwood door were all one could see of the main building, which otherwise was nothing but a long, grassy hill that seemed to smoke from its depths.

The scrawny seventeen-year-old stepped inside. He was greeted by darkness. The grassy sod between the floor supports smelled musty, and after three steps, he opened the inner door.

"Drink!" Erik was standing by the barrel right behind the entrance to the hall, his red hair matted with sweat. He grinned at Tyrkir, dipped the ladle into the sour milk, and handed it to the slave. "Our first harvest. Thanks to the gods! You will see how we get our steer and cows through the winter. Come spring, we'll have done it!"

Tyrkir quickly emptied the ladle. He dipped it in once more and drank again. Despite their difference in class, he and the son of farmer Thorvald had formed a deep friendship, even with Erik being three years older. "Tastes better than any beer back home!"

"This is home now." Erik clenched his fist. "Forget Norway. This is Iceland, and by Thor, this forsaken rocky land will not defeat us. Never."

"All right. I believe it. But the hay will only get us through a month." Before Erik could respond, Tyrkir added, "I know. We've found three more meadows with good grass. I know."

Erik threw back his shaggy mane and turned around. "It's getting better, Father. Our wise German thinks so, too. All will be well, you'll see."

He got no answer from the high seat near the center of the great firepit, which stretched like a glowing band through the main hall. The light from the embers flickered over the rows of rough beams supporting the ceiling before it faded into the dark of the two side rooms.

"Father, tomorrow we should drag the ship higher up the beach. Who knows how long this good weather will last."

There was still no answer. Erik squinted toward the fire. No wave of the hand? No nod from the mighty head?

Tyrkir shrugged. "The master is sleeping."

"Nonsense. My voice wakes everyone, even those without ears." But the jest quickly died on Erik's lips. The young men shot a glance at each other, then they both dashed toward the high seat. There was Thorvald, his back stiff, his gray-haired head against the backrest, empty eyes staring into the fire.

"Father?"

Tyrkir put his arms around his friend's trembling shoulders. They stood that way for a long time, as though waiting for the scene before them not to be true.

Outside, noise and laughter echoed down the hall. The other five male servants entered, along with two maids.

Tyrkir rushed toward them, his hands raised in warning. "Quiet! Stop! The master is dead." Unconvinced at first, they quickly saw the hard edge in Erik's narrow, freckled face. Realization set in. The women pressed their lips together; the slaves nodded. One of them let out a groan.

"Go outside and wait until you're called," Tyrkir said quietly before turning away.

Erik was already standing behind his father in the dark. Tyrkir approached him slowly, keeping close to the rough pillars on the right side of the hall. Catching the eye of a dead man could bring terrible misfortune. *Anything but that,* he thought. The danger was too great that the farmer's last thought would burn itself into his mind and torment him for the rest of his existence. He slipped into one of the side rooms and felt along the benches and tables until he found a woolen rag, then quickly started tearing it into small shreds.

The two young men worked together in silence. They were ready. Erik approached the high seat from behind, reached around, and closed his father's eyes. Now no more thoughts could escape from his eye sockets.

Only then did they dare step in front of the dead man. Quickly, they stuffed a woolen shred into Thorvald's mouth and used the other scraps to block his nostrils and ears. They could leave no opening for the spirit to slip out of the body's protective shell so it could go on to perform terrible deeds. Only after they'd sealed every one of Thorvald's seven openings did they step back.

"Why did he have to pass on like that? As a straw-corpse?" Erik muttered, slamming a fist into his hand. "Father was a brave Viking. If anyone was deserving of a seat in Valhalla—"

Tyrkir cut him off: "Not now. Later." He called in the maids, and under his stern supervision, they cut out Thorvald's toenails and fingernails. He threw them all into the fire; nothing could remain of them. Soon, the stench of burning keratin joined the thick smoke.

Erik ordered the other servants to assist him, had them move the tables and benches from behind the high seat, and then he strode in a straight line from the chair to the wall. He scraped the outline of a big square into the wall with his knife. "Begin."

The men removed the sod and earth from the joints, before carefully lifting out the stones one by one. Two of the men rammed their spades into the protective layer, while the other two went outside to work toward them. The earth kept caving in, and it took much effort to keep the tunnel to the outside as narrow as possible.

"It'll do." The twenty-year-old man lifted his father from the high seat. Tyrkir grabbed the feet and walked ahead, and so they shifted the dead master through the opening to the outside. They carried him a good stone's throw from the house, placing the corpse on a rock. "It's far enough."

Tyrkir folded his arms. Behind him, the servants had already begun to relay the bricks and patch the opening. They would soon have the six-foot-thick wall sealed again. "We will stand guard until we're sure the master's spirit won't find its way back into the house."

The two friends stared down at the ship and out to the restless sea. The day was fading. It was July, and the sun was setting again, though its pale glow would keep lighting the night as it wandered east, beyond the horizon to reappear from behind the rim of the earth.

"I mourn him. Had he known of his end, he would have asked me. I'm sure of it." Tears dripped into Erik's red beard. "One quick stab would have secured his eternal joy, but now he has to move to the domain of Hel."

Tyrkir understood his friend's sadness. The thought of his father spending eternity in the dim afterlife under the earth rather than enjoying feasts and joys with the gods was grim. Up there, in Asgard, honorable Vikings rode out every morning to meet on the battlegrounds and measure one another with axes and swords, sparks flying and blood flowing. After the battle, all wounds would close, and the warriors would go back to the shield-covered Valhalla to feast with the gods. Every day was a feast day and a celebration. The vat of mead would always be full, and there would be an endless supply of bacon and meat from boiled hogs.

But as Thorvald hadn't fallen like a warrior—since he hadn't himself determined the time and manner of his death—he would have to wander through darkness and cold to the realm of the goddess Hel. His path would lead him past roaring rivers, until he finally reached the golden bridge across the chasm, which would take him to the hall of the straw-dead. There, Hel reigned over all the shadows. She was awful to behold. The body and face of the cruel goddess were half black and half blue. Only her eyes glowed brightly. She would assign Thorvald his place among the silent masses, where he would endure nothingness, boredom without even the tiniest diversion, until the end of all time.

"The master was always good to me." Tyrkir picked up a pebble and rolled it in his hands. "When he bought Mother and me, I was afraid of him. I was so small and scrawny."

"But you are also wise and clever, and that impressed Father."

The servants called them. Only the fresh sod showed where the opening had been. They had done quick and thorough work. Now they came nearer to help with the body.

"He shall lie there, at the edge of the cliff," Erik ordered, "looking east over the sea. Dig the grave as deep as you can manage."

There was no wood for a coffin; it was too precious. All that grew here in the stormy northwest of Iceland were scraggly birches, and what driftwood they found on the beaches was urgently needed for building houses or making tools.

Erik secured his father's sword. He left him some bread and meat for his journey, and then they wrapped him in sailcloth before lowering him into the knee-deep grave. One last silent nod, and then the two friends formed the burial mound with rocks. They gave it the shape of a ship, the bow pointing due east.

"It's not enough," said Tyrkir. "Every stranger should recognize the master." He crouched down and cut some runes into a stick, then rammed the rod into the middle of the pile. Erik said, "Read it to me."

"'In memory of Thorvald the Brave.'"

"That is good and true." Erik nodded. "We will not forget anything, and he will live forever in our memories." He turned to the servants and maids. "Come to the house. Let's honor your master!"

The high seat between the two richly carved wooden pillars remained empty. After the meal, Erik had the servants tap their only barrel of mead.

Since their departure from Norway, Thorvald had guarded that barrel of intoxicating liquor like his own life. It was meant for their first Yulefest in the new land. Now it was tapped for a wake.

Erik stood close by the great fire. He looked across at the maids, and then at the servants by his side. "Let me call my ancestors!" There was nothing more important than the clan. It was the only refuge. A freeman answered to no lord; he was responsible only to his family, then to his neighbors, and then to his people. Their names formed the chain connecting the forefathers to their children's children. "Grandfather Asvald! Here stands the son of your son. Do you hear me? Bring your father, Ulf, and you, Ulf, bring your father, Oxenthorir, to us!"

Erik waited. The only sound was the crackling of the fire. Suddenly, the smoke stopped rising to the wind-eye, the opening in the ceiling. Instead, it drifted as a thick cloud through the hall, before it again formed a pillar of smoke straight up to the ceiling.

Tyrkir closed his eyes. He quickly thought of his ancestors far away in Germany. *Even if I knew your names, you would not hear me. Never would you come to sit with me, a slave.*

Erik continued. "Today, Thorvald joins you. He was honorable and proud, like you." Erik told of the campaigns and battles his father had fought, how he had built a farm in Norway and had become a farmer and trader. "He was respected and liked at all the trading posts...."

Tyrkir felt a sting. He no longer focused on the speech, his thoughts drifting to Haithabu on the banks of the fjord Schlei. It was where the Vikings had brought him and his mother after their raid on their home far south by the river Rhine.

*I was called Thomas then*, he remembered, *and I was just five winters old. And my mother?* He didn't recall her age, only that she had been beautiful and wise. And her smell when he snuggled up to her—he would never forget that smell. She'd served in the house of a slaver, carefully guarding her child, no longer raising him in the Christian way. "You have to live like these people. You have to think like them, or else you won't survive when they take you away from me."

Getting used to his new name had been hard. She'd begun calling him Tyrkir, instead of Thomas. "There is no god in Viking heaven like Tyr" was how she began every story about Valhalla, teaching him to be proud of his new name.

During the years that followed, Tyrkir had soaked up everything about his new surroundings. He'd only spoken German when he was alone with his mother. Otherwise, he'd spoken Nordic, like all the children in Haithabu. He'd soon learned every custom, and he'd learned to feel and think like them. His time in Germany hadn't been erased, but it had become a distant secret buried deep in his soul, one he rarely touched.

Tyrkir had lived eleven winters when the prosperous trader

Thorvald came with his ship from Norway and took a liking to the slave woman and her child. He'd paid a high price for them. His laughter had been so loud when he squeezed Tyrkir's mother to his side. The small boy had been terrified of him.

During their journey back to Norway, his mother had become sick, and by the time they reached the homestead in Jaedern, she'd had to be carried off the ship on a stretcher. She'd died a few days later. Tyrkir remembered the farmer cursing: "A bad trade! Not once did she entertain me, not once did she work in my household. I paid good silver for her."

Then he'd looked at the crying boy. "I don't want you, you scrawny thing. I'll leave you to the wolves."

Tyrkir had wiped his eyes. "Don't send me away, please," he'd whispered. "I have learned a lot, Master," and he'd shown how he could carve wood with his knife, how quickly he could build a fire. Then he'd dashed across the yard and back. "That's how fast I am."

The master had muttered into his beard. "And what else can you do?"

The little brown-haired German boy knew about herbs and healing plants. "My mother taught me. I also worked in the vineyards back home...."

"Wine?" Thorvald licked his lips. "The little mite knows how to press wine?"

"Yes, I learned it all from my mother," he'd lied. "Believe me, Master. I'm useful." Desperate, he'd spread his arms. "I also know the gods, all of them! Odin, Freya, Thor, and the wisest god, Tyr! He chained the wild hound Fenrir and bound him for all time. Well, he lost his right hand in the process.... But I still have two! Tyr is the best warrior and the wisest scholar. That's why Mother named me after him, because I'll become like God Tyr—"

"Quiet, you grub. None of us will be like a god." Thorvald had grinned broadly. "Your everything, everything, everything is going to clog my ears. All right, you may stay. I give you to my son Erik. And woe to you if you keep him from his work."

In three years, a friendship had grown between the two boys. Erik, the strong, slightly irritable heir, and the agile, sharp-thinking, narrow-chested slave had found trust in each other. And today? They shared their joys and sorrows and were able to settle even the sharpest disagreements without falling out. *It will stay that way*, Tyrkir thought as he refocused on the speech.

"It came to a fight!" Erik had just reminded everyone of his father's quarrel with his neighbors in Jaedern, an insult that Thorvald could not accept without revenge. "By Thor, our fight was honorable. No ambush. We openly faced the enemy. But on the day of the tribunal, the witnesses testified against us. They'd been bribed."

The Thing-gathering had found Thorvald guilty of malicious murder, and the verdict had been the loss of honor. The farmer would only be granted a short period before he might be openly hunted and killed by anyone. Thorvald had quickly sold the farm, equipped his ship, and set sail with his son, some servants and maidservants, a few cattle, and the most necessary belongings. His destination was Iceland, the promised land of emigrants. Westward for seven days, through the ups and downs of the stormy waves. The dragon at the bow defied the sea.

But they came years too late to claim good, fertile Icelandic soil. "No land for you!" Erik clenched his fist. "You, my friends, heard it again and again. No land! We were pushed farther and farther north. It was only here, on Sharpcliff at Hornstrand, that we could finally build the farm." They had all worked hard, including Thorvald, until a few weeks before he'd been overcome with fatigue. Because his limbs would no longer obey him, he had stayed in the house.

"Take leave, friends! Drink with me to Thorvald!" Everyone in the hall grabbed their cups, draining them to the bottom.

Erik looked at Tyrkir quizzically. They exchanged a nod and then Erik walked calmly to the seat of honor. The murmuring ceased—not one sound in the hall—as all eyes followed him anxiously. He slowly stroked the carving on the posts. These supports were like a sacred shrine. The leader of a clan maintained them, and everyone to whom these duties and rights were assigned added an ornament or magical sign at some point. Erik stretched his chest and took the raised seat.

Tyrkir waved the servants and maids closer, signaling them to refill their cups. "Long live our Lord Erik, who is called the Red, and he shall live and protect us. May the gods never deprive him of their favor!" The servants joined in. *Yes, praise to our new lord.* The cups were filled and refilled again. Sip by sip, the sweet mead transformed the sadness of the last hours into the joy of serving Erik.

But the great man couldn't stay on the bench of honor for long. "If the gods have the right, so do we. Let us celebrate!" He waved his cup in his left, and with his free arm, he embraced the hips of one of the two maidservants, pressing her against him, then slowly turned with the girl still pressed to his side and kissed her. Breathlessly, he released the maid and grabbed at the second slave. "And you, Katla?"

As the pretty maidservant pressed closer to her master, much to his delight, Tyrkir noticed the greedy hunger in the other servants' eyes. There was danger in the air. Heated by the mead, they might easily forget that only the lord was allowed to help himself to the women. In three steps, he was beside the maid and pulled her away. "Leave it alone, Katla," he warned quietly. His angry look sobered Erik for a moment.

"Yes, Tyrkir is right," he said. "Two women are not enough for everyone. Let's drink! We do have enough mead!" His laughter was infectious, and soon the hall was filled with exuberant noise until, eventually, heads became heavy.

Late that night, Erik pulled his friend along behind him. "Come with me!"

They left the hall with sluggish strides and trudged through the pale twilight over to the burial mound on the cliff. For a long time, Erik stood there. Finally, he asked, "What now? I am the lord, but you're the clever one. What now?"

Tyrkir stepped close to his side. "Marry."

"What?"

"You must get married, and I say that not only because the farm needs a mistress. You're the last of your clan. You'll need children for the line to go on."

Erik shook his head. His gaze had lost some of its drunkenness. "Just like that? Get married? It takes two. Have you forgotten that? Who am I supposed to—"

Tyrkir scratched at his flea bites. Despite the mead, he somehow managed to arrange his thoughts. He'd thought this plan through, but had not yet dared to propose it to his friend. Now the time was right. "Down at Hvammsfjord, when we asked for land there," he began carefully. "You met the daughter of old Thorbjörn." He pretended not to remember the name of the young woman. "What was her name?"

"Thjodhild," Erik murmured thoughtfully. "Thjodhild of Hawk Valley." The memory seemed to paint her picture in his mind. "Not a bad woman. And she was still free in the spring. She is blond and straight grown. Yes, not a bad woman." He gently jabbed his friend in the chest. "We leave first thing tomorrow. Why should Farmer Thorbjörn have any objections to me? Look at me! I am a son-in-law. He couldn't have wished for a better one."

"You should probably take a bath," Tyrkir remarked. "Otherwise, no one will recognize your beauty."

17

"Don't you dare!" Erik raised his fist, half in anger. "You're speaking to your master." When he saw Tyrkir's bold look, he embraced his slave. "Nothing will separate us, not even a woman. Never. That I swear!"

# THJØDHILD

*A diversion, finally!*

For two weeks, Thjodhild had been longing for this day. The market was held down by the fjord. In the summer, it took place in the middle of the first week of every new month. It was nothing compared with the big market during the Allthing in the fall, but it was good enough for her. Thjodhild measured time by the market days. After every one, she lived off her memories for a while, and then counted the days until her next visit.

Thjodhild had swapped her coarse smock for a shift and a skirt with straps secured by brooches. Over it, she wore a large green shawl held together by a silver clasp. The chain of bronze medallions nestled coolly around the eighteen-year-old woman's neck. She had carefully combed her long blond hair, which fell from under her headscarf and far down over her back.

To be free of all of her chores! No laborious whipping of the salt butter today, no work in the house or stable. To see other people and forget her monotonous everyday life for a few hours.

Her mother had stayed on the farm because her leg was hurting again, so only Thjodhild and her stepfather had saddled their horses earlier that morning. They'd ridden through the upper Hawk Valley, along the brook, past the lake and forest, and finally down to the beach. Some neighbors had joined them along the way, swapping stories, and the time had quickly passed.

*Even the weather is lovely,* she thought. Despite a few fast-moving cloud shadows, the August sun shone down from the glass-blue sky onto the stalls and booths as laughter, shouting, and bargaining filled the small trading place. The bright light and pleasant warmth added to the general atmosphere of cheer.

Thjodhild had been waiting for her father for a while. He was standing at the horse trader's with his big farmer friends, inspecting the powerful animals, reaching into the luxuriant manes as if into women's hair, checking teeth, stroking bellies and the tendons of the front hooves.

"And I say, this mare is stronger!"

"Or maybe you're wrong, Thorbjörn."

"Don't say that! I know more about horses than you do."

A heated argument was brewing. Thjodhild knew this back-and-forth all too well, and a lot more time would pass before the men reached an agreement.

She strolled through the crowd. From the corner of her eye, she enjoyed the hungry looks of the young farmers. The unmarried sons of the wealthy landowners had come for business but were in festive attire, hoping to finally find a bride. Some had already asked for Thjodhild's hand, but so far, no one had pleased her. Since Thorbjörn himself had not had any children but loved his wife's only daughter like his own blood, he would not marry her off without her consent. And so Thjodhild remained free.

"I'll wait until someone pleases me," she often said to her mother while they enjoyed the steam and warmth of the sauna house together.

"Don't wait too long, girl," the old woman had warned just a few days before. She had lost her first husband, Jorund, at an early age and had been glad to have found in Thorbjörn another capable, kindhearted farmer for Hawk Farm. "Flowers are beautiful when they're in bloom, but they wither quickly." She stroked her large breasts and weighed them in her hands. "In the old days, they were firm and taut. And today?"

"Don't worry! I know what I want."

"No, listen to me! The younger brother of the master of the Valt-jof Farm, Ejolf, would be a—"

"Enough!" But Thjodhild quickly softened, lovingly rubbing her mother's back. "Forgive me, Mother. Please understand. No matter how rich his family is, the name already has me shivering." Thjodhild shook her head. "I will never marry Ejolf Dirt."

Though he was now a man, as a child he'd soiled himself, and the unfortunate nickname had stuck. Thjodhild was sure to run into him at the market today. She could already see his grin, hear his boasting. And like every other time, she'd turn away until he finally relented.

The smell of roasted seal meat crept into her nose. No, not just yet. She would eat something later, together with her father. But first, she wanted to take her time looking at all the wares on offer.

Yes, it was a beautiful day. Besides fishermen and artisans, some neighbors were offering what they could spare: to trade a spade for a chain for the cooking pot, two knives for scissors. Thjodhild did not feel like buying household goods today. Instead, she went to the stalls displaying decorated shoulder straps, jewelry, and other treasures. She marveled at an arrangement of small figures carved from walrus teeth, then moved on. She stayed longer at the silver-smith's, transfixed by his gleaming handiwork. *If only I were not so reasonable, I would buy all his bracelets and brooches.* She sighed.

When she turned, she found herself looking straight into a freckled face with dark, smiling eyes for a brief moment before the slim lad stepped aside for her. *Who was that? He must be a stranger, though I can't help feeling I've met him before.* Judging by his smock and shorn hair, he had to be a slave. Thjodhild jutted out her chin. *How dare he!*

A little later, at the potter's cart, he was suddenly beside her again. "You're blocking my view," she barked at him.

"Don't be angry, fair lady."

The warm voice made her pause. "What do you want from me? What is your name?"

"Tyrkir, chosen by God Tyr." He smiled. "No, no, I am not a messenger from the gods. I want nothing, and yet I do want something. Or rather, my master wants to show you something."

A serf looking for customers in an odd way, nothing more. Somewhat amused, Thjodhild nodded. "All right, where is his stand? Take me there."

The first thing she heard was the authoritative voice. "I killed the bear myself in Norway. And believe me, it was a fight to the death!" Then Thjodhild saw the bright red mane above the heads of three women who had surrounded the hunter and were haggling. He rejected each of their bids with the same words: "Too little. By Thor, I shall not sell this fur so cheaply." Finally, the customers gave up in disappointment and went to the next stand.

Tyrkir approached slowly with the slim woman. As soon as Erik spotted them, he wiped his face and drove his hands through his hair. "It is a beautiful day today" was all he could manage. She nodded slightly, and when she bent over the soft, brown-black bear blanket, he secretly motioned to Tyrkir, pleading for help. Tyrkir just smiled.

"How much do you want for your fur?" Thjodhild asked.

"My fur? I'll give it to you for all that you are." Erik's face blushed red, darker than his beard and wild mane.

She looked at him, surprised.

His amber eyes held her gaze. "This is my prize, fair Thjodhild. And I won't bargain, just so you know."

"You know my name?" Before he could answer, she remembered him, his eyes. "Weren't you with us in the spring at the farm?" Of course, he and his father had asked for land all along the coast of

Hvammsfjord, in Salmon Valley and Hawk Valley. "You're Erik the Red who came over from Norway."

"That's me. We settled up north, on the Hornstrand. Now we have a big farm there. Good grass. Even plenty of farmland. We did well."

Thjodhild looked briefly at Tyrkir, then again at the broad-shouldered boy, annoyed because her heart was beating more quickly. "You were never a bear hunter, and yet you had me lured by your servant. Don't think I'll fall into your trap!" Still, the game excited her. *Let's see how clever he is.* "It's a pretty long way from the Hvammsfjord to here." She raised her brows. "No wise farmer makes such a journey during harvest time just to visit our little market."

"I do. Even if you insult me."

Tyrkir held his breath. *Be polite, my friend,* he pleaded. *Don't spoil everything before it's even begun!*

Erik struggled hard against his rising anger. "Perhaps I'm not as clever as you. That may be so. But I know what I want."

"And what's that?" Thjodhild asked.

"My fur," he growled. "I want to sell it to you."

Thjodhild drove her fingers through the bear fur on the wooden trestle: "You mean this fur here?"

"Yes, damn it. And by Thor's hammer, my hide as well. That's why I'm here." His anger grew stronger, bursting out of him. "But with your sharp tongue, I don't know if you're the right one, after all."

"Too bad. You'd give up so easily?" Thjodhild turned away. After a few steps, she called over her shoulder, "Perhaps I'll stop by later with my father. If the bear fur is still available, who knows? Maybe he'll buy it for me."

Erik stared after her and then punched his fist into his left hand.

"Some woman she is," he murmured. "Good riddance. Better you don't come back." As soon as he saw Tyrkir grinning, Erik growled, "Stop smiling! It was your clever plan. Oh, I should—"

"Why are you upset?" Tyrkir calmly stepped toward him. "She took the bait. Believe me."

"That stuck-up woman? Never!"

Tyrkir was about to explain the situation to his disappointed friend when a young farmer appeared in front of them. "You are strangers?" The man had an angular face, angry eyes, and was dressed in tight trousers and a shirt made of the finest linen, along with a brown cape worn on his left shoulder, which covered the hilt of a sword. On his right side, the man carried a battle-ax in his belt next to a knife and coin pouch. "What are you doing here?"

"Who wants to know?" Erik straightened to his full height. At that moment, he wouldn't have objected to a brawl.

"Before you stands Ejolf of the Valtjof Farm. Everyone knows me here!"

They measured each other with their eyes, and in the end, the well-groomed lad was the first to lower his gaze. "All right, not today." He eyed the Red through half-closed lids. "I saw you talking to my Thjodhild. And for a long while. What about?"

"Nothing that concerns you."

Quickly, Tyrkir pointed to the fur. "The beautiful woman liked it. My master gave her the price, that was all." The answer didn't seem to satisfy Ejolf, but he didn't press further. "Well, you're in luck. If Thjodhild wants the fur, then I'll buy it. It would make a fine gift. Name your price."

Over the head of the young farmer, Erik spotted the blond woman, now accompanied by her father, approaching. He crossed his arms in front of his chest. "Too late. I won't be doing business with you. Either I sell the fur to the daughter of Hawk Farm herself, or I keep it." He drew his brows together, then loudly asked, "Why do you say *your* Thjodhild? Do you have an understanding with her?"

"We will celebrate our wedding at the beginning of winter. And then she will belong to me. I have long been in agreement with the farmer." But Ejolf didn't notice who was coming up behind him.

"Liar!" Ejolf flinched at the sound of Thjodhild's voice and spun around.

"There's no truth to this," the young woman hissed at him. "Don't you dare spread such lies, do you hear me? Never again!"

Ejolf muttered, "Thorbjörn, how can you let your daughter talk to me this way? I thought we were good, peaceful neighbors. Here, I wanted to give her this fur. Just like that, for her to enjoy. And in return, she insults me in front of strangers."

The gray-bearded farmer tried to appease him, but Thjodhild interrupted. "Leave it alone, Father! I can speak for myself." She pressed her fists into her hips. "You can give me no pleasure whatsoever, Ejolf Dirt. As a neighbor, I can suffer your presence, but never as a groom."

"Wait and see!" He grinned slyly. "No one else at Hvammsfjord would dare get in my way. You're not getting any younger, and eventually, there will come a day when you'll be happy for me to have you. You'll beg me to."

She abruptly raised her hand, but he ducked just in time. "Away! Go away!" she seethed. "Go to your friends, those idiots, and leave me alone!"

Ejolf was still grinning. "I'll see you soon." He cast the stranger and his servant a sharp look. "You're to forget what you heard, understand? Not a word about it, or you will wish we had never crossed paths."

Erik didn't so much as blink, and as soon as the pretentious man was out of earshot, he mumbled to Tyrkir, "This woman, she'll be a handful."

Still worked up, Thjodhild stepped in front of the Red. "And now to you: Do you stand by what you said to me earlier?"

"What did I . . . ?" Erik frowned, but Tyrkir nudged his elbow into his master's side, and understanding suddenly dawned. "Yes, by Thor. Every word was true."

"All right, then." She turned to her stepfather. "I'll take the fur." No, he could leave the silver in the pouch; they had already agreed on the price. "Please invite this man and his slave to our farm as guests. There you will have time to discuss arrangements." With that, she turned and walked away.

Thorbjörn shook his head apologetically. "My daughter is a little . . . lively."

"That seems to be the truth," Erik replied, releasing a breath.

The farmer and his daughter left the trading place earlier than usual. His guests rode a bit behind them. The afternoon sun glistened in the willows on either side of the stream. Thorbjörn eyed the young woman at his side; she was sitting upright in her saddle, looking off at the black mountain ridges in the east. Finally, he broke the silence. "So fast? Are you sure, girl, that you're not making a mistake?"

She turned her attention back to her stepfather. "He's different from the other men I've met so far."

"And it's not because you want to punish young Ejolf? Oh, child, nobody knows anything about this Erik."

She took in her father's worried expression. "But I feel something new in here. No, no, trust me. My heart alone won't decide. We have plenty of time before we must make up our minds."

Three horse lengths behind them, Erik fidgeted with the halter in his fist. Tyrkir waited patiently.

"It wasn't your plan alone," the giant grumbled. "You are not that clever. Must be providence. What do you suppose? Which god had a hand in this?"

"It wasn't Tyr. He doesn't interfere in these sorts of things. But perhaps he gave God Freyr a hint. He knows something about fertility. After all, we *are* in a bit of a hurry."

"Could be." Erik stroked his horse's mane and patted his neck. After some time, he smiled to himself.

Thorbjörn of Hawk Farm understood how impatient the red-haired man must be. His servants couldn't be left alone in the north for too long during harvest time, but a marriage was not a quick transaction; the terms had to be properly negotiated. It had already cost the good-natured big farmer a lot of effort to explain to his wife, at Thjodhild's request, that her beloved daughter had decided not to choose one of the neighboring young farmers, but instead wanted to leave with this stranger.

Since breakfast, the men had been sitting alone in the spacious living hall decorated with tapestries. Erik's line of ancestors had no flaws, even when he reported frankly about the conviction in Norway and the escape. Thorbjörn had only shrugged regretfully. *Bought witnesses! How quickly anyone could have suffered the same misfortune.* "We are all subject to the whims of fate." No, the court case was settled, and it no longer mattered. "What do you offer our daughter?"

"Well, there's a lot to consider." Erik had feared this question, and now he regretted that his friend was not present for this conversation. He'd give anything right now for Tyrkir's signals and glances. "All right, then. Ten cows in the barn. My bull is hot-blooded, I assure you. Then horses for each servant. Yes, and a good forty sheep. The land . . ." Erik stretched, then told of fertile meadows, and the leeks, onions, and peas abundant in the field. The more he spoke, the more splendidly he painted his property, and he was sure that through hard work, he'd be able to develop it to the size of Thorbjörn's farm in the future.

"I had no idea." The farmer scratched his beard thoughtfully. "Didn't know that it could be done so easily up on the Horn-strand. It's a shame we can't combine our farms. That would please my wife. Not just because of the land—we have enough of that ourselves—but because then she could see the girl more often."

"We will visit you," Erik assured him hastily.

"And you own a ship?"

Relieved to report something that was finally true, Erik raved about his seaworthy knarr, proudly calling her *Mount of the Sea*. Forty servants could comfortably find room on her. He spoke of the red sail, the dragon's head at the bow, and the large cargo hold. "When I stand aft at the tiller, wind, sun, and the North Star are my friends—"

"That's enough," Thorbjörn interrupted. "I like you, yes. I be-lieve you are a man full of energy. Now that I know your for-tune, I want to offer you just as much in return. Thjodhild shall have ten servants and five maids to accompany her to the Horn-strand."

"I do lack women," Erik interjected.

The landowner generously increased the number by another four female slaves. He also offered lumber—enough for a women's shelter—along with wool, two looms, and other household goods. The list went on for a long while, and Erik was astonished at what a rich woman he'd won.

"Do you agree? Is the dowry appropriate to your possessions, if we don't include the value of the ship?"

"I would have taken her for less."

Thorbjörn smiled. "How infatuated and inexperienced you are. If a clever matchmaker were to negotiate with me instead of you, such a confession would never cross his lips." The arrangement of a marriage was a sober deal, he warned. After all, according to

Viking law, in the case of divorce or separation, women were entitled to half the common property. "Take my advice, boy: When we repeat our agreement in front of witnesses tomorrow and they fix the bride-price for Thjodhild in silver, be silent about your feelings. They will only cost you."

Erik swallowed. Was this a reprimand or even an insult? Only after some careful thought was he able to reassure himself; the big farmer had no wish to offend him. He only meant Erik well. "I'll remember that for next time."

"Don't you dare! I'll give you my daughter, and with her and only her, you shall increase the happiness of your clan."

The broad-shouldered redhead understood that, too, and he was glad when he was able to finally escape the living hall.

In the two weeks that followed the engagement beer, he hardly saw Thjodhild. Erik hadn't been able to talk with her much before, and they'd never been alone. Thorbjörg was always watching over her daughter. When the rising unrest in his loins kept him from his sleep at night, he complained to his friend: "How am I supposed to be certain about my wife?"

"You must wait until she lies beside you." Tyrkir yawned. "Your surprise will come on the day of the feast."

The old farmer's wife had resigned herself to her future son-in-law, but she was full of worries, especially as they weren't following the usual waiting period of at least two months before the wedding. She would have liked to see a grand celebration during the three holy nights that marked the beginning of winter. "That would be the best date to ensure my child's happiness." Instead, she had her hands full in August. New cooking pits were dug, goats and sheep were slaughtered, and the freshly brewed beer was fermenting in the barrels.

The bride helped tirelessly and endured an endless stream of advice during the idle hours. "There's not much time left, child." The mother raised her breasts. "But I will give you all the knowledge I can to make you a good mistress." Thjodhild listened patiently.

Though she'd laughed little these past weeks, her step was more buoyant than usual. The appointed date approached. The invitations were issued, and on the day before the wedding, the unmarried daughters of the wealthy neighbors arrived. As Hawk Valley lacked hot springs fed by Iceland's underground fire, they took over the sauna house with their giggling, whispering, and chatting. Usually, the sauna was a place for masters and servants to rest together on Saturdays, or as a warm place for childbirth. Today, however, no man was allowed to enter this area behind the main building.

The first task was to prepare the bath for the bride. Soon, the girls huddled together in the antechamber, nibbling on honey-sweetened berries. They began with stories of boys in general, but little by little, they exchanged more suggestive, pleasurable details as their cheeks grew red and the water bubbled in the crucibles behind them.

"She's coming!" Thjodhild silently acknowledged the joyful greeting. Her expression remained strained. She wore only a simple shift. She had barely slipped it off when the other girls all quickly disrobed. They openly displayed their bodies, cheerfully accepting admiration or mocking consolation, and then led the bride naked into the parlor. A pleasant heat greeted the young women. They drew lots, and two were allowed to sit in the giant vat with Thjodhild while the others served them. As the water hissed on the hot stones, the room quickly filled with steam, and then lukewarm water was poured into the tub.

For the first time, Thjodhild felt the painful realization that she had to say goodbye—to being a child, and to her dreams. *How often did I wash the bride myself?* she thought. *Sometimes I was even jealous. And now today, it is my turn.* She was leaving her parents, her comfortable home. *What waits for me up there in the north, so far away from Hawk Valley? How lonely will it be there?*

"Why aren't you happy?" The girl next to Thjodhild scooped water with her hand and let it run over her neck and breasts. "Tomorrow, you'll have a man. If I were you, I couldn't wait...."

"You're right." Thjodhild pushed aside her worries with a sharp clap. "Erik is strong." She splashed the others. "And now he'll be my husband!" Finally, the tension released and the young women cheered, pouring water over the bride's head, then tickling her until she begged for mercy and rose from the tub with her arms stretched high. The servants thoroughly thrashed and rubbed her back, buttocks, and legs with fresh birch twigs and scrubbed her from head to toe.

A tub of cold water waited in front of the sauna house. Thjodhild emerged, gasped for air, and screamed, immediately followed by the terrified screeching of her friends. Later, they sat together wrapped in cloths. "Remember...?" Stories from the past came to life while they wound the bridal wreath from flowers and leaves. In the evening, Mother Thorbjörg and two maids brought meat soup and a jug of mead. Her gait was heavy; the effort of the past days had made her leg ache again.

"Come sit, Mother," Thjodhild said. "Rest with us a while."

"Thank you, my child." When Thorbjörg noticed the disappointed faces all around her, she had to chuckle. "No, don't worry, you excited sheep. The old hag is leaving now. I won't spoil your last maiden night." She looked at Thjodhild for a long time, then she stroked her knee and smiled. Before she left, she scolded the other girls. "Tomorrow, you'd better make my daughter glow. If I have to give away my girl, then she will be the most beautiful bride of Hawk Valley."

Erik had ridden up the nearby hills with Tyrkir. They'd left the horses behind at the edge of a grove and were watching the setting sun. "This area must be a garden of the gods." The twenty-year-old tore out a tuft of grass and earth and inhaled the smell. "If I'd been allowed to settle here, my happiness would be complete."

"I've never seen you like this before," Tyrkir mocked. "Did Father God Odin, the one-eyed protector of the poets, suddenly blow beautiful words into your ear?"

Erik thoughtfully rubbed the tuft between his fingers. "I just feel that way today."

Both stared at the sinking fireball on the western horizon.

"What are you afraid of?" Tyrkir began quietly, and since he didn't want to mention Erik's lies about the farm on Sharpcliff, he added, "Who knows what our future will bring? I'm sure whatever it is, we'll ultimately win good fortune." He wanted to cheer up his friend. "You get a beautiful, proud wife. And it's good that we'll soon be heading north, because here in Hawk Valley, you now have an enemy."

"Ejolf, the brother of the landlord of the Valtjof Farm?" Erik shook his head. He'd given the man no grounds for a feud. Thjod-hild had never been promised to that braggart.

"Even so, he'll try everything to harm you," Tyrkir said. "And we both know how injustice makes you angry."

"Why are you so clever?" Erik grinned, and his boyish good humor returned. "I wonder why you haven't found a woman yet!"

"That's your responsibility," Tyrkir replied. "You're the master." He raised his hands defensively. "On second thought, better not. With your taste, you're sure to put a cow in my bed. No, my lord, let me find myself a bride, and then I'll come to you."

"Stupid lad!" Erik laughed and shoved him gently in his chest. "No cow! But we take home five new maids with us. Maybe you'll like one of them."

"You marry. I still have time."

They raced to their horses. Tyrkir was the first to jump into the saddle, and Erik galloped after him, past the birch grove and down the meadow hill.

They'd made the blood sacrifice—a special plea to the mother goddess Frigg for happiness, the blessing of children, and peaceful coexistence. Thorbjörg had insisted that the little goddess Var, who heard and fulfilled every promise, also be remembered.

The smell of burnt juniper filled the spacious living hall. Since the hearth fire in Thjodhild's new home could not be consecrated that day, she'd take some of the holy ashes in a leather pouch with her and would later repeat the ritual on Sharpcliff. All the guests had taken their seats; the closest relatives sat close to the honorary chairs, then friends and neighbors.

The host had to pay meticulous attention to where guests were seated because proximity or distance reflected how much respect he showed to those invited. The happy faces around the fire proved that Thorbjörn had not made any mistakes. And when he brought the bride and groom together, cheers and chants of joy broke out in the hall.

It was only with great difficulty that he was able to calm the enthusiasm again: "Friends! Friends, listen to me!" It took him some time before he could continue. "Let's take the oath!" The company went silent. "Everyone in this hall swears by their honor that they will not resent one another's words as long as we drink and the feast lasts. No matter how hard our heads become, no feud must arise from our drunkenness." Women and men solemnly raised their right hands. "With this, I open the wedding feast. Drink and eat, dance and laugh. Be my guests for three days and two nights." Steaming bowls were brought in by the maids. Servants filled the cups from jugs.

"Where is your slave?" Thjodhild was seated next to Erik on the second, slightly lower bench of honor opposite her parents. As a sign of her new status, she had tied her blond hair into a knot at her neck, and a big ring hung from the belt of her light blue dress. Keys were still missing, but she would receive them in her new home. "I want to drink with him and you first, because I can't shake the suspicion that he was the one who brought us together."

"That's not true," Erik countered weakly. "But if you so insist, there might be something to it." He whistled. Tyrkir, standing near the doorway, raised his head, understanding the signal, and squeezed through the rows of benches toward the bridal couple. He looked at his master, waiting for his request.

"No, not me. Your mistress has something to say to you."

Thjodhild handed the slave her jug of mead. "I know you are my husband's friend. And I very much wish that you not only serve me but also stand by me in joy and sorrow, as faithfully as you do him."

Tyrkir regarded her openly. "It's difficult to share love, Mistress. But right after Erik, I give you a place of honor in my heart." He took a sip, then handed the jug back to her. She toasted with Erik and both emptied their vessels.

A sudden noise from outside cut through the celebration—a man was screaming, cursing, his words incomprehensible. Little by little, the party took notice, and the carefree laughter gave way to a watchful tension.

"Come out! You stole my bride! Do you hear me, you coward? Come and fight!"

Thjodhild clenched her hands into her wedding scarf. "It's Ejolf Dirt," she whispered. "Ignore him. Please!"

The jealous man kept screaming outside. The guests were becoming restless; some men felt for their daggers. Tyrkir looked anxiously at his friend and saw the anger building inside him. *Help, great Tyr,* he pleaded silently. *Grant him restraint! Do not let this day drown in blood!*

"How dare he," growled Erik. "Just turns up..." He stared at Tyrkir. "Where is my sword? Bring it here. Also the ax. I'll show this boy that Erik Thorvaldsson is not a cowardly rabbit."

"Right away, sir," Tyrkir said, but he didn't move. "But, are you sure you're not mistaken? I hear the man raving, but he did not mention your name. Perhaps his challenge is meant for another guest."

The giant clenched his fist. "You will obey me, or I—"

"Yes, it's better if you hit me." Slowly, the weedy man crossed his arms behind his back. "Go ahead. You can take out your anger on me and save yourself from the consequences of any hasty action."

Erik snorted and threw himself back so hard, the high seat groaned.

Ejolf's curses were still ringing through the hall.

The bride's father watched the son-in-law sharply, then finally stood. It seemed that his reason won out. "No one will disturb my daughter's day." He called over to the row of benches occupied by the neighboring big farmers. "Valtjof of Valtjof Farm, your brother was not invited. He's entered my property without permission. For peace's sake, go see to it that the hothead no longer bothers us."

The roundish farmer turned bright red but rose from his seat. As everyone looked on, he walked along the fire to the exit. A single sharp order and the shouting cut off, and shortly after, Valtjof returned. He raised his hand before the benches. "Forgive me, neighbor! The lad is still young and unstable." Then he turned to address Erik. "May the gods bless you and your wife with many children!"

His words were met with silence. After a tense pause, Erik pressed out through his teeth, "Forgotten. Every word of your brother. He could not offend Thor in me."

The men in the hall looked at one another, amazed. Each of them had, as a child, chosen a guardian from the circle of gods, one who had dwelled within him ever since, giving to him their trust and confidence. An insult or any kind of offense hurt, above all, their own god, and only revenge could appease his anger.

A murmur went through the rows of tables. The groom had not felt attacked by an equal. For him, Ejolf Dirt was just a stupid ruffian who could not violate his honor. What a noble gesture!

Valtjof bowed deeply. "For your generosity, I am in your debt. Take a bull as atonement from me."

As soon as Erik had accepted the compensation, enthusiastic congratulations were offered to him from all sides. The feast came to life again, now even more cheerful and boisterous. The minstrels took to the drum much too early, conjured up waves of sound with their harps, and blew on the lur until hunger drove them back to the plates.

Erik sat next to his bride, drenched in sweat. Tyrkir knew what a battle his friend had fought with himself. "This victory was hard-won," he said quietly.

"Shut up," Erik grumbled. "Didn't I send you for beer?"

"Forgive me. How stupid of me. The whole barrel, sir?"

They looked at each other, and their mouths twitched.

"Never mind. Just beer. I'm thirsty."

Tyrkir took the cup and pushed himself through the rows of tables.

Thjodhild lightly touched her husband's arm. "I'm proud."

Erik puffed out his chest. "The wedding was good," he said, awkwardly, but only later that night would the real celebration begin. "If you know what I mean."

Her look told him just how well she'd understood him.

Erik had almost overcome the first drunkenness by the evening. Before he and Thjodhild were led to the other house, Tyrkir insisted on pouring a bucket of cold water over his head. "I don't want you to sleep through your surprise."

"You think? I could never get that drunk."

The maidens had shaken out the blankets and decorated the bedposts with bouquets. Embers crackled in the firepot. They were now standing together in front of the wedding room, whispering and giggling. As soon as the bridal parents approached with the couple, they fell silent, and only their shining eyes revealed where their thoughts had strayed.

Thorbjörg pressed her daughter against her mighty chest, as if saying goodbye before a journey into the unknown. The big farmer laid his hand on the groom's shoulder. Then the young women opened the door wide before closing it again quietly behind them as they left.

The couple was alone. Neither said anything, and because Erik just stared ahead, Thjodhild worried that he was as inexperienced as she was. She boldly disrobed, presenting herself to her new husband. "Do you not like me?"

The red one looked up in awe. "A gift." His voice barely obeyed him. "I've known enough women, but you are a gift."

She hadn't expected so much flattery, so she slipped under the feather bed, staying close to the left edge. Erik tore his shirt over his head, then hastily took off his trousers and climbed in from the other side.

"You'll want for nothing with me," he said, but didn't move.

"I trust you."

Slowly, they slipped toward each other. They'd barely touched when Thjodhild hit something hard and cold with her thigh. Frightened, she threw the feather bed aside.

"What is it?" asked Erik.

She held a bronze Thor's hammer in her hand and laughed. She had put this into the bed of newlyweds herself often enough. "And today of all days, I didn't even think of it." She looked down at Erik. Her gaze lingered. "I also believe," she whispered, "that such a... that it stimulates masculinity. Do you understand?"

The journey home went well. It was raining, but the wind was good, and the servants rarely had to push out the oars. Tyrkir stood at the bow by the dragon's head, a vigilant pilot whose calls or hand signals were immediately obeyed by his friend on the aft steering deck.

During the second day, the gentle green coast retreated, and rugged, steep rock cliffs appeared, interspersed with narrow, deeply cut bays.

They'd set out soon after the wedding feast, equipped and over-loaded like a train of settlers. Thorbjörn had taken it upon himself to escort the bridal couple and their servants from Hawk Valley over the pass to the Bocksfjord in the east. At the front, Valtjof's bull pulled the cart with the timber, while each packhorse trudged under its heavy load of presents, new household goods, and cloth-ing.

"You didn't exaggerate." As soon as the big farmer saw his son-in-law's ship, he let out an appreciative whistle. "Your knarr really is a mount of the sea."

"I know none better!" Erik stroked the slender bow like a sweet-heart, and Thjodhild nudged him, a gleam in her eye. "I come first, you Viking!"

They'd fastened the dowry and the wood, and then Erik ordered the bull and horses to be hobbled in the hold—they'd manage the journey north better lying on their sides.

The farewell had been short. The daughter had waved to the father standing on the beach until the ship had slipped out of the bay.

For the past hour, the wind had been blowing more violently.

The waves carried crowns of foam, and Erik navigated even closer along the shore. Tyrkir signaled from the bow deck to avoid the dangerous reefs. The ship's speed had to be reduced, and Erik commanded the line guards reef the sail halfway. "We'll be there soon," he shouted to Thjodhild.

She stood next to him, shielding her eyes against the rain. She saw stony beaches and black cliffs passing behind them; even the small fjords of the morning had been left behind. *Once we're around the next headland, the area will open up again*, she told herself, trying to soothe her increasing restlessness. But even after the next rocky ridge, and the next, she saw no sign of land that would entice a farmer to settle there.

"There, you see?"

"Where?" she asked.

"Up there!" Erik pointed to the ridge of a cliff.

"I can't see anything." She shrugged. "What am I looking for?"

But her giant was too busy and did not answer.

She went forward to Tyrkir. "Tell me, what's up there? And why are we landing here?"

He wiped his wet face. "This here is Hornstrand. Up there, that's Sharpcliff."

When she remained silent, he added, "Well, everything looks better when it's not raining."

Erik left it to the servants and maids to free the horses from their shackles and to get the cargo ashore. With Tyrkir, Erik escorted his wife up the steep path. Twice, she slipped in the rubble, but without complaining, pulled herself up again. She kept her gaze fixed firmly upward. Finally, they reached the top.

Thjodhild stood staring at the smoking mound of grass and earth and the slightly smaller one next to it from which she saw no smoke rising. Finally, she asked, "Is this your farm?"

Erik turned to Tyrkir for help, but the servant shook his head.

Erik gnawed at his lower lip, pushing it back and forth. Finally, he said, "Well, you can't see everything from here. There's another barn between the stable and the house," by which he meant, the poorly covered shed layered with stones.

"You're right. I can't see a thing." *Just as well that it is raining*, she thought unhappily, mopping at her eyes. "Lies? Then everything was a lie?"

"It's not like that at all," he muttered. "Not everything."

She yanked his arm violently. "Look at me, Erik Thorvaldsson! You not only deceived me but you also deceived my father, my mother, and all my relatives. Why, by all the gods? Tell me!"

"Because ... well, because otherwise, you would not have taken my fur."

She pressed both fists against her temples. "How stupid you are. So stupid!"

Before Erik could get upset, Tyrkir suggested they go into the house. They could discuss the matter by the fire in peace, or better yet, tomorrow when the mistress was rested from her journey.

# HAWK VALLEY

Erik first dared hope that things would be all right when he heard Thjodhild laughing with the maids in the pantry three days later. "I knew it." He winked at Tyrkir. "She'll get used to it," he said, more to convince himself, then clapped his hands on his thighs. "Well, that's the truth of it: a woman belongs to her husband, no matter where they live."

Tyrkir was carving the notch on a new whip stick. "You'd better not brag about it that loudly. I think the mistress is laughing because there's nothing else to be done."

The wound tore open again. "This is your fault!" Erik growled. "Why didn't you warn me?"

"I couldn't have guessed, sir, how generous you would be in assessing our estate." *No, no mockery*, Tyrkir scolded himself. *Bad enough that we lured the poor woman into this wasteland.*

"Let's stop arguing about who's to blame. We should focus on how to make her life with us as good as it can be," Erik said.

"Yes, enough."

Looking ahead, that was what the friends were about, rather than arguing over mistakes made in the past. Immediately after arriving at Sharpcliff, Tyrkir was appointed manager of the farm. Although he'd long since assumed the responsibility, Erik wanted to define Tyrkir's role for the new servants.

*Thjodhild shall want for nothing!* This statement was like a command for them both. And they made every effort to make it so. By the end of September, the hay had been harvested, the salt butter barrel had been filled, and dried herbs and roots, pots with honey-sweetened berries, and plenty of fish and seal meat had been cured and stored in the pantry. During the last two weeks of October, Erik and the farmhands built a small house right next to the main building, which was easy to keep warm. "For you," Erik shouted proudly. "I promised your parents. And you see, I keep my word."

He didn't earn any extra thanks. After the first days of her despair, Thjodhild had grown more pleasant, and she didn't withdraw from him at night, but she spoke only when necessary. She quickly found out which maid her husband had been particularly fond of before their marriage. In private, she gave Katla a choice: "Either you keep your knees closed for him in the future and become my confidante, or you can sleep with the cattle from now on, and I will prove to you how demanding I can be as a mistress."

The young woman laid both hands on her left breast. "Never again. And if the gentleman should be too forward, I'll send him to you. Let me be your friend."

"You are a clever child." Thjodhild nodded, and shortly before the three holy nights, she moved into the newly built house with all of her maidservants. This meant no real separation; she continued to share a bed with Erik, but there was now a shelter on the farm for the women that belonged to them alone, undisturbed by the looks of men.

Winter could come.

The first ice storms howled from the sea over Sharpcliff. Soon snow fell, and the wind piled it over the earth and grass roofs. Every day, the servants dug their way to the stable to feed the cattle.

On the deepest night of the year, wrapped in darkness and cold, they celebrated Yule. There'd been no barley to brew beer, and no boar since Erik had no space to keep pigs. Thjodhild, however, understood how to season the soup and then let the scent of the seal meat run through the living hall until mouths watered, and this roast seemed to them to be the most delicious Yule feast.

Days later, Thjodhild was standing at the loom. She evenly guided the weaving sword, and every time she moved forward and back, the weights of perforated shards of clay jingled and tinkled at the bottom of the warp yarns. She watched Erik from the corner of her eye.

*Even if you lied to me,* she thought, *you really are diligent and capable. None of the young men back home can work like that.* He was sitting with his legs apart on the stool next to her, plucking wool from the distaff and letting the spindle whirl in his hand. As was proper for the clan leader, Erik knew how to swing the battle-ax, to navigate a ship, and of course, how to spin a good wool thread. *A man only becomes a man when he has mastered every job.* Thorvald had lived up to this motto and had raised his son accordingly.

Thjodhild paused her activity. She stepped close behind Erik and laid her hand on his shoulder. "I am no longer alone."

He turned around, surprised. "Have you forgiven me?"

"No, never." There was no resentment in her voice, though. "Let's not talk about it, not now. I wanted to tell you that we are no longer alone."

He didn't understand, but Katla standing near her did. She was already whispering the news when Erik finally dropped the spindle. "By Thor, that's good! And after this child, we must have another! Yes, here on Sharpcliff, our family will take root." He stood up and carefully pressed her against him.

But that wasn't enough for him. With mighty strides, he paced before the great fire, crossed his arms, then uncrossed them, only to cross them again, all the time moving his lips soundlessly. Finally, he pulled Tyrkir into the semidarkness of the opposite side room. "What do you say to that? A child. Although she is still angry at me, she is having a child!" He scratched his beard. "That's what I call a good woman."

"She is the best. I knew it right away." They grinned at each other like boys. Erik was to become a father, although the thought also made them a little uneasy.

"Don't I have to give her something?" Erik said. If he could go to a market now, he'd buy her a chain or a bracelet. But until the nights got shorter again, they were locked up in this place.

Tyrkir nodded. "It doesn't have to be anything valuable," he said. "Just a symbol of joy. Still, it will be hard to plan a surprise in such close quarters."

"You can do it," Erik decided.

During the next evenings, Tyrkir sat with the servants in the front part of the hall where the equipment of the house and farm was repaired or replaced. He hollowed out a soapstone with a burin and a knife. It was the last soft stone he had brought from Norway, and his skilled hands quickly turned it into a bowl, the rim of which he notched six times.

Until then, he'd been a lively participant in the never-ending stories of dwarves, Norns, and creatures that lived in the roots of the World Ash. Now, occupied with his task, nobody was allowed to talk to him. First, he drew the design on the outside of the bowl with charcoal, assessed his work with a critical eye, then carefully cut a woman who was breastfeeding a child into the light stone.

For a long time, memories of his home village on the Rhine had been forcing their way back into his mind. This picture? It was not foreign to him. A mother held her son on her knees. What was her name? He couldn't recall.

When Tyrkir was finally satisfied with his work, he called Erik. "Here, the gift is not quite finished yet. I think you should at least contribute a little."

"Not so loud," Erik grumbled. He knotted six thick wool threads together at the ends, placed the bundle in the middle of the bowl, and pulled the loose ends a bit over the six edge notches. He put whale oil in the soapstone container and waited until the wool had soaked it up before he lit the wicks.

Solemnly and slowly, he walked over to Thjodhild. She was standing in front of the loom and didn't notice him immediately. As soon as she saw the shining lamp in his hand, her eyes widened.

"For the child," he said. "I mean, for you, because then you both can keep away the dark."

She took the bowl, her fingertip stroking over mother and child, and she could not hold back her tears. After a moment, she whispered, "We have to be all right, you hear me?"

"I want to, but..."

After that, she talked with her husband more often, sitting with him and Tyrkir, even taking part in verses the German forged for the entertainment of all. The evenings passed more cheerfully than before. But as soon as plans were mentioned, her face again grew hard.

By the beginning of February, the days were already more distinguishable from the nights. One of the servants returned from the stable and quietly gestured Tyrkir to follow him.

A flickering oil lamp was brought into the barn during the short milking and feeding times; at all other times, the cattle were surrounded by darkness—darkness for months. Each pen was separated from the next by a thin, mid-hip stone wall and was only big enough that the animals could stand or lie down, nothing more.

The servant pointed to an emaciated cow, which had sunk onto her forelegs and showed no signs of even trying to stand.

"Is she still eating?" Tyrkir understood the threat. "How many cows can we get through the winter?"

Without a word, the servant lifted two fingers.

"I will talk to the master. Wait here!"

After consideration, only one possibility remained. "We have to put her down," Erik decided with a heavy heart. He'd spent a few hours hoping to hide the defeat from his wife, but the misfortune was not only written on his face but on Tyrkir's and all his servants'.

Thjodhild distributed the stew, waiting until the last person had licked his spoon and put it back into his belt. "What is it?" She looked at her husband, but when he said nothing, she turned to Tyrkir. "Tell me!"

"No, it should come from me." Erik laid both hands on the table-top. When he'd finished, she held his gaze.

"I stand by you, like everyone else here in your household."

Her trust gave him courage. Even if happiness had abandoned them for the moment, it had to return. "Fate is provident, I know it." As soon as the snow melted, he wanted to buy new cows, find more meadows in the area, and work even harder. This year, they'd have more at their disposal than the last. And next winter, every head of cattle would survive. "We'll also buy sheep. And we'll fatten a boar for Yule." His enthusiasm spread to the maidservants and servants. Even Tyrkir clenched his hands full of hope.

Thjodhild leaned back quietly and stroked her rounded belly. *My child*, she thought. *You in there. Have no fear. Your mother will take care of you.*

In mid-April, the first yellow flowers bloomed on the steep slope that led down to the shore. The snow began to melt, except in those areas shaded from the sun, and here and there, it took on the smell of warm earth.

While the women were bathing in the house, the men outside cleaned themselves, cut their beards, and searched each other for lice nests. Although the master had generously left it to each slave to wear their hair long, most of the men cut off their winter manes to win the battle against the nuisances. "We are also building a sauna," Erik shouted. "Every Saturday, we will sweat in steam."

Thjodhild stepped outside. She walked tall and proud, not even a slight bend in her back despite the weight of the unborn child. "Follow me." Without waiting for Erik, she walked over to the grave on the cliff.

"The air does you good." He looked at her with a smile as the wind pressed her dress against her body, clearly revealing her rounded shape.

"I have to talk to you about that." She faltered. She had carefully weighed each word, thinking how to explain her decision. The time had come. She could no longer delay. "My child and I are suffocating here. I will not remain on Sharpcliff, Erik."

He staggered, drawing a sharp breath, as though he'd been punched, then fixed his gaze on the stone ship. "The storms are hard up here. I'd best reinforce it. What do you think?"

"Did you hear me?"

The red man fussed over choosing a stone. Finally, he heaved a boulder up onto the grave.

"Erik! I'm not staying here."

He let the stone fall back and his shoulders dropped. "I have... No, I know nothing. Only..." He shook his head and turned away. After looking out at the sea for a time, he said, "I was as good to you as I could be."

"I know. But it's better this way."

"Better?" Erik's broad back trembled. "It's better for a wife to stay with her husband. And the husband to be with the wife and child."

She stepped behind him, carefully placing her hand in his. "That's what I believe, too."

"What?"

Thjodhild touched him with her belly. The most difficult part was before her. *Great Frigg, goddess of all mothers*, she begged silently. *For our happiness's sake, let me now find the right words!*

"We must stay together, Erik. I wish for nothing more. For the child, and also for me. Together, yes, but not here."

"I don't understand." He was still staring at the water. Suddenly, a jolt went through his body, and he slowly turned around. "You don't want a divorce after all?"

"Never. Unless you lie to me again. I might think about it then."

"You mean, we should leave here . . . ?"

"Yes." He should give up Sharpcliff. She understood enough about harvesting, keeping cattle, and good and bad soil. This area was infertile, and the enemy of every hardworking man. "Should our child grow up here among the rocks?"

"Father chose this place."

"Because he had no other choice."

"That's true." After some hesitation, he mumbled, "But even if I wanted to, I couldn't find another place for us."

Thjodhild regarded him. "There is land enough. Down in Ha-bichtstal. Good land, too."

He lowered his gaze. It was impossible. What would his father-in-law, her mother, and all her relatives say? Erik the liar! He tricked his way into the marriage contract! Impossible. It would be better for her to leave him with the child than lose face like that. "Shame is worse than death."

"Don't worry. I'll talk to my parents myself, and I won't even have to lie. I'll just omit part of the truth. I promise. You'll be received honorably and with open arms in Habichtstal."

"Well, it would be better for the child, that's true," he grumbled. He asked for time. It was a big decision and he wanted to think it over.

Thjodhild felt a dizzying sense of relief. She took a deep breath before continuing. "Yes, Erik. Think of the child and of me." With that, she started to trace the route back to the house, but after a few steps, she turned back. "May I tell Tyrkir about our plan?"

"Yes. He should do some thinking, too. It would be a nice change."

As she walked along the narrow path toward the farm, Thjod-hild patted her belly with both hands. "Since you can't understand words yet, my child, just feel how happy your mother is."

Around noon, the lank manager came out to the burial mound. Since Erik's conversation with Thjodhild, he had not only strength-ened the bow of the stone ship but raised the side walls. "So that Father always feels safe."

"The mistress has a plan," Tyrkir began. "I couldn't have forged a better one." Thjodhild wasn't going to utter a single complaint to her parents about her husband. The harvest had been bad, so the cattle had starved to death. The winter storms had been fierce, so the house was no longer habitable. Tyrkir listed several other reasons she'd planned. When he was finished, he said, "Since we didn't find happiness here, we'll just have to walk a little toward it. Everyone can understand that."

"I think so, too. Maybe it's better that way."

When would they leave? Soon, Thjodhild insisted. The child would not wait, and they'd need a home when it came. With that, Erik was decided.

For the neighbors of Hawk Farm, it should look like a visit at first. Thjodhild had insisted on it. "Trust me, and our reputation will be preserved!"

Erik agreed, because even Tyrkir thought that his mistress was more capable of handling people's curiosity. The servants and maids had been ordered to break up the farm on Sharpcliff, to pack the family's belongings in boxes, and to bring the valuable timber down to the beach. The actual move would take place on the second trip.

Erik, Tyrkir, and Thjodhild set out one morning with only six oarsmen and a strong north wind and were already anchored at the Bocksfjord before sunset the same day. Without much baggage, the horses made good progress along the path. The couple carried only a few bundles of clothing and the family treasure in an ironclad, tightly sealed box. Thjodhild kept the three keys used to secure it safe on the large ring on her belt.

Soon after the pass, the country opened to the west, and the first farms appeared. Erik and his wife greeted everyone they met, asked questions, and told stories. Admiring glances followed them. It was a visit of new beginnings. After a long winter, fresh green shone between the pale brownish, wilted grass. Hazel bushes, birches, and ash trees stood with swelling buds. And Thjodhild was more beautiful than ever. There was no cause for suspicion. The daughter of Hawk Farm was doing well with the stranger; the happy news soon spread all over the valleys.

Yet soon after the first reunion, Thjodhild's mother had grown suspect. "Tell me the truth, child."

Thjodhild leaned her forehead against the cheek of the old woman. "Don't worry. I couldn't have found a better man."

The next morning, Thorbjörn listened quietly to his daughter. From time to time, he glanced at his son-in-law, who stood next to her in front of the high seat, flinching as if being struck as she spun the chronicle of their misfortunes. Thjodhild had long since finished, and her father was still scratching his chin through his dense beard. Finally, he said, "Our family belongs together."

Not one scolding word, no probing questions. Only: *Our family belongs together.* And thus, the decision was made.

Thorbjörn himself spread the rumor: At the request of her old parents, Erik would return to Habichtstal with his wife, because working side by side was the best thing for the future of the clan. The rich lords of the neighborhood nodded in understanding.

Erik emerged from his troubles as if from a dull, stuffy cave, without loss of honor. And with this clear perspective, he could now look forward to renewed happiness.

"Today I'll show you your land." Thorbjörn sat in the saddle of a pink-and-white stallion and rode with Erik and Tyrkir from Hawk Farm northward into a higher side valley. Servants followed, one of them guarding the pot aglow with embers, the others leading horses packed with brushwood and wood shavings.

After about half an hour of riding, the farmer bridled the stallion and had a stake driven into the ground.

"Son-in-law, all the land you can see from this point to the Water Horn is what I'm willing to give you, as well as the hillside that goes down from this valley to the river, where you can build your farm. You'll have plenty of space, and yet we won't be far."

Erik shielded his eyes. Meadowed slopes rose to the mountains in the north and east. A stream meandered through the plateau, and in the northwest the view ended at a wooded hilltop capped by a bare rock peak, the Water Horn. "You are good to me."

"It's not a gift." There was a clear threat in Thorbjörn's voice. "Our new contract now includes your ship." In the event of a separation or divorce, Erik would have to pay out half the value of his wife's ship in hacksilver, as had been established yesterday before witnesses.

"I understand," Erik grumbled.

Stiffly, Thorbjörn stood straighter himself. His face hardened.

Tyrkir watched him anxiously. What came now? The friends had expected a fertile piece of land and some meadows but never dreamed that the farmer would give away half his land. And now, why this sudden long silence? The old man was clever, and he had certainly seen through Erik's lies about the marriage agreement by now. Did he want to see Erik repent? Was his goal not to help, but to teach a lesson? As long as his word was not sealed with an oath, he could still deny the new agreement. *Great Tyr*, the German asked silently, *please help my master find happiness. There's been enough bitter disappointment.*

And as if the prayer had been heard all the way to Valhalla, the gray-bearded man now spread out both arms. "Erik, who they call the Red, who is my daughter's husband, the father of her child, receive my land, bless it as your own, and make it prosper."

Even before Erik moved, Tyrkir jumped off his horse with a relieved sigh. Soon he had an armful of brushwood and piled it on the ground. Erik came to his side, pushing shavings into the embers before igniting the fire. Over the flickering flames, he stretched his clenched fist to the sky. "Hear me, Thor! I dedicate my land to you."

And then the men mounted up again. They rode for a long time to the next hill. And when they could just make out the first fire behind them, they ignited the second. So it went, paying close attention to the distance, with each new fire in sight of the smoke plume of the last, and by evening they'd surrounded the high valley and had reached the birch- and ash-wooded hill below the Water Horn.

In front of the thick forest, Erik pushed the fire once more into the layered woodpile. "Thor, my divine protector. Look here. This is now our land. Live here with my clan and me."

Thorbjörn dismounted and firmly laid his hand on his son-in-law's shoulder. "Let us be neighbors and friends. We are one family. We will endure any sorrows together. But it is now your duty to preserve our lineage."

Erik met his gaze. "You can trust me."

The old man nodded, satisfied. With a wave, he ordered the giant and Tyrkir to follow him. As soon as they entered the forest, a black fluttering army rose from the birch crowns as ravens croaked and screamed above them. "They are the guardians of our border," Thorbjörn explained. "A long time ago, the mountain here trembled. That's why the ravens curse every intruder, as if they fear that even too firm a footfall could shake the rock again."

Tyrkir watched the giant birds. For a while, they circled around the rugged Water Horn before they settled again in the branches. *Not just guards*, he thought reverently, *but brothers of Hugin and Munin*. Surely, they just told the two god-ravens, Odin's omnipresent scouts, about us. And Hugin and Munin will now fly up to the golden high seat in Valhalla, settle down on the shoulder of Odin, and whisper into the ear of the God of All Heaven about who is now the young farmer in Habichtstal.

A rushing sound tore him from his reverie. Before him, Thorbjörn and Erik slowed their pace, and shortly thereafter, they reached the bank of a deep blue, quiet spring lake. Although the picture was peaceful, roaring and gargling filled the air. The friends looked at each other uneasily.

"Come," Thorbjörn said. "I'll show you how closely beauty and horror can live together."

Slowly, they walked along the shore, avoiding overturned ash trees, before coming to a chasm. Next to them, the lake plunged into the abyss. The water hit the fissured rock deep below them, splashed up, and threw itself as a spraying white wave down into the valley. From their position, they couldn't make out where the waterfall hit the ground, only its deep rumbling. Only farther down in the plain had the elemental force turned into a foaming brook again.

Erik pointed to buildings and stables below the steep slope. "Who farms there?"

"Valtjof, our neighbor. He chose a good place for his farm." In winter, the mountain protects him from the ice storms from the north, and in summer, the warm winds from south and west gather down in the basin. "Fruit and grass grow abundantly in his soil."

"Valtjof?" Erik asked, and the blood rose to his face. "His brother Ejolf—that lout at the wedding party—"

"Mind yourself," Thorbjörn warned. "You've forgotten. I demand that you stand by your word."

"Don't worry," Erik muttered.

Ejolf Dreck. With that name, Tyrkir once again grew worried. *Jealousy is a wound that never heals,* he thought. The pair hadn't thought of the rival for months. Tyrkir sighed. *From now on, we'll have to learn to live with him.*

# LEIF

Thorbjörg took care of her daughter by day, and often by night, so much so that Thjodhild sometimes wasn't sure which of them was looking forward to the baby more. Thjodhild enjoyed the weeks on Hawk Farm while her husband and Tyrkir sailed up to Hornstrand.

After loading all their belongings, Erik planned to take the longer route around the North Cape. "Believe me, sometimes you get to your destination faster by taking a detour," he had asserted. After sailing the big northern arch, he wanted to enter the Breidafjord from the west, and then feel his way through the island belt and reach the inner Hvammsfjord. From there, the loads could be transported more easily and by the shortest route to the newly chosen farmstead. "You'll see. By late summer, a fire will be burning in our own hall."

Thjodhild had not doubted him for a moment. After the hard months in solitude—after all the disappointments—she knew that Erik would keep his word.

"Wait with the child until I am back."

It was a promise she could not make when they said their goodbyes. "I do not know enough to promise that."

Goddess Freya would determine the time. That was Thjodhild's firm belief, and also what she'd been telling herself in recent days. Under Thorbjörg's supervision, the sauna had long since been prepared to become a birthing house, and Thjodhild had moved there when the first pain came. Every morning Thorbjörg had come to her daughter's bedside. She'd spread oil over Thjodhild's rounded belly, firmly but tenderly, as if she were stroking the unborn child while at the same time making sure it shifted to a comfortable position for the birth. She always hummed a melody that Thjodhild remembered from her own childhood.

One morning, the experienced woman gently checked below. "The contractions will come more regularly today." Seeing her daughter's helpless face, she added with a smile, "You can help. Your child wants to come into the light. Think of nothing else now."

She let Thjodhild get up. While both walked in the sunshine in front of the sauna house, the old woman told of the night she'd given birth.

Her voice lured the contractions—Thjodhild felt a painful wave, which soon withdrew and then returned after some time. "Breathe, my girl, only we women have the strength to give new life."

As the contractions came at ever-shorter intervals, Thorbjörg led Thjodhild to a mortar full of grain and handed her the pestle. "Crush them! But not with violent blows—the flour should remain coarse. From this, I'll bake you a sweet child's bread after the birth." With that, she left the daughter alone.

Thjodhild's arms rose and fell, and she felt each time how the pressure in her pelvis became more painful. A contraction took her breath away, and she cried out against her will. But before fear seized her, her mother returned with two old maids, and together they led the groaning young woman into the warm room.

As if through a veil, Thjodhild saw the space covered with moss and a cloth. "Kneel down, my little one!" Arms lifted her body with each new wave. Thjodhild noticed her mother's serious face, her calming voice, nothing else until this one great pain stopped all time.

A little scream, bright and demanding, roused her from her exhaustion. *It is true*, Thjodhild thought as she opened her eyes.

She lay on soft furs, saw the ceiling beams above her, nothing else. Her abdomen and thighs were being rubbed with a damp, cool cloth. *Why is Mother silent? Why don't I hear anything from my child?* Thjodhild tried to stand, but she was only able to rise a little before she sank back wearily. She felt tears well in her eyes.

"Mother. Where is it?"

"Soon, my girl. Soon."

She heard the bright cry again, followed by indignant whining. Thjodhild breathed out a sigh. *Yes, it is really true.* And when her mother bent over her and put a rosy warm being between her breasts and said, "You have a son. He is so beautiful," she felt all the distress and pain of the past hours flow away from her. With her fingers, she felt for the wet hair and found shoulders and arms. "I want to look at him. Please!" Immediately, pillows were tucked behind her back. She took in a wrinkled little human with tiny eyes in a wrinkled face. "But he looks so old," she whispered in horror.

The women smiled and laughed. Thorbjörg sat down next to the bed on a wooden block. "That's the way it is, my girl. So the circle of life begins. In a few days, the skin tightens, then the little one grows into a man, has strength, and believes that he always will, but later on in old age, he will again be as weak and wrinkled as he is now."

Thjodhild gently stroked the baby's tiny clenched hands and silently compared them to his father's fists. "I wish you a life full of happiness, my child," she whispered.

Only at the beginning of June did the ship enter the bay at the bottom of the Hvammsfjord. A storm had stopped Erik for two weeks. Tyrkir had been injured. While jumping into the cargo hold, he'd stumbled over a rope and sprained his right foot.

"You'll never be a sailor," Erik mocked.

"And what would you be without your pilot? We'd only go around in circles." But the pain had remained. The first boatman had had to take Tyrkir's place at the dragon's head because his swollen foot had made standing on the swaying planks torture. Now Tyrkir was glad finally to be able to return to land.

From the ship, he spotted young men on the shore. They were laughing and yelling. Some raced their horses on the shallow pebble beach while others faced off half-naked and measured their strength wrestling. As soon as the boat approached, the men ceased their wild play. A distraction! Three of them waded into the water to help pull the knarr farther onto the beach, but a shrill whistle at their backs made them halt. "We won't touch that tub!"

Tyrkir squinted. The order had come from one of the riders—Ejolf Dirt! He sat in the saddle, his blond hair held back with a headband, his angular face pale with rage. "Come back now. We don't help strangers."

By then, Erik recognized the man, too. He watched silently as the three boys turned and, shortly after, left the beach with their leader and comrades. "Well, I could have done without that welcome."

"Just forget him." Tyrkir snapped his finger. "Ejolf and his cronies weren't here at all."

"What do you mean? I'm not blind."

"Excuse me, Master." Tyrkir gave a small shake of his head. *Blind? It would be better*, he thought, at least when it came to that Ejolf and those precious idlers.

Halfway into the high valley, servants paused their work in a meadow and waved with their rakes before coming to meet the ship. One asked, "You are Erik, the husband of Thjodhild of Hawk Farm?"

"What about my wife?"

"She is well. Be glad you have become a father. Of a son!"

For a moment, Erik froze, then he swung off his horse with impressive speed as he usually did only in battle, and stormed toward the servant. "Say that again!"

"Father... as I said." The man took a few cautious steps back. "People everywhere are talking about it."

Erik punched his fist in his left hand and turned to Tyrkir. "Did you hear? I'm a father! That's what I call a good woman." He pulled a piece of hacksilver from his belt pouch and handed it to the messenger. "Here, take it! Happiness must be paid for. Otherwise, it won't last long."

From that moment, the men's progress felt painfully slow. Erik couldn't ride ahead to see his son since Tyrkir was unable to work with his injury, so the young father had no choice but to lead the trek past Hawk Farm and to their destination.

Finally, they reached the slope close to the Water Horn. The crates were unloaded. While the timber was to remain on the cart, two carved beams for the high seat were carried by Erik himself to the place where the new house was to be built. "Come closer! Hurry up!"

As soon as the servants and maids had gathered around him, he called down Thor's blessing on this spot. But his impatience shortened the solemn moment.

He pointed to the nearby meadow creek. "Pitch our tents there," he ordered the women. "And you, Katla, take care of the food. There are still enough supplies."

He divided his servants into two groups. One, he instructed to collect stones for the walls, the other to cut out sod and peat bricks from the swampy meadows down by the river. "Tomorrow, I'll be back. And you'll be sorry if we're not ready to start the construction!" He pulled Tyrkir into his side. "Did I forget anything?"

"The only thing missing is the whip," his steward remarked. "Then you'd be a true slave driver."

"Don't irritate me. I'm a father now," Erik threatened. "Besides, you can't run from me with your foot." Without warning, he grabbed Tyrkir, carried the wriggling man to a horse, and swung him into the saddle. "We'll go see my son!" He got on his own horse, let out a howl, and spurred the animal on.

Shortly before reaching Hawk Farm, he reined in his mount. Surprised, Tyrkir looked at him from the corner of his eye. "Have you forgotten something?"

"The name. What will my son be called?" Erik couldn't approach the child unprepared. As soon as he acknowledged the newborn, he had to call him by his name to keep the evil powers at bay.

They let the horses trot. Thorvald, like his grandfather? After great-grandfather Ulf? Or Oxenthorir? No, Tyrkir said, it would be better to choose a new name. "It has to distinguish him, because he is your firstborn."

"Yes, his name will bring him happiness." Erik ran both hands through his shaggy hair. His gaze wandered over the buildings in front of him and farther, over the extensive property of Hawk Farm. "All this will one day belong to my son." And in that moment, he knew the name. "Leif. Because he is my heir."

"Leif." Tyrkir practiced the name several times.

"Yes, Leif. That is the name of my son." The father tapped his chest. "And I found the name, not you. Don't forget that, you know-it-all!" He slapped his thigh. "Yes, now I also know a name for you. Tyrkir the Know-It-All—that suits you."

"Very imaginative, my lord. When I consider the thrift with which you normally use your brain . . ."

They were greeted by the dogs barking, then by the servants, and soon Thorbjörn came out of the house to receive the men. He asked about the journey, and it was clear how hard he was trying not to tell the news right away.

Erik also kept to formalities and said, "Except for the storm, there were no difficulties. The servants and the crew are in good health. Our cargo wasn't lost—"

"You can tell me later!" the old man interrupted. "Welcome, son-in-law. But now I want to tell you about—"

"It's a son, isn't it?"

"You already know?" Thorbjörn seemed almost disappointed.

"The whole valley talks of nothing else." Erik couldn't hold in his excitement any longer. "How is my wife? Where is the child? I have to see her, right now."

"Then follow me." The gray-bearded man led the friends to the sauna situated behind the residential building, giving the young father the right-of-way while remaining near the entrance with Tyrkir.

Erik hesitated, looked at his mother-in-law, then at the men standing by the door, and blocked their view with his back. He leaned over Thjodhild, kissed her hair, forehead, and pressed his lips to her soft mouth.

*How much I missed you*, she thought. *Even if the odor of travel and old sweat takes my breath away, I love it.* She turned her head back and looked into his amber eyes. "I couldn't wait. There's been three of us for twenty nights now."

Erik followed her gaze to the cradle. "Show him to me."

"Wait," his mother-in-law interjected resolutely. "There must be order, or I will not allow you to give him the son." Taking the ball of yarn, she pushed Erik aside and freed her daughter from the strand of wool wrapped around her hands. "Tell your husband to at least wash his face and arms!"

"She's right." The corners of Thjodhild's mouth twitched. "Your son's nose is still sensitive." She grabbed hold of Erik's fingers and whispered, "But first tell me his name. Quickly!"

The father straightened up. "If I have to wait"—he grinned

boyishly—"then you must wait, as well." With long strides, he left the room, Tyrkir limping behind him.

Out by the water tub, they both dunked their heads and rubbed their necks and arms until they determined they'd made enough of a sacrifice to cleanliness.

On their return, the cradle had been placed in the middle of the anteroom. Oil lamps flickered on the floor around the child. Tyrkir stood outside the light ring along with the mother and grandparents.

It was clear that Erik had now become aware of the gravity of the moment. He alone had the duty and the right to accept this child into the family or to reject him. A father could reject the newborn child and leave it to the animals of the wilderness if it was deformed or if the family could not afford another mouth to feed.

But nobody even considered this when Erik joined the circle and bent over the cradle. His lips trembled at the sight of his naked son. With his fingertip, he touched the little hands and feet, and stroked the scrotum and the tiny limb. "You shall belong to me!"

Having his sleep disturbed, the baby answered with an angry squeal.

Outside the circle, Tyrkir stealthily watched the mother. *How much I like to be near her*, he noted in surprise. *I hadn't noticed before, but now after so long…* He immediately suppressed the thought. But it was too late. Thjodhild turned her head as if she'd felt the warmth of his musings. She met his dark eyes with a puzzled look, then returned her attention to the father of her child.

Erik lifted the boy over his head with both hands and stretched him toward the sky. "Air, fire, sun, and water—to you, great forces, I offer my son, Leif. Accept him, be his mighty protectors and friends for as long as he lives."

Protesting against the uncomfortable position, Leif screamed and struggled, and a bright stream rained down on his father's face and beard. As soon as Erik tasted the juice, he shouted proudly, "Welcome! Yes, you are my son!"

Thorbjörg pressed her husband's hand. "A good omen," she whispered, sighing.

The father held the rosy, screaming baby before him on the palms of his large hands. Then the mother quietly stepped into the ring of lights to join them. Erik presented her with the child, and she rocked him in her arms, humming until Leif calmed down, then introduced him to his line of ancestors for the first time, singing quietly. This was an important task, and it would be repeated until the child could recite the chain of names himself. This alone would allow him to identify himself as a full member of the clan.

"Leif, you are the son of my Erik, and Erik is the son of Thorvald, and he had Asvald as his father, and Asvald was the son of Ulf, and he had Oxenthorir as his father." With the familiar sound, the little one soon closed his eyes and fell asleep.

Thjodhild turned to her husband. "We should choose the godfather now."

"But who? I know no one suitable." Someone had to be found. Among noble families, it was even the custom to switch firstborns for a few years. Erik shrugged. How could he choose between the neighboring farmers if he didn't even know them? "I leave the decision to you."

"I only know one to whom I would entrust my son." Thjodhild looked over to Tyrkir. "Come into our circle!"

He hesitated. Was it out of shame for his forbidden thoughts earlier? Was it because the honor startled him? He did not know.

"What is it?" Erik rumbled. "My best friend won't take care of my child?" The solemn ceremony was already taking too long for the eager father. And Leif, roused by his father's loud voice, whimpered. "Shall I drag you over here? Are you trying to insult my wife?"

"No, Master." He cleared his throat. "Nor will I ever." *Move, fool, and don't delay the ceremony any longer,* he ordered himself. He limped to the young family.

"About time," Erik growled.

Irritated by the harsh tone, Tyrkir snapped back, "Why are you rushing me, Lord? I have the right to think about such a duty."

"Know-It-All..."

"Stop it!" Thjodhild warned. "You can argue later if you still feel like it." She carefully placed her child in the arms of the freckled steward. "Swear before us, the parents and the grandparents, that you will support Leif as a friend and teacher."

Tyrkir looked down at the boy. How warm he felt. How soft his skin was. He managed to return Thjodhild's gaze without embarrassment.

"The great Tyr be my witness, I will be a faithful teacher to Leif, using all my skill and knowledge."

Erik clapped his hands. "Well, that's done." He went to his father-in-law's side. "My tongue is dry from all the talking." Surely there was reason enough to celebrate!

Thorbjörn did not need to be asked. Yes, a sip for the child, a second for the happy homecoming, a third so that tomorrow the building of the house could begin under good fortune. After that, they'd surely come up with some reasons for the fourth sip, and those that would surely follow.

Over his shoulder, Erik called to his friend impatiently. "Come now, or do I have to carry you?"

"You go ahead!" said Thorbjörg, holding Tyrkir back. First, she wanted to look at his foot, and she would not tolerate any objection. "As godfather, you now belong to my family." She treated the swollen ankle with herbs and ointments; the injury wasn't that bad, she said, and with a little more rest, Tyrkir would soon be able to walk without pain.

She showered him with advice until it became too much for even Thjodhild, and so the patient was freed from her care.

After four weeks, the exterior walls of the main house were completed, and the roof was sealed with turf. Inside, the seat of honor for the head of the family was set between the two elaborately carved supporting beams.

On a bright summer's day, Thjodhild and two maidservants from Hawk Farm set out to visit the construction site. Erik embraced her with a laugh. The servants came from all sides and gave the mistress a warm welcome. As her mother had told her to, she first inquired about Tyrkir's foot.

He looked at her and tried not to show his uneasiness. "Say thank you to Thorbjörg. She saved me. Without her remedies, I would surely have lost my foot."

"Don't mock," Thjodhild scolded. "Even if Mother is sometimes too worried, she really does mean well."

"And *I* am serious." With an exaggerated gesture, Tyrkir put his hand on his chest. "I am saved, Mistress."

Thjodhild laughed. "Silly man. Oh, it's good to see you again."

*She suspects nothing*, Tyrkir thought with relief. How he had fought those forbidden feelings for her in many sleepless hours! He hadn't been able to defeat them—he knew that—and he didn't want that anyway, but at least he'd suppressed them enough so that they didn't endanger his friendship with Erik. This first meeting was a test for him, and he had passed it.

Later, Erik led his wife alone through the new hall. A cone of light fell through the wind-eye directly onto the wide high seat. He shone the torch into every corner. "We're not finished yet." The ditch for the great fire still had to be laid with stones. The side aisles needed to be raised. The dining benches were missing, and there were still no shelves hung on the walls. "We need more wood. But we'll get that in the next few days up on the Water Horn."

He pulled her farther inside and opened the door to the sleeping chamber at the back, holding the torch higher, swinging it back and forth. "Well, what do you think?"

The wide bed could not be overlooked. A fragrance floated through the room—a mixture that Thjodhild loved. She found the sizable hay sack next to the timbered frame, and the peeled beams, ornately decorated at the head and foot ends, added to the smell of fresh wood. She leaned against her husband. "I shall gladly make my home with you here."

Gently, he wrapped his free arm around her and touched her breasts. Since Thjodhild was breastfeeding, they were bigger and fuller than before. "When ... I mean, it's been a long time since we ..."

"Yes, Erik. I long for it, too." Her hand slipped from his belt down. She stroked slightly over his hips and closer to the middle. Already, at the first touch, she felt his excitement. She let him go immediately. "Forgive me. Now, after the birth, I do not know how long we have to wait."

Erik held her tightly in his arms. "Gently ... Just say when. Believe me, I can be very gentle."

Her fingers wandered back to the middle, as if drawn. *If my body wants it*, she thought, *then what harm can there be*? She looked into Erik's eyes. "Now."

"What do you mean?" he asked, surprised.

Thjodhild fidgeted with his belt. "Right now." She had already opened his trousers and pulled them down.

But the torch was in the way. "Wait!" Hindered by the bulge of cloth around his ankles, he hurried to the wall in hopping steps.

There was no iron holder, so he rammed the shaft between the bricks.

Meanwhile, Thjodhild had thrown the hay bag onto the bed and laid herself on it. Despite her desire, she had to smile as he came back in the same awkward way.

He looked down at his ankles. "It's your fault. If you don't give me time, how else am I supposed to come to you?"

Thjodhild pulled her skirt up to her navel. As he kneeled between her legs, every joke was forgotten. "Be careful, Erik," she whispered.

At first, there was pain, but quickly her desire absorbed it. When Erik began to pull away, she felt for his arm. "No, don't go. Stay beside me for a moment. I want to feel your skin. I missed your smell so much."

Both watched the flickering light on the beams above them for a long time. Finally, Erik broke the silence. "Even if I don't have beautiful words, providence is good to me. You and Leif and our new land—that's a lot. Do you understand what I mean?"

She rolled to her side and snuggled up to him. "Here we start anew. Yes, Erik, here we've found our happiness. And we will hold on to it."

# THE LANDSLIDE

The weather changed from one hour to the next. Rain whipped the men's faces, yet soaked to the skin, they continued to work. It took longer now to have the two horses pull the branched trunks from the forest. Since the day before yesterday, Tyrkir had been digging with five farmhands below the Water Horn. Ax strikes and the breaking down of the trees had filled the days with noise so the ravens, disturbed in their peace, had withdrawn with outraged croaking to the rugged rock top. Tyrkir's gaze had wandered up to these scouts of the god-ravens Hugin and Munin.

Even now, as Tyrkir, his men, and the draft animals once more stomped into the cleared aisle, he looked around for them. *They watch our every step, as if we've desecrated their holy realm*, he thought. But then, just as quickly, he chided himself. *What are the ravens to you? We need wood, and the forest is our property. We'll be working here two more days, and then peace can return to the mountain lake, and the guards will be able to retake their posts in the crowns of the birch trees.*

The closer the men came to the mountain ledge, the harder they had to fight against the wind and rain. Even the roar of the waterfall was drowned out by the howling elements. They had cleared the forest over a width of ten horse lengths, and only a few bushes were left between the felled trunks and stumps. The storm brushed and dragged at the foliage without protection. Giant clouds drifted above their heads, and like a torrent, the rain hit the exposed surfaces and washed the soil off the porous rock.

"Two more! Shield the nags!" Tyrkir shouted at the servants. "Watch out for the ropes! Then we're done for today!" They could get the rest of the trunks out tomorrow.

The troop reached the farm late in the evening. Protection and comfort under a sturdy roof. What a gift on such a day! Soon trousers and smocks were drying on the line near the great fire, and meat broth, prepared by Katla, warmed the men from the inside.

Tyrkir, wrapped in a fur blanket, sat with Erik. "As long as the storm continues, there's little point in continuing," he said.

"It doesn't matter. Our people have to go up to the forest again." Erik put down the fishbone he'd been using to clean his teeth. "We need the timber. When Thjodhild and the boy come in two weeks, I want everything in the house to be ready."

How well Tyrkir understood his friend. The memory of the farm on Sharpcliff and the despair on Thjodhild's face when she saw the miserable buildings for the first time was still too fresh. Now Erik wanted to offer her a home they could be proud of.

"So, we're agreed," the steward said, yawning. "I'll send the men out early in the morning." If the ground in the aisle was too soft, they could at least load up the trunks already piled at the edge of the forest and bring them here. "I'm going to lie down for a while." Grinning, he looked toward the sleeping chamber.

"Yes, just make yourself comfortable, Know-It-All!" Erik scowled. As a reward for his carving work on the double bed, Tyrkir had claimed the right to sleep there until Thjodhild moved in. Meanwhile, his master had to make do with a spot by the servants' benches. "Two weeks to go. By Thor, then, at last, it is over!"

The storm intensified overnight. Below the Water Horn, the rain washed away all the moss and topsoil from the cleared area to the mountain ledge. The roots of the tree stumps lay exposed on the bare rock. Unhindered, the water penetrated deeper into the stony cracks. Small chunks detached themselves from the porous edge, rolling into the valley. An enormous gust seized the ash nearest the edge of the aisle, crashing and tearing and toppling the tree next to it. The next tree, a birch, also buckled under the force. As if pulled by an invisible chain, the weather protection of the forest gradually collapsed.

When morning dawned, the wind had died back, though the rain was still pouring down, penetrating deeper into the fissured rock. Dull fractures shook the mountain ledge. Immediately, the ravens lifted themselves out of their sleeping niches, lamenting and circling over the rugged rock.

A crack opened. It gaped from halfway across the length of the aisle all the way to the lake. Stone and mud slipped and sank slowly into the depths. It took with it trees and the whole front part of the mountain ledge, tearing away the lower rocks as the avalanche grew, all of it roaring into the valley with a mighty crash.

Valtjof's farm was crushed as if by a giant fist.

Silence set in, and the rain stopped. Soon, the first blue spots appeared in the sky.

Ejolf Dirt had been drinking and playing dice with his cronies on a neighboring property, and he had spent the night there. He was torn from his sleep by the distant rumble. With a pounding head, he staggered outside. "What's going on?"

A servant pointed mutely up to the Water Horn, following the path of the landslide with his finger, before finally stopping at the massive mountain of mud and debris far back in the valley. "A great misfortune, sir."

"My brother!" screamed Ejolf. He stormed back into the house. Soon after, he reappeared with Hravn Holmgang, one of his closest friends. On the way to the stable, they strapped on their swords, then pulled out the horses and jumped into their saddles.

When Ejolf reached the end of the valley, he found nothing left.

His brother, along with his family, and all of their wealth, had been buried by the avalanche. All that remained for him were the sheep, the young cattle in the summer pastures, and the charity of his relatives. The realization hit him like a blow: his carefree life had come to an end.

"Who caused this?" he lamented.

Hravn put an arm around his shoulder. "The gods have destined it this way."

"Never! Why should the gods punish me?" Ejolf freed himself violently. "For what crime? Tell me!"

Hravn picked up a boulder that any other man could have only lifted with difficulty. He possessed the strength and speed of two men and was known as a fearsome fighter. He'd earned his fame during the Holmgang, where according to the duel's strict rules, he'd killed every one of his opponents. "Do you see this stone? Thousands and thousands far bigger have fallen here. No man possesses such power. It was fate, believe me!"

Without answering, Ejolf climbed up the mountain of debris. He stared up for a long time. The waterfall had become broader, and the demolition site looked as if Utgard-Loki, the master of the empire of the giants, had come himself and knocked down the ledge with a mighty blow.

"There's a border up there. The area belongs to the Habichtshof. So it was land from the Habichtshof that killed my brother." Ejolf rammed his fists into his sides. "And who is settling on the slope to the plateau?" With one single movement, he was back by Hravn Holmgang's side. "That red bastard!" Hate glowed in his eyes. "Who knows, my friend, if he didn't cast a spell to bring about my misfortune."

Ejolf rejected every one of Hravn's attempts to console him.

"It was intentional, I feel it. If you're not a coward, come with me. We'll ride up there and see for ourselves."

Tyrkir had sent the five servants ahead. He wanted to follow with the horse and cart and bring them closer to the slope below the forest so the trunks wouldn't have to be hauled as far. "Don't wait for me," he'd ordered. "There's still a lot of wood in the clearing. Move out as much as you can until I can join you."

The morning air was fresh and clean, and the slaves quickly reached the forest. But as soon as they entered the aisle, their two draft horses snorted and shied. Neither shouting nor whips were of any use—the powerful animals refused to be commanded and would not move from where they stood.

"A troll?" suggested Ketil, the most experienced and oldest servant. "Or an undead? Maybe he was here looking for shelter from the storm."

Fear washed over the men. If there really was an eternally damned spirit nearby, they had to drive him away. Until they did, they couldn't begin their work. The danger of being banished was too great.

They took the axes from their shoulders, spread out, and shouted, striking the tree trunks to the right and left of the clearing, rustling in the bushes, and making as much noise as they could.

Step by step, they continued to work their way forward, paying attention to the depressions and branch forks at the edge of the aisle. They did not look ahead.

The troop reached the yawning abyss and the shouting died. The men stared into the depths, following the trail of devastation, and saw the mountain of mud and scree in the valley. "There was a farmyard there," Ketil whispered, as if he didn't want to make the disaster worse.

"The farm of Valtjof," moaned the man next to him. "Oh gods, do not let our neighbors lie under the rubble!"

Tyrkir jumped from the cart box and led the horse by its halter. He searched for a convenient path between the rising hills, one they could also use on their way back to haul the wood. He thought how juicy the grass was. He looked up to the forest. *From up there, we'll bring in more hay than from all the meadows on Sharpcliff together. There will be enough food for cattle. We'll never have to fear winter again.*

Two riders appeared on the ridge to his left. Tyrkir shaded his eyes. Against the cloudy sky, he couldn't see who was riding, only figures in blowing coats who were driving their horses up to the birch forest. Fish robbers! There was no other explanation—brazen fools. No one else dared to fish trout from a lake that did not belong to him.

The riders had reached the wood yard in front of the aisle, jumped off, and disappeared from his view. "Be glad that I'll be the one to drive you away," Tyrkir rumbled. "If Erik were here, you wouldn't get away that easily." He pulled the halter harder, but in vain, for the horse set the pace and refused to be yanked out of it.

The slaves were still standing at the point of destruction, paralyzed by the scale of the disaster, all trying to understand what had happened. They didn't hear the two men coming.

"Criminals! Cowardly murderers!"

The servants turned in terror. Ejolf Dirt and Hravn Holmgang stood two horse lengths away. "Didn't I say so!" Ejolf said in a menacingly soft voice to his friend. "Not the gods. These villains caused the landslide."

The giant shrugged his shoulders. "It may be so, or it may not be."

"Look at them! Guilt is written on their brows. Why else would they be here so early?"

Old Ketil shook his head violently. "Please, Lord, do not judge us prematurely!" He dropped his ax and walked toward Ejolf with his palms open. "We logged here, nothing more. No man can kick off a mountain."

"Yes, yes, you worm. First, you felled all the trees and then enlarged the rock cracks with iron rods. Now my brother and his family are lying under rubble and mud."

"Never." The allegation took Ketil's breath away. "No, Lord, believe me. Valtjof was a good neighbor and a friend of our lord. Why should we break the peace with him?"

"My brother was a friend of Thorbjörn, not of your master, that sneaky red intruder."

Ketil raised his hand to vow. "All the gods are my witnesses—"

The blade flashed, and Ejolf cut off Ketil's forearm. "A liar may not dare seek help from the gods."

Blood splashed from the stump. Despite the pain, Ketil insisted, "Neither Erik nor anyone else is to blame for this misfortune." He gathered strength and staggered toward the slender young farmers. "You and your friend, you are liars . . ."

With a slight step to the side, Ejolf let the old man pass, then hacked the sword blade deep into his shoulder. Without a sound, Ketil fell to the ground.

Hravn hesitated, and then his expression changed. "No one must insult Hravn Holmgang."

"I swear it," Ejolf said. "He and the others over there, they are cowardly murderers."

"That's true."

Erik's servants looked around, afraid. The abyss yawned behind them. Their only hope of escape was to flee past the two men.

They swung their axes, screamed, and stormed forward. Hravn did not even reach for his own weapon. He snatched the hatchet from the first man that tried to pass and split his skull with it, grabbing the next like a doll, breaking his spine, and throwing the lifeless body aside.

Ejolf had lowered his sword, letting the remaining two men come close. "Show me what you've got," he taunted, dancing back and forth. "Come on, hit me!" They tore their weapons back at the same time but were too slow for the experienced fighter. Ejolf separated the first head from the torso, avoided the ax blow of the last of the four servants, and drove the blade deep into his belly.

Finally, Tyrkir was satisfied. The cart stood on a flat surface, and he had secured the wheels with stones and wrapped the horse's halter around a boulder. He had not been able to guide the carriage any closer to the last meadow slope below the wood yard. *We'll easily manage the first haul to the farmyard by evening*, he thought. *Erik can relax. Our Thjodhild and his son won't lack for anything when they join us.*

Pounding hoofbeats made him look up. Bent over their horses' manes, the two riders rushed away along the ridge.

"You can count on my Ketil." Tyrkir whistled appreciatively through his teeth. "As old as he is, he has lost none of his courage. He still defends the land as if it were his own. In gratitude, I'll drain a well-filled jug with him tonight," Tyrkir said aloud as he climbed the slope.

It was quiet at the clearing—too quiet. The heavy draft horses stood immobile right in front in the aisle, and Tyrkir didn't see the men at work. He called out to them, but there was no answer. He called out again, this time louder, more demanding.

The sky suddenly darkened. The nags neighed and fled back toward the wood yard. Out of nowhere, the ravens were upon him. The black army fluttered up and down above his head in a confused frenzy. Claws pulled at his collar and coat sleeves, and beaks snapped at his ears. For a moment, there was only wild screeching and the flapping of wings. Then the guards flew away and let themselves drop farther ahead into the treetops to either side of the aisle. The cawing did not stop.

Driven by a grim sense of foreboding, Tyrkir ran ahead and discovered the dead. For a moment, his heart seemed to stop. *Maybe*—

The word drowned out the horror that filled him. Maybe one was still alive? Maybe he could help him? Save him? But Tyrkir's hopes were destroyed as he took in the severed head, the bleeding wounds, and the faces frozen in pain and fear.

He went from one to the next and closed their eyes. One last service—there was nothing more he could do. Farther into the woods, he discovered the old servant. His limp body trembled. With his legs, he tried to push himself forward.

"Ketil." Tyrkir immediately fell to his knees and gently turned him to his back. "Friend. My good friend."

Ketil opened his eyes at the sound of Tyrkir's voice. "Where? Where are you?"

Tyrkir bent over the tortured face. "Here, friend. Be still. Everything will be fine. I will take you down into the valley."

"No, leave me!" The words came in bursts. "I—I am going away from here in a moment. Stay until then!" The old servant's breathing was labored, and only after some moments did he manage to speak again. "It was Ejolf . . . also Hravn. Revenge . . . because the mountain broke off."

Tyrkir did not understand and believed that the embrace of death had already confused the spirit of the old man. "Don't be afraid! It was Ejolf and the Holmganger? Are you sure?"

"Landslide." Ketil lifted the stump of his arm weakly. "Up ahead . . . The mountain has buried the Valtjof farm. All are dead."

Tyrkir looked over his shoulder, horrified, but he couldn't see a thing. "I'll be right back."

"No, please stay!" The old man's eyeballs rolled restlessly. "I forgot."

"What, my friend?"

Ketil pushed the bloody stump onto his chest with great effort. "Which god . . . ? Who also lost his hand?"

"It was Tyr." Tears rose to Tyrkir's eyes. "The great, courageous Tyr."

"Yes, tell me!" Ketil pleaded, looking into the young steward's face. "What . . . what did he do?"

And Tyrkir quietly told of the futile fight of the gods against Fenrir. Tyr, alone, had succeeded in chaining the monster because he had pushed his right hand deep into its throat. "He sacrificed his hand to banish the evil forces forever."

"Thank you." Ketil nodded weakly. "Now, I know it again." He closed his eyes and sighed. And then he was no more.

Tyrkir crouched next to him for a long time, overcome with grief and loss, before realizing that the reality was much graver. It was not just these cowardly murders—Valtjof, their neighbor and friend, was also dead!

Tyrkir gathered himself and went to the site of destruction. To his right, far away, the mirror of the great lake flashed, a peaceful view embraced by the sun, but right there, deep below him, lay a muddy grave. Tyrkir felt a sharp coldness rise within himself. "Our happiness was also crushed there," he muttered. The wheel had been set in motion, and no one knew whom it would roll over before it completed its journey. The mountain had buried the farmer and his farm, and Ejolf blamed Erik for this misfortune, so in retaliation, he and the Holmganger had killed the servants.

And all because of this? Tyrkir picked up a birch branch. Little by little, he tore the twigs from the trunk. Jealousy is a wound that never heals. "That vicious Ejolf!" He had deliberately not waited, all to frustrate any possibility of a peaceful settlement. "Battle and blood, that's what he wants. Nothing else." Erik would have to act if he didn't want to lose his reputation.

Tyrkir gathered the plucked green twigs with his foot. *How quickly the leaves will wither*, he thought as he passed the corpses. Later, he would return to recover the bodies and bury them.

The two horses were grazing near the wood yard; one whistle, and they followed him down to the carriage. Tyrkir did not climb onto the carriage bench. Peace should last for just a little while longer, so he led the carts and animals on foot back into the valley.

"Damn, where's the wood?" Erik had only glanced at his friend. "What is this, Know-It-All?"

When Tyrkir didn't answer, Erik stepped forward, furious. "By Thor, I should—" He stopped and narrowed his eyes. "What's happened?"

"I'm alone." Except for the freckles, all the color had drained from the steward's face. "I returned without our servants."

"And when—?" Confused, Erik stopped himself. "Oh, you mean the others are still up at the Water Horn waiting for reinforcements because they alone cannot load the trunks. Why didn't you say so? Come on. I'll go myself. How many more men do you need?"

Tyrkir shook his head. "None today." His heart was so heavy. He would have given anything to preserve his master's newly awakened happiness. Now he had to be a messenger, and as soon as he had spoken the news, he would, without hesitating, walk the path determined by fate at Erik's side. "The servants are dead."

Erik stroked his beard, drove his hand through the shaggy mane. Finally, he muttered, "And we needed the wood so badly for sleeping benches and shelves."

"Erik! Didn't you hear me?" Tyrkir stepped closer. "They're lying up there in their own blood. Slain."

"Don't say that!" Erik's broad shoulders rose. "Who would kill our men?"

"Not here." Tyrkir was already walking ahead. Slowly, his friend followed him to the bubbling stream. Close to the bank, they stood together. While Tyrkir reported what he'd seen, Erik's face changed, and when the steward had finished, it was a mask.

"Ejolf and Hravn." Erik barely moved his lips. "Did they have any right to act so heartlessly? Tell me!"

"No."

"Should I sue the murderers at the Thing in two weeks?"

It was just a question. Erik had already made up his mind. Tyrkir quietly confirmed to him what they both knew: Erik was still considered a stranger in Habichtstal. There was little chance of him winning at the court gathering. "Surely Ejolf is already riding from farm to farm and will leave no doubt that you are to blame for the landslide. Until the Thing, he'll stir up all the neighbors against you. And you know, the more supporters he can win, the easier it will be for him to pull the judge to his side."

Erik went to the brook, dropped down, and slapped the cold water onto his face, over and over, then dipped his head in before throwing back his dripping hair. The cold didn't help. "Damned, damned Ejolf!" A scream broke from his chest, wounded and wild. With his fists he pushed against the sky and roared.

Only after some deep breaths did he manage to speak again. "Injustice," he whispered. "I can never let it stand." On his knees, he pointed to the glowing red ball in the west. "Do you see the sun? It doesn't set—the night belongs to the day. No more darkness. I wanted to give Thjodhild and my son the long light and hold them here in my arms."

Tyrkir waited quietly. Finally, his friend rose, and a dangerous glow appeared in the amber of his eyes. "Revenge—that right belongs to me." The mourning was over. Almost matter-of-factly, Erik said, "I must regain my honor. Otherwise, Thor will find no peace in me."

"So, you want war?" Tyrkir replied. "Then I'll hand out weapons to our servants today?"

"Leave it!" The peace in Hawk Valley should be disturbed only briefly and as necessary. The red man had resolved to take his fight to the two murderers alone.

Tyrkir met his master's eyes. "We are two. Even if I lack your strength, I can watch your back."

With a bitter smile, Erik put his hand around the neck of the slim man and pulled him to his broad chest. "Thank you, Know-It-All."

Side by side, they climbed upstream. First, they had to plan for the farm. A troop would salvage the dead the next day, and the wood had to be brought down. Immediately after his return, Erik wanted to continue with the extension of the house, so Thjodhild's move would be delayed by only two weeks at most.

He didn't waste a thought on the fact that this vendetta could mean his own death. Tyrkir looked at his friend with admiration. *That's better*, he thought. *It's enough that I alone am afraid.*

"No sleep," Erik announced. "We'll ride as soon as we've prepared the weapons."

Before their revenge could begin, they'd have to go to Hawk Farm. Erik would not go and fight without the blessing of the family and, above all, without Thjodhild's consent.

While Tyrkir dragged the armory chests outside the house with the help of a servant, Erik briefly informed the other servants of his plans. He divided the work and determined the place where the dead were to be buried. Afterward, he selected four fast horses, ensuring that each hoof and tendon was carefully checked.

Tyrkir was satisfied with the condition of the weapons. Thanks to the fat-soaked rags that had wrapped them, the blades of the long-stemmed battle-axes, daggers, and spearheads showed no signs of rust. The usual armament, which they carried with them daily or had ready at hand in the house, would not be sufficient for the upcoming battle.

For the first time since their arrival in Iceland, Tyrkir held the well-made bow woods, the sinews and arrows, the shimmering chain shirts, and the cutting and stabbing weapons. After checking each object carefully, he laid it in the grass, separating those intended for Erik's use from those he'd use himself. Nothing could be left to chance—the slightest damage, break, or torn bow-eye could mean death. He had the servant rub the round helmets with a mixture of seal fat and sand, after which he mixed ashes with his own saliva to polish their surfaces. The metal had to shine, flashing to frighten the opponent. Then Tyrkir turned his attention to the round shields.

As Erik led the bridled horses to the forecourt, Tyrkir had just decided on five shields, all made of tightly joined wood. The leather and the pointed horn on the metal arch in the middle of each was undamaged.

"It's been a long time," Erik murmured at the sight of the arsenal. "The last time we were armed so was when my father and I prepared ourselves in Norway."

"It'd feel easier if the weapons stayed in the chest." Tyrkir sighed. "Back then, we won and yet lost."

"Not a word of that! We will punish the murderers of our servants. That's the end of it. There will be no war between the families."

"That's how it should be," Tyrkir said, quietly hoping that providence would be kind to them.

Both men silently put on their undergarments of thick, tightly woven cloth, tied their leather shoes, wrapped the leg protectors up to the knee cuffs of their wide pants, and then put on their chain mail. Each pulled the knob of his sword into his belts and put two daggers within reach next to it.

"Just the cloak. That'll do for now," said Erik as he pulled the strap of the hunting horn over his head. "Or else, Thorbjörn might think we're about to attack Hawk Farm." The servants tied the battle-axes and spears, shields, bows, arrows, and quivers to the spare horses along with the travel bundles. Before Tyrkir fastened the polished helmets to his saddle, he silently showed his friend the dents from earlier fights.

"So what? That's how you know how much they can take. Even your Know-It-All head stayed whole under there. What more do you want?"

As they left the new farm on the slope, blessings for success and for a happy return accompanied them until they finally ebbed away.

The friends rode in silence. Fog capped the snow-covered mountains in the distance, gray veils of haze rolling along with them on the nearby hills. No night and yet no day. The singing swans, disturbed by the riders, rose out of the meadow with shrill cries.

Soon, the men had reached the pastures of Hawk Farm. As always, the dogs struck first—this time louder, angrier—and the servants came out of the main building faster to see what the commotion was. Only upon closer inspection did they recognize the armed men as Erik and his steward and ran back inside to wake their master.

Barefoot, in a roughly woven nightgown, Thorbjörn stepped outside. With one look, he took in the armor and weapons. The determined faces of his midnight callers made any question unnecessary. "Come into the hall."

After Thorbjörg and Thjodhild emerged from their sleeping rooms wrapped in their capes and had greeted the young men sleepily, the big farmer sat down on the high seat. "I'm listening."

Erik's chest rose and fell. He started twice but struggled to explain the facts calmly. Finally, he turned to Tyrkir. "You explain. You know better than I what's happened."

Thorbjörn interrupted the German's report only once. "The ravens—what did they do? Were they silent when Ketil died?"

Tyrkir tried to remember, recalling the scenes one by one. He moved from one corpse to the next and heard the screeching. At the same time, he closed the lids of the disembodied head, then kneeled next to the old servant. "Silence. When Ketil asked me about God Tyr, and I told him about the hand, there was no sound from the trees."

"That's good." The big farmer twisted a finger through his beard. "Go on. What happened after the man died?"

"Nothing important."

"That's for me to decide, boy."

First grief, then fear made Tyrkir rise. He recalled looking down into the valley at the scree. "I tore green twigs from a branch and thought how quickly they would wither." He explained how he'd found the two horses grazing quietly and closed with how he had led the carriage down into the valley on foot. "As I said, nothing important happened afterward."

The sentence faded away in the hall. For a time, only the crackling of the smoldering embers could be heard.

Thorbjörg broke away from Thjodhild. Her leg slowed her walk to the high seat, but there, she stood tall with a gaze that showed no weakness. After a slight nod from her husband, she laid both hands over her heart like a shield. "The birch leaves must not wither until the murders have been avenged. Hear this, son-in-law. Even the dead must not be touched until you have purified our family honor."

"What? But I've already ordered my people to take them down to the farm."

"You cannot!" Never before had the old farmer's wife scolded him so harshly. "Do you want to break the spell that supports your just cause? How can the gods help you when they can no longer see the reason for your revenge?"

"I didn't think," Erik mumbled, and shoved his friend in the side. "You should have warned me."

Because Tyrkir felt responsible, he defended Erik without hesitation. "Calm yourself, Mistress. Our error can still be rectified." He suggested sending a messenger right away to change the command. Nothing would be touched at the scene of the murder. Quietly, he added, "Thank you for reminding us."

The words brightened the old woman's features. Fighting was a man's business. But Thorbjörg had not been gifted with magical powers, and she often lamented this lack of ability. Still, she would certainly not have let the two young men go on their quest without herbal potions and an incantation. She not only fulfilled her duty as a housewife to always remind the men of their revenge but she also ensured they received divine support and the family's encouragement for the weighty task.

She turned to her daughter. "Why are you silent?"

Thjodhild fidgeted with the hem of her cape. "Soon, Mother. Everything is so new . . ." she whispered. "Give me more time!"

Thorbjörn saw her distress and called out for a servant, gave him precise instructions, and sent him to the new farm on the hill. Turning to Erik, he said, "Whatever happens, I will support you with all my wealth and my loyalty. But before you set out, we should please God Thor with a gift."

Together they went outside and entered the fenced-off sacrificial garden. Erik took the chicken the farmer offered, opened the animal's breast with a single cut, and tied it to the top of the stake by its claws. While blood dripped on his silver Thor's hammer, he looked up at the sky. "Don't think me arrogant, great friend, but lend me some of your strength! Only so much that I can regain our good fortune." He carefully put the amulet back into the coin bag at his belt.

Thjodhild felt her mother's disapproval. *Be calm, Mother. I will fulfill my duty.* She accompanied the men to their horses. *My heart must be silent*, she thought. *I must not say anything about how afraid I am for my son's father, nor about my concern for Tyrkir. He has more courage than strength. I am the wife of a Viking.*

She gave Erik both of her hands. "Blood for blood. Revenge for the sacrilege that was done to us." Uselessly, she fought against the tears. "And . . . and return to me!"

Erik wanted to pull her close, but under the eyes of his parents-in-law, he resisted the urge. "Don't worry. You won't have to wait for me long."

Thjodhild went to the steward. "Take care so that Leif doesn't lose his good teacher. He and I, we need you."

Before Tyrkir could answer, she turned away and returned to the house.

# THE HOLMGANG

As the sun rose higher, the friends rested in a sheltered hollow. They kept their swords and shields within reach as they stretched their tired limbs. Erik chewed on a blade of grass and watched the drifting clouds. Tyrkir had rolled up his coat and pushed it under his neck. *The morning is so quiet and peaceful*, he thought. How long would it last?

The lower Hawk Valley opened up before them. The river gleamed like a silver ribbon, broadening and becoming an oval mirror in the form of the great lake in the distance. There, on the lower bank, behind the woods, was the Spiel Farm. Hravn Holmgang and his clan lived there. "Do we ride directly to the lake? Where do we start the search?"

Erik spat out the stalk he'd been chewing on. "From house to house. I want to have my back free." He pointed to the settlements, small and large. "We inquire about the murderers everywhere. Everyone should know that we're hunting them, and why."

"But we'll lose time. Somebody will warn them."

"That's what I want, Know-It-All." Erik sat up. "No one can say afterward that I killed them in an ambush."

*Oh, great Tyr, give him sense*, begged Tyrkir. *He challenges men who train with their weapons every day, and now he won't use even a little cunning.*

"How long has it been?" Tyrkir began cautiously. "I mean, when was the last time you fought? Swung an ax or hurled a spear?"

"Why do you ask when you already know the answer?"

"Three years is a long time."

"I haven't forgotten," Erik whispered. He pushed his hand through his red mane. "Father took care of that. . . ."

Week after week, Thorvald had trained his son in hand-to-hand combat. Bruises and open wounds were no excuse to interrupt lessons. Only when the son had defeated the father a few times had the old man been satisfied. "You'll also have to remember quickly what he taught us." Erik stood. "Come. This is our day."

The pair shared a flat loaf of bread, washing it down with sour milk, then strapped their swords back on and put on their helmets. The nose bridges changed their faces, pairs of eyes separated by cold metal. They took their battle-axes and spears with them, riding to the nearest farm.

"We're looking for Ejolf Dirt and Hravn Holmgang."

"They're not here." The farmer eyed the armed riders warily. "Is there a reason why you carry so much iron with you?"

Erik enlightened the man in brief words, and immediately they rode on.

"That man is lying," he grumbled. "I know it. Did you see his eyes?" He paused. "You talk to the others, Know-It-All. You'll do better than I."

By noon, they'd reached the upper shore of the lake. They'd asked at four houses on both sides of the stream, but no, the men they sought were not there, and no, nobody knew where they were.

"There! See that man?" Tyrkir pointed to a horseman he saw leaving the homestead where they'd last inquired. The man rode at a wild gallop, making a wide arc, and then headed straight for the Spiel Farm.

"That's good." Erik nodded, satisfied. "Now we know exactly where our prey is. This dog will lure the weasels out of their den." He quickly reached for his spear, making sure the shaft readily slipped out of the leather quiver on the side of the saddle and that the long-stemmed ax jumped into his other fist, before replacing each.

"If we'd had to go to the courtyard first, it would have been bad for us. They could have quickly spread out in the stable or barn."

Tyrkir was quietly amazed. His friend was often sluggish in his thinking, but now he was a hunter who carefully sought to avoid any mistakes.

They rode around the densely packed buildings at a safe distance until the sun was at their backs. Atop a hill, they climbed from their saddles.

"What now?" Tyrkir looked down at the green roofs. White columns of smoke quickly dissolved in the breeze, leaving behind only the smell of a wood fire.

"We wait. And if it takes too long..." Erik struck his horn lightly. "I blow them out."

They didn't have to wait long. The door of the main house swung open, and fully equipped, Ejolf Dirt stepped outside with Hravn, followed by five armed men. So Ejolf had anticipated an attack and had already gathered his horde.

"We should have brought some servants with us." Tyrkir's tongue stuck to his palate. "There's still time. We could retreat and gather reinforcements."

"I'm not a rabbit." Erik watched closely as the men led their horses out of the yard and approached the hill. Only Ejolf and the giant wore chain mail shirts—the rest had protected themselves with thick, quilted-leather jackets. Within shouting distance, the troop formed a spread-out line of attack.

"I'll make my demand," Erik whispered. "You take care of the rest. Our success depends on you. Do you understand?"

"No."

"Don't tease me now, Know-It-All! I'll tell you quietly what you should say. Just make sure you do it right."

Ejolf Dirt took a few steps forward and greeted Erik with an exaggerated wave of his arm. "Look. Visitors. I can't say that this pleases me, but what makes you, intruder, keep honorable men from their work?"

Despite the mockery, Erik controlled his temper. "Atonement for my five servants whom you murdered. I demand the full fine for each one."

Laughing, Ejolf summoned the Holmganger and the others with a signal, and they joined his laughter. But when he raised his shield, silence immediately returned.

"Never before have I paid money for manslaughter, not one gram of silver. Even my friend Hravn has so far only bagged, but never relinquished anything. You speak of murder? No, I avenged the death of my brother and his family. With that, the balance is restored." He bounced slightly on his knees. "But if your ugly red comb swells, we will gladly trim it for you." He gave his men a signal, and with spears in their fists, the attackers moved as one, drawing their semicircle closer around Erik and Tyrkir.

Tyrkir looked around surreptitiously. The escape route was still open—into the saddles, up and away. This pride—this damned sense of honor—what good was it if it only brought death?

But Erik did not move. "Let them come a little closer," he whispered. "Then tell them something about cowardice! Seven against two. I want to fight each one alone."

Tyrkir understood. It wasn't a good plan, but it at least offered them a small chance of survival. With his hands raised high, he stood in front of his friend. "You cowards! My lord has nothing but contempt for you."

Surprised, Ejolf faltered and ordered the cronies to stop. "Contempt? Tell your red rooster that he'll be slain by men who are respected throughout Hawk Valley."

"My master will defend himself. He may die, yes, but the honor will remain his. Your reputation, however, will be blackened. Cowardly mutts, that's what they'll call you and your people in the future. Do you think any woman will ever want to dance with you at a feast? No, she will turn away, her face full of disgust."

Tyrkir saw how his words affected the vain man and added, "What everyone has always thought about you, today you've proved. I can already hear their scorn. 'Yes, Ejolf is all hot air, when he has a superior force at his back.'"

Pale with anger, Ejolf shouted back, "What does your master demand?"

"A fair fight." Tyrkir let his arms sink to his sides. "Nothing more."

Behind him, he heard the quiet voice of his friend: "Excellent, Know-It-All. First, you target the bastard, then Holmganger."

Tyrkir continued loudly, "Your people have nothing to do with it. We, too, could have come here with men, but my master does not want war. This dispute concerns only you and Hravn. If you're so brave, then face my master, and if you are defeated, let your friend try his luck."

"You! You certainly have a smart mouth." Ejolf pointed threateningly. "That tongue—I should cut your fucking tongue out!"

Behind him, Tyrkir heard Erik whisper, "He's not so stupid. You would make a clever gode. Well done, my friend. He doesn't have a choice now if he doesn't want to lose face."

Below the hill, Ejolf consulted with Hravn. There was a violent exchange of words between them. Again and again, Hravn struck his chest, and despite his efforts, the slender leader had trouble appeasing him. Finally, they came to an agreement.

"As you wish," Ejolf Dreck shouted up to the hilltop. "My friend only regrets that he'll be deprived of the fun since I get to fight first, and only the corpse of Erik will be left for him. As compensation, he may take weapons, horses, and you as a slave.

Your master has succeeded in his demand, but I choose how we fight."

The duel was to be carried out on horseback, and then, if necessary, on foot. Ejolf selected a meadow near the lakeshore. Only death would bring victory. Until then, no one but the two fighters would be allowed to enter the battleground. He chose the west side for himself, with the advantage that Erik had to ride against the sun.

"Fine by me," the Red growled.

"My master agrees."

"Tell him to hurry," Ejolf jeered. "I want this little business done in time for dinner."

Tyrkir turned. "Do I have to answer him?"

"Leave it!"

The skin on Tyrkir's freckled face was pale. His heart beat painfully. "By the great Tyr, defeat the braggart! I will kill him myself before I become a slave to that chunk of meat."

"Don't worry. You are, and will, remain my slave." Erik managed a weak smile. "No, you are much more. You are my only friend, and we will remain together for a long time yet. Now, help me prepare."

Tyrkir hung two spare shields on Erik's saddle horn and wished him luck and all of Thor's powers. There was nothing more he could do. Erik jumped on his black-and-white-spotted stallion and trotted ahead to the lakeshore.

Tyrkir wished for lightning as he mounted his horse and pulled the packhorses behind him—a bolt of lightning hurled from Valhalla to burn their enemies. But nothing happened. Scattered clouds drifted above him in the blue sky as the sun glared down.

Beyond the battle turf, Ejolf's gang had rallied around their leader. Ejolf's brown horse danced, and he let the spear circle above his helmet like a light walking stick, accompanied by shouts and exuberant laughter. He seemed to be preparing for sport, not a bloody fight, and for his companions, the winner had already been determined.

When Tyrkir reached his lonely position on his side of the field, Erik gave him a silent nod. He rode out into the meadow, his shield covering his chest, his long-stemmed battle-ax shouldered, his lance still stuck in its leather quiver. The sturdy figure seemed clumsy in the saddle, almost too big for his short animal.

Ejolf Dirt spurred on his brown horse with sharp, chopped-off whistles, and shoved his heels into its flanks. Rider and horse merged into one. He set straight at his opponent in a wild gallop, the blinking tip of his lance pointed at the Red's upper body.

Erik waited calmly, and only at the last moment, pulled his spotted horse aside. The thrust missed him by a hand's width, and before the enemy could rein in and turn his horse, Erik rode straight south toward the water, turned back, and waited.

Howling, the filthy man charged again, noticing just in time the danger of plunging past his opponent and into the lake, and tore back his horse, its front hooves leaving furrows in the turf. "Come!" he shouted, waving his spear. "Come, red dog! Show what you can do!"

Erik didn't let his enemy out of his sight but slowly steered his stallion westward along the embankment. Though Ejolf threw mockery and curses at him, only too late did he realize that Erik now had the sun at his back. In wild anger, the boaster hurled his spear.

Erik blocked the projectile with his shield, knocking it aside, but the force of the impact and the violent movement made him stagger in the saddle.

In an instant, Ejolf was up again. He swung his ax, striking Erik, again only hitting the shield and splintering the wood, and the charge was over. Ejolf made an arc and prepared himself for the next attack.

Tyrkir fell to his knees at the edge of the meadow. "You won't make it fighting that way," he lamented. "You're too slow for the man."

"Come on. Fight like a man," Ejolf goaded. "Otherwise, I'll chop you up piece by piece." Again, he let the reins go, confidently circling his weapon over his head. Erik fended him off with the half-shattered shield; at the same time, he quickly delivered a horizontal blow to his opponent's side. The chain mail tore, and blood stained Erik's ax blade. Ejolf briefly curled over, stunned. "A lucky strike, nothing more."

Erik didn't respond. Instead, he clicked and let his spotted mount run directly toward the enemy in a restrained tölt.

"Finally. And here I was thinking you were too afraid." Ejolf lifted his shield slightly. In his right hand, he weighed his weapon. "Come closer. Which arm would you like to lose first? Or should I just cut off your ugly head?"

Erik still didn't say a word. His lips tense, he watched the eyes of his opponent. Another two horse lengths separated the fighters, and smoothly, without rocking his rider, the steed continued tölting.

Erik reared, hurled his shield to the side, and with his free hand reached for his spear while pushing himself out of the stirrups and jumping back over his stallion's croup. The horse was startled, leaping toward Ejolf, who shied away.

That moment was enough for Erik. He charged his enemy, his ax whirling around from his right, and hurled it hard from close range. One spin in the air, and the blade hit the enemy's face with a dry crunch.

The weapon stuck under the edge of the helmet like a grafted, second nose, right where the right eye had been. Ejolf Dirt was frozen in his saddle. His men cried out. But Erik's task was not yet complete. He pushed his spear into the dead man's chest with all his might. The corpse tilted back and hit the ground.

There was not a sound. Breathless silence lay over the battlefield. The victor calmly gathered his weapons, whistled to his pony, and walked beside him to the edge of the meadow.

"My shield was no good," he growled.

Tyrkir looked into his master's sweaty face. "We still have four."

"You're bleeding, Know-It-All."

"Don't. This is no time for joking."

"No, really. What happened to your lip?"

The skinny man touched his mouth and looked at his blood-stained fingertips. "Fear." His knees trembled. "I was afraid for you."

"I don't understand. Why?"

"Because—" Tyrkir broke off, his rising anger helping him overcome his fear. "Damn you, boasting like that braggart. If Thor hadn't stood by you, you'd be—oh, never mind. You've won."

"And you expected . . . ?"

Loud shouting interrupted them. Ejolf's companions kneeled by the dead man. Hravn Holmgang stood beside them, his legs apart, and screamed at Erik: "This fight was not fair!"

"What?" Erik rose. He grabbed his friend by the shoulder and pushed him in front of him. "I'm counting on you to speak for me again." When they were close enough to not have to shout, Tyrkir said, "You say my master has broken the rules? Only a blind man could make such a claim."

Hravn's brow furrowed and he thought for a long time before replying. "We agreed on a fight on horseback. Your master has jumped off."

Briefly, Tyrkir explained why the giant was wrong. He both posed questions and answered them, deliberately not allowing Hravn to speak. Finally, he concluded: "How could my master have fended off the next attack? With a broken shield? There you are—you understand. He had to fight on foot. Ejolf himself had already come to this conclusion. Or don't you remember now?"

"I can't talk to you," Hravn complained. "I know that you're twisting everything to the advantage of your master." He put his fists to his hips. "It's no matter. I don't want a duel with that coward. I challenge him to a Holmgang. Then we'll see if your master can also fight on the leather hide." He grinned broadly. "Tomorrow at sunrise. I'll wait for him here. My men will prepare the place." He turned away without another word and followed the other men who were already carrying Ejolf's body toward Spiel Farm.

Where to now? The friends exchanged a look. Back to the high valley? They would only find safety on their own land, but Tyrkir calculated that there would be no more than two hours left for rest before they'd have to go back.

"I need sleep," Erik announced. No long ride, and no hiding, either. He pointed to the hill above the homestead. "We camp there. Everyone will see us, and they'll also see that we're not afraid of anyone."

Tyrkir was not very happy. "I'll keep watch," he said. "If we voluntarily offer ourselves on a plate, who knows if those mush-brains won't get hungry at night?"

"Oh, friend, I'd worry about the dirty one, but Hravn? He's a killer, but not a sneaky mutt."

They found a place on the hill and settled down, loosing their horses to graze nearby. The shackles on the front legs gave them enough freedom but prevented them from running away. The sun had long since settled behind the snow-covered mountains, far off on the horizon of the Hvammsfjord. Its light was a red streak that slowly wandered north. Bread, dried meat, and sour milk were the only provisions the men had taken with them.

"It's a poor meal for a man who has to fight," Erik growled as he looked down on the grass roofs of the Spiel Farm. "I can smell the roasted meat up here. I'm sure that giant is filling his belly and topping it off with beer." He lay back and pulled his coat under his chin. "That's already unfair. What do you think, Know-It-All?"

"I hope he drinks until he falls over. Then I'd feel better for tomorrow."

*Tomorrow?* Tyrkir shivered. His friend had never fought a Holmgang. Back in Norway, they had often watched as spectators, but nothing more. He had seen the fighters on the leather square, ten cubits in size. The judge gave the signal. Strike after strike, the fighters took turns hitting each other. If shields broke, new ones were handed over. How many shields could be used before the fight had to be continued with only a weapon? "Do you know the rules?"

Instead of an answer, Tyrkir heard even snoring. *Yes, you just sleep*, he thought. *Since you must be hungry, you should at least gather strength from your sleep.* He looked back up the valley toward the Water Horn. The mountains rose black against the bright sky. *Will Thjodhild find peace tonight? Certainly not. She is sitting in her chamber, maybe standing outside and waiting for us. Yes, she keeps watch, just like me.* He tried to warm himself with that thought.

Many spectators had come from the neighboring farms. Not just men but women with their children and youths wearing caps and rough capes. Clouds had darkened the valley. Nobody laughed. Nobody shouted. The tension dampened any noise. The sacrificial animal had been brought by two servants a few moments before, so the beginning of the spectacle could not be far off.

The people stood at a respectful distance and watched an old, hunchbacked man who had been entrusted with being the judge. The movements with which he prepared the square for the Holm-gang seemed almost cumbersome. He was driving the last peg into the fourth corner of the leather mat. With every blow, he bent farther down, and when only a small stump protruded from the eye-let, he looked up at the sky between his spread legs, grabbed one of his earlobes, and muttered a spell.

Tyrkir did not understand him, nor did he wish to. This strange man was from the enemy's clan, and who could say if he was invoking a spell for Hravn's victory? Would he really be just and impartial? Out of caution, the two friends had held intimate con-versations with both Thor and the wise Tyr before they rode down from the hill and arrived at their assigned place next to Holmfield.

Erik did not know the rules, except that no battle-axes could be used. Tyrkir closely observed Hravn and his weapon helper on the other side of the floor. Since they were tightening the helmet's chin strap, Tyrkir immediately checked the leather strap under Erik's chin, then the fit of his chain mail, his sword belt, and his daggers. The leg splints and the knots of the bootstraps came last.

"There, what's that for?"

Both stared across the field. Hravn had his sword tied to his right forearm, where it dangled loosely from a loop. As a test, he grabbed his spear with both fists, took a thrust, threw it aside, and had the sword grip in his right hand with just a short flick.

"By Loki, he's a cunning one," Erik growled. "It certainly makes things easier."

"Do you want me to fashion something similar?"

"No, damn it. I didn't practice the trick. I'll just end up stumbling over my own blade."

Tyrkir suppressed a sigh. So now the opponent, apart from his size and experience with the Holmgang, had another advantage Erik couldn't match.

In the meantime, the judge had checked the battlefield. In awkward hops, he followed the foot-wide corridor marked by four sticks along the edges of the mat. With one last look, and satisfied with his work, he stood next to the sacrificial animal. "Hear me!"

He had to repeat the request before quiet was finally restored. When all eyes were on him, he began in a shrill, nagging voice, "Who's asked for this divine judgment?"

"I, Hravn Arisson." Accompanied by his helper, the giant stepped forward.

"Aha. And who have you challenged?"

Hravn's fist pointed at Erik.

"Aha!" The old man moistened his lips. He seemed to be visibly enjoying the honor of his office. He resumed the prescribed ritual. "If the opponent seeks a judgment, may he give his name and come forward."

"Erik Thorvaldsson!" The red one approached calmly, Tyrkir following with his master's shields on his back. Because he didn't know how many they were allowed to use, he'd brought all the ones they still had.

The judge laid his head back and looked intently from one fighter to the other. "I have nothing to say about the cause of your quarrel. My task is to supervise this Holmgang. Anyone who violates the rules shall be banned. Do you understand me? Ah, good. Then hear and obey."

He announced the rules in a strident singsong. The fighters were not allowed to leave the leather mat. Anyone who set foot outside the hazel twigs would be warned with a cry of "He's giving way!" If a combatant crossed the border with both feet, he was judged to have fled. That meant he had sacrificed his honor, and the victor was allowed to kill him when and where he chose.

"You will alternate exchanging blows. Each fighter has three shields. If one breaks—" The referee interrupted himself, barking at Tyrkir, "What's this I see? Three, not four! Three! Can you not count?"

The steward immediately threw one of the shields aside.

"Ha! There is no cheating with me. I will keep an eye on you and your master." He moistened his lips again. "If one shield breaks, the weapons helper will pass on the next one. If all the shields are unusable, the fight will continue without them." The judge faltered; he had forgotten something but could not recall what.

Hravn Holmgang bent his head to him. "The price, you idiot."

"Ah. I heard that today is not about house or property. If one of you can no longer lift his sword, he must pay three marks of silver to the victor to redeem his life. If he is dead, the winner receives the same sum. Therefore"—he snapped and held out his hand to both armored men—"hand me the treasure to keep!"

The giant had his silver handy. Tyrkir had his friend's purse. He took a few pieces and handed them over. "That'll do."

Because there was no time to use the belt scale, he'd given more than necessary. *A judgment of the gods?* he wondered. *No, the reason why we're here doesn't matter. This is a murderer, and Erik wants amends for the crime. But the Holmgang erodes that distinction. Suddenly, each man's demand for justice is equal. They even fight for the same sum.*

The arbitrator threw the silver into a bowl and resumed his place beside the bull. He touched one of the curved horns and looked up at the gray clouds. "After the Holmgang, the victor will sacrifice this animal to honor the gods."

Finally, all preparations had been completed, and the spectators crowded closer. From the expressions on their faces, there was no doubt as to who would win, only the suspense of how long the stranger could hold out against their hero's assaults. And after the victory, there would be roast and beer in abundance!

Each fighter grabbed a shield and took his position in the field. Both weighed their spears in their right fists. Since Hravn was the challenger, Erik was allowed to lead the first charge.

The judge slowly stretched his arm. "Victory to the strongest!" And he gave the signal.

Like in a dance, the men simultaneously set one foot on the leather square, followed by the other. Erik stayed close to the edge, shuffling two steps to the right; Hravn followed. Erik took four quick steps to the left, again the same movement mirrored on the other side.

*Two predators in a far-too-tight cage*, Tyrkir thought. *There is no room for dexterity.*

From a standing position, Erik jumped forward and hurled his spear. Hravn stepped aside, and the weapon flew past him, over the heads of the spectators, and was lost. The giant yanked his spear back, Erik immediately protected his head and chest, but the opponent dropped the shaft, and the hanging sword jumped into his fist. With a mighty blow, he struck a deep notch into Erik's shield, the sharpened tip cutting into the Red's chain mail shirt. Hravn laughed and picked up his spear again.

As Tyrkir handed his friend the second shield, he whispered, "Are you hurt?"

Erik gave a small shake of his head. With a roar, he rushed forward, surprising his opponent, because he didn't strike at him but hacked through his spear shaft. The lopped-off half with the long spearhead spun, landing on the left edge of the mat. Threatening growls rose from the giant's chest. He swung out wide, and Erik's shield splintered. The Red hit Hravn with the same force and achieved the same result.

"We are at a disadvantage," Tyrkir warned as he handed over the third shield.

And then the last protection was shattered. Erik held only the sharpened metal hood over his left fist. Although he'd managed to penetrate Hravn's second shield with his next blow, the blade even hitting the underarm of the chain mail, it didn't wound.

"The shield walk is finished. All weapons may be used," the arbiter announced, pointing to Hravn. "You have the next strike."

The giant took his time. Armed with his third shield, he planted himself before Erik with his legs spread apart. "Your cunning won't help you now." Hravn's sword cut through the air. Erik fended off the blow with his blade. Dancing, Hravn expected the counter-blow, which did not break through his cover. Blow followed blow after blow, sparks flew, then the giant hit the left upper arm of his opponent. The ruptured iron mesh turned red. Erik's left arm sank.

Hravn intercepted his next blow with his sword blade. A piercing, sharp noise, and Erik's sword was broken—only the stump remained in his fist.

A murmur went through the audience. Outside the hazel passage, Tyrkir moaned.

The giant threw his shield aside and grabbed his sword with both hands. Although Erik swerved, the blow hit him on the side of his helmet. Dazed, he stepped to the left. He didn't fall but managed to stay on the leather mat by a foot's width. It was his turn. Searching for his opponent, he lifted the stump of his sword.

Hravn considered the gesture a strike. "Now, I will finish you. You will atone for the death of my friend!" And he let the broad side of the blade crash against Erik's helmet. Erik fell to the ground near the spearhead, which he had cut off at the beginning of the fight.

Above him, the giant sneered. "Your blow. What are you waiting for?" He looked triumphantly over to the onlookers. "Patience, friends! The feast will begin soon."

Laughter carried from the crowd; even the judge howled cheerfully, and the first chants about the invincible Hravn began.

Erik arched his back and slowly pulled himself to his knees, resting his right hand on the short segment of the spear shaft. Then, swiftly, he shot up and drove the sharpened point under the chain mail, deep into the body of the giant.

Hravn roared, staggering back and forth. He raised his sword, swayed, and then he took his strike. Momentum pulled him forward, and he stumbled over Erik, lost the weapon, and fell facedown into the grass outside the hazel passage.

Horrified, the arbiter rushed to Hravn's side and bent over the moaning man. The giant rolled onto his back. He tried to pull the iron out from between his legs, but in vain, and the huge body began to tremble, limbs twitching uncontrollably.

Tyrkir could hardly believe Erik's luck. "He f-fled," he stammered. But the judge was silent. "Didn't you hear me, old man? Hravn lost by the rules. By all the gods, announce it: Hravn has fled! The fight is over. My lord has defeated him."

Only reluctantly did the judge remember his office. Tears wet his wrinkled face as he turned to Erik. "It must be so. But it wasn't your spear—it wasn't your weapon that wounded him. But it must be so."

Loudly, he announced, "Hravn Arisson has fled. The gods have passed judgment. This is the victor."

There was no cheering. Silently, all eyes followed Erik. Exhausted by the battle, he left the leather carpet and picked up the pieces of silver from the bowl.

"Kill me," gasped Hravn. "Do not leave me lying here like this. Kill me!"

"You're already dead." Erik turned away. The arbiter stood in his way. "The sacrifice for the gods? Do not sin!"

"Enough blood has flowed today."

Now the spectators were growing restless, feeling betrayed about the feast they'd been promised. Muttered curses and threats became louder.

Erik paused for a moment. He picked up his opponent's weapon and rammed it into the bull's neck, then hurled the sword far away from him. Without even acknowledging the judge or the gawkers, he nodded to Tyrkir and mounted his horse. Stiffly erect, the Red rode off.

On the shore of the lake, just before the forest began, Tyrkir caught up with his master. He led the pack animals behind him but did not dare approach Erik.

Halfway up, rain started to fall, and the wind whipped the water from the Hvammsfjord into the riders' necks.

"It was the rain," Erik finally grumbled. "That's what caused the landslide, not us."

"Should I have a look at your arm?"

"Leave it! Thorbjörg can do a better job than you."

Thjodhild didn't know how many times she'd climbed the basalt boulders above the path. She hadn't heard her mother's quiet admonition. "Stay in the house, child! No woman should show her worries so openly. The man will come back or he won't. You can't do anything to change that."

When her daughter wrapped the scarf around her shoulders again, Thorbjörg stopped her at the door. "What will they say in the valley if servants bring him back hurt and see you? The proud Thjodhild stood like a sheep on the stones looking for her lost lamb. Your husband won't like that. Not even if he comes back healthy."

"Silence, Mother!" Thjodhild suppressed her anger. "Forgive me, but I can't stop my heart. I must be the first to see what's happened to Erik and Tyrkir. And I need to be alone."

The old woman heaved a great sigh. After a moment, her eyes softened. "Do you think I don't know how hard these hours are for you? I just want you to become a lady of the house, respected by everyone, my little one. But go if you must."

Thjodhild climbed the rocks many a time. She'd found a spot

below the highest boulder, hidden from view. From there, she could see down to the ridge in the valley and spot every rider long before they reached Hawk Farm. But so far, she'd seen nothing. The gray of the night gave way to the lighter gray of the day. Thjodhild hadn't slept, and still nobody had come around the black rock and up the path. Now rain clouds obstructed her view.

Disappointed, she was retreating to the house, when ... there! Weren't those black spots moving among the black stones? She wiped her wet eyes, and the outlines grew more defined. Riders—two of them—riders with packhorses! Thjodhild waited until she was sure. A towering figure, and next to it, a slender one, both men sitting upright in their saddles. Upright—that was enough. She quickly left her lookout.

Back in the house, she stopped near the door and pressed her forehead against the beam. She sighed in relief and her heart pounded against her temples. *Calm yourself*, she pleaded, but how could she, now that all her fear had been transformed into joy? *Oh, curse it! Mother is right. I'm still far from being the wife of a Viking. I'm nothing more than an unrestrained silly goose.*

Thorbjörg watched her daughter from the loom. She waited until the slender back tightened, then went to her with a shoulder cloth in her hand. "Now everything will be all right, my little one!"

"How do you know?"

Her mother gave her a smile instead of an answer. "Give me your scarf and take this dry one. After such a ride, every father rejoices when he is received not only by his wife but by his son."

Finally, they could hear voices outside. The farmer greeted the riders. Erik spoke little, but Tyrkir explained briefly what had transpired. There was no laughter. They were voices devoid of the joy of victory.

The door opened and Erik entered, followed by Thorbjörn and Tyrkir. The fighter's drawn face lit up at the sight of his wife and little Leif. "How good to see you..." He saw his mother-in-law and dutifully greeted her first. "Both murderers are punished. Our honor is restored."

"I'm so proud." Thorbjörg handed him a cup of sour milk. His hand trembled, and before he could bring the drink to his lips, he sloshed half of it into his beard and over his chain mail.

Thjodhild rushed to his side. "You're hurt?" The shredded ring mesh on his left arm was soaked, and blackish blood coated up to his fingertips. "Oh gods."

"My muscles and bones are still good." To prove it, he moved his hand, drawing in a sharp breath.

The old farmer's wife waved at him. "Come into the kitchen with me this instant." First, she wanted to wash out the wound with a brew of veronica, then apply a powder of crushed bedstraw, then leaves of plantain, and then a bandage. She assured him that he was in the best of hands and she would hear no protesting.

Thjodhild gave Tyrkir a smile. "Drop your arms."

He obeyed, and while she watched him put his helmet and sword aside, he suddenly longed for a touch from her—a little tenderness after these miserable hours. She seemed to sense the desire, smiling again, and stroking little Leif instead. "We are happy you're back. Both of us."

The moment passed. Thjodhild calmly handed the boy to Tyrkir and went to give her mother a hand. Erik slipped his chain mail over his head. He could pull out his right arm himself, but it was painful when the iron rings were loosened from the scabbed wound. Blood once again seeped from the deep gash.

Thjodhild brought fresh warm water and cut long strips for the bandage. She did not dare ask what had happened; Erik said nothing. Later, he sat silently, exhausted, next to her at the great fire. Tyrkir reported in detail about both fights.

The farmer had him tell the end of the Holmgang twice. "You

kept to the rules, son-in-law." Thoughtfully, he turned his finger in his gray beard. "Only bad that the judge was from Spiel Farm."

As soon as Erik had stretched out on the hay sack, weariness overpowered him. He lay there with his mouth open, gasped, and then snored.

The master of the house had gone to bed with his wife. The servants had also gone to rest. Tyrkir sat alone by the great fire. The glow from the embers flickered across his face.

"Is it really over?" Unseen, Thjodhild had sat down next to him.

He glanced at her. "Yes, the murders are avenged. But . . . I care only about Erik. He fought well. You should be proud."

"What are you trying to tell me?"

*Tell? I will never be allowed to tell you how I feel about you.* Tyrkir shook his head. "Anyone else would have triumphed after such a victory. But he carries it as a heavy burden."

"It's good that he has you as a friend."

"Us. He needs you and your son, just as much as he needs me. Only together will we find happiness."

# TO BE READ FROM THE RUNE STONE OF REMEMBRANCE:

The inscriptions are weathered. The eye can decipher only a few words and lines with difficulty:

... **THE YEAR 934:** War, blood, and devastation... Denmark... defeated by the German king Heinrich I... Archbishop Unni proclaims Christianity in the conquered territories of the north. He cannot convert the wild Danish king Gorm, but he succeeds in winning Prince Harald Blue Tooth over to the new teaching. Hate and mistrust are sown between father and son...

... **THE YEAR 965:** The runes become clearer: For thirty years now, King Harald Blue Tooth has ruled. Again, a battle against a German ruler is lost. During the armistice, Bishop Poppo proclaims Christianity in front of Harald. The pious man carries a glowing iron and shows the king that his hand is not burnt. This miracle removes Harald's last doubts about the power of the Christian God. He is baptized, and with him, the whole Danish army. Blue Tooth forces his ally, the Norwegian Jarl Hakon and his entourage, to accept this faith as well. But no sooner is the insidious Jarl back in his homeland than he mocks the hated doctrine... Again, the rune stone tells of war, blood, and misery... because Harald Blue Tooth devastates the coastal areas of Norway...

... **THE YEAR 981**: Bishop Fredrekur comes to Iceland with a ship. Because he doesn't speak the language, Thorvaldur Konradsson accompanies him. Only a few landowners are impressed by the sound of the bell, the incense, and the singing. The missionaries are met with hatred, insulted, threatened with clubs, and often enough that they move on quickly...

The first messengers of faith have entered Iceland! But this news does not reach Hawk Valley. The sharp wind from the fjord drove the rain clouds out of the valley and over the mountain ridges to the east. For two days and two nights, the sun has been shining and the water in the river gleams as blue as the sky...

# ⦰XENS ISLAND

Thanks to the care Erik received, he quickly recovered from his injury. He never spoke a word about the fight. When Thorbjörg was not nearby, he stood and secretly planned with Tyrkir about continuing the extension of his house. As soon as the strict mistress caught him, she sent her patient back to bed under a torrent of insults. "Thick skull! I decide when you are healthy!" To ensure the success of her healing arts, she finally ordered that Leif should sleep next to his father after breastfeeding.

Thjodhild cooed over the arrangement. "How well you fit together. And be careful, you must not wake him!"

"Babysitting! What have I become?" Erik complained and looked at the small head of golden curls on his right side. "That's no job for a man." But he obeyed the women all the same, and a new optimism tinged life into the house.

The big farmer, on the other hand, was worried. Since the Holmgang, no neighbor had stopped at Hawk Farm to refresh himself over a chat and a cup of sour milk. In fact, all who approached sped their steps or spurred their horse, as though they wanted to pass the homestead as quickly as possible.

On the third morning, hoofbeats lured the gray-bearded farmer outside. Half hidden behind the towering basalt boulders, he watched a farmer pass the house meadows in a fast tölt. He was wearing his Sunday best.

Before he had disappeared behind the ledge farther below, there was more clatter. Four of the neighbors from the upper valley followed. The hooves of their strong horses whirled through the air. They carried their heads high, and behind their bulging manes, the riders sat almost motionless in their saddles. They were all clothed in festive capes and fur caps.

Thorbjörn stared at the dust cloud. "But today is Thursday," he muttered as he returned to the house.

During the morning, he withdrew to his high seat, where no one was allowed to approach him without being asked. At lunchtime, he leaned silently over his wooden bowl and soaked chunks of bread in his gruel.

Tyrkir, to the delight of Thjodhild and his servants, presented a verse about Erik and his childminding skills. Only Thorbjörg noticed the change in her husband, but she said nothing so as not to disturb the serenity of the shared meal.

The sound of horses clopping, neighing, and snorting carried inside.

In the living hall, Tyrkir interrupted his verses. The riders did not pass by but appeared to be drawing closer. Now the dogs sensed the visitors, and the barking became louder. All eyes flew to the weapon stands to the right and left of the door. Some servants made to jump up to arm themselves.

"Stay," ordered the landowner. "Only those who have a guilty conscience greet their visitors with an ax in their fist."

"So, that's it." Thorbjörg took a deep breath. "You believe . . . ?"

Her husband looked at her. "I've feared it. Now I hope that we'll be saved from the worst."

A powerful voice shouted, "Thorbjörn, lord of Hawk Farm, here waits Ulf Einarsson, the gode of all valleys on this side of the Hvammsfjord. I have honorable men with me. We come in peace and ask you to welcome us outside your house."

The big farmer wiped his shirt sleeve across his face and smoothed his beard. Before he reached the narrow corridor, he hesitated, then turned back and instructed four servants to arm themselves. "For safety only. Wait here. I'll call if necessary."

He stopped in the open doorway, and his squat, slightly bent figure blocked Tyrkir's view and that of the others in the hall.

Thorbjörn silenced the dogs with a sharp whistle. "A good day," he began. "And what an honor for my family that the judge himself set out to visit us. Welcome, Ulf, and also you, my friends and neighbors."

"Yes, the grass is good," replied the gode. "This summer, we do not need to make any more sacrifices for the hay harvest."

They exchanged pleasantries, talked about sheep, horses, fishing, and as if by chance, Ulf Einarsson steered the conversation toward the distribution of the driftwood washed up on the beach. The quantity was sufficient so that every farm, including the forest owners in the upper Habichtstal, could be taken into account. "Except for your son-in-law. As I was told, he cleared enough."

"It doesn't matter. You mustn't exclude Erik," demanded the big farmer. "He received land from me and thus the same right as all of us."

"Your friends, Thorbjörn, came to me and brought charges against him." The judge's tone became brusque. "Where is he hiding?"

"Hiding? No member of my family needs to hide. Or do you wish to offend me, Gode?"

"Be calm! The matter does not concern your clan, only this Erik. And I must assume that he is somewhere in your house."

"Because he ... because he recovers from the wounds," Thorbjörn explained with painstaking control. "It was an honorable fight."

"Nobody wanted to wait for the Thorspitzthing in two weeks. We've held a council. Let Erik come out, or if he's too weak, lead us to his camp."

"Nobody shall dare to cross the threshold of my house!"

In the hall, the servants gripped the shafts of their axes and spears more tightly. Thorbjörg beckoned Thjodhild to hide with the maids behind the kitchen in the storerooms. At her quiet command, Tyrkir went into the sleeping chamber to inform his friend of the situation. When he returned a little later with the undressed Erik, the exchange of words outside had become sharper.

"You are all on my land. Do not force me to break the sacred privilege of hospitality."

"Be reasonable, Thorbjörn," the judge barked. "You're putting the peace of your neighbors at risk. For the last time: Surrender the defendant!"

"It's not me that's causing trouble. It's you and your jurors."

Inside, at the great fire, Erik growled, "Maybe they want the prize money back for Hravn? No matter. What else can they want with me? I have nothing to be blamed for. Still, if we wait any longer, it could grow dangerous for Thorbjörn. Let's go outside."

Tyrkir held out Erik's shirt to him. "Here, I'll help you." Erik waved his servant off—"There's no time"—and slipped through the corridor of peat and sod. "Calm yourself, father-in-law. It's all right. Let me talk to these men."

The old man reluctantly cleared the exit, and Erik stepped outside. His appearance, naked except for the bandage on the upper arm, struck the gode speechless. Even the twelve festively dressed farmers could not believe their eyes.

Tyrkir pushed in beside his friend. Silence reigned. Strengthened by the presence of his father-in-law and steward, Erik stretched his chin toward the delegation. "Why are you staring at me like that? Do you think that I lie in bed with my coat and cap?"

"You . . . you don't know . . ." Ulf Einarsson took a moment to regain his composure. "I am the highest judge in this county. You could show me a little more respect."

Surprised, Erik scratched his chest hair. "You wanted to see me immediately. Here I am. What have I done wrong?"

The gode hissed through his teeth. "Be it so. Let's not lose time talking about customs and decency. A complaint was brought against you—a complaint because you insidiously killed Ejolf Dirt, the brother of our friend, Valtjof."

"Thor be—"

"Silence! You also killed Hravn, Ari's son, in the Holmgang."

Erik nodded. "That's true. Enough people were there to witness it."

"You only managed to win because you broke the rules."

Tyrkir saw the tremor, saw the fist, but his friend controlled himself.

Erik breathed heavily. "Who says so?"

"We hear this not only from the family, but we have the word of Orm the Hunchback who was appointed judge. Everyone who was there has testified."

Now Thorbjörn raised his hand. "Ulf, in the name of our friendship, my son-in-law is being wronged. The witnesses are all from the same camp. Let him and his servant tell you how the fight unfolded. Only then make your judgment."

"Two voices against more than twenty? Even at the Thing, the matter would be clear. No, Thorbjörn, however much I respect you as a friend, the jurors and I have deliberated and come to a unanimous decision. It's a matter of securing peace in the district."

The big farmer's shoulders dropped.

"But I ask a favor of you," continued Ulf Einarsson. "Tell your son-in-law to at least get dressed. Even a rag would be better. Damn it, I don't want to pass judgment while I stare at a cock and ass!"

Without waiting for an invitation, Erik tore his shirt out of his friend's hand. He could only pull it over his head as his injured arm got in the way. Tyrkir tried to help, but without much suc-cess—both were too clumsy. "By Thor," Erik cursed, irritated by the bulge of cloth in front of his face. "These idiots. All this effort to take a few pieces of silver away from me? These pretentious bas-tards."

"Not so loud," warned Tyrkir. "Or else . . ."

"Come on." Erik stripped off the shirt again. "You've all seen. I can't manage the shirt. Are you satisfied now?"

The gode waited with a frozen expression. Finally, Tyrkir wrapped the shirt around the naked man's loins.

Erik glowered at the men. "That's enough. Say what you have to say and then leave me alone."

The judge waved his hand, and his jurors immediately formed a semicircle behind him, taking off their headgear. "Erik Thorvalds-son, you have been accused of the cowardly murder of two men, and you have been found guilty."

As if after a blow, the giant shook his head. Next to him, Tyrkir held his breath. *No*, he begged silently. *They can't take things that far.*

"In consideration of your honorable father-in-law, the council has shown leniency and has not, as the law permits, banished you and declared you an outlaw. Hear your punishment: Within two weeks, you are to leave Hawk Valley and my court district. Anyone who finds you in our territory after this period may kill you with impunity. This exile shall last for three years."

Erik stood, pale and rigid. Tyrkir looked at the blue sky. *Did you not hear him? The verdict has been passed. The community has excluded us. Hear, gods, injustice has happened.* But no god inter-vened.

The gode and the festively dressed farmers walked back to their horses. In the saddle, Ulf once again addressed the condemned man. "It would have been better had you never come here. In my valleys, there is no room for troublemakers or murderers." Turning to Thorbjörn, he continued, "I regret that you gave your daughter as a wife to this stranger. Nevertheless, you will remain our friend and good neighbor in the future."

With that, he gave the signal to leave the farm. The riders parted ways. One cloud of dust went into the upper valley, the other hovered lower down on the rocky outcrop before blowing across the river.

"Shall we rest?" Tyrkir bridled his horse and let it trot up next to the wagon's carriage bench. "All you have to do is give us a signal."

"Am I old and sick?" Thjodhild sat wide legged, with her skirt up to her knees and her boots pressed against the footrest on the bench. She looked briefly to the side. "A short break is enough for me, just like you."

"I thought only because, as a woman..." Tyrkir wiped his sweaty, freckled face. "Well, we men have it easier... if you understand what I mean. We don't have to squat down."

"Get out," she snapped, but she could barely suppress her laughter. "Take care of the animals. I'll be fine."

"Forgive me. I didn't want..." Tyrkir hastily turned his horse.

"Don't be angry," she shouted after him. "You mean well, I know." As soon as he had disappeared behind the wagon, her face grew serious again. "I like it when you're worried about me."

They had been on the Hvammsfjord shore road since that morning. The wheels of the wagons groaned at every hole and hump on the stony tracks. Now and then, Thjodhild turned around and peered through the half-open tarpaulin into the interior. Despite the bumps and swerves, her child still slept.

His cradle was lashed with ropes between the crates. He was bedded on the bearskin, hay sacks, and blankets underneath, and the silver chest with the three locks was at the very bottom. "Oh,

Leif, you know nothing of the grief your parents now must endure."
She looked out to the fjord.

Erik accompanied the trek on the water. He had only raised the
sail halfway. His *Mount of the Sea* lay low and glided along near
the shore, loaded with lumber, barrels, tools, and weapons. Katla
stood at the head of the dragon and watched for shallows. The
other maidservants were assigned as line guards, while Tyrkir and
the servants drove the horses and guarded the covered wagon on
the coastal road.

Erik's hair shone from the stern of the ship. *You really can't be
overlooked*, Thjodhild thought. *So proud, so courageous, and yet so
stupid when it comes to me.*

The night after the verdict, Erik had come to their sleeping
chamber. Standing in front of the bed, he had offered her a divorce.
"Just say it. No woman should have to stay with an exile."

"And is that your wish?" She sat up against the pillows.

"Never mind what I want. Here you can lead a peaceful life."

"Erik, I asked you a question."

He kept poking his toes against the bed box and finally mumbled, "You, at least, should not be without happiness."

"We are no longer on Sharpcliff. You are not to blame. At my
request, you defended the honor of the family. You fought for us. I
should leave you because of false testimony? We belong together,
Leif, you, and me, and Tyrkir. And the four of us will start anew,
together."

She drew him closer and put his hand on her breast. "But now . . .
I think if we are careful, we don't have to learn it all over again later.
Or do you think it'll harm your arm?"

Despondency had turned into relief. Erik had lay down with her,
his gaze full of desire. "Best not to ask the mother-in-law first."

The memory of that night made Thjodhild smile. Rarely had
Erik been so tender with her. She slapped the reins of the two

horses lightly on the croup. Or was it only the injured arm that hindered him? No matter. It had been beautiful.

To her left, the hills were green, and the dark mountains loomed behind them. One mountain giant after the next, some still snow covered, pressed shoulder to shoulder westward out onto the large peninsula. Thjodhild was unable to see the glacier from here. *Not yet*, she thought. *I should be able to see it when we turn away from the fjord's shore and drive across the high valleys to the other side of the peninsula. But only if no clouds are covering it.* The glacier dominated the outermost headland with its two white humps. Mysterious powers emanated from it. It either rewarded anyone who dared to climb up and disturb its peace with happiness, or it punished them with misfortune, like a capricious god.

As a young girl, Thjodhild had seen the incredible sight three times, always from a safe distance. Each time, they had sailed through the Breidafjord, around the cape of the Snowy Rock Peninsula, to visit the relatives of her stepfather who lived down there on the shore of the South Island. And now she was on her way to them again. *When we get there, maybe I will climb the snowy rock and our life will finally be good.*

"Visit my cousin Einar Sigmundsson on Warm Spring Slope," her father had suggested. "You can overwinter with him. He has two daughters—they must be your age. And it may well be that he sells you land, enough for you to settle in the area. Then you won't be with strangers as you begin again."

Thjodhild's mother had pressed her close and stroked her back. "It's quite far, little child, but I promise we'll visit next year. And if you need anything, send a servant. Your father and I will help you."

*We don't lack hacksilver*, Thjodhild thought. Since sheep and cows had to stay behind in Hawk Valley, Thorbjörn had paid his son-in-law more than a fair price for his livestock, and Erik also still had his father's fortune. "So why worry?" She looked behind her again. "Sleep peacefully, my little one. Before you know it, your parents will have built a new home for you."

The more the sun edged toward the horizon, the greater the number of seagulls that moved with the ship, a banner of bright white plumage over deep blue water.

Horn call! Erik gave a signal from the ship that he wanted to anchor in the bay.

Tyrkir overtook the covered wagon. "I'll find us a place to camp," he shouted to Thjodhild and drove his horse along the road in a fast tölt.

Later that evening, the smell of smoldering peat and wood lay over the grassy hollow. After eating meat broth and bread, Katla and the other maids had rowed back to the ship. The servants slept rolled in blankets with the animals. With a clear view of the water, the wagon and two tents stood around the fire. Erik poked at the embers. "So, this is what my farmstead has become."

"Don't think of that anymore!" Tyrkir looked at Thjodhild as she breastfed her child. *I could never have carved it as beautifully as the reality.* Thjodhild loosened the second breast brooch on the straps of her dress, switched Leif to the crook of her right arm, and let him continue his meal.

"What are you talking about, Know-It-All?" asked Erik.

"I ... I mean ..." Tyrkir forced himself to focus. "We cannot return to Hawk Valley, you know that. So, we'll look for land down on the South Island and build a new farm there."

"If it were only that easy."

Thjodhild interrupted. "Easy? Certainly not! But I have a strong husband and a clever steward. I trust in them, and I am not afraid. As long as we stick together, things can only get better."

Erik saw the challenging looks the two were giving him and stopped poking at the embers. "All right, I get it." He pushed the stick deep into the grass. "Yes, you're right, I'm sorry. Whining only clouds the eye. Enough of that, or I'll end up walking past our happiness even when it stands before me."

The horn call sounded over the water even earlier than the day before. Tyrkir rode out onto a cliff to check on the ship. Through the funnel of his hands, Erik called out: "Carry on for another hour. Then make camp. I'll join you in the evening."

The *Mount of the Sea* turned about and headed for the archipelago, which dotted the exit of Hvammsfjord as it opened into Breidafjord.

His eyes were bright. No, he didn't want to sit. Since he had returned from his excursion, Erik had been walking up and down through their small camp. He had not even eaten dried fish with his people but had chewed on it as he hiked restlessly from the tents, past the covered wagon, to the horses and back. The valley, surrounded by three steep, grassy humps, was far too narrow for his excitement.

Thjodhild took Katla aside. "What's with him?"

"I don't know exactly, but the lord has forbidden us from talking about it." The maid pressed her index finger to her full lips. "It's supposed to be a surprise."

"Well, aren't you a fine friend!" Thjodhild grumbled.

She'd have to wait. Finally, the slaves were back on the ship, and the servants had gone to their sleeping places.

"Don't run around like an excited bull that can't find a cow. Come to the fire and tell me what's going on!"

Erik stood with his legs apart in front of his wife and friend. Almost solemnly, he announced, "I have discovered it. I know where we will build our new farm." Before Thjodhild and Tyrkir had recovered, he asked them to follow him. With long strides, he left the camp and led them to the beach. There, he pointed past his ship to the countless brown-black and green spots in the water. "There. You see?"

"Very nice," Tyrkir remarked dryly, thinking, *The wind got you today, you big Viking.*

"I see only the islands." Thjodhild hesitated, but then put her hands on her hips. "No, I don't see anything! And if you really believe—"

"Wait. Wait!" Erik positioned himself close to her and led her gaze over his index finger. "There's a big island back there, do you see it? And just behind it, a second one. I was there. Both are uninhabited, and there is no land marked off, so they don't belong to anyone. There is water—fresh spring water. There's enough room to breed sheep, room for horses and dairy cattle, and our farm."

Now Thjodhild also stretched out her index finger. "But those are islands."

"Yes, lush grass and lots of space." Erik took a deep breath. "That's all I need."

"But I want more!"

"Damn..." Anger rushed through Erik. "Oh, you explain it to her, Know-It-All!"

But before Tyrkir could speak, Thjodhild brushed a strand of hair from her face, clearly upset. "By Freya and all her cats, don't you dare! We're going to my relatives. And there, we'll buy land."

"To live by the mercy of others? I've had enough of that! My own kingdom is what I want. Land of which I am the lord where no one has the right to chase me away."

"Don't be a fool!" Thjodhild barely managed to restrain herself. "There is no such land, Erik. There are neighbors everywhere, and you'll have to get along with them. And to be a gode? You've come to Iceland much too late for that." She saw how his face became rigid and turned to Tyrkir. "I don't want to live in a wasteland again. If he has forgotten that, then remind him. You're his friend."

*That's right*, Tyrkir grumbled silently. *When the masters run out of arguments, they call on their slave to take the blows, and from both sides!* "Maybe next time, if you don't mind... Oh, never mind. I think it would be better if we didn't commit to anything right away. First, we should look at the islands together tomorrow. Maybe we'll like them? Or maybe Erik's first look was deceptive, and we won't be able to settle there at all? Both could be possible." He looked from his master to his mistress and was relieved when their faces softened.

Yes, they agreed. They would wait until tomorrow and then decide.

*That's good*, Tyrkir thought. *The war is postponed.*

They had almost reached the tents and the wagon when Erik stopped, slowly pulling the battle-ax from his belt. "No farther," he whispered.

Tyrkir had also spotted the three figures on the ridge of the left hump. He felt for his dagger.

The men stood there, motionless. Against the bright sky, there was no way of telling whether they were carrying weapons. A quick glance to the horses. Even their six servants had already noticed the strangers and were ready to fight.

Thjodhild clawed at her scarf. "Leif is sleeping in the wagon. I have to go to him."

"Stay!" Erik slowly walked across the hollow, whispering to the slaves as he passed them. "As soon as I whistle, two of you storm up the slope with me, the others attack from either side." He stopped at the foot of the hill. "Who visits us so late at night?" he called out.

"Peaceful farmers." The slightly smaller man in the middle raised both hands. They were empty. "We smelled the fire and came to take a look. Who are you?"

"Who wishes to know?"

"Thorgest, the lord of Breida Farm. Half an hour's walk from here." He put his arms on the shoulders of the two men to his left and right. "These are my sons. Hardworking lads, yes, very hardworking—and very strong."

Erik introduced himself, but he only mentioned his name and said he was on his way south. For two nights, he wanted to camp here in this hollow with his people.

"A good choice, yes. Sharpcliff offers protection against the wind."

"What did you say? What is the name of this place?"

"Sharpcliff, because of the steep hills here. May we join you?"

Erik had already raised a hand in invitation, but Thjodhild shouted from behind him, "Not tonight! Please! We are tired!"

The red one lowered his arm again. "Then tomorrow. We'll visit you. We could probably use some fresh water and bread."

"Come only if you can. Guests are very welcome at Breida Farm. We haven't heard any news for a long while." The farmer and his sons swung their caps to say goodbye and disappeared from the ridge.

Grinning uncertainly, Erik embraced his wife. "Don't mind the name. There are friendly people here." Nevertheless, he sent a servant to each of the three grass mounds. "I don't think we need guards. But it's better to be safe."

"Sharpcliff?" Thjodhild shivered. "Those men stood up there like ghosts. I'm glad they're gone." She went to the wagon and carried Leif into the tent.

Erik was still grinning, gently shoving Tyrkir in the shoulder. "They'll be our new neighbors. You like it here, don't you?"

"Can't say yet." Tyrkir shook his head. "And if you want my advice, don't call these farmers neighbors in front of your wife. Not until she agrees."

"Yes, you're right, Know-It-All. But those islands... I know there's good land, and I'm sure she'll . . ." Erik didn't want to sleep. "You rest, my friend." He was going to think and plan.

They left early. Since it wasn't far, Erik took only two oarsmen with him. The rest of the servants stayed with Leif, the horses, and the equipment in the camp.

Guided by Tyrkir, Erik skillfully steered his ship through the shallows between tiny islands and reefs. The water rippled. A light breeze refreshed Thjodhild, catching her hair. "Back there!" From the steering deck, she pointed east over the low side of the ship. "The sun is over Hawk Valley."

"I hadn't thought of that." Erik touched her shoulder. "You wouldn't be far from your parents here. They can visit us often."

They entered a small bay by the outer island. Erik jumped off the boat and carried his wife to the beach, which was covered with black pebbles. Alongside a gushing stream, they climbed up to a meadow terrace.

"Here you'll find enough room for the house and the farm buildings," he explained to the two. "Just look around! The location couldn't be better." The bay would be the only harbor for larger ships and could easily be defended from here. He didn't forget to point to the rocky step on the other end of the island, which would offer protection from northerly and easterly winds.

Tyrkir listened to his master, impressed. *Not so dumb at all*, he thought. *Once Erik's got something in his head, he becomes quite the talker!*

"Come on!" Erik ran more than he walked as he guided his companions. Eider ducks startled and fluttered, circling their nests in a wide arc. At the top of the island, the view stretched over hills and hollows. Thjodhild and Tyrkir breathed deeply the smell of the sea and fresh grass. Erik dug into the ground with his bare hand. "Here, just feel it! The soil is good for onions and leeks, and we can grow grain, too." He straightened up again. "We can also collect eggs. There are more than enough birds. And yesterday, I saw lots of seals out on the cliffs near the open water. We have meat and lard right in front of our noses." Full of expectation, he turned to Thjodhild. "Well, what do you think?" Then he growled at his friend, "Say something!"

Tyrkir watched the blond woman from the corner of his eye. He couldn't sense disapproval in her expression. *The great Tyr be praised*, he thought. *No, our Viking has not exaggerated. This really is an excellent place.*

Erik thought the silence had stretched too long. "Have you nothing to say?"

Thjodhild met his gaze. "And where will we put our sheep to pasture?"

"What?" And then he understood. "You mean...? You think...?"

"Yes. I could settle here."

"Well, I..." The giant wiped his eyes with the back of his hand. "Oh, so, the sheep? Right there in front." The sister island lay just beyond. It was bigger, rockier, yet there was enough grass to breed wool stock. "We'll build stables and barns over there, as well. In summer, we can use rowboats, and in winter, we can walk across the ice. We'll..." He was becoming more and more enthusiastic. His inner eye already saw the farm: chickens cackled, and the udders of his cows gave enough to make butter, cheese, and delicious sour milk.

"Not so fast, dearest!" Thjodhild embraced him. "We don't own a single cow."

"Not yet." He pressed her tightly to himself. "I know, I'm too impatient. We can't start until the spring, as soon as the snow has melted. I'll build you a house for the women, right next to the sauna, I promise. And we'll spend the winter with your relatives."

Since there was no wood for a fire, he had his servants collect stones from the beach, and while Thjodhild explored their new empire on foot, the men erected a landmark on both islands. The solemn ceremony of appropriation would take place the next morning.

"Bliss, Know-It-All!" he shouted on the way back, pointing at the two islands. "There it lies. Our bliss!"

"You are my master." Tyrkir grinned. He'd been infected by Erik's enthusiasm. "How could I dare contradict you?" *And I have no desire to. I, too, feel that this land has been waiting for us.*

Thorgest of Breida Farm laughed a lot, and when he laughed, he pushed the chin forward, exposing only the teeth of his lower jaw. Erik had made his request while he was still in the yard, and Thorgest had nodded and invited the strangers into his living hall. "We must get to know each other."

And since then, he'd been entertaining his guests. His throaty laughs were just bearable for Thjodhild. To distract herself from his foul stories, she tried to figure out which animal he resembled. Dog and seal were out of the question, as were horse, ram, and ox. Maybe a predator, but which one? Even that comparison was weak—the farmer's noises did not fit. Finally, she gave up the search.

In the meantime, Thorgest had completed the tale of his wild bachelor years and was now telling about how he'd started a family. "My wife died soon after the birth of my youngest, Odd." He pointed to the muscle-bound son who squatted to his left at the foot of the high seat. With his chin on his knees, the boy, through half-closed eyes, watched the visitors, who were seated on the bench of honor.

"Well, she'd already started to waste away after giving birth to my eldest—that splendid fellow there, my Toke. I always wondered how such a thin woman could push out such strong sons." He pushed his foot into the young blond giant's side. Toke was lying to his father's right on the stomped peat floor.

"The two of you drained your mother from the inside, and then kept at it when you made your way into the world." The rest was drowned out in chuckles. "Well, she died." He laughed, but none of the guests joined in. It didn't bother him. "I didn't take a new woman, but..." His tongue licked over the lower row of teeth. "Well, I always make sure that there are maids on the farm with soft thighs. In the beginning, it was easy, but now the boys also want to go into the hay, and that can sometimes lead to arguments when the old man wants to check the fresh produce first."

Toke and Odd grinned while their father on the high seat slipped back and forth, almost choking at his own joke.

*Disgusting*, Thjodhild thought. With a side glance, she saw the slight smirk on Erik's and Tyrkir's faces. *And you two are no better. Wait until we're alone again!*

The farmer's laughter stopped abruptly. His face became calm and sober. "Let's get down to business." He nodded to Erik. "You're asking for a storage shed?"

"Only if you can spare one."

"I've got plenty of room. That's how I make my living." Thorgest owned five barns. Only one, which stood outside the fence in the middle of the house pasture, was used for his own winter fodder. His farm was conveniently located on the road to Thorsness on the next peninsula, which was where the Thing was held twice a year. And so he rented room to anyone who wanted to store goods, horses, or carts during the court days—a convenient and profitable business. "I have a good reputation with the merchants. Everyone knows me and knows that everything is well guarded here. What do you need the barn for? I thought you were on your way to the south."

"Yes. But also not, at least since yesterday." Erik leaned forward.

ERIK THE RED

"Yesterday—no, this morning—I lit my fires on two big islands outside in the fjord and took possession of the land for myself. We are neighbors, Thorgest."

The farmer and his sons sat up. Toke was the first to get his bearings. "The big one can only be Wiltgrass Island."

"Wait until we farm it, then all you'll see is dark green." Erik grinned.

The farmer leaned back. "And you want to settle on Oxens Island? Of course, because from there, it's easier to take the ship out to the Breidafjord." He ran his fingers over the backrest. "So far, nobody has come up with this idea."

Odd stretched his arms sluggishly. "And everything has to be boated over. That would be too much work for me."

"Nobody asked you to help!" Erik snapped.

The father intervened before a quarrel broke out. "If I understand you correctly, you want to store your household goods in the barn."

That, and the lumber, the covered wagon, and the horses, Erik explained. Also, his family's two valuable high-seat beams. Anything he didn't have to take to the south during the winter. That way, he and all his household could continue the journey more comfortably on the ship.

Thorgest looked at him for a long time. "I haven't heard of you, even though I have cousins in Hawk Valley. You seem to be new to Iceland?"

Thjodhild trembled and quickly glanced at Tyrkir. He leaned forward, ready to support his friend. So far, Erik hadn't said anything about himself and his past, only that he had courted the daughter of Hawk Farm.

"I came over from Norway." Erik stretched out the sentence. "Because I'd heard that life was better here."

"I haven't heard that, either, but yes, it could be. Never mind, it's none of my business." Thorgest flicked his thumb and index finger. "In any case, you are welcome as a neighbor. And since you want to live so far out on the water, we won't get in each other's way."

Thjodhild breathed out. As greasy as the farmer had seemed so far, these words had earned him some of her affection.

"My shed is not cheap. And you have to pay in advance, you understand?"

Erik did not haggle over the sum, immediately agreeing to the price.

"Done!" Thorgest jumped from the high seat, and the men sealed the deal with a handshake. "Here's to good neighborliness next year! Your belongings are in good hands with me, and I will fatten your nags." When he saw the worried look, he added. "Just a joke. We know something about horses. You'll find them strong and without fat bellies." He pushed his chin forward, showed his teeth, and laughed again.

The guests were to stay for dinner. They could use his barn starting tomorrow. He didn't press with other curious questions, instead enjoying his beer, telling dirty stories, slapping the maids on the ass, and raving about the ferocity of his offspring.

After saying their farewells, Thjodhild was glad to have finally escaped that laughter. "That man! And his sons are no better." She glared at the Erik and Tyrkir. "But you had your fun, too."

Tyrkir shrugged. "That's the way it is when there is no lady to pay attention to customs and decency."

"A men's household," Erik said weakly.

"Shame on you!" Thjodhild punched them both in the sides. "Get behind me! I'll do without your grinning mugs, thank you very much."

# THE FISHING HAUL
# OF THE GODS

Both babies were lying naked on a blanket in front of the house. The girl was playing with a rattle, trying to guide the smooth wooden stick to her mouth. She reluctantly shook the toy and crowed when the little stones inside hit each other. She kicked her legs. The boy lay quietly beside her, sucking on his right fist. By the time the south wind from the sea had reached the top of the hill, the midday sun had turned it into a gentle breeze, caressing the pink skin of the little ones. Gudrid had been born at the beginning of March that year, Leif in May—a white blond and a golden head.

Their mothers sat next to the blanket in the grass.

"We have beautiful children," Thjodhild said with a smile.

"They are healthy, that is the main thing. Nevertheless, I am proud..." Hallweig paused. She struggled for air, her lips turned blue, and she rubbed her chest. "It's tight again, so tight."

Concerned, Thjodhild looked at her. "If my mother were here, she'd know an herb that could help."

"I don't believe it. So often... we've had a neighbor from Eagle Farm visit. Grima is a wise völva. Her magic... has saved many." Every sentence took effort. "She gives me tea. But it doesn't help much. Since I had my baby, the trouble just comes, and then... I have to wait until it passes." The small, roundish woman lay back. After some time, her breathing calmed, and fresh red returned to her lips. "Thank you. You're so patient."

"Don't say that!"

"It's true." Hallweig turned to her side and rested her head on her hand. "I'm glad that you and your family are here. Together, we'll have a beautiful winter. And our husbands get along with each other. That's important, don't you think?"

"It seems almost like a miracle to me." Thjodhild smiled, sighing. "Erik is not always easy, but one simply has to like your Thorbjörn."

"Yes, I am lucky."

After they were welcomed a month ago by Thjodhild's wealthy uncle, he had decided that Erik, Thjodhild, their child, and Tyrkir should go to Warm Spring Slope with his son-in-law. Although the house was very spacious, Thorbjörn Vifilsson could no longer offer accommodation. Many visitors had come through since the Allthing and had named him the goden for the South Island area. Without further ado, Erik's farmhands and maids were accommodated with Uncle Einar and his second son-in-law. Since the family farms were not far from each other, this was an easy solution for everyone.

"What's your Erik like?"

The question surprised Thjodhild. Although she and Hallweig had developed a deep fondness for each other over the last few weeks, she hesitated. She'd never talked to a woman about her husband. *Who would I have to talk to?* she thought. *My childhood friends have long since become strangers to me, which only leaves my mother, and she'd have only given more well-intentioned advice.* Thjodhild looked across the plain down to the water. White spray rippled on the waves.

"You don't have to answer."

"No, it's fine. My Erik..." Thjodhild wrapped her arms around her knees. "How can I describe him? You know, he has all the good qualities you could wish for as a woman, but somehow, they have not yet made peace with each other, perhaps because he has too much of everything. First, there is his pride, which almost cost him his life. Diligence and perseverance. He proves he can work every morning when he's out fishing with your Thorbjörn. Add to that his strength. Also, as a fighter, I know no better. And he is loving to me. And he knows how to run a farm. Oh, I could list many more traits. Of course, he has a Viking skull that often makes me furious. Sometimes, I wonder about his wits, but then he behaves like a boy again, and I gladly forgive him. You see, Erik is still full of edges, not smooth. He is still searching. But now we have our islands. When the house is built and we have settled in, then maybe he will..."

Hallweig nodded. "Being settled, that's it. A man must have a place so that he can come to rest. Even if he travels by ship over the summer to do business, he finds peace with his family when he comes back."

"Maybe." Thjodhild swayed back and forth. "It would be better if my Erik stayed at home and managed the farm. You know, he gets angry easily, and I wouldn't be there with him in a foreign country to soothe him. We've had enough misfortune already."

"And your steward, this German, are you satisfied with him?"

*Satisfied?* Thjodhild closed her eyes. *I think about Tyrkir far too often. I know it's not fitting for a respectable housewife. But it helps my heart through the more difficult hours. And since I will never betray this secret, it cannot do any harm.* As lightly as she could, she said, "He simply belongs to us, and it is good that Erik has him as a friend."

The women were startled by a moan. Gudrid had lost her wooden rattles. She struggled and began to scream. Leif immediately joined in.

For two weeks, the farmhands and farmers of the south had been roaming the mountains and gorges. They had searched on horseback for the free-range sheep and driven them from the summer pastures into the valleys. Little by little, they filled up the large, fenced-in gathering place in Warm Spring Valley, and by mid-September, the bleating drowned out even the cries of the kittiwakes above the cliffs.

Each owner recognized his own animals by their differently cut ears and pulled, dragged, and chased them from the inner circle through a gate into his compartment.

Days of slaughter followed, a lot of beer was drunk, and in the evening, the men lay naked in the hot spring pond, chatting and stretching and drinking on.

Erik enjoyed the carefree time with Tyrkir. By the side of Judge Thorbjörn, they were no strangers to the neighbors.

"Soon, we'll have that much meat in our own stores," Erik assured his friend as they strolled from the bath to the house, crimson red and soft-skinned. "And on my island, it'll be easier for us to catch the sheep."

Tyrkir looked at him from the corner of his eye. "Easier, yes. But also lonelier."

"I don't need neighbors—" Erik stopped. "If they were like these, maybe. But I can do without the ones we've had so far. Leave it alone, Know-It-All. We'll build our domain alone, and if we want to see people, we'll go to them by ship. That way, we choose. I prefer that."

*How much have you suffered?* Tyrkir shook his head. *My strong friend, I wish so much that the gods will be kind, and that this time, our hopes will be fulfilled.*

The last light of autumn passed and then the beginning of winter. The new judge wanted to give his first big feast on Warm Spring Slope.

Thorbjörn Vifilsson walked up and down in the courtyard, his high forehead wrinkled. Deep in thought, he stroked the strong bridge of his nose. For each guest, he had Tyrkir push a glowing needle into the tanned cowhide. Relatives and friends had long filled the first column, and the names of the influential lords of his district had not caused any difficulty, either. Still, now the gode tortured his brain to remember the small farmers of the remote areas. "Write down Geirrod of Bird River and Sindri, the Flatstone Collector." He shrugged. "There are getting to be more and more—I'm afraid those who can't find a bench or stool will have to sit on the floor."

"Don't worry! There may be angry faces at the beginning of the feast." Tyrkir pushed the needle into the embers. "Once everyone's had enough beer, the close quarters won't bother them, even if your hall bursts apart like an overstocked wicker basket."

"Stop your mockery!" Immediately friendly again, the judge explained, "I must not forget one single man. Otherwise, he will feel offended, and who knows when I may need his vote. I have to be able to count on everyone. You see, my office forces me to run an open, generous house. That's how it is—hospitality for everyone. But between us, hardly any of those characters really please me."

Tyrkir tried to control himself, but the urge was too strong: "What about my master? He does not belong to your district. So his vote is of no value to you?"

"Watch your tongue." With two steps, the tall, slim, impressive man was beside him. "Don't you dare talk to me like that."

Undaunted, Tyrkir lifted the wooden shaft and watched the judge over the glowing red needle tip. "I must know. Erik believes in you. A disappointment would be bad for him."

"What kind of person are you?" Thorbjörn's anger had vanished. "Why is a slave so concerned about the welfare of his master? I've been asking myself that for some time."

Tyrkir bent over the cow skin. "If he succeeds, I succeed."

"Answer me."

The needle did not touch the leather. "I'm Erik's steward, but above all, I'm his friend."

The corners of the gode's mouth, framed by a carefully trimmed beard, twitched. "I admit, I'm jealous. I don't know whether any of my servants talk about me like that. No, don't worry. Erik means a great deal to me. I would leave the rudder of my *Sea Bird* to him in the roughest seas without hesitation and lie down to sleep." The gode rubbed the bridge of his nose again. "Askel! Askel the Lean must also be invited." After a deep sigh, he added, "I must keep a watchful eye on him. He can easily spoil the spirit of a feast."

"Does he drink too much?"

"No. Too little." Thorbjörn looked at the first rune of Askel's name. "His consumption of beer isn't the problem. It's his stories that worry me."

"I thought stories lift spirits at a feast. I, too, partake in this art. . . ."

"That's often the case, but Askel always tells of only one man and his miracles. He must have first heard of him at the royal court in Denmark. And since his return, he has been transformed." After a pause, Thorbjörn added, "Askel is a Christian, if you understand what that means."

Tyrkir bent even lower over the cowhide and thoughtfully etched rune after rune. Memories came flooding back. He was a little boy. The village on the Rhine emerged from the fog of time. He clearly saw the crouched stone church. Inside, candles burned, and above them hung the picture of the woman and her child. Her name came back to him now: Maria. And also, the name of the son.

"What are you writing? Jesus?"

Tyrkir stopped abruptly. "Didn't you just dictate that name to me?"

"Not that I know of. Jesus is the name of the man—this miracle worker." The judge laughed. "You amaze me again. No, Askel is called the Lean by all. I could not invite this Jesus, even if he lived in my district and gave me his vote."

Tyrkir burnt over the last characters with two wide lines. "It was an accident."

Thorbjörn's hand landed hard on Tyrkir's shoulder. "Really?"

"I must have heard the name before. Believe me, it has no meaning for me."

"That's how it should stay. Not everyone thinks as generously here as I do. The Icelanders take their faith very seriously. Askel is a loner—they tolerate him only because he's from here. But if a stranger appeared with a strange god? It could be dangerous for him."

"So far, I get along well with my friend, the great Tyr." The German heated the needle again. "Why annoy him?" He wrote next to the struck-through lines in beautiful runes: the Lean.

No one had sent excuses; all those invited had come to Warm Spring Slope.

It was raining, and an icy wind drove down from the snowy glacier. To at least offer the gods drink and food in a dignified form, Thorbjörn decided to perform the sacrifice outside. While he asked Odin and the crowd of gods to the table and begged their blessing for the three-day banquet, the company, covered in coats and cloaks, bent their knees. All the men had bared their heads; the women concealed their faces in their hands. Only one stood outside the fence, his back turned, and his folded, scrawny hands stretched to the sky.

Erik nudged Tyrkir. "What is he doing?"

A quick glance was enough. "Leave it! Better that you ignore him."

*So that must be Askel the Lean*, Tyrkir thought. *Did I forget to tell Erik about him? Or was it cowardice?* Since that morning, he'd remembered some of the things his mother had told him about this Jesus.

The sacrifice was offered and Thorbjörn Vifilsson spoke quickly. The company rose, wanting finally to be dry and warm, but their host held them back. "Let us first take the oath of peace." He loudly called to the figure beyond the fence. "Askel! That applies to you, too. Or may you no longer take even this oath?" Some laughed mockingly, others only looked at each other, shaking their heads. The Lean One did not care. With a thin smile on his lips, he entered the meadow of the house. "To make a promise is as sacred to me as it is to you."

No word could be taken as offense during the feast. Even if the beer heated heads, no grudges should arise, and above all, no feud should be instigated. "So be it," all those invited affirmed.

Thorbjörn was satisfied. "And now, let us greet the winter with roast meat and beer! The feast may begin. But since there are so many of us and the room will be cramped, follow my request, esteemed guests, and do not rush into the house. The slave of my friend Erik will let you in, so everyone will find his due place."

In spite of the cold and wet, no one dared protest—it was not just their neighbor but the new gode who had invited them, and his wish was tantamount to an order. Tyrkir unrolled the cowhide and called the names according to their rank. Whoever was closest to the high seat was first to be allowed through the narrow peat corridor and into the warmth. Immediately after entering, they presented their cloaks and swords to the servant, while a second slave took the gifts. In return, everyone received a well-filled jug.

The great fire crackled. Fish-oil lamps flickered on the tables.

The hall smelled of soups and roasts. Soon, all the benches were occupied, no stool remained empty, and the simple peasants and fishermen crowded on the steps to the side aisles.

"Music! Music!" Thorbjörn demanded loudly as he approached his place between the ornately decorated supporting beams, shaking hands along the tables of honor. The players raised their flutes, reached for their harp strings, and stamped their foot-bells. Their melodies danced brightly over the buzz of expectant laughter and gossip.

The women had the rear area of the living hall near the kitchen rooms. Here the farmers' wives had spread out their skirts at first, but soon, they also had to move closer together. Even the finest woven fabrics were no longer on full display, so all that was left to impress jealous neighbors was flashing gold and silver jewelry— combs, necklaces, brooches, and bracelets.

Tyrkir had already stashed a wooden block for himself near the entrance that morning. Relieved, he sat next to the armory servant and enjoyed an unobstructed view of the hall from the front of the great fire. Not far from him, Askel squatted, holding his pointed knees and staring up at the wind-eye.

Erik had been assigned the place right next to Thjodhild's uncle. It was obvious how proud he was of this distinction. His face was shining as he dedicated the first toast to Einar Sigmundsson, and they both indulged in the freshly brewed beer.

Tyrkir thought to himself, *Perhaps it would've been better if we'd bought land here on the South Island. I've never seen my Viking as carefree as he's been these past two months.*

On the bench of honor to the left of the great fire, he saw Thjodhild whispering and laughing with Hallweig. She also appeared to enjoy every day at the side of her new friend. And what was to happen in the spring? The sight of Thjodhild dispelled his worries. *My. . . .* Even in his thought he did not allow the word *dear*, and so he corrected himself. *My mistress. She wore that light blue dress at her wedding. Maybe the fabric is not as finely woven as the cloth of our hostess's green dress, nor do bloodred stones sparkle on her hair clip. But if I had to choose, then Thjodhild would be—*

"Hey, are you dreaming?" His neighbor nudged him for a second time. "Or do you not want to drink with me because you can write, and I can't."

"Do you think so little of me?" Tyrkir clumsily grabbed the offered jug. "But slowly! My stomach is still empty."

"That's what it's all about." The armory servant laughed. "First, we drink until our bellies are full of beer, and then we stuff down the roast. Only then does the fun begin!"

"I'll remember that." Nevertheless, Tyrkir did not finish his drink. The lessons resumed immediately. "No, no. Down with it. By Loki, I suppose you from the north don't know anything about celebrating?"

Tyrkir tried to explain that he had to stay sober for his master and that he wasn't a big drinker.

The servant did not accept excuses. Instead, he saw it as his duty to teach the weedy steward the art of getting drunk quickly. "For three days and two nights, we are as good as our masters. We must take advantage of that, my friend. Here, down with it."

And Tyrkir drank. *No quarreling, no sharp word during the feast,* he thought. *I also took the oath. Today I will not be able to escape this man.* And he drank.

The strong, bitter beer rumbled in his stomach. He was not allowed to listen to any speeches, not even the verses in honor of the host. When the wooden boards with roasts were finally handed around, the smoky hall was already spinning. He tasted the fat, fought down nausea, and the voice of his teacher still droned in his ear: "Drink! It'll be easier!"

Was it his seventh? No, twelve, definitely twelve. The jug slipped from Tyrkir's hand. Waves sloshed the ship, and he noticed that he was sinking and wanted to get up; he slowly tilted sideways from the block and slept.

"Too bad," murmured the armorer. "A decent fellow, even though he can write. But he's not good at drinking."

The planks of the boat creaked, groaning very close to the ear, then farther away. The water tasted rotten. Tyrkir tried to turn in the ups and downs. It didn't work. A bag full of meat lay on his chest. No, it must be fish. *We went out with Thorbjörn. But why did we put the catch in a bag?*

The question woke him. With his eyes closed, he tried to get his bearings. Only snoring men could create this constant grunting and snorting. *So, no ship, I'm in the living hall. The beer knocked me over, too early, like a boy—much too soon. At some point, the rest of the party must have also fallen asleep.*

He sensed the weight on his chest, felt a beard and chin. Tyrkir opened his eyes and looked into the armory servant's open mouth. Every time he breathed out, a rancid, sour smell washed over Tyrkir's face. *First, pour the belly full of beer, then stuff down the roast!* The memory made Tyrkir gag.

He lifted the snorer's head slightly, slid out from underneath it, and laid it on the stamped peat floor, then pushed himself up with the help of the stool.

The hall looked as though a long battle had taken place. Here and there, fish-oil lamps still flickered. Tyrkir recognized motionless figures in the bluish smoke. Peasants and fishermen slept stretched out or rolled up wherever the drink had overpowered them. Some were still holding on to their jugs. Most of the lords lay sunk over the table boards, their faces in the middle of their leftover food.

Tyrkir groped his way along the firepit to the places of honor.

He found Erik next to Thjodhild's uncle. The men were leaning their heads against each other and snoring in the same rhythm.

Where were the women? The rear part of the hall was empty; bowls and cups had been cleared away. How clever they are. He pressed his aching temples. *If I hadn't . . . I would have been in bed in time . . .* He turned back and tried to reach the exit.

"A beautiful morning!"

"Who says that?" He almost stumbled over the gaunt figure in front of him. Askel was half propped up, his gaze keen and earnest. "Our Savior has nothing against drinking, but drunkards are an abomination to him."

"Who do you mean?"

"Jesus Christ."

"All right." Tyrkir continued with erratic movements. *Not him, not now,* he thought, as he stumbled out through the hallway.

It was cold when the wind hit him, and snowflakes bit into his face. He breathed deeply, panting with pain at the same time, the air piercing his chest like an ice dagger, deep into his stomach. He coughed, choked, and puked out the night. *Great Tyr, I must sleep. Only sleep.* With difficulty, he reached the barn. The smell of hay welcomed him, and he let himself drop into its softness.

Snow fell all day, soon covering the grass roof of the house, ankle-deep in the inner courtyard, and still it continued to come. The guests didn't care. Little by little, the feast resumed again. Thorbjörn skillfully knew how to steer the mood. He had knife swallowers, fools, and singers perform. There was entertainment for every taste, and the wealthy landowners and simple farmers and the ladies gratefully praised their new gode.

Tyrkir did not return to the festivities until the evening. He was greeted by a great noise. The tables in the front had been pushed aside. Two men of unequal stature measured their strength in a wrestling match, their upper bodies bare. Yelling and shouting cheered them on.

*Nobody missed me.* Tyrkir grinned. *Not even my drinking master.* The weapons servant had his arm around another victim's shoulder. With a solemn expression, they simultaneously raised their jugs. After some gurgling and swallowing, each checked how empty the other's vessel was.

Tyrkir gladly gave up his wooden block and sat with the small farmers on the steps. The noise stopped abruptly. The party was spellbound, following the fight. The muscle-packed man had just taken the head of the smaller one in his arms. Only one more jerk, and he would throw him to the ground. Then the opponent shoved his elbow into the muscled man's abdomen while, at the same time, hitting the back of his knee, and freed himself. While the tall one still moaned and staggered, the little one took advantage of the moment. Roaring, he grabbed his opponent's foot and tore it back. There was no hold; the muscle-packed man hit the ground with his full body. The winner was led to the high seat with a chorus of clapping and enthusiastic cheering, and there received a drinking horn decorated with silver tendrils from Thorbjörn.

"My guests!" The gode spread out his arms until calm returned. "Enough of the competitions." He tapped his nose. "Do you smell what is being prepared outside in the kitchen? Fish, yes. The most delicate white fish meat, as much as you can eat. Never before have I succeeded in bringing in such a big catch. I couldn't have done it alone. Here is the man who drove out tirelessly with me—Erik the Red, my friend!" He clapped his hands until everyone followed his example.

Something forced Tyrkir to look over at the women. As soon as he met Thjodhild's gaze, she smiled proudly. *We think the same,* he thought, and nodded to her. *Yes, that's the way it should be. Our*

*Viking needs friends who openly acknowledge him. And how happy it makes him.* The blood stood in Erik's face as he rose from his seat and grinned awkwardly.

Thorbjörn emphasized his frank statement with a pause before continuing. "And after the roast yesterday, I want to share the whole catch with you today."

*Hail to our judge! Hail to his generosity!* He accepted the acclaim with a modest smile. "Enough, friends, enough! I know that each of you entertains his guests just as well. It will be some time before the bowls are brought in. No more tricks or competitions. No, let's enjoy the anticipation more quietly. Let's listen to the minstrels and singers."

The murmurs in agreement showed how much the company, tired of beer, was willing to relax and be entertained.

"Fish!" The call broke through the hall. "Yes, fish!"

All heads turned in the same direction. Askel the Lean had jumped up. "What do you all know about fishing?"

Before Thorbjörn could stop him, he pulled a log to the great fire and climbed up. "Listen to my story!"

Too late! The judge fell back into the high seat. During a feast, every man had the right to tell a story. To stop him after the announcement would be a violation of hospitality. "We are curious, Askel."

"Brothers and friends." The lean man turned to the men, nodding to the women. "You, sisters, listen." With his stretched finger, he pointed to Thorbjörn. "Our gode boasts that he has succeeded in a great fishing expedition." He smiled compassionately. "How many mornings did he have to go out? A week? No, certainly more than a month. And how often did only a few fish wriggle in his net?"

"That's no story," Erik shouted indignantly. "If you're just trying to mock our host in front of the women, better to be quiet!"

With a wave, Thorbjörn urged Erik to remain silent.

Askel raised his thin shoulders. "I'll tell you the story of the most wondrous fishing haul ever. Our Savior, Jesus..."

A murmur went through the hall. Men scratched their beards. Some rested their heads in their hands, others sighed with resignation. The women exchanged pitiful looks.

"Our Lord Jesus came to a beautiful lake late in the morning. It was quite hot. There, the fishermen stood on the shore, cleaning their nets. They'd caught nothing. Well, Our Savior asks a fisherman to row him out a little. From the boat, he preaches to the men on the beach about the great God, his father."

"What is the god's name?" Erik rubbed his knuckles together. "Odin has no Jesus as his son. Name the god."

Surprised, the lean man looked at the high bench. "Only God, because he is the greatest, and the only one."

"What?"

Thjodhild's uncle quickly grabbed the Red's arm and whispered to him.

"What?" Erik repeated, quieter this time, and then he understood. He leaned back and closed his eyes. "A Christian," he grumbled. "I wouldn't have expected something like that here."

"After the sermon, Jesus said to the fishermen, 'Because you listened to me so calmly, I will reward you. Now go back to the lake with your boats and throw out the nets! Go ahead, I promise you a big catch.'" Askel crossed his arms. "You can imagine the faces of the men. The whole night, they'd had nothing in their nets, and now they were supposed to try again in bright sunshine? 'Don't argue,' said our Lord Jesus. 'Just believe me.' Well, what do you know? One boat really set out, and as soon as the men pulled the nets through the deep water, they grew heavy."

The skinny man's story was met with distrustful looks.

"They reached into the mesh, but there were so many fish, they couldn't haul the net on their own. A second boat came to help. I tell you, both boats were so full of fish, they almost sank just before the shore." Askel looked triumphantly into the gathering. "Believe me, this story is true. Only our Savior, the son of the only God, possesses such miraculous powers."

Instead of applause, the lean man reaped only an embarrassed silence.

Tyrkir hadn't let Erik out of his sight since he'd said the word *Christian*. Erik's lips trembled, and when he looked up, his gaze was filled with burning anger. He slammed his fist onto the table-top. But before he could shout, Tyrkir jumped up. "Nets! Do you know who made the first net?"

He yanked Askel off the wooden block and climbed up, taking his place. "I want to tell you this story."

"We're excited," the gode cried, casting Erik a pleading look before saying, "We're all looking forward to it, aren't we, my friend?"

The red one opened his fist and exhaled. "That's right. My Know-It-All knows how to tell a story."

Slowly, Tyrkir lifted his finger and pointed to the wind-eye high above the great fire. "Follow me out there and climb higher with me to Valhalla. In the golden hall, the gods sit together. Never have they been as angry as they are today. Thor would have bent his hammer between his fists if Freyr hadn't stopped him."

Astonished cries filled the room. Erik bent over. "Is that true?"

"If I say so. The anger is so great that even in Odin's only eye, there are tears of rage."

"Why, Know-It-All?"

Tyrkir's voice grew darker. "The gods have learned that Loki, the black-haired, insidious liar, is to blame for the eternal death of the beautiful spring god Baldur."

Met with silence, he continued. "But now, the measure is full.

The divine community has sworn revenge. Loki is to atone for these and all his atrocities. Odin resolutely climbs up his golden high seat and wipes tears from his eyes. From his place, he sees everything up in Asgard, and here with us, in Midgard. Where is Loki hiding?" Tyrkir covered his right eye with his hand, and as he turned on the wooden block, he peered one-eyed through the hall.

"There!" His finger jumped into the throng of small farmers next to the great fire. "There he is!" Immediately, the frightened crowd shuffled to the side—even Askel took himself to safety—and a gap opened on the step to the side nave.

"'I see a mountaintop,' Odin tells the gods. 'There, the fiend has built himself a house with four doors.' After a while, he raises his eyebrow. 'Very smart. Oh, he is very smart.'"

The audience hung on Tyrkir's every word. When he, like Odin, watched the fiend for too long, the host demanded, "Have mercy. Don't forget us."

"By day, Loki turns into a salmon and swims in the large water-fall near the lake," Tyrkir reported. "Only when it is dark does he return to the house, sit by the fire, and consider what tricks the gods might use to catch him. And because thinking is exhausting, he takes a flax thread and knots it into a mesh."

Tyrkir knotted an invisible net while he continued the story. "The gods set off from Valhalla. They've almost reached the house with the four doors when Loki notices the danger. Quickly, he throws his knitwork over the fire and jumps out, turning into a salmon again as he falls and plunges deep into the whirling water. 'Nothing.' The wise Aesir find the room empty.

"Then, one of the gods bends down. Only a few know his name. He is small, slim." In the zeal of narration, Tyrkir pointed down to himself. "Well, imagine my stature. So, this god, Kwasir, bends down and pulls the charred mesh out of the fire. And because he is very clever, he quickly recognizes what it is good for."

One of the listeners shouted, "Well, with a net, you can catch fish!"

"Right!" Tyrkir exclaimed. "That's exactly what Kwasir explains to the Aesir. Together, the gods sit down and weave a new net. No, not everyone—Odin apologizes because his eye is watering, and Thor shows his hands and claims that his fingers are too thick for such work."

Indulgent laughter rippled from the men. Hallweig nudged Thjodhild. "We know, those two are lazy."

The narrator rocked his head. "Don't be so hard on them! Well, I shall be silent about Odin, but Thor? No, he doesn't hide from work."

Again, happy laughter passed through the rows. Hallweig played along. "Thor only chips in when he wants to."

"But when he does, he does it right. Hear and see for yourself!"

Tyrkir led his listeners to the river. The net was thrown into the waterfall. Thor pulled the lines with the other gods while Loki hid at the bottom between round pebbles, and the mesh slipped over him. At the second attempt, stones weighed down the netting. Again, the fiend saved himself, this time by jumping from the net before swimming back into the waterfall.

"Although Loki is a salmon, the gods hear his mocking laughter. Now Thor gets angry. 'Cast out the net! This time, he won't get away from me!' The red-haired god wades behind the net into the middle of the riverbed. Loki is swimming. Should he go to the sea? Should he jump back over the edge again? Both possibilities are life-threatening." Tyrkir turned his left arm into a salmon for the listeners and made it wag back and forth restlessly.

"There! Loki whips around! He takes the jump! But Thor grabs him from the air. The salmon thrashes wildly. His slick body almost slips out of the mighty fist, but at the last moment, Thor grabs the tail and squeezes. 'You won't escape again.'" Tyrkir clasped his left wrist with his right hand and showed it to the audience. "And because Thor had to grab so hard, that's why, since that day, salmon are so narrow by their tails."

Some of the women practiced the grip, looked at each other, and giggled.

"Go on. What happened to Loki?"

Tyrkir stared spellbound at the gap between the peasants. "There is no mercy. The gods bring the transformed fiend into a cave and tie him to three stones with iron bands. Above him, they forge a poisonous snake on the ceiling. Its poison shall drip onto Loki's face until the end of all time. That is their verdict."

Tyrkir slowly raised his gaze back to the wind-eye. "But you know our gods. Despite all their wrath, they allow Loki's wife to ease his punishment, so she stands next to her husband and catches the poison in a bowl." Tyrkir's voice became quieter. "When the vessel is full, she must empty it out. And only during this time do the poisonous drops fall on Loki's face. And it is then that he winds and twitches so wildly that the earth trembles."

Everybody in the hall was silent, lost in thought. Tyrkir waited before he violently slapped his hands together and stomped his feet. "Earthquake! Now you know why there are earthquakes."

The spell was broken. The listeners thanked Tyrkir with cheers, shook the tables, and the lamps and beer jugs swayed as if in an earth tremor.

Erik jumped up, waved his friend to him, and embraced him. "Oh, Know-It-All!" He proudly presented his friend to the rich lords. "Look here, this is my steward!"

Thorbjörn watched with a smile. "Dear neighbors and relatives, I think praise alone is not enough. Our storyteller should sit closer to us until the end of the festival, even if he is only a slave." Without waiting for agreement, he assigned Tyrkir the place next to Erik and his own father-in-law on the bench of honor.

Maids carried steaming fish in from the kitchen, and soon the conversations were lost in enjoyable smacking.

Erik had soon swallowed his first fish whole, but for the head and tail. He toasted his friend and pointed with the bone over to Askel. "You know," he grumbled, "a fellow like that... Oh, forget it. I don't give a damn."

# SNOW-ROCK GLACIER

"I want to see him!" Thjodhild was walking with Hallweig above Warm Spring Slope when she pointed to the snowy glacier.

"You mustn't press him." The friend shaded her eyes. A coat of fog hung around the elongated ridge of the summit. "He only receives visitors when he has fully undressed." She winked. "In that, he is very much like a vain man."

"I haven't met one like him yet." Thjodhild smiled. "No, seriously, I'm glad we can finally see the glacier again."

Weeks ago, the mountain had emerged for the first time from the long winter night, a mere shadow in the clouds, and only for a few moments. Then, on the day Erik had sailed away with Tyrkir, the servants, and maidservants, the two humps already shone in the sunlight, as if Snow Rock had put on his crown to bid them farewell.

Thjodhild's thoughts had hurried over the mountains to the north side. *Surely Erik has reached our island in the meantime.* She knew what the new farm would look like. During the prolonged darkness, Tyrkir had been building models with leftover wood. He made the residential building, the stables, and barns according to Erik's ideas, and a women's shelter right next to the sauna. Even the roofs were covered with grass, and in the yard, there were chickens and sheep. A small, peaceful world on a tabletop. "Just some toys for Leif for when he grows up." The two men had tried to dismiss their work, yet they could hardly hide their pride and impatience.

Thjodhild said quietly, "Now is the time, Hallweig. If it's true that mysterious power emanates from the snow rock, then I'll have to climb up to him soon. We need happiness."

"Who knows if what people say is true? You best just rely on your men."

"They come first." Thjodhild looked at the glacier again. "You know, a little support from the snow rock would be enough for me. And I feel—no, I am quite sure—that he is well-disposed toward me."

Hallweig reached under her left breast. When she noticed the look her friend gave her, she smiled. "Don't worry. Right now, I'm fine. I just thought maybe I should accompany you. If herbs and spells don't help me, perhaps the snow rock can alleviate my misery?"

Yes, together! Thjodhild immediately agreed. They could walk slowly, and nobody had specified how high the glacier had to be climbed for its power to work. "When do we leave?"

"Well, it's April, and the weather is getting better day by day." Hallweig winked again. "I told you how vain he is. Let's give him until the day after tomorrow to prepare for our visit."

"If only Erik expected me like this..." Thjodhild liked the idea more and more. "He lies there like that, freshly washed..."

"Quiet!" Hallweig looked around. Though there was no one about, she lowered her voice. "Not that anyone can hear us."

"So what? How do you think men talk about us?"

Erik and Tyrkir had started work immediately after their arrival on Oxens Island. They did not allow themselves or their servants a break for four days. Deep trenches were dug near the stream and filled with stones. "No storm should harm our house," the builder had announced almost solemnly as he walked along the floor outlines. "Erikshof! We will grow old here, my friend. And so will Leif and his sons."

That day, at first light, Erik had sent out his maids and slaves, ordering them to bring all the driftwood from the beach to the construction site on the meadow terrace. Now, he was sailing through the reefs and islands with Tyrkir and four boatmen. "I wonder what our horses look like," he shouted to his friend from the tiller.

"I'm sure they have fat bellies."

"I'll bite Thorgest's ears off if they do."

A fresh, bright April morning arched across the mountains of the peninsula. There, on the north side, the wind blew too sharply from the fjord, and the *Mount of the Sea* approached the shore slowly and under very little cloth.

"First, the lumber and household goods must be loaded, so that our work can move forward. We'll come back for the horses later."

"You'd better let the farmer at Breida Farm keep his ears at least until then!"

"Yes, yes, Know-It-All," Erik barked at him. "Sometimes, I listen to you, and I wonder which one of us is the slave."

Tyrkir bowed his head guiltily. "I know, my lord and protector."

The friends only managed to stay serious for a moment. They were full of hope and were not in the mood to mince words. The winter was over, and they were finally putting into action what they'd been planning for so long.

The ship entered the bay. Erik anchored in the same place he had the summer before. "Sharpcliff," he murmured to himself as they crossed their old campsite between the three steep hills. "Unbelievable when I think of our Sharpcliff in the north."

"The gods have swapped the land for us. It's a good omen!" Tyrkir said.

"What?" Erik breathed deeply. "Yes, you're right. Providence is on our side."

Beyond the shore road, they followed the path through the

slowly rising meadows. No green yet showed under the brownish grass wilted by the snowmelt.

A wooden gate blocked access to the fenced area. Tyrkir shouted, waited, then shouted louder, but no servant or maid came to greet them. Nothing moved, neither at the four warehouses nor on the forecourt. Only the column of smoke above the main house showed that Breida Farm was inhabited. "What do you think is going on?"

Erik turned around. The view was clear all the way down to the shore road. "Nobody comes up here without being spotted a long way off."

Tyrkir felt uneasiness creep up his neck. He looked at Erik.

His friend's face had also shifted. "Maybe it's the spot death? It does like to come over the winter months and take everyone away."

At that moment, the door of the house swung open. Angry barking tore at the silence. Three big shaggy dogs rushed outside, barking, and raced across the forecourt. They were already at the shoulder-high gate, jumping against the boards, snarling and barking again. A sharp whistle called them back.

"What do you want?" Thorgest had stopped halfway to the gate and crossed his arms.

"What do we want?" Erik slapped his flat hand against his forehead. "Don't tell me you don't know me anymore."

Like a stranger, the farmer leered at him, gradually approaching, only exposing the lower row of teeth shortly before the gate and emitting a throaty laugh. "The Red One. Now I remember. Look at Erik!"

"I am your new neighbor. Have you forgotten?"

Thorgest didn't respond. His laughter turned into a cough, and he gasped, collected the mucus on his tongue, and spat it against the gate.

Astonished, Erik raised his fist. "Hey, what are you doing?"

"Wasn't meant that way." Thorgest's grin froze. "I've heard a lot about you over the past months. My cousin from Hawk Valley was here."

Tyrkir held his breath. What game was this fellow playing? From the corner of his eye, he saw Erik opening his fist and running his hand through his hair. "I don't care. I kept to the verdict. If you deny us the right of hospitality on your farm, it's fine. I won't quarrel about it. Give me my household things and horses. That's what I paid for."

Thorgest hunched down to the dogs and scratched their neck fur. "Do we agree to that? The stranger thinks he paid, but we think it was too little."

"Don't you dare!" With one small leap, Erik was on the gate. "Give me my things!"

The dogs jumped forward, snatching at the intruder. Erik retreated just in time.

Thorgest watched them for a while. Finally, he silenced them with a single whistle. "Remember, I can always rely on my darlings," he warned Erik. "Let's get down to business. But because I now know you, I want to show you something first." With that, he raised his arm.

His two sons appeared from either side of the main house. Servants stepped out of the shade of the barns. Tyrkir counted eight men armed with bows and arrows. They approached slowly. Each of them picked a safe position above the path and stretched his tendon.

"So now we'll finish the trade in peace." Thorgest wet his lower lip with his tongue. "You get your nags. I keep the rest."

Like after a blow, Erik took a few steps back. He wanted to scream. Finally, he caught his breath. "Cheater! I'll rip your ass open, you bastard!" He already had his battle-ax in his fist.

An arrow struck the upper spar of the gate.

"That was a warning!" Thorgest laughed. "My Odd is a good shot. Be careful!"

Tyrkir quickly stepped up to his friend and whispered, "Put the weapon away! He just wants to irritate you. We are defenseless and outnumbered."

Erik's lips and bearded chin trembled. "You talk to him!"

Calm. Calm and time to think—that's all Tyrkir wanted. "Give us the horses. We'll talk about the lumber and tools afterward."

"Very reasonable." Thorgest gave another hand signal. From the elongated stable, servants drove the herd outside with calls and whistles. There was no exuberant neighing and hoofbeats; no stallion used the opportunity to break out into the pastures. The ten horses trotted listlessly across the forecourt, down to the path.

At his back, Tyrkir heard a sharp hiss. "By Thor, that's just slaughter cattle," Erik said. The manes were matted, the ankles fat, and the bellies round. The horses might have been useful for a leisurely outing, but none of the stallions were fit to fight. "Ask him why?"

Before Tyrkir had a chance to speak, Thorgest ordered: "Back up! Even farther!"

Only when he was safe from a quick attack did he open the gate, guarded by his dogs. He let the herd out and pushed the spar back in place again. "Well, do you like my gift? It cost me a lot of food to get the nags ready. And now, go! Our business is finished."

"You can't just keep our property!" Tyrkir screamed, struggling to keep his composure. "That's against law and order!"

"Your master is a killer! The law no longer applies to him." Thorgest spat against the gate. "He should be pleased that I even gave him his horses."

*Great Tyr*, the steward pleaded. *Let me find the right words.* "My master had to leave Hawk Valley for three years. That was the verdict. The goden's verdict does not apply here. Here, Erik has the same rights as you."

"Never," Thorgest roared furiously. "My cousin! My cousin is the brother of Hravn Holmgang! This red bastard murdered a relative of mine! Law! Justice! Ha! If I could, I would chop his head to pieces."

Tyrkir felt a hand on his shoulder. "Leave it alone, Know-It-All."

Astonished, Tyrkir turned his head. "Give up? You want . . . ?"

"Let's go!" Erik's voice sounded strangely calm. "To him, I'm a murderer."

But they hadn't even tried. Tyrkir stepped closer to the gate. "Do you want more silver? Name your price."

Thorgest was silent.

"We need the timber and our tools."

Silence.

"At least, give us the two high seat beams. They are worthless to you, but we'll pay you a good price. Without them, there will be no happiness in the new house."

Thorgest rubbed his knuckles together. "Nothing. I won't give you a thing. I don't want that killer as my neighbor. He should leave." Hate and triumph made his voice reedy. "And the high seat beams? Oh, I'll make good use of them. I'll chop them up, throw them in the fire, and cook myself some soup."

"You wouldn't dare!" Tyrkir said, his voice dangerous. "Our beams are the shrine of the family. If you even damage them, the gods will punish you."

Erik grasped his friend hard by the arm. "Come, now. There's no point." Despite fierce resistance, he pulled Tyrkir away from the gate and ordered his three servants to follow them with their horses.

"Go! Don't let us see you here again! May your ship sink! Murderers! Damned murderers!" More and more curses flew after them.

Tyrkir fought back tears. When they were out of range, he broke loose. "Maybe I could have managed. But you? You just give up. What are you going to say to Thjodhild? Tell me!"

"Silence, slave!" Erik went to strike him.

"Go ahead! What are you waiting for?"

The moment was immediately over; Erik's mighty shoulders sank. "You know very well I am not a coward."

Tyrkir couldn't ask the master for forgiveness. He looked past Erik to the islands in the fjord. "And now? What will we build our house with?"

Then Erik whirled him around and pulled him so close, their faces almost touched. "Nobody steals the high seat beams of Erik Thorvaldsson." The dangerous glow filled his amber eyes again. "By my honor, I'll take what's mine!"

Slowly, the lump came loose. *How could I have doubted my Viking?*

"I am a damned fool. You're planning an attack, and we have to get our people first."

This time, Tyrkir felt no fear as he had the year before when Erik swore revenge on the murderers of his servants. Today, he wanted satisfaction himself. The shame suffered, the injustice—they had to be atoned for. "But it will not be simple. Breida Farm is easy to defend."

"I want my property, not war. How we manage that, let that be my concern. This is one area I know more about than you do." Erik stretched his lips and turned around. For a long time, he stood and looked at the hilly terrain leading up to Breida Farm. The haystack, just an arrow's flight west of the fence, caught his attention. Finally, he mumbled, "Not tomorrow, but in two days, I'll have my beams back."

Hallweig and Thjodhild had risen in the dark. Neither the quiet mockery of the lord of the house nor the worried warnings of the maidservants had kept them from executing their plan. Today they were going to visit the glacier.

They were still sitting next to each other by the hearth fire with their upper bodies uncovered and nursing their children. During the day, the babies would be fed sweet milk porridge.

Thorbjörn came out of the sleeping chamber dressed only in a shirt. He yawned, then looked at the little ones sucking their breasts greedily. "And I? You go out of the house, and I should starve?"

Hallweig pointed to her free bosom next to Gudrid. "Please! I have enough. Help yourself!" When he made a face, she laughed. "Oh, you want something else? Soup, bread, and cheese are waiting, and you don't need me for that." With a deep sigh, she said to Thjodhild, "Men. They go out on their ships, often stay away for months, and we don't say a word. But if we want to leave the house for even a few hours, they'll pull their hair out and worry about a famine."

Thjodhild patted the back of her fully fed Leif. "It shows you who's really the head of the family."

Thorbjörn could not come up with a clever reply. "You're conspiring against me." Suddenly busy, he walked through the hall, but just before he had reached the exit, he shouted over his shoulder, "I am not just the master of Warm Spring Slope. Don't forget that. I am also a gode."

Without paying him any more attention, the women put their children back in the woven cribs and began to dress for the hike. First, the woolen, long undershirt. Hallweig took two pairs of trousers and handed one to her friend.

Thjodhild hesitated. "Do you really think so?"

"They keep the men warm, so why not us?" Hallweig climbed in with quick movements, securing the fabric with a belt above her hip, and fastening the wide tubes under the knee with straps. "When we put the dresses over them, they'll barely be noticeable."

Thjodhild was still fidgeting with her belt when the landlord returned. "The weather . . . Wait, those are trousers! You can't—"

"Yes, we can." Hallweig calmly reached for her leather boots. "I sewed these trousers for you. Today is a good opportunity to try them out myself."

"Two women are just too much for me." The judge surrendered with a laugh. "It's cold outside," he reported, "but the clear starry sky promises a beautiful day." Unprompted, he brought over two pairs of snowshoes. "For safety's sake. Who knows what it's like up there."

Hallweig and Thjodhild refused. They only wanted to climb as high as their boots would allow.

Under the protection of darkness, Erik and Tyrkir waded ashore with eight servants. There was no noise, no unnecessary words. Their faces were soot-blackened, and besides axes and daggers, the men carried bows and arrow quivers instead of spears. Three of them also carried full sacks on their shoulders.

Katla and the other two maids had remained in the bay on the knarr. Their mission was to wait. No matter how long it took, and no matter what happened, they were to wait for the men to return. The ship had to be ready to set sail at any time.

Below the shore road, Erik gently poked his friend's chain mail. "Remember, the sun must first dry the wilted grass. When the stalks start moving in the wind, it's time. Watch out for the ember pot."

"Don't worry!" Tyrkir tried to hide his tension. "Make sure you get the high seat beams out of the warehouse. That'll be difficult enough."

For a moment, two rows of teeth flashed in Erik's blackened face. "That's right, Know-It-All. I'll be glad when we meet here again later." He silently left in an easterly direction with five of his slaves.

Tyrkir watched the group until the darkness swallowed them up. *May Thor help you*, he asked silently. *And you, great Tyr, keep an eye on my men and me!*

His three servants, laden with sacks, trailed him. "Follow me!"

Although there was no danger from any starlight, they ran west for half an hour under the protection of the embankment. Only when the landscape started to rise more steeply did the men cross the bank road. "Watch your feet—" Tyrkir stumbled, catching himself, but the firepot on its chain jostled and lost its lid. The embers shone like a signal. Quickly, Tyrkir put down the pot, fumbled around, and burned his hand as he replaced the lid.

There was no path through the hilly meadows. As if that wasn't enough, the ground was littered with small humps, hardly visible during the day. Now, they made every step more difficult. The group's progress was slow.

Tyrkir looked anxiously at the sky yet again. The stars faded, and far in the east, the first gray stripes appeared. "Faster," he said quietly, and knew immediately how pointless the order was. Behind him, the servants gasped under their load, hampered by the bumpy ground.

When the buildings of Breida Farm appeared as black outlines far to their left, Tyrkir stopped. "Rest!" He put down the crucible and scurried up the next hill.

Just a short arrow flight away, halfway to the yard, he saw the barn in the pasture. They were a little late, but they had reached the right elevation. *It is not my doing*, he thought. *The gods are with us.* He retreated immediately. Preparations needed to be made before the sky grew even brighter.

"You two, come with me!" To the third servant, he said, "Guard the embers, and if we're surprised, stop our pursuers with your bow!" They left one sack behind and raced hunched around the hill into the open pasture.

"Damn," moaned one of the servants. "We'll never make it."

"Shut up." Tyrkir, too, felt exposed. They had quite a distance to cover. What if someone at the farm was already awake and happened to look in their direction? All the same, they had to get to the shed. Otherwise, the plan would fail. Two sheep jumped up and fled from the troublemakers, bleating loudly. The men's hearts pounded, their breath fled.

At last, undiscovered, Tyrkir and his men crouched behind the haystack and out of sight. Now they could move more freely. They opened the sacks, reached into the wood shavings, and pulled out iron rods and spades.

They worked silently on the back wall. The peat was not thick, and the inner wooden struts caused hardly any noise as they broke. Finally, the hole was big enough. The three men pulled hay outside, distributed it, making sure there was enough in the opening, and then mixed in the wood chips. "Get back," whispered Tyrkir. "Don't forget the tools." Ducking, the two servants ran off. With one last look, he followed them. Behind his back, dawn colored the eastern horizon.

Thjodhild walked slowly, but still too fast for her friend. She waited on a hill next to the stream. Hallweig climbed up to her, breathing heavily. "I've become an old woman."

"Only if you keep talking such nonsense. We have time. No matter how unpredictable Snow Rock may be, he can't run from us."

Thjodhild pointed to the glowing mountain peaks in the east. "We should rest here and wait for the sun. It will be easier in the warmth."

Gratefully, Hallweig sat down on a stone. "How do you feel in your trousers?"

"I wouldn't have thought how pleasant they are. There is no cold draught from below."

"When we get back, I'll sew trousers for us," Hallweig decided. Two pairs that fit better and were more inconspicuous to wear under their dresses.

Thjodhild looked down along the bubbling stream and into the valley. Where the rocks were piled higher, she could still see snow that had not yet been melted by the April sun. The pastures were pale brown, and down in the plain, the manor houses lay scattered all the way to the sea. Columns of smoke rose from the roofs into the transparent morning. "It's so peaceful."

"Yes, let's enjoy today. No one is asking, 'Where is the salt? Shall I add wood, Mistress? Do I have to milk?' One day without maid-servants and work." Hallweig hugged her knees. "And no children's screaming. I enjoy that, too."

*She's right*, Thjodhild thought, and was surprised that when she thought of Leif, a quiet feeling of guilt crept up. "They are still so small and need us."

"We provide enough—" Hallweig broke off and looked up, agitated. "It would be nice if our families were to come together, wouldn't it?"

"You mean Leif and Gudrid?"

"Yes, they should marry later."

The thought inspired Thjodhild. She squatted on the stone next to Hallweig, and both planned the future of their children. Sufficient land would have to be chosen in time for the couple. No, not over on the island in the Breidafjord. Here, on the south side, was where they should make their home. Perhaps the farm could even be built beforehand.

Hallweig stopped, thoughtful. "The only problem will be, how do we convince Erik and Thorbjörn? If the proposal comes from us, they're sure to reject it."

"Don't worry. We are the real heads of the family, don't forget that. We'll gradually prepare them for it. They won't even notice.

And when the time comes, they'll sit down, frown, pull at their hair, and tell us the weighty decision afterward."

Hallweig sighed and leaned her head against her friend's shoulder. "Since you've been here, I've felt free and strong like never before."

So they sat, thinking about the marriage of their children until the sun rose over the mountain edges and flooded the valley with light.

Around noon, Tyrkir decided to strike. The wilted grass had dried. The wind came from the west and had even freshened a bit, favoring the venture. Behind the cover of the hill, the steward had the bows stretched, and every tendon carefully checked. "All depends on the first shot. The second could already betray us. You don't have much time. Still, aim calmly and only shoot when I give the order!"

The arrows were wrapped at the tip with fat-soaked cloths. Tyrkir sprinkled wood shavings into the embers. A small flame rose, and the men lit their arrows. Final glances were exchanged. They were ready—they climbed the hill.

In a line, the four men stepped out from their cover, pulling the feathered shafts up to their lips. Only one breath to estimate the distance. "Now!"

The flaming arrows hissed from the strings, four torches ascending; even before they'd finished their flying arcs, the archers had thrown themselves flat to the ground. Tyrkir stared at their target. Too short. He spotted two arrows a good horse's length from the barn, smoke rising; the third had almost reached the hay they'd scattered outside and was still burning. Where was the last arrow? Had it hit through the hole in the side of the barn? Or was it lying somewhere else, extinguished?

Too much was at stake to wait and see. Over by the farm buildings, no one seemed to have noticed anything amiss.

"We'll have to shoot again!" The group quickly retreated to prepare new arrows. It took longer for the cloth wraps to catch fire, but then the men were climbing up the hill again. "Wait!" Tyrkir crawled up alone.

Fire! His heart cheered. The wilted grass had ignited, and the wind drove the flames toward the barn. Flames rose from the hole in the back wall. "We did it," he told his men, and he let them shoot the burning arrows blindly over the hill toward the target.

From his position, Tyrkir watched with bated breath as the blaze raged through the barn. A dull roar set in, then the roof burst, sod and stones swirling high, as a pillar of fire pierced the sky.

Calls rang over from the farm. People ran back and forth. Maids and farmhands with wooden buckets and vats rushed out of the stables. Dogs barked. Now Thorgest and his sons could be spotted in front of the house. The shouting increased, but the barked commands were louder still. The food supply was on fire!

Tyrkir could imagine their shock and horror. They had to try to save some of the hay and extinguish the flames. The pasture gate was pushed open. All the farm people stormed to the brook in the meadow. They drew water and ran toward the fire, the farmer first, with Odd and Toke and the three dogs close behind.

Tyrkir turned his attention from the pasture to the other warehouses. He saw no movement there. He scanned the yard. Erik should have already come from the east, but there was nothing— nothing to be seen of his friend and the other men. *Great Tyr, help me!* Tyrkir hit the grass with his fist. *That damn Viking!* Suddenly, he stopped.

The gate of the barn swung open. His prayers had reached Valhalla. Erik strolled out of the storeroom. *Why didn't I see you before? It doesn't matter.* Erik's men followed close behind, with pairs carrying a beam on their shoulders. The fifth servant pressed the gate shut again, covering the rear.

Without any further caution, the group moved at a run toward the fountain.

Tyrkir glanced at the pasture. The people from Breida Farm were still fighting the flames. He turned his attention back to his master. Erik had already opened the main gate. The way down through the meadows was long, and there was no protection up to the shore road. Only one glance in their direction, and they'd be discovered. *Faster!* Tyrkir had to force himself not to spur his friend on loudly. *Faster? How pointless!* Weighed down by their valuable load, the group couldn't go any faster.

"Father!" Toke had turned around and stretched his hand toward the path. "Father!"

Instantly, the farmer was beside him. Odd dropped his bucket of water. The three roared and cursed. From his place, Tyrkir made out *ambush*, and one other word: *thieves*.

Then the old man shouted orders. His sons raced away, accompanied by four servants, jumping over the brook and toward the yard.

It wouldn't be long before the pursuit began. Tyrkir left the hill. "Move!" Glow pot, sack, and tools were left behind. He had to try to reach Erik as soon as possible.

He definitely wouldn't make it in time, but if a fight broke out down at Sharpcliff, or on the beach, maybe he and his three men could still help his friend.

Though the snow was blinding, Thjodhild was hot. Her eyes almost closed as she stomped ahead with small steps, Hallweig following her tracks. The women had not spoken for an hour. Each struggled with the unusual effort. Sweat seeped from their necks into their cloak collars, and the underwear stuck to their skin. *Why do we torture ourselves so much?* Thjodhild wondered. *If it is true what they say about Snow Rock, then he must have long since noticed us.*

*That must be enough for him.* She stopped resolutely and turned around. "Should we climb even farther?"

Hallweig stepped into her shadow. "I thought you'd forgotten me. Let's turn around and leave the glacier alone." As soon as she had spoken, her face lost all color. "There! O Freya, help us!" She stared over her friend's shoulder up the snowy slope. "There! Look!"

Thjodhild turned her head. A cloud drifted toward them from the height of the glacier. The sky above remained blue to their right and left, and the day continued to shine in the sunlight. No, this was no cloud. It was a massive, round, dense gray fog. Black threads emanated from inside of it, transforming into reaching arms. "The s-spirit..." she stammered, "... of Snow Rock! People were not lying."

The formation approached them silently. Thjodhild thought of fleeing, running away, hiding. Immediately, the fog grew and filled the width of the snow slope. Too late. Although it had not yet reached them, they were already at his mercy. Hallweig trembled, grasping her heart with a groan, her lips turning blue.

"Stay calm!" Thjodhild supported her weight. "Let's sit down!" In her arms, her friend went slack. Thjodhild struggled to hold her up, sinking slowly into the snow and resting her head on her lap. "You'll feel better soon."

"What... what?" Hallweig whispered, her eyes closed. She felt for the hand on her cheek and held it tight. "The glacier punishes us."

"No, don't be afraid! I'm with you." Thjodhild looked up. She couldn't scream. Directly above them, the fog billowed, contracting and expanding like a gray beating heart, the black tentacles oscillating around the two women and sinking down into the snow. Now, the rest of it sank down on them. Thjodhild leaned protectively over Hallweig. The haze enveloped them. Thjodhild felt no weight—only silence, painful silence.

Before Tyrkir had reached the three humpback hills below the bank road, he already heard the beating of iron against iron, the roar of the fighters. He ran faster—his companions couldn't keep pace as the noise rose from the hollow in the middle of Sharpcliff.

Tyrkir rushed onto a ridge between the hills. His first objective was to locate Erik. His friend was fighting off two enemies' shields and axes. Like bloodhounds, they jumped before the giant, stabbing him with their spears, and tried to break his cover. One of them was Odd.

At second glance, Tyrkir grasped the extent of the horror. The beaten ones lay scattered all over the place—here and there, a man rolled in his own blood. *Our servants are all unfit to fight, or dead,* he noted with horror. Four of the opponents were defeated, but the last two were pressing Erik hard. He evaded them again and again, their wild attacks pushing him backward step by step, farther into the middle of the valley.

Tyrkir looked around for his three men. They'd almost reached him. "Hurry up!" He looked down again. "Hold on, Erik. We're coming!"

Then one of the injured picked himself up—Toke, the farmer's second son, got back on his feet. A short sword flashed in his fist. He staggered around blindly, then found the fighters. With his blade outstretched, he moved toward the back of the Red.

There was no time left to wait for reinforcements. Tyrkir rushed off. Running, he reached for the ax on his belt. He jerked and pulled, but the weapon would not slip out of the leather loop. Toke had already come within two horse lengths of Erik.

*I have to cut him off.* That thought alone drove Tyrkir on. He left the ax and pulled out his dagger. Storming up from the side, he covered Erik's back just as Toke reached out for the strike. Tyrkir managed another warning call for his friend, then saw the ax edge coming toward him. He saw nothing more but felt a hot burning in the left half of his face and then dropped to the ground. Knocked off balance by the force of his own blow, Toke fell over him and died with a deep sigh.

No matter how hard Tyrkir tried, he could not shake off the lifeless body. His mouth filled with blood and he choked. With immense force, he turned his head to the right until the blood drained out of the corner of his lips and he could breathe again.

The surrounding noise grew. *The men have come*, he thought. The beating, the pounding became more violent. Then he heard a marrow-shattering roar, and a second one rose immediately. Death cries, then silence reigned.

*What's happening?* Again, Tyrkir tried to free himself from the corpse. He was too weak and only managed to move his legs helplessly.

"You're alive!"

Erik's voice—never before had Tyrkir found its sound so soothing. *No, you are alive*, he thought. *Thank Thor, my Viking is alive!* Valhalla had not fallen to the earth. Colors—red, yellow, blue, and green—flashed before him. He felt lifted by them as if on to a rainbow. He felt so light.

"Hey, Know-It-All?"

Almost regretfully, Tyrkir opened his eyes and looked into his friend's sooty face. He wanted to ask, but only strange sounds came from his throat.

"Stop talking." Erik grinned, but there was deep concern etched into his face. "The way you look, you won't get a word out, anyway."

*What about me?* Tyrkir groped for his left cheek. Immediately, Erik grabbed his hand. "Don't! We must take care of you, but you are lucky. The blood is drying, and the bones still seem to be whole. That's the main thing. A bit is missing from your ear, but nothing too bad. Somehow that flesh on the side will surely heal together again."

My face! With the realization came a deep pain. Tyrkir groaned.

"I know, little one." Awkwardly, Erik stroked his forehead. "I know."

"Lord! There, over there!" One of the servants pointed to the southern saddle between the hilltops. Four horsemen, led by the farmer of Breida Farm, trotted down into the valley.

Erik whispered, "Stay like this. Play dead! I'll come back for you later." The giant jumped up with his ax in his fist. After a few steps, he bent down again, yanked the dead Odd up from the ground by his shaggy mane, and dragged him into the middle of the field.

"Thorgest! Your sons have fallen!" He waited. The news caused the troop to stall. "They attacked me and my men. For this, they received their reward."

"You red bastard!" The father's pain mingled with the curse. "You entered my yard. You are a thief. Arsonist! You miserable murderer!"

"I was in the right! You stole from me. This is not my fault. You alone are to blame for this bloody day."

Thorgest raised his spear threateningly. "No one will listen to the word of an outlaw. I will rip your heart out of your chest and give it to my dogs to eat."

With a jerk, Erik pulled the head of the deceased higher and set the ax edge to the face. "Don't move, peasant! You'll be gathering Odd and your Toke in tiny pieces. I have also lost men. Each of us should bury his dead in honor. Wait until I set sail with the ship, then you can fetch your sons and the others!"

Thorgest laughed, coughed, and spat on the ground. "Cowardly bastard, you think you can just get away with this?"

"Be assured, Erik the Red will not rest until he has shoved your insults back into your mouth so that you may choke on them."

The lord of Breida Farm was silent. After a long pause, he

shouted, "So it is war! We will let the weapons rest for today. We'll each take our fallen and prepare them for the long journey to the realm of the dead. But then we will meet again."

So it was war. As soon as Erik and Thorgest had agreed to it, the anger was gone. Like their own negotiators, they calmly settled the terms. Each party was given one month to gather enough men. Even before the Thorsnessthing in June, the fight was to be fought here at Sharpcliff.

"Give me proof," Thorgest demanded at the end. "Show me that you want to keep the peace today!"

Slowly, Erik put his battle-ax back into his belt loop, let go of the dead man's hair, and spread his unarmed hands. For a while, he stood like that, defenseless, in front of the spears of the people of Breida. "Now you," he demanded. The farmer pushed the tip of his spear into the ground next to his horse. Even for an inexperienced archer, he offered an easy target. The proof had been provided from both sides.

Obeying an inner drive, Erik grabbed Odd under his armpits and laid him down next to his brother. With a calm gesture, he closed both of his eyelids. "The sons are waiting for their father. Is that enough for you?"

Wordlessly, Thorgest gave his people a sign. They turned their horses and rode off over the southern saddle toward the shore road.

"Quick now!" Erik ordered the three surviving slaves to first bring the high seat beams, then the dead aboard. He kneeled next to Tyrkir. "Everything will be all right, little one. Everything must be all right!" He picked up his friend and carried him down the path to the beach. "Get a blanket," he shouted to Katla.

When he reached the ship through the hip-deep water, the maids had already taken off their capes. They accepted the injured man and lay him down gently. Despite the flames in his face, Tyrkir felt their soft arms, looked into their worried eyes, then the colors washed over him again.

The gray surrounding the two women lifted. The fog moved away and broke into four equal parts. The tentacles also went slack, and each fog quarter stretched wide. Like pale cloths, they floated up to the four cardinal points and lost themselves in the distant blue. As if nothing had happened, the snow dazzled, the sun warmed them again.

Thjodhild dried the sweat from her friend's forehead and cheeks. After some time, Hallweig regained her strength, and her breathing calmed. "I dreamed," she whispered, "a carriage came out of the fog toward me. Cats were pulling it. Freya sat on the carriage bench and held the reins. I waved to my goddess to take me with her, but she did not stop. The wheels rolled over my heart."

*No luck*, Thjodhild suspected. The glacier had decided against them. She told herself it was all a lie. No mountain possessed the power of the gods.

"Forget the dream!" She resolutely helped Hallweig up. "I don't know what the fog means, but there is one thing I do know—we shouldn't have come here. Let's turn back." She walked ahead, and Hallweig stayed close behind her. "We'll make it, no matter how long it takes. The children are waiting for us." They remained silent, and neither dared to look around at Snow Rock.

Down in the valley, the farms lay scattered all the way to the sea. Smoke stood above the roofs. The picture was so peaceful.

# TYRKIR

"There's been a fight. Over on the north side." The news reached Warm Spring Slope after four days. A daredevil trader had ridden with heavily loaded baskets on horseback over the not-yet snow-free mountain road and was the first to offer his goods this year in the house of Thorbjörn Vifilsson. "Blood was shed."

Thjodhild paid no attention to the seal teeth and whalebone, coveted by every household. "Where? Who fought?"

Hallweig also took little interest in the treasures spread out on the table. "Do you know more?"

"Not much." The merchant shrugged. "I came from Thorsness, and before I went up into the mountains, I heard about the news. Must have been farther east at the fjord. Near Sharpcliff."

"Think!" Thjodhild barked at him.

"Some stranger . . . Yes, now I remember. He attacked Breida Farm. That was it. But why are you so interested?"

Without a word, Thjodhild stood and hurried to her sleeping chamber.

Hallweig watched her go. "Were there any dead?"

"Name me a fight in which there is not at least one head cut off." The merchant grinned. "I've often wondered if I should add human bones to my offerings."

"Go!" But Hallweig gathered herself. "Wait! Do you know anything more?" She chose a large piece of bone—many needles and combs had been lost or broken over the long winter, and new ones had to be carved.

171

In the evening, both women badgered the gode—he had to send servants to the north side. They needed certainty, no matter what was discovered. The truth would be easier to bear than to have to wait, to hope, and then be disappointed.

They did not have to persuade Thorbjörn—he was deeply concerned and acted quickly. By morning, he had two of his men mounted, had given each a spare horse, and had ordered them to ride over the pass to Breidafjord without stopping. "Ask around. Listen. But be clever. I don't want anyone to be suspicious or to know who hired you."

As soon as the servants left, Hallweig confronted her husband. "Why the caution? Don't you stand by Erik?"

"Silence. This is a man's business." With that, the judge turned to pass the women and go back into the house, but his gaze fell on Thjodhild, who was glaring at him, her lips pressed together. Thorbjörn rubbed his finger over the bridge of his nose. "If the worst has happened up there on the beach, I need time to prepare revenge for Erik's death without his murderers seeing it coming. It's precisely because I stand by my friend that I have ordered caution."

Though the women still remained doubtful, he continued inside.

After a moment, Hallweig nodded. "Thorbjörn never breaks his word."

"I trust him." Thjodhild tugged at the knot of her headscarf. "Perhaps I'm unfair, because . . ." She sighed.

"No, we shouldn't talk as if the worst has already happened."

At lunch, the little son of a slave stormed into the hall, forgetting every rule. He ran to the lord's table. Even Thorbjörn's punishing gaze didn't seem to bother him. The boy beamed up into the gode's face, struggling to catch his breath. "There is . . . I have seen it. The ship. On the shore . . ."

The judge grabbed the boy's shirt and shook him. "If you don't talk sense right now, little fellow, I'll cut out your tongue!"

That alone was enough to widen the boy's eyes and shut his mouth.

"Now, from the beginning!" Thorbjörn put the boy down. "What did you see?"

No longer beaming, the boy stepped out of reach of his master and, close to crying, took a deep breath. "I just wanted to say the ship's arrived. Lord Erik's. Down at the shore. I recognized it by its sail. It's all red. I was playing by the rocks, and I ran as soon as I saw it."

Thjodhild's hands crushed the flatbread she was holding, and the pieces flew across the table. *Let it be true,* she pleaded silently. *I can't stand tricks, not anymore. What a day this is. Ice and heat are poured over me almost at the same time.*

Thorbjörn rose. "You're a good boy. Come on, we'll go see together." As soon as he stretched out his hand, the little boy screamed and fled from the hall.

Thjodhild tried to pick up the scattered pieces of bread, but they kept slipping through her fingers. Hallweig saw her distress. "I won't just sit here waiting. Let's go see for ourselves."

The ship's crew had already made their way up the winding path from the shore through the plain and was in the last ascent to Warm Spring Slope. Thorbjörn and some of his men had run toward the small group.

Erik was glowing. "Your husband is alive," Hallweig said. "Praised be Freya, nothing has happened to him. But most of your slaves are missing."

Thjodhild nodded. Though relieved, a new wave of fear washed over her. *Where is Tyrkir? I'm afraid for both men, even if I'm not allowed to admit it.*

Her gaze was fixed on the wounded man being carried by the

group—a small, slender figure. Tyrkir? Yes, it was him, he was alive, too. At least he was still alive. But his entire head, except his forehead and eyes, was wrapped in cloths. He was supported by men on either side. Because he had little strength to walk himself, they led and carried him up the steep path. Thjodhild's heart urged her to run to his side immediately. Her mind commanded her to stay. *You can't betray yourself! Show sympathy but not concern!*

Shortly before the group reached the courtyard by way of the house meadow, Hallweig grabbed her friend's hand. "The poor man with the bandages must be your steward. He looks in rough shape."

"Since Tyrkir is still on his feet, the injury can't be life-threatening." Thjodhild heard the words passing her lips and was amazed at the objectivity of her tone. "He is not strong, but he is tough. I know him."

The women did not take a step toward the arrivals. Erik embraced his wife with a longing look. Still, as was customary, he first stepped before the lady of the house, greeting her clumsily. "I return from the Breidafjord with only a few. Fortune did not follow us. Please grant us hospitality again under your roof, even if it brings more work. Because my friend . . . well, you can see, he's wounded."

"Welcome, Erik." Hallweig smiled. "Get some rest. And don't worry about your steward. He will not want for care." She ordered the helpers to take Tyrkir to the sleeping chamber and hurried ahead.

Erik held his wife tightly in his arms. Thjodhild hid her face in his broad chest. "Your son is well," she said. "Yesterday, he laughed, and when he sees you, he'll surely laugh again."

"We won't build a house for Leif on our island." He stroked her hair. "The ground there isn't good enough for us."

"Oh, Erik... Right now, I'm just glad you're back." She gently freed herself from his embrace. "What about Tyrkir?"

"It's nothing serious, but his face got a slap. He saved my life."

"I have to look after him." Thjodhild kept her composure until she reached the door, but alone in the hall, she hurried to the sleeping chamber just as Hallweig carefully removed the dirty cloth wrappings from Tyrkir's face.

He was crouched down on the bed. Now he saw the slender figure, and his gaze came alive. In the darkness of his eyes, joy and fear flickered in equal measure.

"Can I help?" Thjodhild asked.

Hallweig nodded. Tyrkir, on the other hand, shook his head weakly.

*What are you afraid of?* Thjodhild asked herself as she cut the bandage on his temples with scissors. *No matter how battered you are, it won't scare me.* But as the last piece of cloth and the healing leaves were removed, her breath stopped for a moment. Then she was flooded with loving care and compassion. The left half of his face was massively swollen. A deep, blackish, crusted wound festering at the edges had split his face from the ear to the corner of his mouth. The upper part of the ear was missing, and the inflamed flesh had grown over the auditory canal.

Tyrkir tried to read Thjodhild's gaze. *No, she is not disgusted*, he thought gratefully, and his fear about their reunion slipped away. He struggled to move his lips, finally managing to form the barely comprehensible words: "I won't need a mirror anymore."

It took her a moment to understand, but then his joke helped her suppress her emotions. She gently stroked his hand. "Not immediately, but soon. Don't worry."

"What does he mean?" Hallweig asked while she stroked a paste of fat and crushed bedstraw onto a soft cloth.

"He doesn't want a mirror."

"I can't believe how vain men are. They get their skulls split almost in half, and their first concern is for their looks."

The women smiled. Tyrkir wanted to laugh along with them, but even as he tried, a sharp pain shot through the left side of his face.

The ointment cloth was carefully laid on his cheek, and a new bandage was wrapped over it. This time, more skillfully so that the uninjured side, including eyes, mouth, and nostrils, remained free.

"That's all we can do for you today." Hallweig looked at him thoughtfully. "Tomorrow, I'll send for our völva at Eagle Farm. Grima has to look at the wound. Don't worry, she'll preserve what she can of your beauty."

Erik remained silent as he examined his boot tips. He wanted to give the judge time to decide on his own without the pressure of his gaze. The Red had not embellished or omitted anything, nor had he insulted the farmer of Breida Farm nor described himself as a hero. He had not made any requests. If Hallweig's husband was going to stand by him, he would have to act of his own volition for a just cause if he wanted to avoid the stale aftertaste that would linger, no matter who won the war.

Thorbjörn left the high seat with smooth movements. He pulled out his sword and pushed it into the compacted earth in front of Erik. "Together, we are strong."

Even faster did the Red's weapon jump into his fist, and sword handle bobbed next to sword handle. "How can I ever thank you?"

"Not a word of it. Friendship does not keep score." With his high forehead furrowed, the gode paced before the fireplace. He murmured more to himself than to Erik, "Our courage alone won't prevail against a superior force."

He considered names. Most of them, he rejected immediately.

Finally, he'd narrowed his list down to five lords whom he might win over to join their fight. "Two live here on the south side, the others have their farms up by the Breidafjord. We have enough time." He would send messengers across the mountains to catch up with the servants who had left that morning. "Those two had orders to inquire discreetly about your well-being. Now, instead, they can recruit allies for our fight."

Erik kept pushing his fist into his left hand. "I don't like sitting here idly for three weeks. I can't leave the work to you alone."

"Who says you'll be idle? You'll open our weapons chests, supervise the blacksmith so that every blade is sharpened. Not only do we have ten slaves to arm, but we have to prepare them." The two ships, the *Mount of the Sea* and the *Sea Bird*, had to be equipped with tents, provisions, and combat equipment from spears to shields. Thorbjörn stretched his lips. "You understand more about all this than I do. After all, I haven't fought in five years."

Erik stared at him in horror. "Then I really have a lot to do."

From one day to the next, life changed on Warm Spring Slope. Carefree laughter no longer came from the kitchen or stable; maidservants and servants were nervous about the imminent war.

Erik was tough with the selected men. Every morning, he made them run until they were breathless. After that, he instructed them in archery and the use of spear and ax; he ordered them to fight each other in pairs without a weapon. Only in the afternoon were they freed to do their usual work on the farm.

Tyrkir knew when his friend was going to leave with the judge. "They won't sail without me." He was soon able to pronounce this sentence clearly enough that it wasn't only Thjodhild who understood him.

"Only if we allow it," his nurses replied. "First, the wound has to close completely. You'll stay here until then."

"They won't sail without me." His will and the herbal ointments from the sorceress of Eagle Farm accelerated the healing. After two weeks of obedient boredom in the sleeping chamber, Thjodhild and Hallweig freed him from the last bandage. Satisfied, they examined the success of their care by lamplight.

Tyrkir did not trust their expressions. "Give me a mirror!"

"Wait," Thjodhild pleaded much too quickly.

"Am I so deformed?" He looked from one woman to the other.

Hallweig pushed her lips out and shook her head.

"And you? What do you think, Mistress?"

"No, not bad." Thjodhild grasped his hand. "Please, come with me to the house. I'll prove it to you. And I'll give you a mirror later."

After so long in the semidarkness, the daylight outside was dazzling. With Hallweig, Thjodhild led Tyrkir to the house meadow. The children lay side by side on a stuffed mattress. "Bend over them, say something. Or play with them."

Tyrkir kneeled down to the little ones. He smiled and tapped Leif on his round belly, gently stroking Gudrid's cheeks. "It's been so long. I missed you." He found it difficult to form the words; his lips were too unpracticed.

But the two of them pedaled merrily, waving their arms, their eyes beaming at him.

"You see, neither is afraid of you." Thjodhild pulled a mirror out of her skirt pocket. "There's nothing to be worried about." She handed him the hand-sized silver disc.

Tyrkir didn't recognize himself. *My face consists of two halves*, he concluded in horror. *One human, the other . . .* He found no comparison.

A deep red scar, two fingers wide, ran from the left corner of his mouth. It pulled his lips, furrowed through the freckles, stretched over the cheekbone, and ended in a bulge under the ear hole, where the actual ear used to be. *Half my face resembles the undead.*

"Children have kinder eyes," he muttered. "It doesn't matter that they don't scream at the sight of me."

"Then I have kinder eyes, too." Thjodhild reached for the mirror. "What are you moaning about, anyway? You could just as well be lying with the other corpses in the pit on Oxens Island. Be glad you are healthy and here with us!"

Her anger drove a shameful blush into his face. *You fool*, he scolded himself. *You've been afraid of her judgment for weeks, and if she can look past your scar, that's all that matters.* "Forgive me. I must learn to get used to my new beautiful face." His smile was not entirely successful. He left the house meadow and walked over to the edge of the rock above the cave plain.

Shaking her head, Hallweig watched him. "With your steward so thin, he's not fit for war. You should order him to stay here."

"If only I could." Thjodhild sighed deeply. When she noticed her friend's astonished expression, she quickly added, "He doesn't need our help anymore. That's what I meant. Erik's in charge of him again now."

The dispatched servants had returned to the farm on Warm Spring Slope. Of the five landlords questioned, three had decided to support the party of the Red with a small retinue, not because they supported his cause but because they would not deny a request of judge Thorbjörn Vifilsson.

"This is a bad omen," Erik grumbled. "The unconvinced fight poorly."

"Be grateful!" The gode tried to persuade him. "It doesn't matter why they're joining us. We now have a total of thirty-five armed men on our side. I'm not sure your enemy can put up nearly as large a force."

The evening before their departure, Erik seemed transformed. There were no more doubts or worries. While eating with Thorbjörn, Tyrkir, and the ten servants he'd trained, he laughed and encouraged the men. He was now their leader, and he was focused on only one goal. "We win. Because the gods and justice are on our side." Fists drummed on the tabletops—his supporters tried to push away the last of their fears with the clatter.

When the bowls were emptied, Erik rose. "Listen to what I have to say. Hear and be my witnesses!"

His solemn tone silenced the conversation. With both hands, he stroked back his hair. "I don't want to go into battle with any guilt. Only when the heart is light can the arm fight with its full strength."

Tyrkir was amazed at how charismatic his Viking suddenly sounded. *I'm curious . . .* He didn't get any further in his thoughts because Erik was now standing in front of him. "Here's my steward. See his scar. He intercepted a blow that would have killed me. I owe him my life."

He told the audience how Tyrkir had come to his father's farm in Norway, and he frankly acknowledged the friendship that had grown between them, the lord and his slave. "Today, it is my solemn intent that all differences between us be abolished."

The servants present exchanged stealthy glances. *Freedom! To be a master yourself!* Which of them had not dreamed of it?

Erik's outstretched finger shot out at the steward. "Get up!"

Tyrkir obeyed immediately.

A grin twitched on Erik's red-bearded face. "That was my last order to you, slave." Serious again, he laid both hands on the shoulders of the slender man. "I, Erik Thorvaldsson, ask the father of my father and his father and also the father of my great-grandfather, the great Oxenthorir, to join us in this hall." He waited for a few breaths before continuing. "In the presence of my ancestors, in the presence of Lord Thorbjörn Vifilsson and his slaves, I release you, Tyrkir, who is called the German, into freedom. From now on, you can go wherever you want, build your own house, look for a wife yourself, and keep cattle and slaves. Your word shall be valid, not only in contracts and business but also at the Thing. Your voice now has the same weight as that of any freeman."

The blood rushed into Tyrkir's face, and his scar throbbed painfully. *My Viking,* Tyrkir thought. *My friend, you are giving me a gift I have never longed for. But now that I have it, it fills me with pride.*

Erik didn't wait for the applause of the goden and the servants. He also didn't give the newly appointed freedman the chance to speak. "That's enough, all of you!" The ceremony had lasted too long for him already, and the well-worded speech had been difficult. "So?" He looked at the friend. "Decide, as a freeman."

"What?" Tyrkir groped for the scar and covered it with his hand.

"Well, Know-It-All, get used to it! From now on, I have to ask you. Are you joining us on the ship tomorrow or not?"

Despite the quiet chuckles all around them, Tyrkir swallowed his anger. Now was not the time to return the jibe. *But just wait, you Viking. Someday you may regret your generosity. An equal friend may say more to you than a slave.* "I will accompany you."

Fresh beer was served. The soldiers handed the jug from mouth to mouth, shouted the praises of the new master, invoked the prowess of the ships, cursed the enemy, and always found new reasons to continue drinking. Meanwhile, Erik, the goden, and Tyrkir once more went over the plan.

The next day, they would embark. The combat gear was stowed away—nothing was missing. Katla and three slaves had taken care of the provisions and tents. Thjodhild had chosen the long-serving maid as their companion. None but Katla had enough insight and experience to support the men in their dangerous enterprise.

With favorable winds, they hoped to meet Styr's ship around noon. Styr was the only landowner on the south side who could be recruited. The meeting point was Oxens Island. The two allies from Breidafjord also wanted to meet there with ships and fighters.

Thorbjörn nodded. "Until then, we should remain unnoticed. Just now, before the June-Thing in Thorsness, many knarrs are crossing the fjord, so ours won't stand out."

"And how we proceed from there"—Erik slowly clenched both hands into fists—"will be my decision once we've arranged the day of the battle with the Breida farmer."

Thjodhild was still awake when Erik lay down beside her. She stroked his chest, then kissed him. They pushed toward each other. Goodbye—how much more beautiful and yet weightier.

Later, they lay quietly. Again, Thjodhild reached for her husband's hand. "Please, dearest. Leave Tyrkir here. He's still too weak. The scar could break open again. Command him to stay!"

Erik chuckled. "Too late. He'll join the fight. I can't give Know-It-All any more orders, because he's now a master like me."

The news worried her. *My Tyrkir no longer belongs to the family? What will he do? Stay? Or form a clan himself?* Thjodhild could not ask, however much she wanted to.

Which side would the gods take? On the morning of the battle, a storm swept over Oxens Island, whipping the rain against the tarpaulins on the meadow terrace. Down in the bay, the masts of the ships groaned.

Tyrkir watched his friend with his cap pulled deep onto his forehead. Anger stood out on Erik's wet face. Despite his sacrifices, his god seemed to have forgotten him. How else could Thor send them such weather today? Wind and a cloudy sky was all he'd asked for, and now?

"Postpone!" Tyrkir shouted against the howling of the storm. "You must . . . postpone the war—" That's as far as he got.

"Shut your crooked mouth," Erik barked, then paused, shocked at his own words. "I didn't mean that. I'm sorry." He pushed his slender friend in front of him back into the tent. "Am I to become the joke of the fjord? At Sharpcliff, the Breida farmer stands ready with his people and waits for us."

Tyrkir stepped closer. "That's just how it has to be. We won't get any of our ships safely through the reefs and islands." His speech could not keep pace with his thoughts, but he tried to express himself clearly. "And even if we succeed, in this storm we can only land in one bay. Thorgest will find out immediately and will have his people guarding the beach. Before we're off the ships—before we even reach the shore—more than half of our people will have already fallen victim to their arrows."

"I know that!" Erik punched his fists together. "Damn. I'm bleeding honor here. There must be another way. And we must find it today or all our efforts have been in vain."

Tyrkir didn't answer. Apart from Judge Thorbjörn, the allies had only committed to this one day. Their word was valid today, and today they would dare the impossible. But he doubted whether they would be ready for battle tomorrow, let alone in a week if the weather remained this bad.

Thorbjörn stepped into the tent. He painstakingly shook the rain off his cap. "We have to give up on our plan." The meeting was scheduled for noon. Before that, two ships were supposed to bring troops ashore, unnoticed, and far away from Sharpcliff. And when the third ship ran straight into the bay at the agreed time as expected by their opponent, the other men were going to surprise them from both sides.

Thorbjörn shrugged. "I was thinking. We still have one chance. It's unlikely to succeed, and no matter what, it will lead to the loss of many lives. Split up into dinghies, the entire army could row into the bay by Sharpcliff, despite the waves. The most capable fighters would have to try to reach the shore. In such a storm, even the best archers can only hit their target by chance."

"And then?"

"Once our vanguard has cleared the beach, we masters will land with the main troop."

There was silence. The wind pressed against the tarpaulin.

Tyrkir forced himself not to object immediately. Despite all his anger against the Breida farmer, they could not carry out a plan that meant the inevitable death of their own people from the outset. Any peace acquired in this way wouldn't last long. With a silent warning, he stared at his friend and the judge.

Erik scratched at his beard, then pulled his battle-ax halfway out of his belt. "I've never sent others ahead before me. This is my revenge, so I have to be the first on the beach."

"I expected and feared you'd say as much." Thorbjörn sighed before he continued. "A stray arrow may hit you before you can look your enemy in the eye. Without even getting to fight to cleanse your honor, you would have thrown your life away senselessly." He grabbed Erik's arm. "There's no other choice—"

"It's all right," Erik interrupted him. "I know what I have to do. Today there will be no war. And I have to tell this sneaky bastard before noon. Damn it, I can already hear him laughing."

The judge immediately promised to accompany Erik on the dinghy. But first, he wanted to visit the three allied lords in their tents. "At least I can spare you that walk."

Again alone with his friend, Erik smacked his forehead. "Wrong! I did everything wrong. Every child knows how quickly the weather changes here. I should have brought our people ashore yesterday. Erik the Red, the great leader!"

"Stop feeling sorry for yourself."

Amazed, the giant looked down at his steward. "How dare you talk to me that—"

"Don't threaten me!" The scar on Tyrkir's face flamed bloodred.

"Yes, yes, I know." In spite of the imminent disgrace, Erik grinned. "Master Know-It-All."

"Get used to it, Master Erik!" Now Tyrkir had to laugh, too.

The friend shaded his eyes. "If you could see yourself right now, you wouldn't be laughing."

Suddenly serious, Tyrkir said, "It doesn't matter. I...I will accompany you to the Breida farmer." He turned away the left half of his face. "I don't deserve your mockery."

"That was also wrong. Forgive me." Erik put his arm around Tyrkir's shoulders. "I'm glad you're here with me. Without you, it would be even harder."

# THE JUDGMENT
# OF THE THING

A few steps below the summit, the shoulder bag burst open, and the lucky stone rolled down the mountain. Tyrkir rushed after it, throwing himself over it, but it slipped from his hands, rolling on. He again succeeded in catching it, but it tore his fingers bloody, rolling faster... *Do not give up...* Tyrkir jumped after it, landing painfully. With bruised limbs, he slipped farther on his belly, his clothes shredded, his body chafed... *Do not lose it!...* There, right in front of his eyes, the lucky stone dropped... and now Tyrkir, too, sped over the steep wall and fell. Seagulls circled, screeching. Far below, he saw the dark water splashing as his stone hit the surface.

Tyrkir sat up with a jerk. Though his scarred skin hurt, he felt the pain as consolation. *No, I am not falling into the abyss.* He carefully wiped the sweat from his face. Next to him, Erik snored evenly. *I am in our tent on Oxens Island.* He was fully awake now. It was the third time this dream had haunted him.

More than a week ago, he'd rowed to Sharpcliff in the dinghy with Erik, the goden, and ten armed men. From a safe distance, they'd waved a white cloth, only wading ashore after the people of Breida Farm answered with their own white rag.

What a test for Erik. As soon as he'd canceled the fight, the farmer cursed him, calling the red one a cowardly thief and a murderer before spitting at him. With great difficulty, Thorbjörn Vifilsson had finally succeeded in calming the scorned man. "The war is only postponed. Name another day!"

But the master of Breida Farm had laughed until the drool flowed into his beard. "The bastard missed his opportunity. Now the court will decide. I'll sue at the Thorsnessthing. And by all the gods, he will need more than the fingers of four hands to count my witnesses."

The following night was the first time Tyrkir had lost the stone.

The nightmare had returned after a messenger from Thorsness had delivered the complaint in proper form: "You are ordered before the Thing."

"What good will that do me?" Erik had asked.

"If you don't appear, you'll be given the severest sentence. Find some witnesses and see that they get you justice."

Until the day before yesterday, all three allies had remained loyal. Thorbjörn had been able to swear them in for the trial because of his experience. "Even if you weren't there for the fire or the fight, you must praise our friend, his bravery, his nobleness. He has been wronged." Their missing memories were filled in by the prospect of a considerable sum of hacksilver.

The day before, however, the landowner of Swanfjord had broken off his tents. "Try to put yourself in my position. I live here. My neighbors are also the neighbors of Thorgest of Breida Farm. So far, nobody knows that I was going to fight on your side. And I would have done so. But the war has been called off, and I've kept my word. That should be enough. The neighbors won't understand if I raise my voice at the Thing for a stranger. You understand. Peace between neighbors is more important. . . ."

Erik had turned away and climbed up the rock step at the end of the campground. There, he'd stood until the landowner had sailed away with his slaves.

The first two times Tyrkir had the nightmare, he'd wiped it aside after awakening—*Don't think about it. It will fade*—but it had come back more clearly, the pictures sharper and more painful. *You need to explore it,* Tyrkir ordered himself. *Otherwise, it will overpower you. When we sail to Thorsness tomorrow for the Thing, the dream must not paralyze my mind.*

He pulled up his legs and put his chin on his knees: *You carry our lucky stone up the mountain and lose it. You run after it, but it slips away each time.* Tyrkir smiled bitterly. It took no great wisdom to interpret the meaning so far. The end—that was all that mattered. *Remember it exactly! As soon as the stone sinks into the black water, you wake up. Perhaps that's a good sign? Hope for Erik, Thjodhild, and for me? The dream proves that we're not meant for the abyss, even if it may look like that right now.*

At first, Tyrkir wanted to wake his friend, but he immediately pulled his arm back. No, Erik needed the sleep to gather strength for the Thing. *I'll tell him about the dream later. Later, when we have found real happiness.*

The flat area stretched into the Breidafjord from the mountainous, snow-covered peninsula like a crushed wolf's skull. The sky stretched above—high in the blue, isolated bales of cloud traveled east. There was no more night, only this one day, and its light no longer faded.

Every June, during the Allthing, all freemen of West Iceland traveled to Thorsness on the outermost headland.

The visitors thronged in the tent city, as well as on the market set up near the court area. Faces were washed, hair combed, and a strong smell of beards tamed with seal fat followed the travelers. Some even braided their beards into greasy pigtails. Rich or poor, every man wore his best festive robe: soft baggy trousers, decorated belts, and coats or cloaks of colored woven fabric, the most splendid of which were decorated with collars of silver fox. Friends were greeted with beer and joviality; enemies were avoided as much as possible. The oath of peace was the reigning commandment of this week.

No one paid attention to the two unkempt men in their midst. Erik and Tyrkir had pushed their caps deep onto their foreheads as they wove through the crowd in search of Thorbjörn's hut. At the market, Erik hesitated at a jewelry stall. "If things were any different," he grumbled, "I'd buy a nice brooch for my Thjodhild here."

"Maybe later." Tyrkir pulled him on.

*Avoid notice, avoid conversation.* Thorbjörn had impressed this on them aboard his *Sea Bird*. The gode had agreed to defend his friend. "Everyone in the tent town now knows your name, Erik. They've all heard about the events in Hawk Valley and about the fight at Sharpcliff. The Breida farmer will have made sure of it. But very few people know the face of the man who bears that name. Thorgest will want to point you out as soon as possible. But if you remain invisible for as long as possible, he won't be able to stir up the mood against you before the trial begins. We can use that advantage."

It was evident that Erik was struggling with this. "What . . . what kind of odds are those?"

"Trust me. We have a chance if you do as I say. No matter what lies and malice are brought against you, stay silent. Leave the response to me. As hard as it may be, keep your temper!" After this advice, Judge Thorbjörn had hurried ahead with Styr, the farmer from his southern district, and Ejolf, the lord of the nearby Hog Island. The most urgent task for these new allies was to recruit more honorable men. Thorbjörn wanted to test their reliability. Erik needed witnesses, many witnesses.

The gode in charge lived in a stone hut during the Thing days, where he was surrounded by the tents of his followers. Thorbjörn

Vifilsson, too, had set himself up in a temporary but spacious accommodation covered with canvas.

"Wait!" Immediately after entering, he assigned Tyrkir and Erik a place in the farthest corner. He turned again to the guest sitting on a stool next to his chair. "I can count on your voice? Good. When the time comes, I'll call you as a witness to my friend's cause."

The man rose. After a stealthy look at Erik, he asked, "What about the reward? We haven't discussed that yet."

"An oath in court shouldn't be bought." Thorbjörn smiled thinly. "But you have my word, your worries will find the open ear of your gode in the future."

This promise was enough, and the guest hurried away. Thorbjörn watched him go. "I'm not entirely convinced about him, but who can look into another man's heart?"

The creases in his forehead smoothed. He shouted to his friends. "Welcome to my dwelling! I offer you shelter." Unfortunately, it was no comparison to the farm on Warm Spring Slope. There were no housewives to cook for them, and since Katla and the maids had been left behind on Oxens Island, they'd have to eat at the meat and fish stalls.

"I don't care," Erik growled. After some time, he slapped both hands flat on his knees. "Damn it! I don't know what I'm doing here. Why can't I settle my feud with the Breida farmer myself?"

Alarmed, Tyrkir watched the judge. *Don't be angry with my Viking*, he pleaded silently. *It's not ingratitude, he just feels so powerless.*

Thorbjörn crossed his arms. "Do you think I would have let myself be elected judge if the office didn't mean anything?" Coolly, he assured them that he was not interested in accumulating wealth, as was said about some of his fellow judges. "In every clan, the head takes care of justice and the law—that's how it ought to be. But we don't make those decisions independently, you know that very well."

He pointed in the direction of the Thing place. "Since yester-day, the speaker has been standing on the holy rock, proclaiming our laws. We have all committed to obeying them. If we did not, there would be no community, no peace between families." The judges in their districts were usually the only ones responsible for ensuring the observance of laws, but if there were severe crimes or disputes that couldn't be settled, the Thing Assembly was called.

By then, Erik had regained his composure. "If it had any pur-pose..." After a pause, he continued bitterly. "I've yet to hear of a man who got justice at a Thing."

"Do you mean to offend my office?" Thorbjörn snapped. "Our laws are good. They regulate life."

"Yes, by Thor, I know. A severed ear costs half a man-price, a pierced eye only a quarter, but if the nose or foot is missing, the perpetrator has to pay a full man-price. Anyone who lets his cows graze on another's pasture—"

"Quiet!" The goden's eyes blazed. "I stand by you, and you mock—"

"Don't!" Tyrkir stepped between the two men. "Don't risk your friendship! Please, Thorbjörn, let me explain it for him, and be patient with me if I still find it difficult to speak clearly." With his hand, Tyrkir shielded his scar. "Erik has long wanted to tell you how grateful he is for your help. But he's also worried about the outcome of the trial. He's been accused at the Thing before."

As quickly as his lips allowed, Tyrkir described the trial in Nor-way. Even then, few witnesses had stood opposite the many oath helpers on the plaintiff's side. Despite clear evidence of innocence, Erik and his father had been convicted. "Erik does not mean to disrespect the laws or your office. The judge announces the sen-tence, the selected jurors determine the verdict as required by the community. My friend is anxious because the individual with the most people on his side is the one who ends up being right."

Visibly affected, Thorbjörn pulled Tyrkir next to Erik and grabbed both of them by the shoulder. "I freely admit: True justice cannot be won at the Thing. There's still a long way to go. But from year to year, we'll improve order in Iceland together. And I'll contribute to it. That's why I'm fighting for Erik."

"Thank you." The giant looked at him gratefully. "That's what I wanted to say, anyway."

A landowner in a blue cape with chest panels embroidered with red eagles entered the hut. He hesitated at the sight of the three men standing so intimately together. "Am I in the right place? I'm looking for the goden responsible for the south side of Snow Rock."

"Welcome!" Thorbjörn detached himself and gallantly asked the gentleman to his high seat. "I am the judge."

"At first, I thought . . ." The guest briefly looked over his shoulder at the two inconspicuously dressed people in the background. "No, I might have guessed who the master was here. So, Ejolf from Hog Island told me you were looking for witnesses."

Thorbjörn inquired kindly about the man's name and origin, then explained the case. He spoke skillfully, asked whether the man could follow him, and left no doubt about the honor of his protégé.

Erik listened in amazement, before finally nudging Tyrkir slightly with his elbow. "He can talk, but you—that was even better."

Now it was Tyrkir's turn to be amazed. Twice, his friend had thanked him in such a short span. That meant a lot for his Viking pride.

The speaker on the sacred rock lowered his arms, falling silent. The seagulls, no longer curious, sailed away across the water. The quiet settled across all present. The assembled men outside the consecrated circle stood and waited for the next sign from the sage. Some faces clearly showed the effort it had taken to follow his words. He had spoken the laws of Iceland in a formal language, but only one-third of the whole, as custom dictated. By his election, he had been chosen as chief judge and speaker of the Thorsness Thing for three years. And so that the laws would implant themselves in even the most ponderous skull, he would only bring the other thirds to the attention of the next June court, and the one after.

The wise man descended from the rock and entered the plaza, which was cordoned off with hazel sticks and ropes. He walked through the still-empty rows of benches to the altar stone in the middle. "Those of you who have concerns, those of you who seek answers to questions, you may now bring them to the Thing in a civil manner!"

The silence lasted only a moment, then all the throats seemed to scream at the same time. Everyone tried to drown out their neighbor—only their own request was urgent. Some hefted rattles, not caring that these made even their own words impossible to discern. Like a rock in the tides, the supreme judge stood next to the sacrificial stone, taking in the cries.

There were two islands of silence in the rear rows, far apart from each other. Plaintiff and defendant, each surrounded by their followers. Squeezed in by Erik and Thorbjörn, Tyrkir watched the Breida farmers on the other side of the plaza through the throng of shoulders and heads.

Thorgest had seen Erik and tried to point out the enemy to his witnesses. Shrugged shoulders, another look, more shrugs. *You didn't succeed, Tyrkir,* he thought, satisfied. *You, sneaky villain, could not present my Viking as a sacrificial animal.* Erik had only entered the Thing place toward the end of the proclamation of the law, and even then, he still wore a full hood under which his face remained half concealed.

Tyrkir's gaze was fixed on the man next to the Breida farmer.

The fur hat, the sharply cut mouth, the beardless chin—it was Ulf Einarsson, the gode in charge of the Hvammsfjord. *Great Tyr, why did you allow our enemies to become so powerful?*

He quickly gave their advocate a sign. Thorbjörn bent down to him. "Over there, standing by Thorgest, is the judge who banished us from Hawk Valley last year for manslaughter. And of all people, the farmer has chosen him as his advocate."

"Are you sure?" Thorbjörn paused, thinking. "That means this case is doomed. I must prevent it from being brought here."

Tyrkir saw Thorbjörn's desperate expression and nodded with a sigh.

Most of the screamers by the barrier soon ran out of breath. Only those who had spared their voices now reached the ear of the judge: The driftwood was to be distributed more equitably. If a farmer was not able to bring in enough hay for the winter, his neighbor should help him out and not drive up the price. Who owned a stream? Could a farmer living near a spring divert the water and thus dry out his neighbors' meadows downstream?

For each case, the chief judge proposed a just solution. If the majority agreed to it by their affirmative cries or raising their fists, only then did he rule. He would include the new commandment or the addition to an old one in his law proclamation at the next Thing.

With a sweeping gesture, the judge now laid his hand on the sacrificial stone. This marked the end of the general question time. He touched the open iron ring next to the blood bowl.

"This is the time for the high court. Whoever wishes to present a dispute may now bring his complaint."

The crowd retreated. Near the barrier, only the two groups of unequal size remained. More than thirty men had gathered around the Breida farmer. He stepped up to the rope and called, "Hey, Red! You're right to hide your face. You're facing honorable

Icelanders here. Your guilt torments you so much, you can't even bring yourself to lift your head!"

Before Thorbjörn and Tyrkir had realized it, Erik was at the barrier of the court. He threw back his hood and pushed out his chin. His mane and beard faded against the red rage in his face. He stood with his fist raised, mouth open. Enemies and gawkers awaited his outburst, but the giant conquered himself and said nothing.

The supreme judge nodded in his direction, then barked at the farmer, "If your tongue is too long, bite it off. But don't dare violate the order at the Thing again!"

With a firm grip, the trial leader pulled the defiant plaintiff away from the barrier. Ulf Einarsson spoke at him with a raised finger, and only when he was sure that Thorgest would be silent from now on did he set off on his way to the Law Rock.

Ulf Einarsson collected himself at the foot of the roughly carved stone. All eyes now rested on the figure. Finally, as if a call from Valhalla had come to him, the gode threw his hair back, tightened his spine, and climbed up step by step.

"Hear me! Thorgest of Breida Farm has summoned many witnesses to this court and appointed me his advocate. I raise a complaint against Erik the Red"—with an outstretched arm, he pointed toward the small flock around the giant, and waited until all eyes had followed him—"against Erik the Red for a punishable arson. He set the barn of Thorgest ablaze with fire arrows. In addition, I raise a complaint against Erik the Red for a punishable theft. He robbed valuable goods from a warehouse of the Breida farmer." The voice echoed far across the Thing place.

At the barrier, Thorbjörn listened with a stern expression. His counterpart knew the proscribed phrases; hoping for a formal error would be a waste of energy. "Moreover, I raise a complaint against Erik the Red for a punishable first attack. He jumped on Toke Thorgestsson at Sharpcliff and injured him. That blow became a death wound. I raise a complaint against Erik the Red for another punishable first attack. He also jumped on Odd Thorgestsson and injured him. That sting became a death wound. . . ."

Next to Tyrkir, Erik hissed, "That's what happened, but it's not the entire truth."

"The gode only says what he has heard from the deceiver, and what is useful to the deceiver."

"Oh, Know-It-All, let's just walk away."

"Don't you dare! Think of your wife. Your son! Maybe a miracle will happen, some sign . . ."

The words *Hawk Valley* made both friends turn their attention back to the stone. ". . . for treacherous manslaughter, he was banished from my court district for three years, of which only one has elapsed." Murmurs rose in the crowd. Ulf Einarsson did nothing to quiet them. "Four murders! A stranger comes to Iceland and brings death to four men."

"Justice!" Thorbjörn stepped forward with quick steps. Raising his fist, he shouted, "I demand to be heard! The esteemed Ulf wrongly brings up the complaint from Hawk Valley. It has long been atoned for, he imposed the punishment—"

"Quiet!" the chief judge interrupted him. "I'll call you when your time comes." Then he turned his attention to the prosecutor. "The first conviction does not belong in front of this Thing!"

The gode looked annoyed. "Then I ask the assembly to forget what I said about the shameful murders in Hawk Valley."

Thorbjörn returned to his friends, pale with anger. "That fox," he whispered to himself. "All the jurors know about it now."

On the rock, the accuser raised his voice again. "I demand that Erik the Red become an outlawed, peaceless man because of this suit. A man whom no one may feed, clothe, or protect. I declare him stripped of his goods and possessions. Half of his property is to go to Thorgest. The other half, to the jurors, who are to confis-

cate the goods and chattel according to the law. This I make known
to all who will hear me."

Applause and calls of the audience rang out, rattles were enthusiastically shaken. The complaint had been well presented and,
above all, was understandable for everyone. A stranger had dared
to disturb the peace. There was no place in the community for a
convicted murderer. Erik and the small group of his followers were
met with glares and looks of contempt.

In the meantime, Ulf Einarsson had left the rock. He took his
position next to the chief justice in front of the sacrificial stone.
The Breida farmer approached at his signal. He grinned mali-
ciously and coughed but was careful not to spit out the slime. His
witnesses were called. One after the next, they entered the sacred
area. Each declared his name and origin and then had to place his
hand on the iron ring next to the blood bowl and swear that the
complaint was correct.

Behind Thorbjörn, his friends, and the two landowners, the
newly recruited six men nudged each other stealthily. Without
words, everyone knew what their neighbor was asking himself.
Was it wise to continue to stand by the defendant in the face of
this parade of witnesses? What harm could they, could their family
suffer?

The big farmer in the blue cape nodded to the group. They
had not yet publicly taken sides. He hooked his thumbs into his
belt and stepped up to Thorbjörn. "The situation is this..." He
explained his doubts—the incident at Sharpcliff now appeared in
a different light, and he could no longer, in all honesty, stand up
for the innocence of the Red. "I ask you, on behalf of the rest of the
group, to release us as witnesses."

Before Thorbjörn could answer, Erik grabbed the cloth of the
cape, pulled the finely dressed man closer, then immediately
shoved him away. "A mutton belongs to his flock. Go! All of you. I

release you of your word of honor. You don't need to be afraid of me."

"I'm not against you, you have to believe me. Only, in this trial, you will—"

"Go!" growled Erik. "Before I really do commit murder."

The six men backed away from the court barrier, relieved when they could disappear into the crowd.

Tyrkir pressed his hand on his scar. The blood pounded there painfully. "What now?"

Sweat beads ran from Thorbjörn's forehead. "I will object to the complaint. That hasn't changed."

Erik smiled bitterly. "It's hard to believe, but your skull is almost harder than mine. We both know how this game ends. Well, get this over with." He grabbed Thorbjörn by the shoulder. "But our Know-It-All is to take precautions. For later."

Erik's plan met with no opposition either from Tyrkir or from the two remaining faithful. After a short deliberation, Thorbjörn also agreed. "I still hope that you will get your due here on the Thing. Nevertheless, we should plan for your security in any case."

The swearing-in of the witnesses at the sacrificial stone was completed. The chief judge raised his voice: "Whoever wants to raise an objection against the complaint in this dispute may speak now or forever remain silent."

Thorbjörn walked straight-spined to the Law Rock.

Like the six renegades just a few moments ago, Tyrkir withdrew step by step. He was greeted by the spectators with applause and murmur. "You're smart. No honest Icelander should stick by this red stranger."

He felt the well-meaning pats on his back like fist blows and pushed himself through the smell of seal fat, only breathing a sigh of relief when he'd left the assembly behind.

Thorbjörn's *Sea Bird* lay half-beached, squeezed between fourteen other ships in the harbor about an hour's walk back on the headland. While their masters visited the Thing for a week, the crews had settled ashore. They sat in groups around a large fire, drank beer, laughed, chatted, and roasted pieces of meat on long, pointed sticks.

Tyrkir tried to attract the attention of his people by whistling, but his lips failed. *I must practice that again*, he thought angrily.

He approached the fire, trying to go unnoticed, and found a slave who belonged to the *Sea Bird*. Tapping him on the shoulder, he murmured, "Thorbjörn's orders. Come to the ship immediately. The others, too. But no fuss. Time is pressing."

"Why?" The slave choked down a bite. "Is there an argument? Has the oath of peace—?"

"Don't ask, lad." Tyrkir jerked his head around to reveal his scar. "Do as I say!"

The sight frightened the servant. "I'll pass the message on quietly. I've got it." He pulled himself up. With the rest of the roast still on the stick, he shuffled through the camped groups.

Tyrkir watched as the boy nudged a comrade with his foot, then bent down and whispered something to him. Both were chuckling—it must have seemed to the people gathered around them as if they were swapping dirty stories.

Tyrkir nodded appreciatively. The servant went on, finding the next man. Little by little, the slaves rose up. Some reached between their legs and walked toward the beach as if to release their bladders. Two supported each other, swaying as if drunk. Without arousing suspicion, all ten of the goden's slaves had soon left the feast.

"My friend's case does not go well." Tyrkir looked sharply into the surrounding faces. "Make sure you get the fog out of your skulls. You may soon have to prove how much faster the men from Warm Spring Slope are than those drunkards there by the fire."

It had always been easy for him to give clear orders, but since his injury, he struggled with every word. Finally, the ten men had understood what was expected of them. "Your lord, my friend, and me, too, we count on you."

Uncertainty lengthens every path. Finally, Tyrkir returned to the Thing. The rock of the law stood empty—Thorbjörn had finished his defense. The spectators had again stepped forward to the barrier and were engaged in quiet conversations with their neighbors. The verdict was clearly still pending.

Tyrkir squeezed through the crowd. Only reluctantly was he given room. A muscle-bound landowner growled, "Slowly, little one. Otherwise, I'll rip your head off. You missed the best part." He stretched out his arm like a crossbeam. "Who are you, anyway? Hey, your face? Didn't I see you with Erik earlier?"

Without answering, Tyrkir ducked under the muscled barrier. In front of the rope, the crowd was tightly packed. He searched until he got a clear view of the sacred place.

The twelve jurors had left their benches and were consulting with the chief justice. To the right of the altar, the Breida farmer's witnesses stood around his advocate. They exchanged stealthy pats on the backs, fat grins on their faces.

On the other side, Erik waited with Thorbjörn and the two landowners. The friend had put his fists to his hips. His bearded chin raised high, he stared boldly at the gawkers. *That's how strong you are, my Viking*, Tyrkir thought. *But what use is pride and respectability against such numbers? We couldn't even buy a handful of testimonies.*

The jurors returned to their benches, and the supreme judge stood before the sacrificial stone. With his eyes closed, he remained there, waiting, until silence fell over the Thing place.

Slowly, he opened his eyes. "By the power of my office, I will now pronounce the verdict. The complaint and defense have been adequately presented to the assembly by honorable speakers. According to our sacred laws, I pronounce Erik Thorvaldsson, also called the Red, guilty of cowardly manslaughter of Toke and Odd, the sons of Thorgest of Breida Farm."

No murmurs rose outside the court barrier; no emotion crossed Erik's face; nobody on the plaintiff's side moved. This judgment had been expected by all. After a pause, the wise man raised his voice again. "As punishment and atonement for his deed, the murderer is to pay a double man-price to the aggrieved farmer."

The Breida farmer laid his hand on the shoulder of Ulf Einarsson. Two man-prices, the prospect of two hundred marks in silver, satisfied him.

For a moment, Tyrkir felt a quiet hope rise. Would that be the only punishment? He watched as Thorbjörn nudged his protégé. Erik did not move.

"However, since the guilty man's timber and household effects are still held unjustly in the Breida farmer's barn, the twofold man-price will be accounted against these. It is thereby deemed paid in full."

A shout of anger burst out of Thorgest, and the judge from Hawk Valley had to silence him with a hard grip.

*Oh, great Tyr, will you show mercy to my Viking?* Hope grew in Tyrkir. Next to the sacrificial stone, Erik moved for the first time, scratching his right cheek.

The chief judge looked from one party to the other, then turned to the assembly. "Although the murders in Hawk Valley have been atoned for, the new homicides further taint the reputation of this man. The rot must be cut out. Otherwise, it will poison all the flesh. In the interest of our safety, and to give comfort to the father who lost two sons, Erik the Red shall be stripped of all rights and honor for three years. He can leave the country or live here in Iceland like an animal, with the animals in the wilderness. In three days, counted from this hour on, anyone may pursue and kill him without consequence. Whoever accommodates him, nourishes him, or clothes him, however, is himself subject to the law. After the punishment has been served, Erik Thorvaldsson shall be cleansed again. He may then return to our community as an honorable freeman."

The supreme judge turned to the Red. "Will you obey the verdict?"

Like a tree caught by a squall, the giant back bent abruptly. With the crook of his arm, he shielded his eyes.

The spectators held their breath. The sentenced man had to agree to the punishment and carry it out himself because, except for the plaintiff, there was nobody who could enforce it. That was the law. If the condemned man did not comply, his deed would have to be declared unforgivable. His spine would be broken right here on the sacrificial stone, like that of an unworthy criminal who had raped women and girls or had killed a defenseless cripple.

"I repeat my question!" The chief justice's tone grew more severe. "Do you obey the verdict?"

Erik dropped his arm. His face was wet with tears, but there was a fire in his yellow-brown eyes. "Because I have to, I, Erik Thorvaldsson, will submit to the verdict of the Thing. For three years, I will bury my revenge in me. But forget—" He looked over his shoulder up to the rock of the law, then more for himself, he added, "Injustice was suffered by me, not my opponent."

Before the judge could respond, Thorbjörn whispered, "Quiet! The verdict stands. Do not say another word until we've left the holy place!"

The chief justice nodded approvingly and did not punish the condemned man's last remark. "That concludes the matter," he shouted to the freemen. "We haven't discussed everything yet. But first, eat your fill. Do not drink too much!"

The gode of Warm Spring Slope walked ahead with his head raised high. Erik followed him, and the two landowners brought up the rear. The Breida farmer sputtered with anger. He was trying to motion to his people with hand signals, but he was still not allowed to leave the sacrificial stone.

The group slipped unhindered under the rope, and the spectators cleared a wide passage. Tyrkir used the opportunity to break away from the crowd and join his friend. Erik glanced at him. "Yes?"

The answer was just a nod.

"That's good." They moved faster.

As the custom dictated, the crowd closed back together behind them. The banished man should have enough of a lead to hide from his hunter. The five heard the outraged shouting of Thorgest until it was lost in the laughter and noise of the crowd.

There was no time to go back to the tent town to collect the few belongings they'd brought with them. Thorbjörn sent only the two landowners to his goden hut. "You stay there! I'll catch up with you tomorrow."

He hurried on with Erik and Tyrkir. It wouldn't be long before Thorgest was on their heels. Even though the grace period lasted three days, the hunter had to keep an eye on his quarry. It would take too much time and effort to find his trail. Anyone who killed a banished man could claim all his possessions; that alone made the hunt worthwhile.

Finally, the harbor came into sight. The three men slowed their pace. The servants who were camped there should only realize what was going on as late as possible. Before they turned from the road down to the bay, Tyrkir looked around once more. "Time is running short."

From the tent city, riders were dashing over the headland at a fast tölt, dragging dust plumes behind them.

"Let's go. Don't worry about them," Erik growled. With long strides, they hurried through the middle of the feast, past the fire, and approached the pier.

Thorbjörn uttered a suppressed curse. His *Sea Bird* still lay half-beached amid the other knarrs. "By all the gods! My ship should have been out in the open water long ago."

Erik grabbed his steward by the neck. "What's going on? Only the dinghy was supposed to be waiting for us. And where are our people? Damn, it's going to be close now."

With a jerk forward, Tyrkir freed himself from Erik's grip. "I came up with another plan. Trust me." He pulled himself up the side of the ship and sat astride the gunwale. The servants were huddled in the hold. "Have you prepared everything?" Their smiling faces were enough for him. "Then let's go now!"

The slaves all rose simultaneously. They scurried to the bow and jumped ashore to the right and left of the dragon's head. Tyrkir shouted to the two gawking men, "What are you waiting for? Or are you planning to have a chat with the Breida farmer?" His words were barely audible, but his look toward the camp underlined their meaning: the pursuers were already rushing down the slope.

Hastily, Thorbjörn and Erik swung themselves over the gunwale. The servants pushed the ship off the beach. As soon as there was enough water under the hull, they used the rudder ports as stirrups to jump aboard. They stretched out their arms to their companions, and soon the last man was lifted over the railing.

The knarr detached itself from the row of ships and slid into the open water. Now the fugitives had been discovered, and the shouting around the fire grew. The servants stumbled to and fro; Thorgest and his friends punched their drunken minions, gradually gathering a boat crew and kicking them to the harbor.

In the stern of the *Sea Bird*, Thorbjörn pushed the tiller forward. The knarr turned slowly. The slaves had taken their seats on the benches and pushed the long oars out through the ports. Light strokes on the port side of the ship supported the turning maneuver.

Erik stood next to Tyrkir and watched as the knarr of the Breida farmer was pushed into the water. "I intended to disappear in time." He clenched his fists, then opened them again. "I didn't want a race. Oh, Know-It-All, you gave away our advantage!"

"Wait and see!" Tyrkir pulled the good half of his mouth into a grin. "We're already safe now."

"What? Did they also cut away your mind at Sharpcliff?"

The oars plunged evenly, pulled through, slid forward again close over the curling waves, plunged in again, and the *Sea Bird* picked up speed.

The two friends walked past the mast to the aft. On the steering deck, Thorbjörn received them with little confidence. "We might be able to escape if we reach the island belt with a small lead. Something has to work out for us on this miserable day."

Erik stared past the stern to the harbor. "I don't understand."

The ship of the pursuers was still bobbing back in the bay. Thorbjörn turned his head. "Why...? But they should have turned long ago!"

Tyrkir crossed his hands behind his back. "Yes, should be child's play... if you have a rudder blade," he said lightly. "Even just using the oars, it would take a little longer. A knarr should at least have one of those." He fell silent, enjoying his friends' puzzled expressions.

"Stop it," Erik barked.

"It's simple. That barge is drifting because the rudder and oars are neatly stacked behind a pile of stones at the end of the mooring." Tyrkir shrugged. Because he didn't know which knarr belonged to the Breida farmer, he'd let the servants "lighten" all fourteen ships. "As I said, we are already safe."

"Sly boy." Erik wiped his forehead. "Know-It-All, you're good for something after all!"

Where to? Farther northwest? There was nothing more there than impassable, bare mountains, and nowhere on Iceland was the winter more severe than there.

Where to? Deeper into the south? Too many people had settled there. A banished man could only survive in the wilderness, and only then if luck was on his side.

Yes, there was the desert of the banished: fields of solidified lava as far as the eye could see, a little green around ponds hidden in crevices here and there. No man voluntarily went there, so the outcasts dwelt at the few oases and fought and tore each other apart over a stray sheep or a few bird eggs.

"I don't want to become a beast."

"Patience, Erik!" Thorbjörn had reassured him and Tyrkir two days ago. "You'll find enough shelter here in the Twin Bay for a time. Wait for me and let's think in peace." With this, he was back on the ship to pick up the two landowners from the Thorsness Thing. To any questions from the tent city, he had only one answer: "The condemned man submitted to the verdict. As is my duty to my friend, I gave him a head start, nothing more. As my last service, I bring his ship to his family."

Together with Styr and Ejolf, he had then broken down the tents on Oxens Island and stealthily brought the *Mount of the Sea*, along with all its belongings and the maidservants, through the maze of countless islands and reefs farther north up to the secluded bay.

The associates had been sitting on the beach with Erik and Tyrkir for hours, advising them. There was no danger of being surprised. A little farther out, Thorbjörn's *Sea Bird* was acting as a scout, and the ships of the two landowners were anchored across the narrow entrance to the bay. Their crews were aboard, bows and arrows ready. Should a pursuer discover the hiding place by chance, he would be duly received.

A soup simmered over the fire. Katla did not move from the cooking place; with a worried look, her lips slightly open, she listened to the men's planning.

"This is beneath me." Erik refused. He even rejected the offer of spending the three years somewhere in a remote cattle hut on the south side of the goden's district, well taken care of by friends.

"Why?" The judge rubbed his nose hard. "Your wife could even visit you there from time to time in secret."

Tyrkir backed the suggestion. "Down there, it would also be easier for me to look after you. Nobody will notice if I disappear from Warm Spring Slope for a few weeks now and then."

"You mean well." Erik took a flat stone and threw it over the water. After a few skips, it struck the side of his knarr. "Do you want me to lose my pride completely? In front of Thjodhild? In front of you, Know-It-All, and you . . . ?"

He broke off. A new idea replaced the lament. "It would be better if I left Iceland. An outlaw is free to do that. That way I'm not violating the Thing's verdict. I could go back to Norway . . . No, that's where they chased me away. No, better still farther down to that trading place. What was the name, Know-It-All? You know. Where my father bought you and your mother?"

"Haithabu, on the banks of the Schlei." Tyrkir nodded thoughtfully. "Not a bad idea."

Hard clanging made them all turn. Katla hit the ladle against the soup pot. "I'm going with you!"

"Don't you interfere," Erik barked at her. "See to it that we get something to eat."

She shot him a reproachful look. "That's why I want to go." The maid puffed out her chest. More to herself than the men, she murmured, "That's why I won't leave you alone."

To this point, Ejolf from Hog Island had only listened. Now he said, "So late in the summer, you still want to dare the long trip to the southeast? The wind is no longer favorable for it."

"I don't care."

"If anything, I'd sail west."

Grinning slightly, Erik looked at the landowner. "So, to the west? Very good. Only there is, unfortunately, nothing there. Should I frighten the whales as a ghost of the sea?"

"Mock away! But here at the Breidafjord, we hear that there's supposed to be land."

"Who told you that? Who's seen land there?" The others also stared at Ejolf, wishing to hear more.

"I can't swear to it, but my brother-in-law told me." He told them about Gunnbjörn, the son of Ulf Crow. The young merchant came back from Norway one summer and was driven west beyond Iceland by a violent easterly storm.

After a few days, the wind had eased. Rain set in, and heavy clouds hung over the ship. Finally, the weather cleared up. "And then Gunnbjörn saw rugged rocky islands in the haze a few sea hours away. Something rose behind it, gray or blue. In any case, it covered the whole horizon. Either it was a mountain, or there was a giant. Gunnbjörn didn't dare to get closer, and because there was finally a westerly wind, he took advantage of it and went back to Iceland."

"How long did it take him?"

"I don't know exactly, but less than a week."

The audience was silent. Erik kept scratching his beard. Eventually, he grumbled, "Land where nobody has been before. If I find it..."

Tyrkir rose and looked west across the bay. "Then it's yours."

Silently, he added, *My Viking, don't lose yourself in a dream. If there's really land there—land that's habitable—only then is it valuable.*

"What is it, Know-It-All?" Erik's gaze had gained a new glow. "Or does the newly freed master want me to go alone?"

"Why do you ask when you already know the answer?"

With a ladle in her fist, Katla stood tall before her master. "Don't you dare say no. I'm coming with you, and so are the other two girls. After all, you must be taken care of."

The giant wanted to reach for her but remembered himself in time. With a look at Tyrkir and the others, he said, "No slave has the right to demand anything! You follow me because I command it. And now give us some soup."

The grace period had expired four days and three nights ago. Erik's friends didn't care. Although they now had to reckon with punishment themselves, they tirelessly attended to the equipment and condition of the *Mount of the Sea*. Lines were checked, the red sail was set and reefed again, the spare cloth was checked for tears. With great effort, the maids greased the outer wall with seal fat.

Since only Ejolf lived near the Breidafjord, he had sailed to Hog Island and returned with provisions: barrels filled with salted meat and dried fish and full leather skins. "Thought a sip of sour milk now and then might do you better than water." He almost lovingly patted the two smaller skins. "I filled these with mead. Drink it when you've found the coast and think of me. But if there's no land, you can at least get drunk again before you..." He didn't finish this sentence. "You have to get out of here. And soon." The Breida farmer had assembled armed hordes. They were searching for the banished man island by island, and they had already come dangerously close to the Twin Bay. "It won't be long before they find us."

"I can't put you in any more danger." As soon as the sun rose again on the eastern horizon, Erik wanted to leave the hiding place. "If I have the sun at my back, I can't miss the right course. Besides, it's looking good for us." With an easterly wind and a cloudless sky, the weather promised to stay constant.

Erik whistled and waved to gather the maids and his small team. "Break down the camp. Stow everything aboard. I'd better not find a cup or ladle anywhere. And then sleep."

The ten slaves he'd trained for the war had been left to him by Thorbjörn. It wasn't much, but enough to crew the ship. Erik cheerfully turned to the judge and the landowners. "I'd better memorize the smell of fresh grass and earth now. Who knows when we'll be on solid ground again?"

Tyrkir stretched out next to his friend. He didn't want to sleep, but at least he tried to rest and enjoy his last hours on land. For a long time, he stared silently into the pale sky. His thoughts wandered across the mountains to the south side of the snowy rock. Poor Thjodhild. She knew nothing of the canceled war, nor about the court ruling. How hard the news would hit her!

He sat up and hugged his knees. "Are you awake?"

Erik just grumbled.

"Is it hard for you to leave without saying goodbye to her?"

"Be quiet." The friend turned his back to him.

"Say it!"

Only after some time did the answer come. "She is my wife . . ." Erik's voice became fragile. "And strong. She'll have to understand. . . . And we'll come home again. Thorbjörn will tell her that. I will miss her, and the boy. . . . By Thor, be quiet now!"

Tyrkir looked at his friend's trembling shoulders but remained silent. *How empty my heart will be without Thjodhild. But you can never know it, my Viking.* He stared at the ship. *No matter where it takes us, we must come back.*

The call of an eider duck broke the silence. Tyrkir listened. It didn't come from anywhere in the grass behind him. It was coming from across the water.

Again, he heard the call, this time much closer. It wasn't a duck cry. Danger! The scouts on the *Sea Bird* had sounded the alarm, and the knarr crews at the entrance to the bay had passed the signal along.

Erik had also heard it. "Onto the ship," he ordered in a low voice through the funnel of his hands. "Hurry up!"

Immediately, Thorbjörn and the two landowners were on their feet. Nobody had to be told. The maids ran into the shallow water, the servants lifted them on board, the masters climbed in themselves, and Erik grabbed the tiller. "Let's go now!"

Rudder blades clapped into the water. The *Mount of the Sea* quickly drew away from the shore. It reached the narrow gate of the bay where the two guard ships had already left their hiding place and were waiting.

"Knarr to the south," Erik was informed when his ship came alongside the other vessels. "Half an hour away."

Without hesitation, he urged his faithful helpers, "Better you climb across and disappear. I can do this alone."

The judge shook his head. "We'll be with you until you reach the open sea."

There was no time to argue. Now Thorbjörn had taken command; he sent Ejolf and Styr to their own ship. They should take the *Mount* in the middle. "Sail!" he ordered his friend. "Set a full cloth. Your red sail will be hard to spot between the others at a distance. They'll take you with them, and as soon as we reach my *Sea Bird*, it will join behind us, so no one will know for sure which egg our fleet is carrying away in its nest."

A weak wind barely reached the sails. Side by side, the convoy fought the ups and downs of the waves. In the meantime, the pursuer had sighted the ships and changed course. No doubt they would try to cut them off.

"This brainless fool," Thorbjörn cursed. "Does he not see that we're the greater force? If he comes too close, we'll turn him into a ghost ship." Resolutely, he raised his arm. "Hold your weapons ready!" His order had been addressed to the escorts' crew. "You, too," he ordered the ten slaves on the *Mount*.

Tyrkir had gone pale. "Do something," he whispered to Erik. "Before another misfortune happens."

"You're right." The giant left the tiller to his friend and quickly went midship to the gode. "I didn't know that you were so battle-addicted. I always thought I was the ruffian and you were the more prudent one."

"What choice do we have? After my failure at the Thing, I want to at least deliver you safely to the open sea. I swore that to my-self."

"You're a true friend. But perhaps we can do it without a battle." Erik suggested that as soon as the pursuer had come within calling distance, he would lie down in the hold with the provisions. "Let them come close and ask for me. You are the skipper here, and you are just transferring my knarr to the south side, as you announced in Thorsness. And since we haven't passed the glacier yet, we're actually going in the right direction."

The gode rubbed his forehead with the back of his hand. "Why didn't I come up with that myself?"

Erik was silent. Suddenly, the breeze increased. To the right and left, the sails swelled. The red cloth also turned into a bulging wind belly. The men on the tiller adjusted course, and the formation skimmed faster and faster across the crests of the waves. The *Sea Bird* flew in their wake.

One eye squinted shut, Erik estimated their distance across his stretched thumb and compared speeds. After a while, he grinned.

"No battle today. And no questions, either. He can't stop us any-more."

The tension faded, and the judge sighed from the bottom of his heart. "Would have been the first time that I ..." He waved his hand. "I'm really much better at other things."

Standing next to each other at the mast tree, they watched as the pursuer finally gave up the hunt and turned back. Only a swarm of hungry seagulls held their speed effortlessly. "It'll be a good day," said Erik.

The four ships reefed their sails when they reached the tip of the snowcapped peninsula. It was time for farewells. Styr and Ejolf from Hog Island came aboard the *Mount* once more.

"When I find the land, I'll come back." The red one looked gravely from one man to the other. "I will never forget this—what you did for me. And if one of you ever needs help, I'll give it freely, I swear." They reached out their hands; then Ejolf and Styr returned wordlessly to their knarrs, accompanied by Thorbjörn.

While the crew set the red sail again and the *Mount* detached itself from the formation, Erik called after the goden: "And tell Thjodhild, three years is not long. Tell her that!"

Tyrkir stood at the stern stem. He waved. When the friends' ships became smaller, he whispered, "Three years. That's three long winters and three summers." He turned around and went forward to the dragon's head. The wind bit his scar, tasting salty on his tongue. He shivered.

# HALLWEIG

Thjodhild did not cry. She'd listened to Thorbjörn with a stony face. When he fell silent, she took her son off the play mat and carried him outside through the hall. It was raining. The clouds hung low. She left the courtyard of Warm Spring Farm and walked spine straight along the narrow path to the steep cliff. There, she hid the little one's head on her breast. The view to the west found no horizon; it was sucked up somewhere between the sea and the rain clouds.

"Both of them. They both left us alone." Thjodhild pressed her lips together to stop her chin from trembling. *I would have gone with them. Whatever lies ahead, I belong at your side, not Katla.*

The thought of the maid alarmed her. Her helplessness turned into burning anger. Katla, with her round bottom and rocking breasts. *No, don't be unjust,* she reproached herself. *When the men started their war against the Breida farmer, you sent the maid aboard yourself. Because she is capable. And now, instead of you, she goes with them on the* Mount *into the unknown. Surrender to your fate!*

Thjodhild smiled bitterly—what a cursed phrase. *As soon as Erik desires it, Katla will obey with joy.* No, no breach of marriage. If a housewife is ill, absent, or just in a bad mood, the master used his slaves. "I must also accept this terrible tradition," Thjodhild whispered. "But get used to it? No, I will never get used to it."

Leif thumped her with his arms and complained loudly about wetness and cold. "You're right, we have to go back. It's enough that your father and your godfather are wandering around out there in the rain."

The rumor of Erik's banishment had probably reached every farm in Hawk Valley long before. Thjodhild feared the lies, and as soon as the weather improved, she had Thorbjörn send a servant to her parents. Through him, they should learn the truth: Erik was not a murderer, even if it seemed so now.

Hallweig felt that her friend, full of sorrow, was withdrawing more and more. At the end of August, she asked Thjodhild to help her sew the long-promised women's trousers.

"Will you leave us?" Hallweig had bent deeper over the fabric.

"What makes you think that?"

"I don't know exactly. Maybe because you've been talking more about your mother in the last few weeks."

Thjodhild absently pushed a loose strand of hair from her forehead. *It is true,* she thought. *In my dreams, I am often at home again. But I don't want to go back there.*

"Believe me, Leif and I feel safe here." Nausea rose up in her. She breathed rapidly against it.

"Are you ill?"

"No, no. I'll be all right in a minute." Thjodhild had resolved to remain silent until she was sure herself. But Hallweig's searching gaze demanded an answer. "Something has been going on in me for some time now," she began slowly. "My body is changing."

It was not necessary to say more. "Really? And I thought . . . Can it be, then?"

"It is possible. Erik was with me the night before he sailed to Breidafjord. And since then, the blood has been absent."

"Such happiness." Hallweig embraced her friend. "No, you must not leave, promise me. You must have your child here with me— with us—on Warm Spring Slope. Nowhere else."

"What about the father?" Thjodhild still struggled against her joy. "Only he can admit a baby into the family. He will be away for at least three years."

"Don't think about that now! Men just get in the way of child-bearing, anyway." There was enough room in the sauna house, and Grima of Eagle Farm would have to be called in time. Hallweig's cheeks glowed—she planned as if the birth were imminent. "Our Grima is the best midwife on the south coast."

"Slow down. It'll only come after the next snow."

"I should hope so. The little one must have properly grown fingers and toes." A thought drove the lady of Warm Spring Slope to the table. "Our trousers! I'll extend the waistband of yours immediately, or they won't fit over your belly." Breathing sharply, she picked up her needle and fabric again. "What will it be?"

Thjodhild raised her shoulders.

"Then it will be a boy." When Hallweig saw the puzzled look, she added, "I knew immediately that I was carrying a girl. That's why you will have a son."

"I didn't even know that particular wisdom." Thjodhild was trying to remain straight-faced. "You really are a clever woman." The corners of her mouth twitched treacherously, and as Hallweig returned the smile, they both laughed, each happy to hear the laughter of the other. Hallweig struggled for air, coughed, and continued to giggle. For the first time since Erik and Tyrkir had left, Thjodhild felt cheerful.

Hallweig stood, turned in a circle, and held her trousers in such a way that the air puffed up the legs. "Well, what do you think?"

"I'll still fit in them, even if I'm carrying two children."

"It has to be soft and comfortable. The fabric nestles up. Come on, get in."

Thjodhild detached the pins from her apron skirt and slipped it over her head.

"The shift, too. Or we won't see anything."

Naked, Thjodhild sat down on the stool. One foot after the other, she put her legs through the holes of the trousers, stood again, and unrolled the fabric cumbersomely until it reached over her hips. "I still have to practice that."

"The men can do it faster, that's true." Hallweig threaded a woolen cord through the loops in the waistband and loosely knotted the ends. "Fits." She looked at the figure. "How beautiful you are." After a while, she said breathlessly, "I can understand why the men like you."

"So far, nobody has seen me in pants."

"That wouldn't be good, either. No, I mean, the men look at you more than they look at me."

Quickly, Thjodhild reached for her shift. "Who? Who do you think likes me?"

"Erik—you know that yourself. I can't even blame my Thorbjörn. Yes, and you certainly please the newly appointed freedman, our little scarface."

Thjodhild pulled the long linen shirt over her head. "Tyrkir? He doesn't count, even if he's free now. He belongs to the family." She turned her back to Hallweig while she took off her trousers and dressed again. "Besides, our steward is Leif's godfather." *You must find a distraction from your thoughts of Tyrkir*, she ordered herself. *You'll betray yourself.* "What makes you think men don't look at you?"

Hallweig didn't answer. Thjodhild attached her straps with the pins again. "I find you very desirable."

She heard suppressed whimpering, immediately followed by a scream—not shrill—and yet it struck Thjodhild to the marrow. She whipped around. Hallweig had her mouth wide open, like a drowning woman. Her fingers were tugging at her neck as if trying to widen her throat. She sank, and before Thjodhild could reach her side, she hit the ground.

"You'll feel better soon." As she had so often during an attack, Thjodhild sat next to her friend and rested Hallweig's head in her lap.

The face was waxy, the lips blue. "Hallweig?" She tested her breath, felt for her heartbeat. Nothing.

In Thjodhild's eyes, the lights in the hall faded. Suddenly, she was surrounded by roaring and hissing. A red sail appeared from a deep swell. Erik's ship. It was hurled up by a wave, disappeared, and emerged out of the spray again. The storm drove the *Mount* mercilessly toward rugged rocks. *No*, she thought. *Not rocks. Those are teeth in the gaping mouth of a huge black monster. It wants to devour Erik and Tyrkir.* Tears ran down her cheeks.

She stroked her friend's hair. "You too? You go on the journey and leave me alone, too. Oh, Hallweig. I'm afraid."

# TO BE READ FROM THE RUNE STONE OF REMEMBRANCE:

The runes have to be exposed with a stick.

... **THE YEAR 982:** Prince ... Olaf Tryggvasson ... His father was treacherously murdered in Norway by twelve men. His mother fled from the enemies while pregnant. She gave birth to her son on a small island off the coast. But the pursuers found the hiding place. Olaf was sold as a slave, kidnapped, and freed. He grew up in Russia at the royal court and became a respected army commander there. One day, he meets the young convent pupil Dankbrand in Wendland. The shield of the novice is painted with a cross. Olaf asks, and Dankbrand tells him about the suffering of Christ and the miraculous power inherent in the cross ... Prince Tryggvasson is deeply impressed and buys this shield ... Olaf, nineteen, often thinks of Norway, his father's country ...

... **THE YEAR 983:** Jarl Hakon has defeated his opponent, and the blood of three hundred and sixty men has seeped into the battlefield. Now he is the unchallenged ruler of Norway. He even denies his liege lord, the Danish king Blue Tooth, the taxes owed him. Jarl Hakon enjoys life at the court of Trondheim. He marries, but his wife is not enough for him, and driven by greed and lust, he shamelessly searches for adventures with other women ...

**... THE YEAR 984:** In Iceland, Bishop Fredrekur and his companion are met with deep disgrace and hostility, but through Thorvald, he steadfastly continues to proclaim the new doctrine to the stubborn. In June, the two pious men even dare to go to the Thing. Fredrekur orders his friend to raise his voice for God the Almighty from the rock of the law while he stands silent. Monstrous! Finally, two men openly blaspheme the bishop: In his skirt, he looks like a woman, and surely, he'd had nine children conceived by Thorvald! That is too much for his righteous friend, and he kills the detractors in front of the assembly. The missionaries must hide. Two hundred men move to smoke out the bishop and Thorvald in their dwellings. Before they reach their destination, a swarm of birds flutters around the heads of their horses. The riders are thrown off, break their arms and legs, injure themselves with their own weapons, and abandon the murder plan.

**... THE YEAR 985:** In the spring, Bishop Fredrekur and his friend give up. They board the season's first boat to the east. The attempt to introduce Christianity to Iceland failed...

# THE DEPARTURE

Leif had stormed the lookout with his wooden sword drawn. The highest place on the basalt boulder in front of Hawk Farm belonged to him alone, and his mother was forbidden from helping his younger brother up. He let the weapon swirl over his head. "I am tall!" The west wind tugged at his red-golden curls. Triumph shone in his blue eyes. "Everything belongs to me." Leif ruled over his grandfather's lower meadows and the road; he even regarded the river his property.

"Where are your slaves, my lord?" Deferentially, Thjodhild looked up at her eldest. She squatted on the stone beneath him and had to hold two-year-old Thorvald from behind by his wool shirt so that he would not risk the climb. "A Viking without servants is no master."

"You are my maid." Leif beamed at her, then pointed with the point of his sword at his brother. "And he is my servant."

"Don't you at least want to appoint Thorvald as a steward? After all, we're celebrating your fourth birthday today, and at such a big feast, a gentleman dispenses favors."

Leif scratched his forehead, then rubbed his chin thoughtfully, a gesture he'd copied from his gray-bearded grandfather. Finally, the decision was reached. "All right. But I don't give him freedom as Father did with Uncle Tyrkir. He remains my slave."

"Very clever. And now let your steward come to you."

Leif received his brother. Like a dog, he ordered him to sit down beside his feet and not move.

"Be alert," Thjodhild said. "As soon as someone comes up the path, let me know."

She leaned back. Except for a few white spots, the May sun had already melted the snow from the steeply rising slopes beyond the lowlands. The river had also become quieter after freeing itself with crunching and crashing from its thick frozen winter cover over the last few weeks. Only a few ice floes floated on the water now.

*Four years ago, I gave birth to Leif*, Thjodhild thought. At the beginning of May. That much she remembered, and it was enough for her. But not for Thorbjörg. "Tomorrow is the anniversary of the day," she'd announced the day before. No matter how hard it was for the old woman to move with her stick through the house and stables, life on the Hawk Farm continued to follow her lead. "It was the tenth day after the change of the moon. I know it. Finally, I got the child out for you."

Why argue? When Thorvald was born in April two years before, her mother had also been there. The sauna house, the smell of moss and oils, her calming hands, while the intervals between contractions became shorter and shorter. "I felt so sheltered." Thjodhild sighed.

*And it was right that Father came to bring me home from Warm Spring Slope after Hallweig's death.* "You cannot stay with a widower. There will be talk. With us, you can wait in peace for your husband's return." There'd been no agonizing questions about the Thing, the banishment, or how Thjodhild's life should go on now.

At first, her parents had only spoken of Erik when Thjodhild asked them to. When Leif became aware and curious, his grandfather relieved her of the difficult task. During the past winter months, Leif had been allowed to climb the high bench with him as often as time allowed.

"Your father is a brave, strong man. Together with Uncle Tyrkir, he undertakes a long journey on the *Mount of the Sea*—that's his ship. And believe me, I have never seen a more beautiful and faster ship. One day they will land on a strange island…" So Thorbjörn started the story regularly and told his grandson about wild adventures.

Leif listened with his mouth open, afraid of the trolls, sea snakes, and dragons, and his eyes lit up when Erik and Tyrkir bravely defeated the fiends. "Me too." The boy clenched his little hands. "I also want to cross the sea."

"As soon as your father returns, you must ask him."

"When will he finally come?"

"Patience. It won't be long now." Thorbjörn twisted his finger in his beard and murmured mysteriously: "First they sail to the island where the sheep have two heads. But I'll tell you about it next time."

How many more stories would the grandfather have to invent for his grandson? Thjodhild jumped up restlessly and looked past her sons to the headland farther down in the valley.

*This is where I stood, my heart threatening to burst with fear, because I didn't know how the battle against the murderers had ended after the landslide. Oh, I hate this waiting for you.* "No Viking housewife is allowed to show her worries," her mother had warned at the time. "The man comes back, or he doesn't. That's the way it is."

Thjodhild pressed her fists against her temples. *I've managed so far. Just a bit longer. The third year of banishment ends in June. Until then, they cannot turn back, and even then, you must remain patient.*

"Mother? You're crying. Are you afraid?"

The worried tone in Leif's voice brought her back. "No, no. The stupid tears come from the wind." She picked up Thorvald. "You two are my protectors. Why should I be afraid?"

"No one's coming up the road today. I don't feel like standing guard anymore. I want to help the blacksmith when the horses get iron shoes. I can do anything today, you promised."

"In a moment, my Viking. Because it's your birthday, I also get a wish. Say your name, please, nice and slow and clear!"

"But only once." The four-year-old crouched in front of his mother. "I am Leif, the son of Erik. And Erik is the son of Thorvald..." With every name, the boy struck the stone with his wooden sword. "... and Asvald was his father, and Asvald was the son of Ulf, and he had Oxenthorir as his father."

In the second half of May, the stars faded, the night's darkness became twilight, and the mountain ridges crouched against the pale sky like the backs of giants.

A shadow. It moved quickly on the slope above Hawk Farm. It disappeared, reappearing a good bit farther down. Then suddenly, a figure stood on the rock directly above the roofs—not tall, coat hung around slender shoulders; a bright spot shimmered under his cap, and nothing more could be seen of his face.

In the inner courtyard, both guard dogs lifted their muzzles. They couldn't tell where the scent was coming from and trotted around, growling, until they finally struck. Their barking lured a servant out of the servants' house. Immediately, the canine guards fell silent.

Dressed only in a shirt, the servant shuffled sleepily to the stable, then to the residential building. Nothing unusual struck him. "Down," he ordered the dogs, wanting to return to the servants' house. Halfway along, a small stone hit him on the shoulder. At the same time, he heard a voice: "Wait!"

The servant spun around. "Who's there?" He looked around, afraid.

"A friend. But if you scream, I must kill you."

"Don't! No!" With both arms, the slave tried to protect himself. "By Odin, I'll shut my mouth. Where are you, damn you?"

"Up here. Above the house."

Finally, the servant made out the stranger. Although he stood there like a shooter holding a bow ready to fire, the weapon itself could not be seen in the semidarkness.

"Why are you sneaking around in the night?"

"Don't ask. Go and wake your master. No one else. Tell him a good friend is waiting here. Tell him it's about the bearskin he bought for his daughter years ago. Hurry!"

Before the slave obeyed, he called the dogs to him with a soft whistle and showed them the figure above the roof. "Watch!"

The stranger did not move. Only the panting of the dogs could be heard in the night's silence. Finally, the servant returned, accompanied by his master. The old man had decided against putting on a breastplate. Both men were still in their thin nightgowns but armed with spears. Both held shields above their heads. They slowly stepped out of the shadow of the house.

Thorbjörn peered up under the edge of the shield. "Who dares to disturb our peace?"

"Send the slave to bed!"

"I am no fool. Say who you are!"

"You know me. Think of the bearskin! You didn't buy it. My friend gifted it to your daughter."

Thorbjörn took a step back. "Either you are a ghost or . . . ?" He carelessly dropped his shield and spear to the ground and ordered his slave, "Go to sleep! There is no one up there. You have seen nothing, heard nothing!"

"But, my lord . . . ?"

"Silence! Take the dogs with you. And not a word to the others, or, I'll drown you in the river. Leave me!"

Only when the servant and guard dogs had disappeared into the servants' house did Thorbjörn look up to the rock again. The spot was empty.

"Here I am."

The old man turned around. "Come closer!" He stared into the face. "I can't believe it."

"You're only allowed to look at this half, then you'll recognize me better." Tyrkir turned the scarred side away.

"Is my son-in-law alive?"

"Why else would I come to you at night like a thief?" There was no time for long explanations. At the moment, Thorbjörn should only know what was necessary: The friends had discovered a country in the west. There had been no losses in their retinue. Erik was well, but the punishment did not end until after the June Thing. The banished man had to be careful until then. "Our ship lies well camouflaged in a bay above the Salmon Valley. For three nights, we hiked over the mountains to get here."

"We?" Thorbjörn stared at the slope above the house. "Are you saying that my son-in-law is hiding somewhere up there?"

"No, but he's waiting for me not far from here."

"You reckless fools!" Full of worry, the old man grabbed him by the shoulder. "Hardly a man survives three years in the wilderness. You've made it to within a month. Why on earth are you putting yourself in danger?"

"We had no choice." Tyrkir grabbed the old man's wrist and held it. "We only want one answer from you: Do you have news of Thjodhild and the child?"

"They sleep."

"I do not feel like joking."

The landlord shook his head. "I'm an old fool. Forgive me, boy! How can you know what's happened?" He'd conquered his shock. "What I said is true. Thjodhild is asleep here on Hawk Farm, and in her chamber lies not only Leif but also little Thorvald."

She's here! Tyrkir took a deep breath. He needed a moment to process this good news. As calmly as he could, he asked, "A second child? From whom?"

"Don't you dare!" The old man smiled. "Thorvald was your friend's farewell gift. And I think the father will accept him with pride. A naming and a homecoming! In the summer, I'll organize a splendid feast."

"Forget that," Tyrkir said. "Erik has a great plan, but I cannot say more without his consent." He hesitated. "I don't like it, either, but the truth is that Erik won't be able to see his family again until next summer. You have to explain that to Thjodhild."

Thorbjörn turned away. He paced the yard with wide strides, staring up at the dark mountain ridges on the other side of the river valley, then returned resolutely. "You ask too much of me. My daughter has a head of her own, as you know. You must tell Thjodhild yourself that she must wait one more year. Right now. Wait here." He left Tyrkir standing and disappeared into the house.

*O my poor, proud Viking,* Tyrkir thought. *Even before you've begun to put your plan into action, an essential part is already going wrong.* And it was precisely what the friends had argued so fiercely about over the last few days at sea. "No, only when I've succeeded will I surprise Thjodhild. I will not see them before."

"Isn't it wiser to include her and listen to her advice?"

"I won't let my plan be talked apart."

"Don't you miss her? After such a long time? Or are you afraid of her because—"

"Quiet!" The giant suddenly yanked his slender friend forward, then shoved him away again. "What is it to you? After all, Thjodhild is my wife."

Tyrkir immediately backed down. With each additional word, he could have betrayed his own feelings. "I see it differently, but maybe you're right."

To avoid her, Erik had not sailed to the south side of the snowy glacier. Instead, he'd steered his *Mount of the Sea* into a remote bay at Hvammsfjord. As soon as the knarr was camouflaged with bushes and driftwood and the camp was set up under overhanging rocks, he'd taken his friend aside. "Forget our quarrel! We'll secretly go to Hawk Farm. Old Thorbjörn can tell us what's going on, and he can send a messenger over to Warm Spring Slope."

Tyrkir ran his fingertip along his scar. *This time, the gods stand by me. You may have planned, my Viking, but fate determines what happens.*

The door opened. Thjodhild ran past her father, hurrying toward Tyrkir. "What luck," she whispered. Her gaze ran over his face, and for a moment, their eyes met.

"Forgive me for disturbing your sleep!"

"You'd be sorry if you hadn't!" Thjodhild wiped her emotion aside and tightened her shawl around herself. "I already asked Father, but he just mumbled something into his beard. Where's Erik?"

*If I lie now, she will never forgive me.* "Farther up in the valley. He's still outlawed until July—he has to hide. He's waiting in our old farmyard."

"Let's ride!" There was no chance to explain or object; Thjodhild was already going back to the house. Over her shoulder, she ordered, "Saddle the horses! Tyrkir should lead them down the road. I'll be right behind you."

On the way to the stable, Thorbjörn chuckled. "Weren't you sent here on a different mission? I thought my son-in-law didn't want to see her." He did not receive a reply.

Thorbjörn brought three horses outside. When they were harnessed, he was still grinning. "I told you, my daughter has a mind of her own."

Tyrkir looked at him openly as he said goodbye. "We're both

agreed on that." He wrapped the three reins around his right fist. "I just hope Erik hasn't forgotten."

"Good luck," the old man called after him quietly. "And send him my greetings. Tell him the summer feast should last six days."

They rode through the semidarkness higher up into the Habichtstal. No matter how hard Thjodhild pressed, Tyrkir wouldn't tell her anything about the trip. "We are back safe and sound. Erik will tell you more."

After the silence had stretched on for some time, she tried again. "And I thought you cared about me."

A hot wave rose in Tyrkir. Despite the dimness, he turned his face away. *If you had any idea how many dreams I've had about you the past three years, you would be frightened. It cannot be,* he admonished himself. *The truth would destroy every hope, every chance of happiness.* "You're the mother of my godson, the wife of my friend. I will always care for you."

"Very wisely spoken," teased Thjodhild. "You would have made an excellent judge." She clicked at her horse and rode on silently in front of the German.

There was rubble on the way from the road up the slope. Only the remains of the wall still hinted at the house that had once stood there. Now, in the twilight, it looked hostile.

Thjodhild slipped out of her saddle in the courtyard. "Where is he?"

"Patience!" Tyrkir also dismounted. Through funneled hands, he mimicked the strange flight song of the snipe, sounds that tumbled down like a ladder from high above. The answer came immediately. Once again, Tyrkir let the little bird fall to the ground from a lofty height.

A jump, stones rolling, then quiet steps, and the giant came out of the ruins. "I saw you coming." With outstretched arms, he walked to meet Thjodhild. She ran toward him, burying her face in his chest. "Finally, I'm right." She sighed. "It was so cold without you."

He stroked her hair, inhaling the scent. Just to say something, he finally muttered, "The fire in our old living hall no longer burns."

She pressed firmly against his body. "Oh, Erik. We'll light a new one. Somewhere."

When his hand touched her back, she whispered, "Do you still remember how you showed me our chamber back then? Show it to me again."

"You mean now? Didn't our Know-It-All tell you anything?"

"Not a word. Now, come! First, I want to feel you. We can talk later."

Over Thjodhild's shoulder, Erik grinned at his friend. "You can't help me right now, but I'll need you afterward."

They left Tyrkir alone in the courtyard. Where the bed used to be, Erik spread out his coat. Thjodhild felt how hard the ground was only after the pain and the much too short heaven. "Stay," she begged.

But he pulled himself back and redressed.

"Can't right now!" His voice sounded almost harsh. "By sunrise, I must disappear again with Know-It-All. And since you're already here, you may as well find out what I am planning."

Disappointed, she closed her eyes, just for a moment, then rose from the coat. "At least you should know that I am happy to see you." With a few movements, she arranged her clothes and stroked her hair back. "I'm listening."

"Don't be angry!" He put his arm around her. "My head is so full, it will burst soon. Let's go find Tyrkir. I think you'll be pleased."

Erik was restless. As soon as the three were sitting together in the inner courtyard, he jumped up again. "It's like this—I've found my land. I can live there!" He bent over to his wife. "Do you understand? This land belongs to me. You'll move into a beautiful house. I've not only marked out the place. No, the high seat beams are already standing, and the roof is finished."

"Wait, Erik! Even if we don't have much time, you're going too fast. I don't understand." She turned to Tyrkir. "Explain it to me. One thing at a time."

"As Erik said, we've discovered habitable land. There are fjords, green pastures—it's a good life." Tyrkir calmly replied to the doubt etched across her face. "You can trust me."

The red one clenched his fist. "Damn it, Know-It-All, the way you talk about my realm, no one would want to go there." He took a deep breath before painting the scene for his wife. "Fat grass, more than enough. Soft soil—I still have the smell of the earth in my nose. It's warmer than here. I've seen fish, birds, even walruses, and polar bears. We can go hunting—there are whole herds of reindeer. Wait until I've assigned the settlers to their farms!"

"Which settlers?" Thjodhild pressed her fists against her temples. "I thought you'd discovered a new land without people."

Erik kneeled in front of her. "Until next summer, I want to recruit people here. I'll tell them about how good their life can be, and I'll choose each of them. You see, the area is big enough. Their families can grow, their children and grandchildren will soon become a new people. My people." He was carried away by his own enthusiasm. "Come to Greenland, where even the gods are resting in the meadows!"

"Greenland?" Against her will, she had to laugh. Turning to Tyrkir, she asked, "Did he invent the name or did you?"

Tyrkir could not suppress a matching grin. "It was all his idea."

"Greenland." Thjodhild sighed. "If only it were true, Erik. Well, I suppose I'll follow you with my sons to Greenland." *I have no other choice*, she thought. *I don't want to be without you anymore.*

The giant froze. "I only know of one son."

She gently patted his hand. "Surprised? Now there are two. Thorvald can be my contribution to the new people. If you want to see him, come to the farm."

"We have to go," Tyrkir interrupted. "You can talk about your children later." The sky over the eastern mountains was already turning. The danger would only grow from hour to hour.

Erik pressed his wife tightly to his chest. "Trust me! I will take care of our happiness."

"I hope more than anything that we find it this time."

They reluctantly pulled away.

On the way to the horses, Erik whispered to Tyrkir, "You tell her!"

"Coward," Tyrkir murmured, but he was glad to be alone with Thjodhild for another moment. He took her hand in both of his own. "You asked me earlier how I felt about you . . ."

"I don't doubt it now. You're a good friend to Erik. And the only one I have besides him."

"We won't come to Hawk Valley anymore." He felt her fingers tense. "I know how difficult it is for you." As soon as Erik had put together the settler fleet, he would send a message. "From the moment you arrive with the children in the harbor, your separation will be over."

"So, *another* whole year."

Tyrkir nodded.

"It'll pass." Thjodhild pulled her hand back. "Hurry!"

She stood motionless. The men led their horses up the slope and soon disappeared between the rocks.

Drought. It didn't rain in May. It didn't rain in June. At the Thorness Thing, the free farmers looked worried. The grass could not grow. "Our hay harvest is in danger." They pressed the chief justice with questions.

"I don't have any advice." Animal sacrifices were made in vain. Even in July, only a few drops fell.

"Erik Thorvaldsson, the Red, has returned from his journey. He has served his sentence. Purified and free of all guilt, he once again is one of us." The news flew from valley to valley. It didn't matter to most farmers—the thought of the next winter weighed too heavily on them. But a rumor that was spread along with this news made them sit up and take notice. "The Red has found a new land. There are lush meadows where even Odin lets his eight-legged stallion Sleipnir graze, as does Thor, his bucks."

"Where could that be?" The answer snuffed out any curiosity. "Ride on! You must have misheard."

"Just wait and see! When he visits you, he will tell you himself about his Greenland."

Heavily loaded packhorses trotted west along the shore of the Breidafjord. Two armed men rode along for protection. The goods train stopped at the height of Sharpcliff. The leader ordered a short rest and drove his horse up the path, through the hills to the Breida farm. It didn't take long, and he returned accompanied by Thorgest, the two dogs panting beside them. Without hesitation, the men sat down.

"Hides and jewelry, you say?" The squat farmer pushed his chin forward. "Let me see."

The leader calmly opened a basket lid. "The neighbors along the fjord assured me I could store our goods safely with you. You are an honest man."

Thorgest rummaged through the treasures with an expert touch. "That's true, by Loki." He exposed the teeth of his lower jaw and snickered. "If the price is right, your goods are safe in my barn."

From the side, he leered at the simply dressed man. "You travel around with furs and don't even have a silver fox around your neck. Be honest, is all this yours?"

As if caught, the leader took a few steps back.

"Did you steal it?" the Breida farmer urged. "You can tell me." He patted the bulging purse on his belt. "Maybe we'll even be good partners in this business."

"You've miscalculated!"

Thorgest flinched at the sound of the voice. On the stony embankment stood Erik the Red, and next to him, Tyrkir the German, both fully armed, both holding a battle-ax in their right fists. One breath later, armed servants appeared on either side of them. They pulled the arrow shafts up to their ears.

In a panic, the Breida farmer tried to flee, but riders blocked his way with stretched bows. Only now did Thorgest remember his dogs. But before he could give them an order, they dropped to the ground next to his feet, pierced with arrows.

Horror paralyzed the Breida farmer. "W-we can talk," he stammered. "About everything."

"You have defiled my honor." Erik's voice was cold. "The god in me demands atonement."

With a mighty leap, Erik landed in front of the farmer. He set the ax edge across Thorgest's neck, took measure, and swung it back.

There was no escape. Thorgest spluttered, fearing his imminent death. The flashing blade hung in the air, ready for the blow. Panting, he babbled, "My fault. I cheated . . . you. I'll pay you whatever you want."

"Fight!" Erik looked at the ax in the farmer's belt. "I'll give you time. Come!"

With the last courage of despair, Thorgest reached for his hip and succeeded in pulling out the short ax. He didn't get any further. The giant jumped up, his boot tips hitting the farmer's arm and wrist in a double strike, and the weapon whirled into the ditch beyond the path. Disarmed, Thorgest sank to the ground. "Kill me," he whimpered. "End it! Kill me!"

"Now, now. What are you asking of me?" Erik placed the massive ax head in front of him and rested both hands on the handle. "You were beating me. Every one of my servants will testify to that."

It took Thorgest a long time to raise his head, his eyes almost bulging out of their sockets. "Don't toy with me!"

"No, you filth, I'm serious. I must offer you a settlement." He waved to Tyrkir. "You handle the rest. I can no longer stand the sight of him."

"My friend demands all the silver you carry as compensation for his stolen household effects." Tyrkir snapped his fingers.

The farmer immediately untied the pouch.

"Very good. And now, return to your farm. Tell all your neighbors that there was a fight between you and Erik, and because you pressed him hard, he had to abandon his revenge. You have made peace. Understand? Good. Then don't hold us up any longer, peasant!"

Thorgest scrambled up. "Peace." He stumbled up the path to his farm. "Peace. Yes, that's it."

Slowly, Erik let his ax swing back and forth. "Well, Know-It-All, what do you think?"

"Not bad for the future gode of Greenland."

"I think your idea was good."

*How proud I am of you*, Tyrkir thought. *But I'd better not tell you that*. He turned the right corner of his mouth into a grin, hiding his scarred side under his hand.

The rain only came at the beginning of September—too late, much too late. Cows and horses had not found enough grass to fatten them up. Even the sheep brought back lean lambs from the high pastures, and there was hardly any hay in the barns.

The scrawny animals were slaughtered, making the endless night of the winter months on the farms even darker. "Greenland!" Like a spell of light, the word took root in the hearts of the desperate. The stories at the great fires grew; the pastures there became even greener, the harvests even more productive. "Greenland!" All across Iceland, be it deep in the southwest or high in the north, the rumor about this promised land was fueled by the impending famine. And there was only one man who possessed the key: Erik Thorvaldsson, the Red.

In April he moored the *Mount of the Sea* in a storm-protected bay out on the cape of the snowy peninsula and pitched his tents. A rugged area of lava stretched over the headland. The meeting place for the emigrants had been chosen well. "You shall see, Know-It-All. Soon, there will be more ships in our harbor than we can take with us." He stroked back his mane. "And here, around my camp, the people will crowd as they would crowd around a gode hut on the Thing."

"Do your boots still fit you?" Tyrkir asked dryly.

"Why?" The giant looked down at his feet.

"I mean, if your head swells, your feet will have grown as well."

"Are you trying to insult me, *Lord*?"

"No." The weedy one also added a *lord* and waited until Erik grinned before continuing. "Without question, success is surely yours. I knew that if you ever got into it, you would have no trouble finding the words to crow about it. But I didn't expect that you'd advertise our Greenland as cleverly as a fishmonger his catch."

"Not one word was a lie."

Tyrkir raised his shoulders. *My Viking. In your enthusiasm, you kept some truth to yourself. We'll deal with that in Greenland. First, I worry about your wife.* "How will you tell Thjodhild?"

Erik looked at the small tent next to his spacious dwelling. "It's simple," he murmured. "Her father will bring her here shortly before we depart. And as soon as she arrives, I'll send her over there."

"Are you afraid?"

"Well, three years of exploring seems easier now."

Like a hero, Erik was admired and courted at the June Thing. He sat with Tyrkir in the tented stone hut of his friend from Warm Spring Slope and received new applicants every day. The Breida farmer's witnesses from the trial four years ago were turned away without a thought. And from the men who were willing to give up their farms in Iceland because of the lack of pasture or the severe famine, he chose carefully, selecting men with hard hands and honest eyes. He didn't even examine the ships of the vainly dressed farmers who talked big. "You've come too late. There are twenty seaworthy knarrs, already loaded, lying outside at the top of Snow Rock. I've chosen five more. That's enough."

As soon as he was alone with Tyrkir and the judge from Warm Spring Slope, he urged Thorbjörn again, "Come with us! Your *Sea Bird* will sail beside me at the fore. We can have a good life in Greenland."

"The idea is tempting." Thorbjörn thoughtfully stroked the bridge of his nose. "But I want and must be considerate." After Hallweig's death, he'd given his daughter Gudrid into the care of the seer of Wagle Farm. "The little one only counts five winters. She has uncles and aunts. Her grandparents are still alive. With her mother already gone, I would like Gudrid to grow up under the protection of my whole clan. Who knows? Maybe I'll follow you with her later."

"Whenever that may be, you will always be welcome."

Thorbjörn Vifilsson promised to come to the cape with his daughter before the fleet left.

On the ride back to the settler camp, Erik kept looking up at the sky. The clouds quickly drifted inland from the west. The wind was not yet allowed to turn; the rain was now welcome. The weather was not supposed to change until August. Only then would the easterlies be stable for at least two weeks in clear skies.

*I will order sacrifices*, he resolved. Each clan had to slaughter an animal to appease Ran, the cruel wife of the sea god. He clenched his fist. Ran, who threw her net at ships, who sent her nine wave-daughters to perform the Death Dance with the seafarers before stretching out her claws to the unlucky ones herself. Only this goddess could now ruin his grand plan, his happiness.

Tyrkir had been trudging through the lava scree since early morning, going from one tent village to the next, counting and filling his leather-covered writing board with strokes. Wherever he went, he was greeted first by dogs barking, then by the smell of meat soup. Each wealthy shipowner had been assigned two or three families for the journey. The strangers had already moved closer together. The children played and quarreled in front of the makeshift accommodations. *Yes, run and rave as much as you can now,* he thought. *Who knows how long you'll be crammed onboard next to the cattle?* Cows stared at him. Horses shuffled and snorted, pegged sheep and goats chewed on tufts of hay, and chickens excitedly cackled in their pasture cages.

Women and maidservants worked around the common cooking fire. Some slaves greased the skin of the rain capes, others mended holes in the fur sacks. At the same time, their mistresses bent over chests and packed indispensable household utensils. Tyrkir was greeted with serious, anxious faces. The tension in the tent villages had grown noticeably since the change in the weather. The departure had to be imminent. But when? He answered questions and tried to ease the fear of the unknown with small jokes.

While his task was just about manageable with the women and children, down in the harbor, it soon became a game of chance. Like bees working their hives, the crews swarmed around their knarrs. Barrels and boxes were carried on board, orders and curses flew; they erected mast trees, rolled ropes, or tarred the planks of the outer walls.

Visibly tired, Tyrkir returned to the main tent.

"How plentiful are the people of Greenland?" Erik asked him.

"With all the confusion out there, I must have counted some of them twice." Tyrkir skimmed the lines on the leather hide. "According to this, however, there are the families of forty-three landowners and one hundred twenty free peasants, plus hundreds of slaves. If I add everything up, then we'll set sail with about a thousand people."

"Distributed among twenty-six ships." Erik wiped the sweat from his forehead. "If we add provisions, weapons, and tools, not to mention the livestock, then our knarrs will lie deeper in the water than I'd like. At the meeting with the captains, remind me that bailers must also be distributed to women and children."

A voice came in from the lively tangle outside. "Where can I find Erik Thorvaldsson?" The friends paused, then both rushed to the exit.

She'd arrived. Thjodhild stood smiling in front of them, holding a son on each hand.

*How beautiful you are*, Tyrkir thought. *Despite your travel hood, I see your hair. Despite the coarse wool dresses, I see your slender figure.* He smiled at himself. *Maybe it's just your eyes that make me see so much more.*

Erik walked toward her. "Welcome." Before he could embrace his wife, Leif stepped between them. "Mother? Is that our father?"

"Yes, boy." Thjodhild laughed. "This is the great Erik for whom we had to wait so long."

Leif curled his nose. Finally, he pressed his fists into his sides. "I'm ready," he reported. "Our luggage is at the ship. We should go out to sea immediately."

"Slow down, boatswain!" The giant happily played along, pounding him against his chest. "Only the skipper gives the orders."

"I'm ready, too, Father," the little one crowed at his mother's left hand.

"Do we have to take him with us?" Leif made a face. "At the sight of the first monster, he'll wet his pants."

"Me too! Me too!"

"Hush now!" Thjodhild pulled her eldest by his hair toward the tent entrance. "Say hello to Uncle Tyrkir."

The boy approached reverentially. So, this was the other hero from the adventures his grandfather had told him. Leif admired the crooked mouth and the scarred side. "Each troll had five swords, I know, but you killed them all?"

Tyrkir pulled him in. "Since you already seem to know all about it, we don't have to talk about it anymore." He looked over at Erik. The friend had the three-year-old Thorvald in his arms. Thjodhild was just delivering greetings from her parents. Thorbjörn had not come with her because he didn't want to leave his wife alone.

The first servant from Hawk Farm had brought Thjodhild and the children. "And I think it was easier for them to say goodbye to me at home rather than to wave to the ship here."

"That's right," the giant mumbled. "What I wanted to say . . ." His gaze fled to Tyrkir, but the German just took Leif by the shoulder.

"Come here," he said. "I carved you a stick. Every sign protects you from a different evil spirit." He quickly disappeared with the boy into the main tent.

Thjodhild frowned. "Erik Thorvaldsson? Why have you suddenly gone silent?"

"See for yourself!" He pointed to the small tent next to his shelter and carried Thorvald over to the sheep.

A little later, she stepped outside again. Her face was pale. "Come here, Erik," she pleaded quietly, and waited until he stood in front of her. "There is a child there. A girl. I don't have to ask who the father is. Where is the mother?"

"Katla? Yes, she is not...?"

"I don't care where she is. When the woman comes, she should immediately disappear with the brat. And now, give my son here!" She tore Thorvald out of his arm.

"That won't be possible." Erik hesitated, then added, "I recognized the girl as my daughter. Freydis belongs to the family."

"Very clever of Katla. At least you chose a nice name." The anger burned in Thjodhild's eyes. "All right, you stud. Now your sons have a sister, but this mare is not going to Greenland."

"I promised her."

"And I said no." Thjodhild knew how little power she had in the decision, so she left him and went into the main tent with Thorvald. Without even acknowledging Tyrkir, she hissed, "Coward! Now I finally know why you wouldn't tell me anything about the trip."

That evening, Thorbjörn Vifilsson arrived with Gudrid. "Save your mead and the supplies for Greenland!" The judge waved at his heavily laden slaves. "I invite you to a farewell feast." He'd brought beer, dried fish, and two slaughtered mutton from Warm Spring Slope.

Thjodhild suppressed her grief and greeted her friend warmly. She kissed his daughter and introduced her to Leif. "You two used to play naked on a blanket."

The boy and the girl looked at each other with embarrassment. "I don't think so," Leif said. "What am I supposed to have played with her?"

Gudrid stuck out her tongue. "You're too stupid for me."

"Stop it!" Thjodhild sighed. *You have no idea what plans Hall-weig and I made for you. But that's not going to happen now, unless fate brings you together again sometime in the future.*

Later, the red night sun swam in the sea. The meal was over. Erik was camped with Tyrkir, the judge, and some skippers around the smoldering embers. They discussed little more than the course, hoping for a steady easterly wind, and above all, that the sky should remain clear.

The noblewomen sat together at a neighboring fire, peppering Thjodhild with questions:

"How far will the families live from each other?"

"Will grain grow there for our bread?"

"Will every farm have enough water?"

"I don't know. Although, I am the wife of the Red One, he's told me even less than you already know."

Her back went rigid. Katla slowly approached the fire with the child. Immediately, the women fell silent. Everyone already knew about the dispute between the leader of the settlers and his land-lady.

The maid had reached Thjodhild. "Won't you have a look at my Freydis?" She glowered with a combination of defiance and pride. "She's two years old. A beautiful child."

"Your Freydis?" Thjodhild lifted her brows. "A slave doesn't own anything, have you forgotten that? Not the rag you wear on your body, not even your life belongs to you."

"But I am the mother."

*And you did nothing wrong*, Thjodhild thought bitterly. At the same time, she felt tense curiosity pressing in from all sides. *How could you have argued with Erik in front of strangers? Forget this jealousy! Every wrong word damages your reputation and the dignity of your family.*

"Katla, you have been an efficient maid to Erik. You prepared food for him, carried his child, and gave birth to her." She gently stroked Freydis's hair. "As is the rule, you would have to raise the little one so that she would serve us later."

The joke made the housewives smile. They agreed with Thjodhild. "But your child will live as a daughter in my family. Be grateful. You couldn't have achieved more happiness for Freydis."

Katla kneeled before her mistress. "I always want to serve on your farm."

*If only I could prevent it*, Thjodhild thought, but said, "That is for Erik to decide."

There was noise and screaming in the harbor. The women listened, the maid and her child forgotten. At the neighboring fire, the skippers lowered their cups. Even a small dispute between the crews so shortly before departure could become a dangerous nuisance on the high seas.

The roar quickly approached the lava hill. With curses and blows, five servants drove a man before them. He fell, so they pulled him up by the collar and pushed him forward. The gaunt figure looked familiar to Thjodhild, but the blood-drenched face offered no way to identify it more clearly.

"Take your daughter and go to sleep," she quietly ordered Katla. "Tomorrow, we'll discuss this more."

Only a few steps away from the men's campsite, the beaten man was thrown in front of the fire by his tormentors like a doll.

"We found him on our knarr, Master." They did not turn to Erik but to Herjulf, the gray-haired merchant from Smoke Bay in the southwest of Iceland. "He was hiding among the weapon coffers."

"You are brave lads. But why, my gods, why do you have to make such a racket about him?" Herjulf didn't waste a single glance on the moaning man at his feet. "Get him deeper into the rubble. Foxes and ravens will do the rest. And then calm down."

"There's something else." The speaker shrugged. "We would have drowned him right away, but he says he is a Christian, and his god punishes anyone who kills another. And since we're going out soon, I thought, better ask first, in case the wrath of this god sends us a storm."

"Christian!" Erik had jumped up. Even before he'd reached the beaten man, Tyrkir and the judge were already bent over the figure and had rolled him onto his back. "It is Askel the Lean."

"Damn it!" Erik smacked his forehead. "We chose only healthy settlers and young, healthy cattle, and then this Christian creeps in among us."

"My Savior..." The Lean One opened his eyes. "He brings the light..."

"Shut up! Greenland is bright in summer and dark in winter, just like here. We don't need your god there." Erik turned to Herjulf. "Let your men take him out of our sight!"

The merchant hesitated. There was doubt in the faces of the other gentlemen, as well. "What's the matter? You don't want—" Erik nudged Tyrkir. "You tell them!"

"Maybe it isn't wise to upset the alien god."

"Know-It-All!" The giant slammed his fists together. "Only Ran is dangerous to us. And we offered her sacrifice. That's enough."

"Damn it! You wanted my advice."

"Don't you dare! I alone give the orders here!"

Quickly, Thorbjörn Vifilsson placed himself between the friends. "Hey, no need to quarrel! Let me help." Turning to Herjulf, he said, "The Lean One was found on your ship. According to the law, the skipper has the highest judicial power onboard, so you decide: Should this Christian be delivered to certain death?"

"Before we...? No, better not."

"The problem is solved." The gode smiled disarmingly. "Askel belongs to my court district. You go to Greenland and leave it to me!" Without waiting, he had the skinny man tied by his hands and feet and put him with the pigs.

The women were relieved to see their husbands' faces relax. They all praised the clever goden. Herjulf sent his servants back to the ship, and the masters sat down by the fire again. Fresh beer was served. It took some time for Erik to calm down, but then he put his arm around Tyrkir's shoulders. "What the hell, Know-It-All," he muttered. "The main thing is the Christian isn't coming to our country with us."

He emptied his cup with big gulps. "Tomorrow, we'll break down the tents," Erik told the group. The settlers and slaves were to board only after the livestock had been safely stored in the holds. "And don't take anyone you don't know with you!" His broad grin proved to all that the incident was over. Erik the Red, their leader, gave the final orders. "From this point on, no one may leave the ship without your permission, and you have one night to settle life onboard with the crew and passengers still in port. At sunrise, we set sail."

He waited until the maids had filled every jug again. "Let's go to Greenland, our green country!" The slogan blossomed in their hearts; it meant hope and promise and was, above all, reason enough to drink and continue drinking.

Tyrkir didn't try to keep up. He looked stealthily over at the women. *Coward.* Not just the word itself but Thjodhild's contempt had hit him hard. At first, he'd been determined to explain himself and to ask for her forgiveness. But now that Askel the Lean was lying with the pigs, he'd come up with a plan. *No, I am not ashamed,* he calmed his conscience. *It's only a small trick, and if it's successful, it will help us all.*

Finally, the women said their goodbyes. At the feast, nobody noticed when Tyrkir stood up and swayed slightly. Everybody had to relieve himself from the pressure of the beer. In front of the main tent, he stood in Thjodhild's way.

"Not now. I'm tired," she said.

"Please, listen," he whispered. "It's about our peace in Greenland."

Thjodhild frowned. As he continued, she wondered, and when he'd finished, a smile twitched in the corners of her mouth. "Do you remember what you said to me at our wedding? Only after Erik do I hold a place of honor in your heart. Maybe the order's changed?" She slipped into the tent without waiting for an answer.

"Don't torture me." He sighed.

In the early hours of the morning, Erik lay down with his wife. Cheered by the beer, he felt the warmth of her skin, and soon the desire for more grew. She tolerated the touching of her breasts, even the bearded kisses. But when he pressed on, Thjodhild slipped away and sat up.

"What's the matter with you?"

"I can't sleep with you?"

Again, he reached for her, but she crossed her arms around her knees. "No, leave me alone."

With effort, he arranged his thoughts. "You're angry because I brought you a daughter. I can't do anything about that now."

"No, that's not it. Freydis should belong to us." Her hand gently circled around his navel.

He lolled there comfortably, and his voice became dark. "Come here!"

"Maybe. But first you have to grant me a favor."

"By my honor, anything you want. I swear."

"Take him with you!"

"Who?"

Thjodhild bent to his ear. "That poor Christian out there."

Like a spring, Erik's upper body shot up. All lust was forgotten. He stared at her like a ghost. "I shall . . . No, never."

"Erik Thorvaldsson, you gave me your word."

He buried his face in both hands and sat there for a long time.

"Why?" he finally whispered without looking up. "What did I do to you? Give me back my word, demand everything for it. The Lean One and his god must not poison my Greenland."

Thjodhild let the silence between them stretch. "Who's to say that you won't break this new oath as well?"

The question offended him, but he tried invoking the Viking honor and respect he owed to the dignity of his housewife. "Peace in our family is sacred to me."

"I trust you, Erik." She grabbed her nightgown and let it slide through her fingers. "I offer a simple exchange: Askel the Lean doesn't sail with us, but Katla stays here, too." Without savoring her victory, she added, "Thorbjörn's taking the Christian back with him, anyway. Give the maid to your friend. As a widower, I think he can certainly use such an efficient maid."

"Now I understand." Erik scratched his beard. "Yes, I agree." Half admiringly, half warily, he looked at her. "What a woman I have! By Thor, you know how to get what you want."

Sighing, Thjodhild lay back. "Thank you. And now..." She stroked his broad back until he also fulfilled her next wish.

A horn call from the *Mount of the Sea*, long and almost lamenting. It echoed across the bay and the beach. A swarm of gray geese rose from the lava scree with excited flaps. The second horn call frightened the seal families on the archipelago, and they silently slipped into the black water. As soon as the third signal had faded, twenty-five ships responded with a seemingly endless cry of joy. "Greenland! Our green land!"

The yard beams were pulled halfway up the masts, and at the same time, the rudder blades dipped in and furrowed through the rippling water.

On the shore, relatives and friends laughed, called out advice and promises, as if this was just a temporary separation. Soon, however, their words could no longer reach each other, and all that remained was for them to wave and shed their tears.

Thorbjörn Vifilsson and Gudrid watched the ships depart, though he'd forbidden Katla to do so. The day before, she'd been allowed to dress her daughter for the last time—no goodbye, just a kiss. Freydis had gladly gone aboard with little Thorvald to play, and there were so many new things there that sister and brother had later fallen asleep rolled into a blanket.

When the fleet reached the open sea, the easterly pushed into the colorfully striped, angular sails. Thjodhild stood at the high curved stern and looked back. The headland quickly became smaller, but the snow-covered glacier had not yet lost any of its size. It wore a veil of clouds around its shoulders, its head crowned with gold from the morning sun.

She had paid him a visit with Hallweig. *At that time, we wanted happiness. But you sent us the ball of fog, which stretched its black arms toward us. And today? What are you giving us for the ride? No!* She abruptly tore herself away from the sight. *I don't want anything more from you.* The glacier has no power over the sea and ships. She calmed her heart.

Next to her, Erik held the tiller. At the bow deck in front, Tyrkir was occupied with the small, round wooden board and the vertical needle in the middle, from which notched lines went out like rays. Thjodhild knew that this was an important, almost sacred, task. As soon as the sun rose higher, he would be able to determine their course by the shadow fall of the needle. Or, at least, so the men claimed, and that was enough for her. *My two men! Yes, we are finally, finally together again.* In the lower hold, she discovered among other children the reddish curls of her sons next to the blond plaits of little Freydis. And far beyond the dragon's head, still behind the horizon, Greenland was waiting, and perhaps a future in which happiness would no longer elude them.

# GREENLAND

On the second day, the sun turned into a pale disc, and the wind coming from the northeast picked up unexpectedly around noon. Tyrkir would have liked to let his friend sleep longer, but he didn't hesitate to wake him. "I'm afraid Ran wants to throw her net at us."

Erik crawled out from under the sealskin. A quick stretch, a short, intense scratching and rummaging in his red mane, and wide awake, he eyed the wobbly, transparent shreds of cloud. His tongue tasted the air, then he took the helmsman's hand off the tiller. "Hard seas ahead." An observation. Erik issued his orders just as soberly. The battle shields were to be anchored to the outer rail. They not only raised the ship's hull but covered the oar ports. The line guards for the square sail were upped to six men, and each had to secure himself with a rope. "You're to tell only the crew. I don't want any unrest in the hold yet." The servant hurried away from the raised helm.

"Now to you, Know-It-All." He had Tyrkir wave a yellow flag until the warning signal was noticed on the next knarr and passed on to the others. During the storm, each ship was on its own, and could only hope to not lose its bearings. "Prepare our people for the dance with Ran's wave-daughters! And stow the shadow needle safely. It won't help us now."

"How bad will it get?"

"Don't know." Erik rubbed his lower lip against his teeth. "I don't like the color of the water. No blue..."

Doubtful, the settlers listened to the pilot. The sun was still shining—what evil could the wind bring? But nobody dared resist his orders.

Together, they stretched a tarpaulin halfway across the hold to the mast tree. Below, the women gathered their children around them. Without being called, dogs, their tail tucked, sought a safe place among them. No barrel, box, or chicken basket was allowed to come free, and the animals' shackles were carefully checked. Erik positioned two chains of women and older children along the inner wall, equipping them with buckets to fight against any incoming water.

"Now, the storm can come!" Tyrkir showed himself undaunted. "Stay calm. We're prepared." But he thought, *How miserable our precautions are!* A ship was not a manor that could be fortified against an attacking enemy.

Finally, he bent his head under the tarpaulin and searched for Thjodhild. She had settled in close to the left wall with the children and had pulled Freydis and Thorvald closer to her sides. For a moment, their eyes met. With a quick smile, he climbed back up to the half-deck aft.

From the northeast, a large gray—and very soon blackening— cloud wedge approached, covering the sky, swallowing all brightness. The first gusts tore the spray from the waves, hurling it at the *Mount*.

"Tie me down," Erik roared. Twice, Tyrkir slipped on the planks. Finally, he managed to wrap the rope around his friend. He fell again, crawled to the spar, and fastened his own safety rope.

"Stay down! I'll manage—" The voice of the Red broke off. Behind him, a wave rose, sank, and in a renewed surge, forced the ship to dance over her back, spewing her foaming saliva at the front of the bow. Another wave was at her heels, rolling up and gurgling under the stern, making the ribs groan and grate.

*No more escape*, Tyrkir thought. *All we have left is to roll from one danger into the next.*

The game was too easy for the daughters of the sea goddess, the melody much too gentle. They were letting the storm draw breath. Erik seized the moment. "Half cloth!" His roar reached the men on the sail lines. He held the tiller with white fists, and although his *Mount* rolled, falling into valleys, and was thrown up crests, he did not lose the reins.

Full of rage, the storm started howling again. It became a terrible demon. The waves wrestled against each other, slamming together, diving under the keel in pairs, shaking the ship and trying to tear it apart.

As if from thin air, a gray-black wall rose on the right side of the ship. It grew higher, standing there for an awful moment, then collapsed with a thunderous roar. The water hit the sail, poured into the cargo hold, and washed over the bow and stern. The next wave threw the *Mount* forward into a trough and threw it up again like a nutshell. Rain whipped the sailors hard; the yard beam crashed more and more violently against the mast, and the sail kept flapping and rattling.

Time had lost its measure. At some point, Tyrkir noticed a servant lying motionless on the planks in front of him. The crew on the halyard was weakened! Without hesitation, he freed the injured man from the safety rope, pushed him toward the settlers in the cargo hold, and took his place himself. Only the shield on the railing stood between him and the daughters of Ran. They screamed, laughed, and spat spray over his head, relentlessly hammering and kicking at his ribs.

Was that a streak on the horizon, or was hope tricking him? Tyrkir closed his eyes, then opened them again. "The storm is clearing!" he shouted to the men next to him. They didn't understand. For them, there had only been the struggle for hours.

"There! Behind us!" Finally, the servants understood. "We'll make it!" The call rang out through the roar, reaching every man on board. "Yes, we'll make it," and with new courage, they leaned into the ropes.

Little by little, the storm calmed, driving the mass of clouds before it. *No matter which power gave the orders*, Tyrkir thought with relief, *now that it has wreaked its havoc, it must also clear.* Soon, a wide sky stretched over the *Mount*, and it rode across the waves as through a hilly landscape.

"Know-It-All." Erik was teetering with exhaustion. "I need to be relieved!" The friend was to check on the people in the hold. "I have to get blood in my arms first."

The salty, cold broth sloshed knee-high in the trenches to the right and left of the keel beam. The assigned farmers and slaves were still scooping tirelessly. Buckets wandered from hand to hand and were emptied over the gunwale. The men's faces were drawn, but they nodded to the pilot as if the rescue had been his doing. He called some maidservants to him: "First, take care of the wounded. Then tend to the cattle!"

Half bent, he pushed himself under the tarpaulin. There he was struck by a sour smell, a mixture of shit and vomit. His eyes slowly adjusted to the darkness. Women crawled around collecting blankets and fur sacks, trying to restore order as best they could. Children cried, and the more soothingly their mothers spoke to them, the louder the sobbing became. Tyrkir questioned one family after another and was grateful to find that no one had been seriously harmed, only suffering a few bumps and scrapes.

He found Thjodhild in the same place he'd last seen her. Pale and exhausted, she leaned against the wall. "Can I help you?" The two little ones lay head-to-head in her lap. Leif crouched next to her, holding a dog in his arms. Despite a bloody scratch across his forehead, he smiled bravely. "How many dragons were there?"

"I didn't count them."

"I saved this one." The five-year-old scratched the dog's shaggy fur. "Me, alone."

"That was very brave of you."

"But we are the winners, aren't we?"

"Don't say it out loud, my boy! You'll call back the ogres."

Thjodhild reached for her friend's hand and held it. "I've never been so afraid."

"It's over for today." To cheer her, he added, "As long as Erik is leading this ship, no storm can harm us. Be proud of your Viking!" Someone called for him. "You and the children should try to get some sleep. Who knows how long the sea will stay calm."

Happy, he returned to the aft deck. Along the way, he announced, "The women and children are safe!"

Erik stood with his back to him, broad-legged, high on the curved sternpost. He was staring east across the sea.

"Crew and passengers, all well. Only one injured. I think he'll be on his feet again tomorrow."

No answer came.

"Hey, aren't you glad? Luck was with us. We should be grateful."

The giant did not even turn his head. Tyrkir came closer and looked at him from the side. "What's happened?"

"Luck? Grateful?" With a sweep of his arm, Erik pointed to the sails of his torn fleet. "You can count, can't you? Tell me, how many knarrs do you see heading for us?" His voice became brittle. "Then tell me I'm lucky. Say it!"

"Oh gods," he whispered, hiding the wide scar under his hand as if to be protected from the truth.

Fourteen ships—as hard as he searched the horizon, there were no more. Fourteen, and before the storm, twenty-five had been sailing in the wake of the *Mount*. Even without asking, he knew what had upset Erik. Ran had stolen almost three hundred people with her net, along with cattle and provisions. "Perhaps they didn't all sink. Maybe some of them survived the storm and only drifted so far that we can't see them."

"If only it were so." The red one pressed his fists against his forehead. "It was I who promised them Greenland. A good life."

"Stop!" Tyrkir hissed. "It's a tragedy, yes, but it wasn't your fault. Focus on the survivors, nothing else! They trust you, I know it. If you doubt now, you take away their courage, and they need it as long as we're at sea. Once we've reached the coast, you'll have to prove all the more how firmly you believe in our happiness."

Erik took in a sharp breath. "And you, Know-It-All? How about you?"

"Well..." Tyrkir shrugged and forced a grin onto his face. "I already know what I have in you."

"Don't." Erik raised his fist, then gave the order to pull up the yard tree. Forward! The red sail inflated and drove the *Mount* farther west.

Yesterday had already been replaced three times by a new today. "When will Greenland finally come?" Leif put his fists on his hips.

"Tomorrow. But wait, I'll take a good look." To please his godson, Tyrkir pinched his left eye and squinted across his thumb at the horizon. "That's right. Maybe we'll discover land tomorrow."

"Uncle! That's what you said *yesterday*." The boy snorted and spat over the railing. *With* the wind, as he'd learned from the men. He spent most of his time here on the bow deck. His godfather had initiated him into the secret of the shadow needle. Much was still too difficult for him, but Tyrkir was amazed at the boy's curiosity and how quickly he learned. "Why don't you help me?"

Leif immediately kneeled beside the sun board. The sharp shadow had advanced in the circle of lines up to the north notch. He scratched his finger through his nonexistent beard. Finally, he was certain. "The sun almost stands in the south. Soon we have lunch."

"Very good. Off with you to your mother. When you've eaten, bring me some dried meat. But hurry!" With his teeth bared, Tyrkir approached the carved bow stem. "Otherwise, I'll have to bite off a piece of our dragon."

"Oh, Uncle." Leif waved him off. "You say that every time."

"That's right. It's about time I thought of something else." Smiling, the pilot looked after the boy as he jumped down into the cargo hold with an effortless leap.

"Land!" No one knew who had called it. Settlers and crew startled. Heads turned. "Land!" Some women grabbed their chests, then picked up their children and pushed to the bow. The flickering of joy was quickly snuffed out. "Land? This is supposed to be our land?"

"No, don't be fooled! We are still far from the coast." Tyrkir waved his arms. "Back! Get to work!" He pointed to the towering, blue-white rock formations. "Icebergs. You see? They float in the sea. They are the guardians of Greenland. Be patient!"

Patience? They'd been sailing for ten long days and bright nights, crowded together, the stench of men and cattle hardly bearable. Their disgust with salted meat grew with every meal; the same went for the softened bread and dried fish. And for a long time now, only the children had been given the tasty sour milk. Ten days in, fear and danger had gnawed away at even the strongest of spirits. The pilot heard the fearful questions murmured from every side: Why was it taking so long? Had the storm drifted them too far off course? Why else would there be icebergs?

"People, have confidence! We're on the right course." His tone became impatient. "And now, go!" The settlers obeyed without grumbling, but he knew the doubts were there, and no command could dispel them.

Leif had already given up two days ago. He no longer asked when they would arrive. Now, with a wrinkled nose, he stared at the icebergs on either side of the knarr. Finally, he shook his head. "I don't understand. They are so far away and very quiet. I'm not afraid of them."

Tyrkir stood tall next to the dragon's head. Before he answered, he gave a signal to his friend astern to change course.

"Come here! What you see over there are just the hats of the giants. But down there in the water, their shoulders are seven times as wide. They turn, and sometimes even rub against each other. And gods forbid if a ship gets in between them. They also clench their fists just below the surface. And believe me, they don't have just two fists."

At that moment, an enormous thundering wall broke off the iceberg on the right and collapsed.

"Danger! Hold on tight! Danger!" Tyrkir shouted his warning across the ship until his throat was hoarse. "Lie down! Danger! Hang on!" He had already torn the boy away from the bow, pressing him onto the planks and throwing himself over him.

The ice wall had dipped into the sea, and after a seething suction, a flood wave rose. Erik managed to turn the *Mount* halfway before it was hit. The ribs screamed and groaned, and the mast and sail swayed. For one breath, they all saw death. Then the knarr righted herself again.

Without letting go of Leif, Tyrkir raised his head. They'd come dangerously close to the iceberg on the other side. "To starboard!" His signal to Erik came too late; he'd already changed course again.

"Thanks to the great Tyr," the German gasped.

"I wasn't afraid." Leif snorted but forgot to spit.

"Is that true?"

The boy nodded. "I couldn't be. You were lying on top of me, so I couldn't see anything."

Around midnight, the horizon before them turned into a vast gray mountain. Tyrkir refrained from tearing the settlers from their sleep with the call of "Land!" and forbade the sail guards to scream. Discreetly, he signaled Erik to join him on the bow deck.

"There's your green land. This is the most difficult part of our journey: What do you want to tell the people?"

"Not a word."

"But you can't hide it from them any longer."

"Damn it, I know that. We're not there yet. They'll see soon enough." Red grabbed Tyrkir hard by the shoulders. "From now on, I won't give people the chance to think. I will suffocate even the slightest sign of unrest. So be afraid of me. After all, you're my friend."

Even before sunrise, every settler family onboard knew—land was in sight. They stared silently at the endless white wall with its countless snowcapped peaks. Even when the mountains gleamed in the morning light, there was no cheering.

Erik gathered the landowners and the free farmers under the mast tree. "One thing you should know: we are now safe from Ran and her daughters."

Without any enthusiasm, the men looked across to the jagged, dark coastal strip. The closer they came, the more inhospitable it appeared.

"Yes, this all belongs to our country, but it is not my Greenland. That is only the backside, you understand? We will sail southward, and on the other side, you'll see its beautiful face. That's where you'll find the green meadows I promised you."

His wooing was not heard by the frustrated farmers. Erik straightened to his full height, a cold light in the amber of his eyes. "Until then, I demand obedience. No restlessness. No whispering among you. If you have any questions, go to the pilot or come to me. Swear it!" Some raised their hands immediately—they knew the law onboard. The others were prompted by another hard look from the skipper. "And now, be grateful that you live." Erik left them standing there and walked back onto the steering deck.

Though his comments had not been addressed to the women, his words soon reached them. Thjodhild tore at Tyrkir's arm. "How dare you?" she said, teeth clenched. "You've already lied to me once. Now..."

"I can explain, but not now. Please. Talk to Erik first. I have to set a new course." He quickly climbed onto the bow deck and bent over the sun board.

With her fists hidden in the pleats of her skirt, Thjodhild approached her husband. "I have to talk to you. Alone." Her expression allowed no objection. He immediately sent the helmsman away and took the tiller himself. "Where are you taking me?"

"To our new home."

"The land there..." She heaved a deep sigh. "Erik, I see only stones, rocks, and reefs—and nothing above but ice and snow. This coast looks even more hostile than the steep beach you lured me to after our marriage with false promises!"

"This is different."

"Erik Thorvaldsson, you have not told the truth. *Again*. And this time, it's not just me." Angry, she pointed to the following sails. "This time is different, and much worse. All the dead are accusing you. How will you stand before the settlers?"

"Silence!"

"No, Erik!" She put her hand in front of her mouth, and barely controlling herself, she whispered, "Why Greenland? Why did you call this icy wilderness that?"

"Because otherwise..." He smiled thinly. "Well, I thought when people heard a nice name, they'd want to go there."

Stunned, she stared at him, tears running down her face. "Even without this deception, I would have followed you and Tyrkir, because we are a family. And if we have to perish there, it would have been the end of Erik Thorvaldsson's clan. But now . . . a whole people? No one should take such guilt upon himself."

"Come closer," Erik said, his voice gentle, "because I cannot leave this place." As well as he could, he wiped the tears from her cheek. "You really would have gone with me no matter what?" He sighed deeply. "Then, the effort was not in vain."

"What are you talking about?"

"I told you the truth. Maybe not quite all of it, I admit, but in a week, I'll show you our green meadows."

"You mean . . ." She clasped her hands and looked into his eyes. "No, you wouldn't lie like that. Or . . . ?"

Thjodhild left him the rudder, looking indecisively toward the bow. Tyrkir was telling his godson something. He rolled his eyes, crumpled his face, and Leif laughed brightly, beaming at him. *Not now*, she decided. *I'll ask him later. If the green country takes too long to reach.*

The storm had driven the settlers' fleet far off course, that much soon became clear to the two friends. On their first trip, there'd been many more icebergs lurking near the coast.

"We are much farther south than I expected," Tyrkir said after one day had passed, and the following noon, Erik came to him on the bow deck. He shielded his eyes from the sun, grinning. "I knew it. Fate is with us."

Before them, the sea was free of ice. "Full sail!"

Their journey turned into a wild rushing party. Driven by a stiff wind, the *Mount* rode around the southern tip and pulled the formation behind it, leading it safely into the mouth of a fjord.

The sails dropped with the yard beams, and no more spray splashed up at the dragon's heads. But before the last cloth was recovered, Erik was already delivering his instructions through the funnel of his hands. All skippers were forbidden to drop anchor. No dinghy was allowed to go to the rocky shore. "We are not at our destination!"

This was a short respite, nothing more. Erik took the onslaught of curses and threats stone-faced. "I have command! Without me, you'll never see green land."

He had his ship row alongside Herjulf's knarr. "Remember this entrance, friend!"

Not much farther down the fjord, there was a protected harbor. On its shore, he had marked out a settlement for Herjulf, who was an experienced trader. They'd already agreed back in Iceland that Herjulf was to erect large storage halls there in addition to his dwelling house. "You will lead the most important trading post in my Greenland. And believe me, I have chosen this place well!"

No matter where the merchants came from, whether from England, the Hebrides, Denmark, or Norway, they would first go ashore here, and they'd be able to store their goods. Herjulf was instantly thrilled by this offer. His only son, Bjarne, had long been sailing the seas as a wholesaler in his stead, and Herjulf felt too old for a new beginning with just a few cattle. But the prospect of being able to set up a new business here in Greenland gave him a fresh surge of strength.

"Set the sails!"

The future master of the trade settlement rejoined the formation. He would return to his Herjulfsfjord only after he'd set down the families entrusted to him and his knarr.

Although no more icy winds were driving the ships north along the west side, the hopes of the emigrants froze from hour to hour. As much as they searched the coast between craggy rocks and scree beaches, they had not yet discovered usable land to provide a living for even three families.

Leif climbed the bow deck. "Should we set the course?"

"No longer necessary," his uncle replied without turning to him. "The shore shows us the way now."

"Even the water below us is greener than the rocks over there."

"Quiet! Even the son of the leader is forbidden to grumble." Tyrkir suppressed a smile and pulled Leif closer to his side. "But I promise you, soon it will be time, and then you'll be amazed."

"Oh, Uncle, you can tell that to Thorvald and Freydis." Indulgently he patted his godfather's hand. "I'm not angry with you, even if you don't know."

"Very kind, my boy."

The steep shore receded into a wide bay, and they sailed past many fjord mouths. Yet not much changed. It was still all lichen-covered reefs and skerries in front of dead rock faces. For a long time, the emigrants sat in the cargo hold silently without looking at each other. Even their dogs no longer raised their muzzles.

Thjodhild could no longer endure the silent accusations of the mothers around her. *Whatever misfortune awaits us*, she thought, *I must have clarity, and I must have it now.* She would only hear new excuses from Erik, so she climbed up to Tyrkir.

"I was just hoping that you would be here next to me," he told her. "We're about to heave to."

Thjodhild waited until the dragon's head was directly pointing toward the mouth of a wide fjord and Tyrkir had signaled the knarr behind them. Then she said to Leif, "Go watch your brother and sister."

"I can't do that." Her eldest tore the wool cap off his head. "Uncle needs me."

She was too tired for a fight. "Never mind, then, but squat down and cover your ears. I want to talk to your godfather."

As he sat on the planks with his back to them, his legs dangling into the cargo hold, she began quietly. "Which demon met you on the first journey and took possession of you? Only those possessed by Loki would dare to lead so many people into misery."

The scar turned bloodred. "Have faith! Just for a little while longer."

"Tyrkir!"

He pointed to the flat shore to the right and left of the entrance. "There—look closely. Those are tree trunks, the best hard driftwood for building houses. Just over there is more than we found on the whole coast of Hawk Valley in one summer. And believe me, every fjord..."

"No more!" she warned, staring into his eyes. "I never imagined you could lie like this." After a pause, she added, "And this from you, my best friend."

"Please don't say that." His lips trembled. "Words can hurt more than any knife, and the wounds heal badly." He quickly turned away, put his hand on the neck of the dragon, and fixed his gaze ahead.

Thjodhild sat down close to her son. *Even if it hurts me, yes, I wanted to hurt you because I hoped I could shake you awake*, she thought. *Now, I'm more helpless than before.*

With the wind of the open sea still behind it, the knarr rushed deeper and deeper into the interior. Shortly before a sharp turn to the right, Tyrkir gave the signal aft to slow down, but Erik waved back angrily, and the servants on the lines were ordered to hoist the full cloth.

His ship flew away from the convoy, leaned low over port, and with foamy spray in front of the dragon's mouth, it rose up again after the bend.

In an instant, the wind was gone. Thjodhild had pressed Leif firmly to her side. Now that the maneuver seemed to be over, she cursed her husband at the tiller, and she was already on her knees, turning angrily to Tyrkir.

Her raised fist froze as she felt a sting. The pain in her chest didn't want to stop. Tyrkir was no longer standing amid dark rock walls. He was now surrounded by brightness. A hilly landscape opened in front of the bow stem, an expanse of green pastures.

Thjodhild let her arm drop. *Are those forests, there, on the left bank? Birches, yes, they must be birches*, she thought. But they were taller than in Hawk Valley. She felt hot and slowly opened her greasy rain cape. *It is not my blood*, she noticed. *It's the sun.*

"Mother?" Leif gently shook her arm. "Why don't you get up?"

"Because I..." She kissed the boy on his forehead, nose, mouth, and cheeks. "Because I can get to you better this way."

Outraged, he tore himself away. "I'm no longer a child."

"All right, all right." She looked up at her friend. "And because I was so stupid." She grabbed his hand and let herself be helped up. "You asked for blind faith. Do you know how hard that is? I just couldn't bear the uncertainty anymore. Forgive me!"

Before Tyrkir could answer, Leif pushed himself between the two and put his fists on his hips. "Uncle, I think we did well. Our course was right."

"Thanks to the great Tyr and, of course, to you. Without you, we would certainly have gotten lost at sea."

In the meantime, the settlers were also beginning to take in the new surroundings. Some rubbed their eyes. Others groped for their neighbors. Finally, cheers gradually blossomed from their silent amazement, soon to be drowned out by the deep, long calls of the horns. Like an echo, they were answered by the next knarr and were quickly multiplied by the ships that followed.

"Our green land! Our Greenland!" The emigrants greeted their new homeland with laughter and tears, waving at the lush meadows as if invisible relatives had gathered there for their arrival.

Thjodhild climbed onto the steering deck. "A free arm is not enough for me. Call the boatman to relieve you."

A little later, she snuggled into her husband's chest, and Erik held her tight. "Even if it was hard," he muttered, "it was worth this."

"Don't let go," she whispered. "At least, until I stop crying."

The wind calmed more and more. The oars were pushed through the portholes. As if driven by long caterpillar legs, the dragon boats ventured deeper into the heart of the summer landscape. Groups of islands appeared, tributaries branched off, and Erik gave them one after the other to the rich skippers. "Ketil, this fjord shall bear your name. Establish your farm and live in peace with your neighbors." He would recognize the borders of his lands by the stone markings that the Red had already erected with Tyrkir on their first journey.

They had also provided for every free farmer. There were no big farewells. The settlers left one by one after a brief plea to the gods to accompany the new venture with benevolence, and the firm promise to come to the Eriksfarm next June for the first Thing of the Greenlanders.

Around noon the next day, only the knarr of Ingolf Arnesson was still following the *Mount*. The last smallholders had been set down along the way with their household goods and cattle; people beaming with happiness waved from the shore after the two ships. And the water turned blue green, the hills became gentler. Far to the east, the mighty back of the endless ice giants glittered and glistened.

Erik had chosen the family of the black-bearded Ingolf as his closest neighbors. He hoped to get along with this open, warm man. His wife, Solveig, had a son and two pigtailed girls the ages of Thjodhild's children. Surely, the women would soon become close.

"I thought of everything. And my realm is in order," said Erik proudly. He left the tiller and led Thjodhild forward to Tyrkir. Together, they stood close while the knarr entered the sun-drenched, wide bay at the end of the fjord. With a sweeping gesture, the giant pointed up to a hill on their left. "Up there! It's not ready, but soon."

She saw a long, stretched roof overgrown with deep green grass, and because she couldn't speak, she just smiled.

The ship went alongside the shore, the anchor fell, and Thjodhild and the two little ones were rowed to land through the shallow water. "I will greet our home alone," she said. She took Freydis in her arms, and Thorvald stomped behind her across the vast pebble beach.

The ascent was slow. *I have time, from now on time no longer runs from me.* Later, Thjodhild wanted to visit the house with the men. She discovered a brook and sat down in the grass. The children crawled around, giggling and picking bellflowers. Thjodhild took in the blue bay, the sky. She closed her eyes, but the smell of freshness and summer continued to paint the picture in her mind. *Happiness.* She sighed. *Come sit with me and hold me tight!*

# TO BE READ FROM THE RUNE STONE OF REMEMBRANCE:

As if hastily etched, the symbols stand close together.

**... THE YEAR 986:** ... Death ... Denmark. Prince Sven Forkbeard doesn't want to wait for his inheritance. He demands half the empire and power from his father immediately. King Harald Blue Tooth rejects the demand of his unloved son. Sven prepares to rise up against the eighty-year-old. An agonizing battle breaks out. More and more people run to the king, and finally, the son has to seek salvation in flight. But an arrow has pierced the old ruler's chest. Harald dies ... Long live King Sven Forkbeard ...

**... THE YEAR 994:** A hundred longships emerge from the morning fog off London. Sven Forkbeard and Olaf Tryggvasson command the fleet. They do not attack but make the king and his people tremble. A raid by the barbaric hordes must be expected. The reckoning works. To spare London, the English king pays the Vikings the incredible sum of 10,000 pounds of silver. No blood has flowed, and yet the treasure chests overflow.

**... THE YEAR 994:** Olaf Tryggvasson enjoys his success. He hears about a fortune-teller and visits him in his hermitage. "You will become a famous king ... You will bring the Christian faith to many men ..." The wise man closes his eyes. "So that you do not doubt, pay attention to the signs: When you return to the ship, some of the crew will rebel against you. You will receive a deep wound. But after seven days, you'll be able to leave your bed, once again healthy, and will then be baptized."

The prophecy comes true. In battle, Olaf is struck, and after a week, the wound is healed. The prince asks where the soothsayer had gotten his gift.

"God himself has given it to me…" The hermit tells him of the omnipotence of the Lord. Deeply impressed, Olaf Tryggvasson has himself and his entourage baptized that same day.

… **THE YEAR 994**: Messengers from Norway come to Olaf. They implore him to wrest power from the smug Jarl Hakon. "You come from the old blood. You are entitled to the crown. Be our king!"

After a night of prayer, Olaf sets sail. With five ships, one hundred and twenty warriors, and a considerable number of priests and learned men, he lands on the coast of his ancestral homeland in late summer.

… **THE YEAR 994**: Jarl Hakon is on the run, not only from Olaf but from the raging farmers from whom he has taken women. He hides with his servant in a pit under a pigsty. Plagued by nightmares, the servant pushes a knife through his master's throat. Jarl Hakon is dead. Without a fight, Olaf Tryggvasson is proclaimed king over Norway by the Thing…

… **FROM THE SETTLERS IN GREENLAND**: After the first hard years, life blossoms. The warm summer compensates for the harsh winter when ice winds descend from the glacier and freeze the fjords. More and more emigrants from Iceland and Norway are looking for a new home in the green land of Gode Erik Thorvaldsson. But from the fifth year on, the Red rejects them.

"There is no place for you to settle down here in the south." He sends the ships two days farther north. There he'd already discovered a second habitable fjord area on his first trip with Tyrkir the German. "Take land in my western settlement and keep peace with your neighbors!"

... **THE YEAR 996:** Already at the beginning of April the hot foehn winds come, break the ice cover in the Erik's Bay, and melt the snow on the heights. In mid-May, the grass, green birches, and pastures sprout.

# FREYDIS

The ravens had fallen silent and were no longer croaking from their clutches in the rocky mountain. They'd become accustomed to the men deep down between the bushes and birches. Tyrkir crouched behind a bush, hardly daring to breathe.

At last. The waiting had been worth it. As Leif had predicted, a reindeer stag stepped up to the clearing. His ears twitching, he checked the weather with his head back, and after he had chosen the juiciest spot of grass for himself, his herd was allowed to follow him.

Neither hunting nor fishing were Tyrkir's favorite pastimes, and he was happy to let others go through the trouble. Still, today he had been urged by his godson: "Come with me, Uncle. You'll bring me luck!" Tyrkir rubbed his scar. *I can't refuse anything to this young lad*, he thought. *And since Erik has promised Leif his knarr for his first trading trip, my peace is utterly ruined.*

For two years, Leif had been buying polar bear pelts, seal skins, and walrus tusks from the fishing troops when they returned with their hauls from the far north. He had even been able to acquire three of the long, white, miraculously twisted skewers of the narwhal. His godfather always had to be present at the conclusion of every deal. "You bring me luck."

What's more, Leif admired his godfather's carving. "We can find you plenty of soapstone. How about you . . . ?"

And Tyrkir started making pots, cups, and lamps in his workshop. Because this work soon became too dull for him, he'd recruited skillful slaves who learned to handle the soft stone under his guidance. Tyrkir went on carving artfully decorated brooches and figures from ivory or bone. But a walrus-tooth belt became his showpiece.

"Uncle, we'll make a fortune at the royal court in Norway."

Tyrkir admired the scene in front of him in the clearing: the reindeers silently lowering and lifting their heads, their branched antlers resembling a forest in winter. Next to the stag, he could see fourteen cows with some young animals. *So there are fifteen strong deer, as many winters as my Leif has now,* he noted. *Perhaps it's a good omen for today.*

"Hej! Yes! Hej!" The call tore through the peace. "Hej! Yay! Hej!" Servants broke out of the bushes from three sides. Dogs barked. The herd was startled, and with only one direction unobstructed, they fled down the valley.

Tyrkir ran after the drivers and the pack without hurrying. Leif had prepared the hunting trap. He'd positioned servants on both sides of the sloping escape lane at regular intervals. They were all screaming loudly, swinging their clubs. The herd didn't dare to break out. Rushed by the high-legged hunting dogs, they fled from the woods into a steeply sloping pasture. Rows of stones closed in on them from both sides.

Already, there was hardly any room, and the animals snorted and collided with one another. Antlers broke as they pushed forward wanting to reach the narrow opening first. And one after the other, they disappeared! There was no escape: the stone funnel ended at a cliff, and in their fear, all the animals jumped over the edge.

By the time Tyrkir reached the prey area below the stone wall, the carcasses were lying next to each other, horns removed, and guts broken open. Ravens were already squatting nearby, hungrily waiting for the bloody intestines.

"Uncle! I knew why I wanted you with me." Leif beamed. "So many skins in one day. Not to mention the meat. Mother will be amazed."

"As long as you don't plan to put reindeer ham on the goods list for Norway now, I'm happy about your hunting success."

Leif briefly scratched his reddish chin fluff. "It might be worth considering."

"By the great Tyr, forget it immediately!"

"Just kidding." Leif waved it off, making sure that the liver, heart, and lungs were put back into the reindeers' bellies. "I'm ready, Uncle. Let's ride ahead to the escarpment." The slaves had to drag the booty home on foot via wooden racks, and that would surely take until the afternoon.

No more Erikshof. Because the house and the farm buildings were erected high above the bay on a broad plane, the property of the Gode Erik Thorvaldsson had been named Steep Slope.

During the ride home, Leif raved about the Norwegian trip at the end of May, and Tyrkir limited himself to simple yeses or nos. Even that was enough to make the young man's plans grow ever bigger.

*You are so like your father,* Tyrkir thought, troubled. *And if your hopes do not come true, you'll ask me how to carry on.* He looked at Leif from the corner of his eye. *No, you are not just the son of my Viking. You have his strength, too. Perhaps even the hair. But your eyes, your bearing, and above all, your movements, remind me of Thjodhild. Besides, you don't share your father's temper and sense of honor. Instead, you weigh the possibilities before you act. Maybe—* Tyrkir smiled at himself—*perhaps you've gotten that quality from me?*

Shortly after they'd ridden down to the pastures, Leif fell silent and bridled his horse. "Do you hear that?"

Tyrkir frowned and nodded. Strange clapping was coming from

the nearby juniper bushes. A child howled, immediately followed by giggling, and again they heard the clapping.

"I know those voices." Both men were already dismounted, creeping to the first bush and peering through the branches. Freydis stood in front of her younger brother. She held out the folded palms of her hands to him. "Now you."

"I don't want to play anymore," Thorstein cursed.

"You have to, or I'll beat you up." With red glowing cheeks, the boy obeyed, pressed his hands together, and bravely held them up to his sister's fingertips. After a short sniff, he struck out at Freydis's hand, but caught nothing more than air.

"You silly!" She giggled cheerfully. "I'll show you again." Freydis won her game. Before Thorstein could avoid it, she slapped him in the face from the right and left so that his head flew back and forth. The seven-year-old howled more from anger than from pain.

"It's your turn," demanded the sister.

Even the bravest should not fight against a superior power. Sobbing, Thorstein hid his arms behind his back. "I don't like this game!"

"I'll show you how good this game is." Freydis struck out, but someone grabbed her wrist.

"Don't you dare!"

She tore her head around.

"Let me play, half sister!" Leif strengthened his grip, and without losing his smile, forced her to her knees. "Come on, get up!"

"Ouch! You're breaking my arm."

"I'm sorry about that." He half pulled her up and released her with a light push. Freydis fell into the grass on her belly. "Sorry."

Immediately, Freydis was on her feet again. "No, you liked it because I'm weaker. And don't you dare call me half sister again. I'm worth as much in our family as you and Thorvald and that little runt there!" Trembling with anger, she pushed the blond curls from her face. "He who strikes a woman is a coward. A mangy dog. One, one..."

Before she could come up with her next curse, Leif said, "Too bad."

"What?" She paused, bewildered.

Leif looked down at her, sighed, and shook his head slightly.

"What do you mean by that?"

"Those slender legs. Nobody would believe that you count only twelve winters. Oh, and those brown eyes. You really are already a beautiful woman."

His flattery softened her expression.

"Only, Sister, as soon as you open your pretty mouth, every suitor will tuck his tail and run."

He quickly moved aside, and her punches missed their mark. "You! You damn dog!" Freydis turned away, stomping, and finally burst into tears.

Tyrkir had taken little Thorstein aside and was now stroking his head. "Well, how about it? Do you want to go with me on my horse?" The boy nodded, and they both went ahead.

"Peace?" Leif cleared his throat audibly. "My horse also carries two. We had a great hunt today. It would be a pity if you missed the arrival of the servants."

Without answering, Freydis ran off, Leif hurrying behind her. However, when she reached the horses, she stopped before Tyrkir and her little brother. Then, gathering her smock dress, she swung herself into the saddle and took off. Leif shouted after her. She laughed, making a wide arc through the meadow before returning. "What is it, Brother? Shall I take you with me?"

"Bitch!"

He climbed up behind her and took the reins. After a while, she leaned against his chest. "And yet I'll find a husband. With my dowry, maybe even a rich one. Wait and see. When you come back from your trip, I might already have one."

"So how many years do I have to be away so that—" When she stiffened and pressed the tip of her knife against his thigh, he wisely chose not to continue.

The news spread like wildfire through the stables, barns, and workshops. "Leif killed a whole herd!" And when the sweat-drenched drivers came dragging the loaded racks to the yard, the servants gathered around to admire the haul. Even Thjodhild came with Thorstein and the kitchen maids from the house to see. Though the little boy's cheeks were still red from the slaps in the face, he now had cream around his mouth. His mother had sweetened his defeat.

"I'm proud of you." She touched the arm of her eldest, and he stroked her hand gently. This small gesture was silent proof of how deeply son and mother understood each other. Leif looked around the clearing. "Where's Father?"

"Where do you think?" She jabbed her thumb over her shoulder toward the heights far behind the yard. "He's building his dam."

"Too bad. I would have liked him to see today's success. But we can't wait that long."

Friendly but determined, Leif sent the servants back to work, ordered his drivers to bring the loot to the slaughterhouse, and followed after them. Thjodhild stayed behind with Tyrkir. "He's become a strong man," she said thoughtfully. "Yet, he is still so young. It's good that you're accompanying him on his journey."

"Don't worry. When you and I met, I was only two winters older than he is now."

"Yes, do you remember? At the market by the Hvammsfjord? I can still see you right in front of me. Weedy, shaved head, and all those freckles. At first, I was outraged that a slave was looking at me from the side. That look..."

"Weedy? Even in comparison to Erik, I wouldn't have called myself that, not even then. Slender, maybe?" Tyrkir smiled. "And today, so many years later, I've gained a belly and lost half my face."

"Hard to believe you're still vain." She reached for her forehead and pulled a strand from under her cap. "And who am I to criticize? Here, you see? They're turning gray."

"Silver," he corrected. "Silver streaks. And with them, you've grown even more valuable."

They looked at each other. Thjodhild masked her awkwardness with a laugh. "We're chatting here as if there's nothing to do. Tonight, there must be a small feast in Leif's honor. I'll send Thorvald over to Ingolf. He should invite his family. How about it? You could put some of your brew on the table."

Tyrkir crossed his arms. "It's wine. I admit that it doesn't taste as good as the one made from grapes, but it's better than nothing."

"Don't be offended!" she scolded. "You men are such sensitive creatures. Erik's trying to dam our stream so that we have enough water for the house pastures, even in dry weather, but every winter, the melting snow washes away his dam, and every summer he starts anew. Yet cursed be anyone who dares to say even one word against his plan. And you? The wise and indulgent Tyrkir? As soon as it's about your wine, you can't stand even the slightest criticism."

"I can if it is from you."

"Well, I don't know about that," she teased, then became serious. "But maybe I'm being unfair. This is where I gave birth to Thorstein, my little Greenlander, and we live in peace with our neighbors. If I think back to all the terrible fights and fears in Iceland, I should really be grateful that a dam is being built and wine is being produced."

Tyrkir watched her as she walked back to the house with a

spring in her step. *It's true*, he thought. *Happiness is finally with us. It has been for a while now.* "And besides, my wine is good," he murmured. He started walking to the cellar he'd dug out for its storage. "At least there's none better in Greenland."

Tyrkir had worked hard trying to make an intoxicating drink over the past years. In the beginning, it was just out of pride. Erik was always in his ears: "Know-It-All, you have to keep your word. Sour milk and water dry out my throat. You came before my father and claimed that you had learned something about winemaking as a child down on the Rhine. That's the only reason the old man didn't kick you off the farm. Now, prove it!"

There was no barley for beer, unless it was bought at a high price from the merchants. There was not enough honey to ferment mead. So Tyrkir had first tried his hand at using roots and the juice of the birch trees, producing a bittersweet swill that barely gave a buzz but kept the head in a fog for days. These failures awakened his passion. Black crowberries—there were enough of them in the mountain meadows, and with only a little goodwill, his berry wine even tasted decent.

From the slaughterhouse wafted the smell of blood and raw meat. The innards were steaming in vats. Leif had assigned only the most experienced servants to cut up the meat. They worked hand in hand—two separated the heads, the next tied each carcass by its hind legs to the top of the wooden rack. Quick, safe cuts, and starting at the hooves, the valuable fur was pulled down slowly. Then the body was divided, and the halves delivered to the servants at the long meat bench. There was no cheering, despite their delight over the successful hunt. To slaughter an animal demanded quiet reverence.

Freydis followed Leif as he oversaw the work. Whether he went looking for hooks in the smokehouse, brought salt pots, or was giving instructions to the servants, Freydis stayed close behind him. Finally, she pulled Leif aside. "Let me, please. Just once, me alone. Please!"

Astonished, he looked into her flushed face. "Let you what?"

Her voice trembled. "Just one of the young animals."

"Tell me exactly what you want."

A strange light flickered in her eyes. Freydis moistened her lips with the tip of her tongue and pulled out her little dagger. "Cut off a head."

"You are—" Leif started again. "Why, by Loki? Our people do the work, and they do it better."

"How do you know if you don't let me try?" She puffed out her chest. "You can watch, and if I make a mistake, you can help me."

He scratched his chin fluff, then found his confidence again. "Well, okay. But not with this toy. You need a dagger with a long blade."

"You are the dearest brother I have." Freydis ran ahead and selected the smallest of the deer. After Leif handed her the sharp tool, she squatted astride the animal and took the body firmly between her thighs. She stroked her free hand up the neck. Her brother was forgotten, his advice did not reach her, as she pricked under the ear. During the cut, she grunted as the blade met with resistance; she had to hack several times until the head was finally off.

Freydis remained bent over the corpse, and abruptly her shoulders relaxed. As she stood up, the strange light in her dark eyes had gone out. She looked at her brother with a soft smile. "Thank you. Did I do it right?"

"Not bad for the first time." He carefully took the knife out of her hand. "Now bring the bucket with the liver into the kitchen. Mother must be waiting for it."

"I'd love to."

Leif stared after her. She happily let the tub swing back and forth by the carrying strap. "I can't figure you out," he whispered. "Such a beautiful girl, but whoever marries you, I don't envy him. He'd better be on his guard all the time."

Grilled liver had been prepared on the griddle over the cooking pit. Before the rare delicacy was brought in, it tickled noses and made mouths water. Guests and hosts had enjoyed the smell like an appetizer. When the steaming pieces were finally placed in front of them, there was no sound but the rattling of knives and the pleasurable smacking of lips, until only the smell of grilled liver remained.

Erik burped, licked his dripping fingers, and lifted the drinking horn. "Blessed is the lord who has such a housewife!" The adults joined in his toast. Erik did not yet put the vessel to his lips but looked sharply over to the young people.

Freydis and Thorvald were chatting happily with the blond daughters of his neighbor. They hadn't met for a long time and were bubbling over with news. Ingva counted fourteen winters, and Sigrid had just celebrated her thirteenth birthday—two lively, freckled girls who liked to laugh too much.

"Silence!"

Heads spun around.

"Thank Thor!" Erik nodded with relief. "At least now I know you're not completely deaf. Now, from the beginning, so you may learn." He rose from his seat. His beard was reddish gray, as was his hair. His figure had become even fuller, granting the giant the necessary respect, even without words.

The young people jumped up obediently. The girls' parents exchanged an appreciative look with the hostess and followed his example. Leif blinked at Egil, who was the same age as him. Both stood next to Tyrkir and tried not to interrupt the landowner again.

"Thanks be to the gods for loving our land and for providing enough food for man and beast." He called Thor, Odin, and Baldur, and praised their merits at length.

Tyrkir thought, *How you have changed, my Viking. The older you get, the longer your eulogies get.*

"But my thanks go not only to the Aesir in Valhalla. They also go to the cook who prepared this tasty meal for us." Finally, he lifted the drinking horn again. "Blessed is the lord who has such a housewife by his side. A toast to my beloved Thjodhild."

Young and old joined in. Together, they emptied their drinking horns and cups. Erik looked to the neighboring table. The adolescents had sat down quickly and were whispering with each other again. "You must be taught some discipline," he grumbled, then made a face. "A toast with sour milk does not work. How about it, Know-It-All? I think we should try that again with wine."

"But only if you don't start with the gods again."

"Don't you dare..."

"Peace," Tyrkir interrupted him sharply, "or there won't be a drop of my berry wine, sir!"

"Be glad we have guests, sir!"

Ingolf and Solveig held their breath. Only when the two friends grinned, and Thjodhild shook her head, smiling with raised eyebrows, did the neighbors relax. There was no quarrel, only friends teasing each other.

After the second sip, Erik brought the conversation to his dam construction and the dream of soon being able to water the meadows throughout the summer. Ingolf Arnesson listened to him with great interest. "If you succeed, then I'll try to dam up my stream. But I don't understand how—"

"Patience! At the next Thing, I'll ask all the landowners to look at my first dam."

Tyrkir raised his eyebrows. "So soon? You really think you'll have the wall finished by then?"

"You take the boy to Norway, and when you come back, you'll be amazed!" Erik turned to Ingolf. "This is how it works." He dunked his finger in the drinking horn and painted the stream and dam on the wooden plate for him. "The water comes from above and here between the rocks..."

Thjodhild discreetly moved away with the neighbor's wife. Erik had found a willing victim, and his explanations would fill the evening as always. The two young men also slowly moved their stools away from the table and turned their backs to the old men.

"Have you heard," Egil whispered. "Farther to the west, there is supposed to be more land."

"Who told you that?"

"A merchant, and he was told by Bjarne, the son of old Herjulf down in the trading post. Bjarne has seen the land."

"Only seen?" They stuck their heads closer together.

"That's it. He didn't step on it." Egil rubbed his hands. "It can't be far, maybe three days. Well, how about it? Don't you want to look for it? You now have the knarr from your father."

"For one trip, that's all. And I'm going to Norway with my uncle." Before Leif continued, he looked around stealthily. "I'm curious all right, though. Imagine if I discovered a new country like my father. Maybe I could..." He grabbed Egil's wrist. "Let's assume my business at the royal court is successful and Father is happy with me. Why shouldn't he give me his ship for a second voyage? And if the wind then drives me west, what can I do about it? Do you understand?"

"But you have to take me with you."

"You have my word. And until then, you won't tell anyone about this new country. I don't want anyone to beat me to it. Promise?"

Egil grasped Leif's wrist, and with firm pressure, they sealed the oath.

Nobody at the table was talking to Freydis anymore. Her expression revealed what she thought: *Horny Thorvald speaks to Sigrid as if he wanted to sell her honey and then eat it with her. And Ingva has had that cow look for some time now.* Freydis followed her eyes and the corners of her mouth twitched. The cow's eyes were on Leif.

"What are you staring at?" She jerked the girl's pigtail. "Hey, your eyes are about to fall out."

"Sorry. I . . . I was thinking."

"Oh, that's what you call it." Smoothly, Freydis moved closer. "Want to know a secret? In two weeks, my brother will sail across the sea to the king. Do you know what that means? There, he'll get to know the good life. There are noblewomen with such tits, the men sit under them when it rains. We can't compete. Who knows if he'll want to come back at all, so better get him out of your thoughts."

"Why would you say something like that?" Ingva hung her head. "I haven't told anyone anything."

"I'm just smart."

After a moment, Ingva collected herself. "No, I don't believe you. Leif will come back."

"And another thing about my brother: He beats women. Even me, his little sister. Be glad if my father doesn't talk to yours about marriage."

"Stop it, please!"

Before Ingva started to cry, Freydis generously gave her more sour milk. "Come on, drink up! I'm only trying to help because you're my friend."

Later that night, Erik lay down next to Thjodhild, still hazy from the sweet berry wine. He stroked her back. "You're beautiful. Such soft skin. You're my beautiful wife."

"Not now," she said. "I'm tired." *And we don't have to worry about having children anymore. My life would be better now if you could just wait until I also want you.*

When he pulled his hand back, she turned to him. "Today was a long, good day, don't you think? Let me fall asleep in your arms."

He did not push her any further. For a while, he stared into the dark silence of the chamber, then mumbled, "Yes, you're right. We have a good life."

At the beginning of June, the *Mount of the Sea* was loaded. Six boatmen stood on each side of the boat, holding the long rowing poles upright in their fists like guards. Veils of mist were still wafting over the bay. On the beach, Erik Thorvaldsson had beheaded a live chicken. He offered it to the goddess Ran in the presence of his whole family and the neighbor's family. Blood was still dripping from the feathered body.

Leif came and caught some drops with his silver Thor's hammer. He solemnly sank on his knee and lifted the amulet by the chain. "My good, divine friend! Stand by us with your strength." He remained silent in worship so that his request could ascend undisturbed into the golden hall.

Much to his father's pride, he had not chosen the uncle's one-armed god, but had named Thor as his protector and dear friend.

The ceremony was over. Leif kissed Thorstein, then reached out his hand to Thorvald. When he approached Freydis, she fell around his neck, pressed her breasts against his chest, and whispered something into his ear. Astonished, he pushed her away. "Absolutely not!" He stretched out his hand to her. "Wish me a good trip!"

"I do so gladly." She grinned and kissed his fingers. "Come back safe, Brother!"

The farewell from the neighbors was warm. Egil whispered,

"Don't forget our plan." And Ingva nodded to him, shook her head, and except for a deep sigh, didn't make a sound.

Leif had said goodbye to his mother in the house, and now he embraced her and let her stroke his hair.

"My boy. I am proud of you and will be happy when you return unharmed." She looked at Tyrkir with silent grief. "My friend, first it was Erik with whom I had to let you go—so often that I cannot count. Now, you accompany my Leif. Take care of him!"

"Don't worry." Tyrkir tried to keep his tone light. "I'll protect your son as best I can. And our ship will find its way back."

Erik had to step aboard himself. On the aft deck, he stood by the tiller. "Come here to me, Son, and relieve me!"

He only took his fists off the round wood after Leif had taken hold of it. "Hold your course, shipmaster!"

"Thank you, Father."

Tears shone in the corners of the old giant's eyes. As soon as he stood on shore again, he turned his attention to Tyrkir. "And woe be to you if my knarr even has so much as a scratch."

"And woe to you," Tyrkir returned, laughing, "if your dam still doesn't hold water when we come home."

The oars were pushed through the portholes. They plowed the water. Freydis ran along the shore and shouted, "Brother! Think it over again."

Leif didn't answer.

"What does your sister mean?" Tyrkir asked while he waved from the back deck.

"Every normal girl would have wished for an expensive cloth or a gold chain. But not my sister. She wants me to bring her a battle-ax from Norway."

Tyrkir let his arms sink. "Freydis has a strange mind, that's true."

"You know her mother, Uncle. Do you think she . . . ?"

"Katla? No, that woman was completely different. Freydis resembles her only in appearance."

High in the east, above the back of the ice giant, the clouds changed color and promised a sunny day.

Leif headed for the middle of the fjord. "Katla was never spoken of at home, but now we're alone, Uncle, tell me about Freydis's mother."

"Not now. I have to get to the bow. Our long journey is just beginning, and we will have plenty of time. I'll tell you about Katla and, if you like, also about your father. How we fared when we arrived in Iceland, how he got to know your mother..."

Tyrkir broke off and went forward to the dragon's head.

# THORGUNNA

Was the fog really to blame? The turning of the wind? Tyrkir was no longer sure why their ship was anchored here in the port of Drimore on the Outer Hebrides instead of in Norway.

When they'd arrived ten days ago, he'd said to Leif, "Let's be grateful to the gods that we found this trading place and didn't drift into the nothing."

Soon after they'd circumnavigated the southern cape from Greenland, the clouds had closed in on them. For a few hours, Tyrkir was still able to determine the origin of the sunlight in the wafting gray through his crystal, and thus roughly determine the course. But in the night, he could not spot the North Star, and in the morning, there was only one direction left for them.

"Stay before the wind!" he'd shouted from the bow. No storm, no troubled sea pressed the *Mount*. As if pushed by a steady hand, it glided over the waves with a full cloth. Tyrkir even found time to tell his godson about Iceland.

Leif was silent during the tales of bloody fights, but when the trial at the Thorsnessthing came up, he interrupted his uncle, wanting to hear the events again before finally saying, "If the number of witnesses, some of whom were bought, can determine the verdict, our holy law does not serve justice. So it is bad."

"No, boy, that would be too easy. Our law helps keep order. It should be improved." Thoughtfully, Tyrkir looked at him. "Maybe that's a task for you. Yes, I can imagine that one day you'll become a great speaker at the Thing."

Leif waved his uncle off. "First, my beard must reach down to my stomach. Now I am young and have something completely different in mind. Do you know, Uncle, that in the west..." He paused and said, "No, I want to complete this journey first."

A fog came up, so dense that Tyrkir could no longer see the top of the mast. They sailed at half cloth, and the horn blower gave a warning signal at regular intervals, but no answer came from other ships. Then, early on the fifth morning, the fog released them, and before them lay groups of islands in the sunlight, spread out like green, hilly gifts.

The crew cheered. Leif embraced his uncle as they approached the land where they discovered a small settlement. There they asked, "Where are we?" and immediately afterward, "Where do we find the largest trading place?" They had been sent on and finally moored in the harbor bay of Drimore.

Receiving a warm welcome, the noblest families of the village had offered them shelter. So as not to offend anyone, and because of their valuable cargo, the merchants preferred to live aboard with the crew. A tarpaulin was stretched out over the long-laid yard tree. They'd promised the wholesalers and noblemen that they'd tell them about Greenland during the banquets in their houses.

That had been ten days ago. Now Tyrkir sat alone on the aft deck and waited. It was a cloudy morning. Over on the beach, the first curious people were strolling past the merchants' stalls. But he barely noticed them. His fingertip ran from the corner of his mouth to the ear bulge and back again.

*I must act. But how? Should I simply command the boy?* He immediately rejected the thought. *No, not a boy. He's old enough, and a man. And yet I am responsible for him.*

Leif had not returned to the ship's tent the night before but had spent the fourth night in the house of the widow Thorgunna. *As beautiful and cosmopolitan as she may be,* Tyrkir thought, *and even though she is the daughter of the wealthiest landowner in the area, I sense that this woman is dangerous. Perhaps some evil force brought us to the Hebrides?*

Leif! Tyrkir immediately spotted the golden-blond head in the harbor crowd; the fifteen-year-old swayed slightly as he approached. He struggled over the ship's gunwale. Without noticing his uncle, he first groped his way to the water tub, dipping the ladle twice with trembling hands before drinking.

He was about to climb into the covered cargo hold.

"Was there roast mutton?" Tyrkir asked loudly.

"I'm tired."

"Hard to believe, as fresh as you look."

Leif shuffled to him, yawned, and stretched out beside the stool. "Oh, Uncle. Last night was the lightest night ever for me, and on the way back, my feet were high above the ground. Believe me, I didn't touch the earth with my boots. I still feel that way. Even as my back lies here, you see, like it's raised above the planks."

"Amazing," Tyrkir remarked dryly. "Was the mead lovely?"

"Everything that Thorgunna offers me tastes and smells good. The honey bread. The fingers, the skin, even her voice."

"I knew that a voice could sound. But that it can smell or taste, that I did not know."

Leif sat up with great effort and embraced his knees. "Yes, Uncle, that's it exactly. Everything changes with her."

"You rouse my curiosity. I'd love to try her mead. Maybe she even knows a recipe to improve my wine."

"Certainly. We can look for berries together in autumn, and then she can help you."

Autumn? Although the prospect frightened him, Tyrkir continued cautiously, "In the winter, it gets too cold onboard for the crew."

"Didn't I say?" Leif looked at him with a glassy gaze. "The farm is big enough. Don't worry! Thorgunna will give you your own chamber, and our people will have room with the servants." His eyelids drifted shut.

Tyrkir gently shook Leif's shoulder. "I can't wait that long, boy."

Leif opened his eyes again. "For what?"

"I need to know the recipe for the berry wine as soon as possible. Do you think Thorgunna would invite me?"

"Of course." Leif swayed back and forth. "Tonight, I'll tell her that you want to visit us tomorrow evening. She has little cat skins, Uncle, and she wraps them around... Oh, you'll be amazed..." His head sank forward and hung over his knees, and Leif was fast asleep.

Tyrkir gently tilted the tired body to the side and covered him with a sealskin. He looked at the face of his protégé: black-edged eye sockets, pale, sunken cheeks, half-open lips bitten to pieces, and blood stuck in the corners of his mouth. *As much as I'd like you to have your first adventure in love, you don't seem to be a match for this woman.*

Late the next morning, Leif had been resting for hours in the tent when a slave came to the harbor and asked for Tyrkir. "My mistress lets you know that it would be an honor for her... No, she would be overjoyed if you..." The servant had forgotten the words and looked up at the sky. "Well, my mistress Thorgunna is glad for you to come to our farm tonight. And by the Virgin Mary, there is damn good food."

Tyrkir threw him a piece of silver. "Give your mistress my thanks. I will gladly accept the invitation with Leif, the son of Gode Erik Thorvaldsson."

"I don't understand."

"We are coming tonight," Tyrkir translated, then he frowned. "What did you just say? Virgin Mary?"

Fearfully, the servant held out the silver piece again. "Here. Take it back. But don't tell that I cursed her by name. My mistress has strictly forbidden it because the priest has also forbidden it."

"It's all right. Keep the money." Tyrkir looked after the servant as he hastily climbed onto his horse. "That, too? What else will I have to contend with?"

He had already followed the sound of ringing bells a few days earlier and had found the small church outside the village. He had known for some time that most families in Drimore preferred the new god to the magnificent crowd of gods in Valhalla. That fact had been irrelevant to him. But now? Thorgunna, a Christian! Was that how she'd been able to fascinate Leif so quickly? How she'd made him forget his every duty so that he no longer wanted to sail to Norway, let alone bring the ship back to his father? Did the new faith give Thorgunna this power over the boy?

Tyrkir closed his eyes and returned to his village on the Rhine. The crouched stone church. The picture above the flickering candles. How tenderly Maria held her son in her arms. *No*, he thought. *As far as I can remember, no evil powers emanated from the mother and the son of God. But who knows? After all, I was still a boy myself and forgot everything except this image. Or has this Jesus changed over the years? It's possible. A son does not always follow his parents.*

The fireplace crackled. Oil lamps flickered all around, their glow scurrying restlessly over the two tapestries, bringing their woven, multiheaded snake creatures to life. As soon as Tyrkir entered the semidark room, he had the impression that their intertwined bodies were moving imperceptibly. A sweet smell made it difficult for him to breathe. Between the wall hangings, he discovered a wooden cross, but only for a moment before Thorgunna captured his gaze.

She conjured her smile from bloodstained lips and teeth reminiscent of a carved ivory chain. "God be with you! How fortunate I am to finally be able to welcome the godfather of my beloved as a guest in my humble home."

There were no drinking horns—the welcome drink was offered by a maid in clay cups. It tasted sweet on Tyrkir's tongue and burned its way down his throat. Rings flashed as Thorgunna's hands moved elegantly while she spoke. "After the death of my husband, I divided our living quarters into two. The narrowness pleases me more. Here, near the kitchen, I entertain my guests, and behind the curtain, I rest. Two fires, and the smoke goes through one and the same eye. Very imaginative, isn't it?"

Before Tyrkir could grasp his senses, she led her guests to the table. At its center, small and large bowls were arranged to form a circular, fragrant focus. She gently pinched Leif's cheek. "You, my star, shall sit beside me. Your godfather may take a seat opposite us on the armchair so that he can always see for himself how happy we are."

Thorgunna turned to the kitchen, clapped her hands, and immediately a maid appeared.

While Thorgunna gave whispered orders, Tyrkir exhaled and used the moment to watch the hostess calmly. Even her back was impressive. Her brown plait was triple looped and held in place by two silver combs. *How long that hair must be when she lets it fall. She doesn't wear a high-necked shift—only a pearl necklace—while gold bracelets adorn her neck and arms. And, why not? It's warm enough in her house. The dark green straps accentuate the white of her shoulders, and how her hips curve below the tight velvet apron skirt...*

"Isn't she beautiful?" Leif reached across the table for his uncle's hand.

Tyrkir pulled his fingers away. "Quiet!"

Thorgunna returned to the table with a slightly swaying gait. "First, there is a soup of—" She noticed the glances of the men and playfully scolded them. "This reminds me of what I learned on our trade trips. Do you know how the ladies greet their guests at noble Christian courts?" She put one foot back and bent her knee, leaning far to allow Tyrkir to take an in-depth look at her lush breasts.

"You have traveled far," he said, and felt his tongue stick to his palate.

"My husband was a merchant, and because he couldn't refuse me anything, I was allowed to accompany him on a few trips."

She looked up at the wooden cross between the snake creatures and lingered for a moment, calmly leading her hand to her forehead, under her breasts, and to both shoulders. Almost apologetically, she said, "I have invited my Lord Jesus to bless our meal."

She sat next to Leif, took a candied root from one of the pots, smiled, and shoved it into his mouth. "This will do you good." She chose another one for Tyrkir. "Take it! Every man likes this spice."

While Tyrkir chewed, his mouth suddenly filled with saliva, Thorgunna chatted about her travels. "As a little girl, I got to know the noble customs of foreign peoples."

"That's why she talks so beautifully, Uncle," Leif said with an enraptured look.

She immediately took another sweet root, but this time did not put it in his mouth. "Wait, my love!" She dunked her finger in another bowl and greased his cracked lips. "Carnation and nutmeg oil. You'll like it better with that."

The maid brought in the soup. Thorgunna scooped out the soup herself and added a different spice to each steaming bowl. "I leave the cooking and roasting of the food to the maids in the kitchen. My passion is to find the right flavors for every single guest."

Leif slurped with evident pleasure, while Tyrkir first tasted cautiously. But when unexpected warmth spread out in his stomach, he kept putting the bowl to his mouth.

Over the edge of her own bowl, Thorgunna winked at him, sipped, and laughed darkly. "These fruits, roots, and herbs come from far away, some even from the Far East." She raised her bare shoulders. "I don't even know where that is. I bought the ingredients in York in the market. I use them to make powders, honey-sugar bites, and brews. But my skill is in mixing them. This is the only way to give them their mysterious effect."

*According to our faith, you would be a sorceress,* Tyrkir thought. But he failed to ask because the Christians probably had a different word for their knowledgeable women.

He was thirsty—very thirsty—and he gladly had his cup refilled.

Cooked fish was served with the main course. Thorgunna sprinkled it with her ingredients, giving Leif a portion seasoned from different pots than the ones she used for his godfather. She entertained her guests without pause. "I love fine English fabrics. I sleep only on silk cushions stuffed with the fluff of eider ducks."

"You should see the bed," Leif chuckled and wanted to throw his head back with laughter.

"Don't, dearest," she admonished sternly. "Why should your uncle be interested in my bedchamber?" Her green eyes rested on Tyrkir again. "I heard you were curious about the recipe I use to prepare my mead."

"Wine," Tyrkir corrected. In an instant, his tongue was heavy in his mouth, and yet he felt no drunkenness. "Wine, that's why I'm here. Because of my berry wine..."

"Take a knife tip from this powder. Whether beer, mead, or wine, no matter what drink you add it to"—Thorgunna stirred a stick in Tyrkir's mug—"this drug causes a wonderful intoxication. But before I tell you the secret, you should taste it yourself. Here, take it."

It was not a command, and yet he obeyed without hesitation.

The bitter sweetness did not run down his throat; it stayed and stretched his head. *I'm sitting in a grand hall,* he thought, and because it was more comfortable, he leaned back.

Her fingers played on his thigh. "Would you like another sip?"

Tyrkir tried in vain to open his mouth, wanting to nod, but it didn't work, wanting to hand her the cup, but his hand no longer obeyed.

"Your godfather must rest, my love."

"So early? I don't understand." Leif hit the table with his fist. "I am a man."

"But not big enough yet."

Tyrkir heard their voices loudly, then quietly, and immediately loud again. The room also changed, from small to expansive to close again. He watched helplessly as she put a yellowish powder into Leif's mead and held the cup to his lips. "You are already prepared for our feast, my stallion. Drink, this will break the last fetter. And then you may prove to me what power you have."

She poured the brew into him in one go. Leif froze, then a tremor went through his body. He jumped up, threw off his cape, and pulled his shirt over his head. "Faster, my love, faster." He snorted through the nostrils, pulling off pants, stockings, and leather boots. Slowly, he bent his upper body backward and pushed his stomach and loins forward.

Thorgunna looked down, pleased, and touched the arrowhead with her finger. "Stay like that," she cooed, "until I call for you!" With a dancing step, she disappeared through the curtain into her bedroom.

When the hall shrank again, Tyrkir saw, much to his horror, that the snakes had curled up and were pushing their glowing heads through the tapestries. Their tongues were flickering at his naked protégé. *I must warn the boy.* But it was impossible. Leif couldn't understand his gurgling and babbling.

Both halves of the curtain moved to the side. Tyrkir closed his eyes and opened them only to slits. *There's no danger*, he thought. *My intoxication is confusing me. There's Thorgunna. Or is it just white skin with a golden shimmer? No, she's smiling at me. Her hair spreads over her shoulders like a cloth. Her breasts are attentive guards with dark eyes. They protect navel and hips, as well as the fleece between her thighs. Now the beautiful one stretches out her hand to me.*

"Come, my strong stallion!"

It astonished Tyrkir that it wasn't he who let out the whoop, but Leif, that he wasn't the naked young man who embraced Thorgunna and kissed her and pulled her into her bedchamber. His eyes widened and Tyrkir floated up, he was so light. There is no Leif, no Thorgunna. Everything that happens here is not real. The sweet mead only conjures up pictures, and why shouldn't you enjoy them? A high bed with a blue sky, silky fabrics piled up on the posts. The woman climbed in, lured with a beautiful white bottom, crawling on her hands and knees into the middle and letting herself be caught up by the man. Tyrkir thought he heard giggles, laughter, even neighing, then screams rose, again and again, casting an eerie silence when they stopped abruptly.

In the distance, the woman appeared and turned into Thorgunna as she stood before him. "You are still awake, godfather. Do you like it so much that my powder won't work immediately?" She put the fingertip on his ear bulge and drove along the scar to his mouth. "You shall sleep, you hear, and forget!"

For a long while, her breasts rocked back and forth like sails in front of his face. A glowing scent rose into his nose, and he thought, *The weather is clearing up, and I can finally set our course again with the shadow needle. . . . Only I don't know where Leif put it. . . . I have to ask. . . .*

His arm stretched long and longer, and finally, Tyrkir managed to follow it with his body. "Be careful, Uncle!"

His knees threatened to buckle; still half-asleep, he leaned on his godson. "Wait, boy." He wheezed and coughed. His mouth was parched, his limbs hurt like he'd been in a long fight. Tyrkir opened his eyes and was startled by Leif's scratched face, his broken lips. "What happened to you?"

"I'm so happy, Uncle. Only a little tired." The glassy expression in his godson's eyes woke Tyrkir completely. *We're still in the house of Thorgunna*, he noticed. Strangely, the tabletop was empty and shiny, and none of the snake creatures in the tapestries were moving. Carefully, he looked at the closed curtain. What was behind it? He tried to remember. *We ate. There was soup, then fish, and we drank. Right. Thorgunna said she'd set up her bedroom behind the curtain, and that I wouldn't be interested.*

"Where is our hostess?"

"I don't know." Leif shrugged. "When I woke up, I was alone in the canopy bed. She's never there in the morning when I leave."

"Canopy bed?"

"That's what she calls it. You have no idea how beautiful it is to lie among pillows and look into the blue silk cloud. Oh, Uncle."

"What are you talking about? Come on, let's go."

One foot in front of the other, they blundered out of the room. At the door, a maid stopped them. "My mistress sends greetings and apologizes. I am to tell you that she would like the young gentleman to pay her his respects again tonight.... Oh, I can't say it like that. You should visit her."

"I'll be on time. Tell her that." Leif grinned to himself. "I will always visit her."

"We'll discuss that," Tyrkir mumbled, and pushed him ahead.

Outside, the rain stung their faces. With every step, they sank ankle-deep into the soaked ground. "Do you float today, too?"

"Yes, look here." Leif performed a small bounce and fell into the mud but didn't appear to care. When he picked himself up, he jumped again. "See how I dance?"

"Even the stupidest mutton can do better."

From that point on, Tyrkir was silent. Every clear thought was lost immediately somewhere in his head. *Later*, he thought, *I will come up with something later.*

Like wet, beaten dogs, they reached the ship. Both hardly noticed the mockery of the crew as they were lifted aboard and fell to their knees in front of the vats.

Water—the cup sat too tight in the leather loop. The ladle slipped out of Leif's hand, and because the bucket was too heavy, they drank from it like thirsty horses. In the onboard tent, they stretched out next to each other. "Oh, Uncle," Leif mumbled. "This woman—I will never leave her."

"Quiet, boy. Be quiet." Tyrkir put his hand over his scar.

Even before the end of his dream, he woke and saw snakeheads turning on fleshy balls that became smaller and disappeared behind a blue silk scarf. He tried to understand the image, and although his mind obeyed him again, he found no interpretation except that the dream must somehow be connected to the evening before.

He reached out for his protégé, but the sealskin sleeping bag was empty. He couldn't find Leif on deck, either, only the guards squatting together rolling dice. "Where is Leif Eriksson?"

Grinning, the first boatman pointed over the harbor square up to the noble houses of the merchants. "Where you both came from this morning."

"Slave!" Tyrkir was already looming above the man. "Don't you dare speak to me in that tone. I'll sell you to some Christian. And I swear to you, their money is just as good to me. I can find a new helmsman on every corner in Drimore. Do you understand me?"

"But, Lord." The man blanched and rose. His comrades quietly stepped back. Nobody onboard had ever seen the prudent pilot so upset before. "I thought..."

"Silence! You only think if I tell you to!"

"Forgive me, Lord!"

"You will keep your mouth shut!" Tyrkir hit his forehead with his flat hand. "Damn, why didn't any of you fools wake me?" He stomped to the railing, exhaled, shook his head, then returned to the men, calmer. "Let's start over again. Speak!"

"I don't know what you want to hear, sir."

"Don't tempt me—" Tyrkir immediately caught himself. "No, you aren't to blame. When did the skipper leave the ship?"

"The rain had stopped, and the sun was still quite high above the west."

"So early? And how was he? I mean, what did he look like?"

The boatman hesitated. When Tyrkir raised his finger, he confessed, "Not so good, sir. Two men had to wipe the dirt off his shirt and trousers and his face. I don't know where he fell. But don't worry, sir. He was in good spirits. The woman must cook well for him. Oh yes, and then he told me something about a stallion."

"A stallion?"

"Must be a special breed. Perhaps the master wants to buy it from the woman?"

"Impossible. Our cargo hold is full, he knows that."

Tyrkir pulled his coat tighter around his shoulders and climbed down the outer ladder.

The boatman bent over the side of the ship. "Forgive me, sir! One more thing. A merchant came to the knarr during the day. He asked about reindeer skins. He wants to drop by again in the evening. What should I tell him?"

"Today, I have no time for business. Put him off until tomorrow or the day after."

At first, the servant hesitated. "Forgive me, sir, but it is only because of the guard. Will you stay the night again?"

"Sit down, throw the dice, and wait for me. I'm looking for a woman. And if I'm lucky, I may even be back soon."

Tyrkir quickly walked across the harbor square. A little off the beaten track, he found fishermen mending their nets. He greeted them, chatted about the weather, and talked about how urgently he had to renew his stock of fish. Finally, he casually asked, "Is there a sorceress in Drimore? A clever völva?"

Immediately, all the heads bent deeper over the nets. "We are Christians."

Even if his first attempt had failed, Tyrkir could not give up. He waited for a time and then tried again. "One who knows how to heal? We come from Greenland, and my friend is sick. There must be a wisewoman living in these parts."

The fishermen remained silent. Finally, one of them grumbled, "Go to Thorgunna!"

"She won't help him if he has no money," his neighbor spat.

Again, the men were quiet. After a while, a man, weathered by age, lowered his needle. "Trude. Even if the priest does not like her, our Trude knows her stuff."

"Where can I find her?"

Tyrkir was directed to the other side of the settlement. He followed the path through hilly pastures, and as he braced himself against the stiff breeze from the north, he asked God Tyr for help. *I need double luck. The boy must be brought to his senses and the sou'wester needs to hold steady so that we can leave this unfortunate spot for Norway.*

He reached a hilltop and smelled a hearth fire. He saw no dwelling in the twilight, but it couldn't be far.

Then he noticed two sheep, just down the meadow slope and around the grazing animals, ravens squatted like a black fence. *Strange*, he thought as he descended.

Immediately, the ravens broke their circle, forming a double row against him. They croaked while the sheep at their backs did not even raise their heads. The closer he came, the more threatening the ravens' calls became. "Give me peace!" Tyrkir deviated slightly from the path and waved his arms. "It's all right. I don't want anything from you!"

When he was almost past them, he saw the stone house. It lay tucked in the hillside, not visible from above because the meadow formed its roof. And it was there that the sheep grazed and the scouts of Hugin and Munin croaked.

"Here I am." He smiled.

The masonry was cracked and crumbling; the door consisted of badly tied sticks and driftwood. Tyrkir carefully pulled it open.

Thick smoke struck him, stinging his eyes. He coughed, and before he could grow used to the weak light, something stroked across his face. Frightened, he looked up. Cat skins with heads and paws dangled from the ceiling. "Trude?"

There was no answer. Slowly, Tyrkir felt his way between baskets and jugs to the fireplace. A foul-smelling brew simmered in the kettle. "Trude?"

Nothing.

He wiped his eyes, and through the smoke, he discovered a sleeping mat on the floor by the back wall. There were no blankets, just a pile of rags. *The völva's probably gone out,* he thought. *I'll wait.* And he sat down on a stool next to the embers. Every niche in the wall was used to store bones and roots and pots. He even found skulls of goats. Dried tufts of herbs and a sieve of human ribs hung on the long string across the room next to the cat skins.

Tyrkir nodded. Even though everything here seemed dirty and

threadbare, the remedies and magic reminded him of the grand parlor of the seeress from Eagle Farm in Iceland.

"Who comes to visit Trude?"

He whipped around. Nobody had entered the room.

"If he will not answer, let him disappear, and let me rest." The voice was slightly muffled, and yet very close.

"Tyrkir. I come to you from Greenland. They call me the German."

"Are you a Christian?"

"The great Tyr dwells in me."

"Strange. Because my black shepherds croaked so loudly, I was afraid that Father Rufius wanted to convert me to his faith again. They sense every Christian, you know, but with this priest, they get particularly angry. All right, I want to believe you. What can I do for you?"

Meanwhile, Tyrkir was sure that the völva was speaking to him from the back wall. "My friend is sick. Can you save him?"

He heard giggling. "From afar? That will cost you more silver, and I cannot vouch for success. Has he broken anything or got pain in his body?"

"No. It's something in the head." Tyrkir looked helplessly at the back wall and raised his shoulders.

"Either you explain to me exactly what's wrong with him or get out!"

"No, don't send me away! A woman's captured Leif with her magic."

"Oh, oh," mocked Trude. "Does the pain of love torment him?"

"It's more me who suffers while he floats above the ground."

"By the three Norns, don't waste my time! Or were you sent by Rufius?"

"No, I don't know him at all." As briefly as possible, Tyrkir described the situation. When he told of the previous night's meal and the mysterious ingredients, the völva interrupted him sharply: "What is the name of this woman?"

"Thorgunna."

He was shocked to see how the rags moved on the mat. Fingers grew out of the heap; arms, and then a face appeared, framed by stringy pale-yellow hair. Trude stared at him from bright, watchful eyes.

"This slut has ruined my business. The sick used to go to my mother. Thorgunna and I learned the art from her. After her death, we were both the völvas of Drimore. But almost everyone came to me, even the richest merchants, because I am more skilled. But then she became a Christian and is now in cahoots with the priest. First, the cross is waved around, then there are the little remedies of Thorgunna, and then they pray vigorously to the mother of this Jesus." Trude stuck out her tongue for a long time. "Just a new scam, nothing more. The medicinal herbs are still the old ones. But the clientele stays away from me." She laughed. "It was good that you came. Now I can prove to this poisoner how quickly I can disperse her concoctions."

Tyrkir didn't want to spark a fight between the wisewomen of Drimore in which Leif could quickly become their victim. "The only thing that matters to me is that the boy has a clear head again."

"By Odin and his three Norns, I swear he will."

Trude peeled all the way out of the mountain of rags and jumped up. She was a wiry little woman, not old, yet not young, either. Her long robe had undoubtedly not been washed for months. It hung down, fraying around her thick woolen stockings. "Sit there and don't you make a sound."

Armed with a silver bowl, she dashed back and forth between the nooks in her walls, took an herb here, a bone there, added brownish little chunks, and while she was crushing the mixture with a pestle, Tyrkir heard her humming.

"That would be the base," she whispered with satisfaction, setting the bowl down on a wooden block. "Now, three eyes from the salmon." As she prepared her remedy, she spoke the recipe to herself in a low voice. "Some urine from the rabbit." She giggled and added a dark powder from a little bag. "A pinch of dried monthly blood, that it may frighten the love-crazed boy."

After she had stirred for a long time, she poured oily liquid from a jug into the bowl. "Rancid seal oil with seagull droppings, improved with beaver's nettle and some hemlock." Trude dunked the spoon, smelled, stuck out her tongue. And Tyrkir was amazed—without touching the slime, she tasted it. Something still seemed to be missing, because she removed the lid from a pot and took out two beads, which she crushed on a board. "Cat's testicles soaked in pepper oil. Makes it hot," she said, and scraped the grease into the brew.

Trude went to the fireplace and let the bowl float on the boiling soup. Three times, her hands ran in opposite circles over the crucible, then she stretched her arms to the ceiling. "Odin, do you hear me?"

She remained in this position, only moving her lips. After several long moments, she took the rib cage sieve, fished out the silver bowl with it, and set it down on the wooden block.

"My part is done." She smiled encouragingly at Tyrkir. "As soon as the brew has cooled, I'll give it to you." She lifted her finger. "Success now depends entirely on you. If you follow my instructions exactly, your friend will be freed from the spell of this slut."

Tyrkir listened, now and then stroking his scar in dismay, but finally he felt prepared for Leif's healing.

As he had been doing for days, Leif returned the following morning. With difficulty, he managed to climb the ladder, and Tyrkir helped him over the railing.

"Oh, Uncle." Grinning and with glassy eyes, Leif stood in front of his godfather. "I feel as light as a seagull."

Concerned, Tyrkir noticed how much Leif's condition had worsened since the previous day. He worried that soon there would be only a shadow left of the radiant Eriksson, the pride of Thjodhild. Something had to be done, no matter what struggle it required.

"A seagull? How beautiful, my boy. Thorgunna is indeed performing true miracles on you."

"You understand me. Heavenly pleasures, Thorgunna calls them, and she wants to enjoy them with me." He touched his swollen tongue with his finger. "I'm thirsty!" He shuffled to the tub. "The mead makes me so thirsty."

Twice he reached before he had grabbed the ladle stem.

Tyrkir stepped in. As if unintentionally, he nudged Leif's arm, and the ladle fell on the deck. "I'll help you."

He pulled the cup out of the leather loop on the tub and filled it half full of water. After a short shake, he handed it to Leif. "Quench your thirst, my boy!"

Leif held the cup to his lips with both hands and drank greedily, emptying it to the last drop. "Uncle..." His face turned gray, the cup slipped from his fingers, and he staggered back. "Uncle, this water..."

A tremble went through the boy's body. Leif buckled, struggling for air, then suddenly straightened up again, groping blindly and screaming like a mortally wounded animal. Finally, he found his godfather. Afraid, he reached out. Waves rolled through his body, accompanied by occasional burps. As his lips began to flutter, Tyrkir grabbed his protégé's shoulders and pressed his hand against Leif's mouth. "Don't spit. Breathe, boy. Breathe!"

Leif flapped around. He was too weak to tear himself away and sucked in air through his bloated nostrils.

Relieved, Tyrkir noticed that the seizures had lessened as the völva had predicted. "But don't wait," she'd warned him. "Use the moment!"

A soft call, and the helmsman appeared on deck. Without letting Leif go, Tyrkir ordered, "Water!"

All the men onboard had been instructed by him. He'd chosen six of the most suitable ones to assist him with the cure. Carefully, Tyrkir freed Leif's mouth and held the ladle to it. "Drink it!" Despite the accusing look, he assured him, "It will help you."

Leif tasted, then he drank in big swallows. "Uncle..." he gasped, "I'm so sick... What was in the cup earlier?" His legs buckled. The boatman jumped to help, and together they held him up.

"Water from our tub, boy. Pure, good water."

"But why...?"

"I'm sure the mead and lavish food didn't agree with you. But don't worry! You're in good hands."

"Thorgunna. I want to rest... because I... because I have to go to my love tonight."

Tyrkir felt the tremors taking hold of the boy's body again. What followed now could not happen on deck before the eyes of the port visitors. Together with the boatman, he brought his godson down to the covered cargo hold. Fish-oil lamps lit the camp. Two servants had buckets and cloths ready. The remaining three reached for Leif's coat, shirt, and trousers, but too slowly.

Before boots and stockings were stripped off, Leif vomited the contents of his stomach. He gagged again, and at the same time, his bowels emptied. Only some of the waste could be caught with buckets and cloths. Though the stench took their breath away, the helpers washed their master clean and covered him with a sealskin.

"Uncle, I'm cold." A second blanket was brought. "Uncle," Leif whispered, exhausted. "Wake me up in time. Because Thorgunna..." He snored with his mouth open.

Tyrkir waved the men to him. "Until our skipper is well again, you'll take your orders only from me. Do you understand?" He waited until everyone nodded and then quietly issued his instructions. The skipper was to be supervised at all times, so two servants were to take turns guarding the ship. "He may not leave. If necessary, tie him up. And have no fear of punishment. You are under my protection." Tyrkir lifted his finger. "Remember, Leif must not drink! No matter how he curses or begs for it, you will not give him a sip. He receives water only from me."

As if a voice had called him, Leif awoke at exactly the same hour as on the previous afternoons. He tried to get up. He did not see his uncle, only the servants. "Bring me my coat..." After a while, he mumbled, "Also my trousers," and was again asleep.

In the middle of the night, he shot up. "Yes, dearest, your stallion is coming to you!" Hands pressed down on his shoulders. Surprised, Leif looked around. "Hey, what are you doing? Let go of me immediately!" But the slaves did not loosen their grip. "This is a poor joke, friends. Give me water and help me with my clothes! Did you not understand? That's an order!" He tried to shake off the boatmen's hands, but they immediately increased their pressure. "Damn it, what's gotten into you?"

"They mustn't let go of you, boy."

Leif raised his head at the sound of the voice and rubbed his eyes. "Uncle?"

Tyrkir moved the stool closer to the foot of the bed. "You're sick, very sick, and have to stay on board."

"But Thorgunna is waiting. She can give me herbs."

"She's already done enough. Her herbs weren't medicinal."

Leif's eyes glittered in their black sockets, and he nodded. "If you're sure, I'll obey."

Tyrkir gave the guards a nod, and they let go of the skipper. Leif jumped up immediately and fled naked toward the exit. But before he reached the steering deck, the men caught him. After a short struggle, his strength was exhausted, and they forced him back into the bed. "You can't do this," he gasped. "I have command of this ship."

Without his calm tone wavering, Tyrkir explained, "Not at the moment, my boy. You're a danger to yourself. That's why I had to take command." He snapped his fingers and instructed two other servants to tie up his sick godson.

Leif cursed—he yelled until he was out of breath—and when he realized that his hands and feet were really tied, tears seeped from the corners of his eyes. "Uncle, why are you doing this to me?"

"Because Thorgunna has robbed you of your senses. I have to save you from her."

"Love. It is love. So infinite. Don't destroy my happiness. Let me go to her!"

Tyrkir said nothing, only held Leif's gaze. Finally, he got up and climbed on deck.

It was cold. Above him, the night sky glittered and sparkled. *I had no choice*, he thought. *And now there's no turning back.* He looked up at the North Star. *How easy it is to determine the course of a ship. And how difficult it is to get my Leif back on the right track.*

"Lord." The helmsman approached with an oil light. "He's asked for water. He says he will die of thirst."

Sighing, Tyrkir took the small bottle from his belt pouch, dripped some of the slimy contents into the drinking vessel, and added clear water. "Come, my friend. We mustn't keep our ship-master waiting."

The struggle lasted for three days and nights, accompanied by screaming and vomiting, unrestrained crying, and terrible threats. Often enough, Tyrkir had to force himself to maintain this relentless discipline against the sick man. On the fourth morning, Leif lay in a deep sleep, and his sunken face seemed to have finally found peace.

"Untie his hands," Tyrkir commanded. He'd keep the foot shackles for now. From the tent entrance, the first boatswain waved to him. "What is it?"

"You'd better come up on deck," the man murmured.

Thorgunna had sent her slave. "My mistress sends her greetings through me and asks if Leif Eriksson would like to give her pleasure, and tonight... Oh, damn it, I just can't remember it. Since he is well again, he should come to dinner with us. My mistress is looking forward to it."

"Send her the shipmaster's regrets. Unfortunately, she must forgo his company."

"Excuse me?"

"He's not coming," Tyrkir translated. "And tell her that Leif is too busy. He will not be entering your mistress's house again."

The servant scratched his shorn head. "By the Blessed Virgin Mary, she will give me the whip."

"I thought you weren't allowed to swear by her name?"

Head ducked, the slave turned around and mounted his horse.

Tyrkir rested both arms on the railing. *None of our people disembarked this morning. Four days ago, the slave was here for the last time, and I sent him away with the news that Leif had fallen ill. And today of all days, he shows up again? How does Thorgunna know the boy is better?*

His scar hurt. *The weather changes*, he thought casually. He looked up at the sky and held his breath. *No, there's no doubt.* The balls of cloud were drifting over the island from the south. *Our wind! If it turns a little more, it will become our lucky wind to Norway.* Into this joy, the thought of Thorgunna immediately crept back again. *So that's why she sent the slave! Her beloved has recovered his strength, and our departure is imminent. She felt this before I knew it myself.* "If only we were already at sea," he murmured.

The open, alert gaze and the prudent instructions of Erik's son compensated the crew for all the toil and doubt through the labyrinth of the last few days. They had suffered with their captain and saved him. Laughter had finally returned to their ship, and the last preparations were easier to make.

After a week, Leif ordered the tent tarpaulin to be removed from the yardarm, then he slowly climbed onto the bow deck. "Uncle, this afternoon, I'll have the sail checked, and then we'll be ready." He lowered his head, scraping his foot across the planks. "We're setting sail early tomorrow morning. If it's all right with you."

"It's up to you, Leif." Tyrkir put the bearing plate out of his hand with a smile. "Skipper! Your pilot reports: We have a steady southwest. Nothing can keep us here in Drimore." When Leif immediately turned his back to him, he was startled and said softly, "It's better this way, believe me."

"Maybe you're right. I have to check the provisions."

Tyrkir watched him go. In silent agreement, both were avoiding mentioning the past weeks. No accusations, no explanations. *How could you be so clumsy now,* he reprimanded himself. *Jokes are not good for an open wound. You of all people should know that.*

The next day, they'd set sail and leave this place behind. Only a few more hours, and then they could finally forget Thorgunna. Tyrkir quickly threw his coat around his shoulders. From the outer ladder, he shouted to the helmsman, "I have another errand. Tell Leif that I'll be back soon."

As troubled as his heart had been that first time, he now happily followed the path through the hilly meadows. Even the angry croaking of the ravens didn't disturb him.

Trude was huddled on her grass roof milking one of the sheep.

Without interrupting the work, she asked, "Are you a Christian after all?"

"Is it important? Your potion worked."

"And why are you still bothering me?" She blew away an annoying strand of hair from her face. "I had fun showing that bitch which one of us is the best."

"I wanted to thank you."

Trude startled, almost knocking over the milk bowl as she whistled at her ravens. "Quiet now!" She looked at Tyrkir suspiciously. "It's been a long time since I've heard that. Repeat it."

"You saved my godson." Tyrkir pulled a large piece of silver from his pocket. "And I wanted to thank you for that."

"Sounds nice." She stroked the teats again. "You've already paid me. Keep your money!"

"We leave Drimore for Norway tomorrow, and you lose me as a customer. Please, take the silver!"

"All right. Just put it in the grass. One of my black sheepherders will bring it to me, and then you can go."

Tyrkir had already climbed halfway up the hill again when he heard the völva calling. "Hey, German! Good luck. I'll put in a good word for you with the goddess Ran. Don't worry. Your ship will get to Norway safely."

He looked back only briefly, then continued walking and waved until he had crossed the crest.

In the harbor forecourt, Tyrkir hesitated at the booth of a jewelry dealer. Two dainty, finely engraved silver brooches tempted him. *I should bring them to Thjodhild.*

"Best English work," the man said, praising his merchandise. "I bought the two pieces at the market in York from the artist himself."

York? Tyrkir immediately had that taste of sweet spices on his tongue again. *No, I don't ever want to be reminded of York.* Without a word, he returned the brooches to the seller and hurried down to the beach.

Fortune stumbled. *O great Tyr!* Tyrkir spotted her from afar.

Thorgunna. She stood in front of Leif, talking with him in her traveling hood and coat. Worse still, two of her slaves were waiting nearby with the horses, and a horse was loaded with baskets and a wooden chest. *My divine friend*, begged Tyrkir, *do not abandon us now!*

Thorgunna glanced at him with a short, evil look, then immediately turned her eyes back to the trembling Eriksson. "Why, star of my heart?" she cooed darkly. "Why won't you take your beloved with you? Give me a good reason."

The thoughts buzzed through Tyrkir's mind. *I must not intervene. For the sake of his dignity, the boy must pass this test himself. But how can I help?* Slowly, he took two steps back. This way, he could at least keep eye contact with the godson, unnoticed by Thorgunna.

The blood had drained from Leif's face. Again and again, he moistened his lips. "Because I do not ... You are from the richest family here. Your father and relatives would hate me if I took you without their permission."

"What does a woman care about custom and practice once her heart is ignited? I will gladly break all family ties and follow you." She offered him her hands. "Have courage, my hero. Abduct me!"

Leif staggered. His gaze fled to his uncle but was immediately caught by Thorgunna again. "I am your happiness," she urged. "Listen only to the voice inside you!"

"That's just it. There are two voices in me, and they fight with each other and torture me." Leif suddenly straightened his back. "No!"

As though she'd been struck, Thorgunna clutched at her cheek. "What did you say?"

"No." His tone was firmer. "In marriage, the mind must give its consent, and the heart can only agree. Nothing more is allowed. Since my mind forbids it, I repeat, no!"

Thorgunna opened her lips and hummed to herself. With a tender gesture, she put her hands under her breasts and let her body swing gently back and forth.

Astonished, Leif watched her, transfixed. "What's wrong?"

"I cradle and comfort our child, because his father is abandoning us."

"No," he moaned, raising his arms, not knowing where to put them, and lowering them again.

Tyrkir had to intervene. "This is a trick, boy. Do not give in!"

Without interrupting, Thorgunna smiled. "Was your old god-father in my bed? Only you, dearest, know what happened there."

"I never gave you my word. As soon as I entered your house, I was in another world. You see, I experienced everything as if through a veil."

"How beautifully you describe our happiness." She batted her eyelashes at him. "I swear by the Virgin Mary and all the angels, it is a son that I carry under my heart."

Leif tore himself away. With his back to her, he stared past his ship over the water. "No!" he shouted to the distant horizon, shouted it twice more, and turned back strengthened. "I will leave Drimore without you. Goodbye."

She released a sigh full of sadness, and with the next breath, her face had changed. A new shimmer rose in her dark eyes. "A woman knows when she has lost, so go without me! But you should not refuse my last wish: give me something that belongs to you and let us sit together by the light of a candle and say goodbye!"

"By Thor, you will never set foot on my ship!" he blurted, then immediately relented. "Forgive me. I mean, goodbye, yes, but not onboard. Here on the beach. I'll see to lights and seating."

After some hesitation, she was satisfied.

Visibly lightened, Leif climbed up the outer ladder. As soon as he'd disappeared below deck, she turned her eyes toward Tyrkir. "You spawn of hell," she hissed, and her tone lost every noble flourish. "I underestimated you, Scarface. It was you. With what poison did you estrange my beloved? Or did someone help you? Tell me!"

"Nobody, beautiful woman. And by the way, I don't understand what you mean." He added mildly, "My godson is healthy again. I am grateful to the gods for that."

"For a heathen to tamper with my business—" Thorgunna broke off as Leif returned with gifts and his first boatman. "Where would you like to sit?"

She chose a sandy spot close to the water. According to her instructions, the two stools were arranged in such a way that the third stool with the candle jug could be placed between them like a small table. "Let's say goodbye alone, dearest."

Before Leif could ask his uncle, Tyrkir moved away, but he remained nearby, full of unrest. New danger was looming. He sensed it, but he couldn't tell how. He sharply observed every gesture of the pair. First, Leif handed over the gifts. Thorgunna admired the scarlet cloak of finest Greenlandic wool, put it around her shoulders, and turned around. "How does it look on me?"

"You are even more beautiful," Leif confessed.

With sheer incredulous amazement, she accepted the belt made of walrus tooth. "I never knew you had such great artists up north."

"There's only one person who could carve that. My uncle."

Tyrkir gnawed at his lower lip. He was annoyed that she'd received his best work as a gift; on the other hand, he felt honored by her praise.

"Your godfather? I always told you he's a valuable person."

Tyrkir was astonished at how smoothly the lie flew from her lips. This woman truly knew how to keep her sail in the wind.

"A ring!" she cheered. "Oh, dearest, please put it on my finger. I'm sure it was your mother's."

"Yes, certainly. Good gold." While Leif took her hand and chose the right finger, his godfather could not suppress a smile. *You understand lying, too, boy. Still a bit awkward, but it serves the purpose.* The ring came from the jewelry and silver box on board, from which purchases were made during the voyage.

"May I kiss you in gratitude?"

Tyrkir immediately bent over. Only briefly did she press her lips onto his protégé's mouth. *No, nothing noticeable*, he thought. But had Leif swayed a little after the kiss? Who'd be surprised, after the passion he'd experienced with her. *No, I was wrong, there's no reason for my uneasiness. I should be glad that the goodbye is going so smoothly and so peacefully.*

"Come now, my star, let us enjoy one last familiar moment." She asked Leif to sit down on the stool right next to the water and moved her seat so that she could shield the breeze with her coat.

"Though you cause me infinite pain, I will not be angry with you." She took off her headscarf, checked the fit of the combs and needles in her pinned-up hair, and lifted the candle from the jug. "Look at me, my love, I want you to remember this image of me."

"I will never forget you," he murmured.

"I hope so." With her right hand, she brought the candle closer to his face. "Don't move! Give me time to see the star shine in the blue of your eyes for the last time." Slowly, she also raised her left hand to the candle.

A needle! Tyrkir noticed the flashing, and before he realized, Thorgunna pushed the tip into the flame. "I prick the light, I prick the heart that I love." Leif sat there motionless, his face frozen into a mask. "There is no other woman for you. And if you ever betray me, you will die."

Tyrkir jumped in. "Bitch . . ."

"Don't come any closer," Thorgunna warned him. Between her thumb and forefinger, the needle hovered in front of the flame. "Don't force me to pierce the light completely, because that would destroy all other happiness for your godson forever. Leif hears only my voice, so be silent until I release the spell!"

She led the silver tip back into the flame. "Dearest, I will raise our son and send him to Greenland as soon as he can walk. And know, my love, you will enjoy the boy as much as you enjoyed me. And I, before it is all over, will be on my way to you." As if placing a kiss, she bent over the candle and blew it out.

At the same moment, Leif went limp, falling from the stool. His godfather caught him before he hit the ground.

Thorgunna rose calmly. First, she flicked the needle into the water, then she looked at Tyrkir with contempt. "Did you really think you could compete with me? I never give up. Mark my words, Scarface. In the end, I always win." With her hips swaying, Thorgunna left the beach. The slaves helped her into the saddle and pulled the packhorse behind her.

"You are not a völva," Tyrkir whispered. He did not know what Christians called such a woman, but he didn't care. "At least now I have taken the boy from you. This is my victory."

After she'd crossed the harbor forecourt and had long disappeared between the houses, Leif awoke from his dazed state. "Where is Thorgunna?"

"Gone, boy. She didn't want to stay any longer."

"Uncle . . ." He touched his lips carefully. "When she kissed me, I felt hot. The blood rushed so loud. Then a bolt of lightning went through my eyes and into my chest. The song? I didn't quite understand the verse. She sang about our child . . . and that it will come to Greenland, and she also wants—"

"Quiet. Never mind." Tyrkir shook him by the shoulders. "How do you feel?"

"My skull is humming like after bad mead." Leif grinned slightly. "Other than that, I'm fine."

"Then let's go!"

"You mean, right now?"

"Yes, right away." The sky was clear, the wind came from the southwest, they'd have visibility for several hours, and at night he could keep his course with the help of the North Star. "We shouldn't stay here in the harbor for another hour."

"Uncle, you want to run away?"

"More than that, my boy. Who knows what else could happen to us here?" Tyrkir put his hand on the left side of his face. "I'm afraid."

Leif laughed. "Let's go. The royal court in Norway awaits."

Orders startled the crew. The anchor rope was pulled in. Four servants pushed the knarr from the beach deeper into the water and then were hauled aboard. "Take to the oars!"

Slowly, the *Mount of the Sea* slid through the harbor. Nobody waved goodbye, and as soon as they reached the open sea, Leif set the red sail.

At the bow, Tyrkir stood tall next to the dragon's head. The wind bit into his scar, and never before had he felt such a pleasant pain.

# TO BE READ FROM THE RUNE STONE OF REMEMBRANCE:

No Thor's hammer, no world tree decorates the beginning of the lines. The cross precedes every inscription.

... **THE YEAR 996:** Without mercy... Norway... Olaf Tryggvasson proclaims the new faith: Christ is Emperor! Olav is King! The people must obey. Those who refuse baptism are tortured and murdered. Rebellious landowners and their families are burned to death. The Cross of the Redeemer will become the torture cross to those who doubt...

... **THE YEAR 997:** King Olaf now wants to convert all the islands of the North Sea. He sends his court chaplain, Dankbrand, to Iceland. The monastic novice Dankbrand has become a proud priest. He is often insulted by the pagans and pays them back with the sword. In the first months alone, the priest slays two mockers.

... **THE YEAR 999:** A berserker challenges Dankbrand to a duel. But before that, he wants to intimidate the priest. "I walk through fire with bare feet. I let myself fall on the tip of a sword and remain unharmed."

"God will decide." Dankbrand blesses fire and sword. The berserker burns his soles, and the tip of the sword penetrates his chest. Because of this miracle, some Icelanders become baptized. But Dankbrand abandons the attempt to bring Christianity to the heathens and sets sail for Norway. In the past three years, he has killed eleven men...

**... THE YEAR 1000:** Olaf Tryggvasson is furious about his priest's failure. He takes Icelandic wholesalers hostage and sends two of them as his ambassadors across the sea to the Allthing of the heathens. War or baptism! The threat keeps the freemen busy, and soon a deep rift splits the Thing. The lawman Thorgeir lies down in his hut and pulls the blanket over his head. After two days, he rises again. From the Law Rock, he warns the assembly, "Woe to our Iceland if we no longer follow one faith and one law. If we tear up the law, we tear up peace. Let me mediate!"

Both parties want to comply with his judgment. And Thorgeir announces that all people of Iceland should be baptized and believe in the new god. But according to the old law, children can still be abandoned, and horse meat can still be eaten. The people may continue to offer sacrifices to the gods, but these must be performed in secret. Displeasure brews. The men from the north and the south of the country refuse to go into the cold water. The priest rides with them to a hot spring and baptizes them there.

**... FROM THE SETTLERS IN GREENLAND:** Two months after Leif's departure, the dam above the waterfall is completed. Satisfied with his efforts, Erik walks across his farm. But the first winter storms bring more rain than snow, and the structure cannot withstand the pressure of the overflowing stream. The following summer, the work starts all over again, but in vain. Whatever is put between the rock-cut is washed away the next morning. "I will win," growls the giant. Though his hair is almost gray, he hasn't lost the will to fight.

Not far from the embankment, on the shore of the fjord, his servants discover a dilapidated hut, a stone ax, and a rotten fur boat. "We are not alone." Judging by the condition of the dwelling, it must have been abandoned long before the Icelandic settlers arrived, but Erik doesn't care. "Even if they have long since died, maybe it's their ghosts that are tearing down my wall." From then on, he has the ruin guarded. Apparently, with success . . .

. . . **THE YEAR 1000:** The newly constructed dam resists the spring floods, and the stream is dammed in the narrow high valley above the waterfall . . .

# FATHER ERNESTUS

The first weekend in August! His big day had come. Erik had asked Thjodhild; Freydis and her two brothers had to obey, and he would not be talked out of inviting neighbor Ingolf Arnesson and his family to the outing. After a ride past the half-mown meadows, through the middle of high grass to the end of the pastures of Steep Slope, the horses finally trotted with loud snorts up the narrow path.

To perform the sacred ceremony, the builder climbed up a boulder next to the dam, crossed his arms, and received congratulations and praise. Even the weather celebrated him—the sun was shining down on his little reservoir from a cloudless sky. "Let us thank the gods!" He raised his eyes and began to greet the community in Valhalla with a powerful voice.

Stealthily, Freydis turned and grimaced until both of the neighbors' daughters started giggling. Ingva and Sigrid were immediately reprimanded by their mother with short, hard slaps. At the same time, the actual guilty party was listening, full of devotion, to her father's ceremony.

Thjodhild had watched Freydis's little game. *What a creature you are*, she thought. Four years ago, soon after Leif and Tyrkir had sailed, the daughter had begun to ingratiate herself with the father. She groomed his brown-and-white pied stallion, brought his cup without being asked. Even on the day of the sauna, she regularly managed to cross Erik's path, as if by chance, and then happened to drop her bath towel. She didn't pick it up immediately and disappear in the women's shelter, no. First, her hair was straightened with an innocent look, then a twist, and finally, while bending down, her bottom was stretched.

Thjodhild shook her head. Erik had never encouraged his daughter to do so, but this young woman actually tried to ensnare her father. She also had sat at his feet when he talked about the dam and asked for details when everyone else had stopped listening. And today? On his day of honor, of all days, she disrupted the ceremony.

"... and may the strong hand of Thor protect the dam from now on so that our meadows will always have enough water, and we can bring rich hay to the barns in autumn!" No sooner had Erik finished than he pointed to the sky again. "A sign. There, you see!"

High in the blue, a white falcon was circling over the lake. "Goddess Freya herself has come to our feast. What great joy."

Thorstein did not share the amazement of the adults. He'd found a stone and was challenging his sister.

"Very well," she whispered. "But you first. Show what you can do!" The eleven-year-old bent his arm back and hurled the bullet far across the lake. The stone finally splashed into the water almost on the other side.

The noise destroyed the reverence of the moment. Before Thorstein could flee, his father jumped down from the boulder and gave him a resounding slap to the face. "How dare you!" he snorted. The anger in his gaze flickered briefly. Then, calm again, the master builder invited his guests to join him to inspect the wall up close.

"I must show you where we drain the water in dry weather without dragging the dam down."

During the walk, Freydis pushed herself behind her younger brother. "You dope. You let me fool you. You're still the same dumb shit you were before."

On the right side of the dam wall, a narrow branch canal led to the wooden lock.

"So, let's assume it hasn't rained for a long time." Erik stood with his legs apart and pointed to the water dispenser. "Four farmhands can lift the individual beams with a winch, as needed."

Horn calls interrupted him. Distant horn calls, dark and long, then chopped off and long again. They blew from the fjord up over the plain.

Both families listened. Finally, Thjodhild broke the silence. "Leif!" She could hardly believe it. "It's Leif and Tyrkir."

Erik pulled at his beard. "Today of all days." He wiped his brow with his sleeve. "Truly. The gods love us."

The dam was forgotten. The young people raced to the horses. Egil, the neighbor's eldest son, got there before Thorvald and Thorstein. The young men were the first to lead their nags down the path, much to the annoyance of Freydis, who had to wait above with Ingva and Sigrid. "You cheating morons," she shouted after them. "I'll catch up with you!"

The descent was slower for the adults, and as she watched children chasing across the meadows, Thjodhild wished she could be with them. *No, not with them. Ahead of them*, she thought. She felt her heart beating. *I would like to greet my boy and Tyrkir before anyone else. How is my friend? Oh, beloved Frigg, highest of all goddesses, give me both back safe and sound!*

The beach below the embankment was in a state of excitement. While the servants were already unloading baskets and leather bags, the young people surrounded the captain and his pilot. Questions, laughter, embraces, and again, questions. Neither Leif nor Tyrkir managed to give clear answers except for *yes* and *good*.

Nobody had even noticed that there was a second ship anchored a little way from the *Mount of the Sea*.

"Father!" Thorvald warned. At once, the cries subsided. Order returned, as custom demanded. Man after man, the ship's crew took up their positions; the sons and daughters who had stayed at home left the returning men behind and formed a semicircle at an appropriate distance. Solemnly and slowly, the lord of Steep Slope rode across the gravel with his wife, followed by Ingolf Arnesson and his wife, Solveig.

Only after Erik had straightened in the saddle did his eldest bend his knee. "The journey was accompanied by good fortune. We only lost three of our servants in a storm off Norway. I return your ship to you safe and sound."

"Welcome, Son, in the name of Thor, our dear friend. Welcome to your father's roof." Although Erik had the second knarr in his sights, he didn't mention it. "You may now greet your mother."

With quick steps, Leif was at Thjodhild's side and lifted her out of the saddle. She hugged him, wanted to kiss him, but didn't. She stroked his hair lightly. "My boy. I'm so happy."

Erik looked down at Tyrkir, and the corners of his mouth twitched. "Welcome, Know-It-All. Why so late? Did you lose your bearings?"

"Is that how a gentleman greets a gentleman? I won't say anything until you dismount."

"I missed that sound." Laughing, the giant swung himself off his horse and laid both hands on his friend's shoulders. "Except for all the work, it was almost boring without you. And we drank all your brew."

"Those who despise my berry wine are not worthy of tasting the best mead. I brought ten skins from Norway—don't even think I'll share this good wine with you."

"You wouldn't dare!"

"Enough, you two!" Thjodhild interrupted. "Before you start where you left off, I demand my rights." She reached out her hand to Tyrkir. "My house was empty without you."

He felt the trembling, took in the warmth of her gaze, and said, "I bring your son back to you." After a short time making sure that Erik wasn't listening, he quickly, almost imploringly, added, "Whatever happens in a moment, you must know that I will never let you down."

She looked at him, concerned, but there was no time to ask for an explanation. Leif joined them, accompanied by the neighbors. Meanwhile, Erik had been staring at the second ship. "Not a bad knarr. Whose is it, Son? Yours or ours?"

"I am the owner. My business in Norway went even better than I had hoped." Leif's words flowed faster. "It's like this, Father. Returning, we rested for two nights at the trading post down at the south cape, and there, with some of the silver, I bought this knarr from the son of old Herjulf. I named the ship *Falcon*, a beautiful name. Do you like it?"

Erik was only half listening to his son. "Strange," he murmured to himself as he started toward the new knarr.

Leif stayed close by his side. "Let's take our time tomorrow to inspect the ship! Tomorrow, not now."

But Erik would not be stopped. Slowly, Tyrkir followed them with Thjodhild and the neighbors.

"Who is that?" Erik asked. His hand pointed up to the quarter-deck. A small figure stood with its back to them. The head was covered by a hood, and the simple tunic was made of the same brown fabric. A rope was tied around his hip as a belt. "Who is that?"

"A friend."

"Why doesn't he ask for shelter?"

"Because he is my guest. And because I don't know . . ."

"I won't ask you again."

Then the stranger turned. Erik blanched and took a step back. With a faint groan, Thjodhild reached for Tyrkir's arm. It was not the face that frightened her—it was the silver cross on the man's chest. "Greetings in the name of the one true God." He bowed his head. "I am Father Ernestus."

Suddenly, Erik raised his fist, making incomprehensible threats, then paused, and his face smoothed a bit. "Oh, now I understand." He gave his son a friendly push. "He's your prisoner." He turned to his wife and the guests. "You see? A Christian snuck aboard on the way, and because my son has a soft heart, he didn't know where to take him." Again, he prodded Leif. "Why didn't you say that outright? Don't worry, boy, this will be done quickly and cleanly. I'll have him put to sleep up on the edge of the glacier with a nice piece of bacon in his teeth. The wild animals will be pleased."

"No, Father. Priest Ernestus is my friend, and he enjoys protection and holy hospitality on my ship." Leif's sparse goatee shook. "No one is to board the ship without my permission, not even you."

Struck to the core, Erik gasped and looked across the bay as if the water would rise any moment. But it remained still. He looked up at the sky, but no clouds came. He turned around, shuffled across the gravel, and returned. "Fine. As if I care. The Christian is yours. I won't touch him."

"Do you promise?"

"You have my word." Erik's smile was tortured. "I trust you. Your parents and your godfather have taught you everything an honorable man needs to know, so you may decide for yourself. Nevertheless, listen to my advice and beware of the Christian's gossip."

With shaking fingers, Leif reached for his neck and fidgeted with the chain under his shirt. When he drew it out, there was no Thor's hammer, but a cross. Slowly, he pressed it against his chest.

Erik staggered, the amber in his eyes dulled, and he sought Tyrkir's gaze. Wordlessly, his friend pulled out an identical cross.

"You too?" Just one statement, then the lord of Steep Slope pointed to the line of boatmen. "I know the crew would not disobey a captain's order."

Tyrkir stepped forward, but Erik raised his hand—"Don't, Know-It-All"—and went to his horse. His hand brushed across the mane. "Treason. My best friend betrayed me." He climbed into the saddle.

No one spoke until Erik had left the pebble beach. As he rode up the path to the farm, Thjodhild whispered, "Poor, sad man. And today was to be your big day." She turned to Tyrkir. "We inaugurated the dam this morning. The wall really seems to be holding this time. He was so proud of his work."

"I'm sorry. If I'd known about the feast, we'd have come into the bay tomorrow."

"I'm so glad you're here." She stared over at the priest. "But I must admit, as humbly as he stands there, Father Ernestus leaves me a little perplexed. Have you really converted to the new faith?"

"Leif was baptized in Norway. As for me—"

"No, no long explanations now," she interrupted. "You'll be spending a lot of time on those in front of Erik. Just tell me one thing: Was your decision the right one?"

"Yes." He looked at her openly. "With heart and mind, yes."

"All right. Then I will join you in the struggle for peace on our slope. I promise you."

"Thank you." With that, he felt strengthened as he went over to Leif.

*Although I do not know how,* Thjodhild thought sadly, *we must try. Oh, my friend, how I have missed you. Your face is still pasty and gray from the journey. Your eyes are enough for me.*

Ingolf Arnesson took the first load off her shoulders. "My Solveig and I think that you and your family will want to be alone today. We thank you for the invitation, and we're going home."

"Understanding neighbors are a blessing. Thank you. But our feast is only postponed. Excuse me." On foot, Thjodhild moved toward the steep slope, hoping to make sense of everything by the time she reached the farm.

The parents mounted their horses and ordered their children with a wave to come along, no grumbling. Even the young people had realized that it was not to be a joy-filled day.

Sigrid quickly said goodbye to Thorvald and he helped her into the saddle. Her sister hesitated, then ran to Leif. The blood rose to her cheeks. "I was waiting for you."

"Let me look at you, Ingva. You're beautiful—" His voice choked suddenly, as if an invisible force was closing his throat. He coughed and finally managed to continue. "Better not. I mean, I'm not feeling so good today. But that's very kind of you."

"See you soon," she whispered, and ran to join her family.

Egil led his horse by its halter. He stopped by Leif for a moment. "Hey, a good ship, your *Falcon*!" Then he whispered, "Are you sticking to our plan? I haven't told anyone. So far, the country in the west waits only for us."

"Leave it for now," Leif murmured. "You see what's going on. First, I have to sort things out with my father. We will go. I'll let you know when."

"That's all I wanted to know." Egil swung himself up. "Good to have you back." And in a fast tölt, he rode after his family.

"Good to be back? I could cry with joy." With a bitter smile, Leif climbed onto the *Falcon*.

In the meantime, Tyrkir had ordered the yard tree to be laid lengthwise, and the board tent erected above it. Provisions and water were carried on deck. Father Ernestus wanted to help, but Tyrkir was unusually strict. "Beware, pious man! We're no longer at sea. If you want to earn respect here, leave the work to the servants."

"As a servant of God, I am sworn to humility. In my convent, it was the rule to do all work. Even Jesus Christ was not ashamed—"

"Damn it, this isn't Saxony. You're in Greenland!" Tyrkir wrung his hands and tempered the tone. "We talked about it often during the journey. The people here do not feel they lack Christ in their lives. They have enough gods and are satisfied with them. Your being here causes trouble, and King Olaf cannot protect you. My godson and I will help you as best we can. Just, please, try to fit in with the old order for now. Do not act as a servant, but as a master who preaches the message of an even greater master."

Ernestus pulled back his hood and thoughtfully stroked the shaved area at the back of his head. "Hearing you explain it that way, I believe you should be preaching in my place."

"I still know too little of what the Bible says." Tyrkir smiled for a moment. "But who knows? I'm a fast learner."

"My uncle's right," Leif interrupted. "We must be smart." He looked up at the house on the hill. "If not, Thor will jump off the wagon and crush Jesus with his hammer before he even has a chance to open his mouth."

Ernestus took his cross in both hands. "The ways of the Lord may be tortuous, but they do lead to his will."

"Amen," Tyrkir added dryly. "We must go. And this particular road is not tortuous, but steep."

To protect the priest, Leif sent two more guards aboard. They received orders to prevent any visitor—if necessary, by force of arms—from boarding the ship.

"My prayer accompanies you," the priest shouted after them.

"That won't do us much good today," muttered Tyrkir. From then on, the men remained silent.

No sooner had they reached the courtyard than Freydis ran toward them. "Brother! You haven't even greeted me properly." She turned in circles on tiptoe. "Don't you like me anymore?"

"Yes, of course."

Tyrkir saw how troubled his godson was. "I'll bathe first. Come along! A little hot water won't harm you, either."

"It's all right, Uncle. I'll meet you later. But let's go to the hall."

With a shrug, Tyrkir disappeared behind the house.

"The old man's finally gone." Freydis pushed herself close to her brother. "Well, you Christian, where's my gift?"

"Tomorrow you can pick out a fabric."

She moved her mouth, and Leif remembered what he'd brought her. "You're still going on about that?"

"You idiot. Don't you dare insult a woman!"

"I wasn't going to."

Mollified, she stroked his dirty shirt and played with his cross. "I could help you wash."

"Leave me alone! You'll make my head explode." He stormed after his uncle.

Freydis had her index finger dancing on her lower lip. "I wonder, Brother, how long you'll get to keep that head. Father won't need an ax. He'll just tear it off."


During the meal, Erik remained monosyllabic, his gaze occasionally settling on his friend. He didn't even acknowledge Leif. It was difficult for the young skipper to respond to his brothers' curiosity, so his tales of travel and adventure, even the royal court, remained lifeless and without color.

"It must have been boring," Thorstein complained. "Did you at least see a whale?"

"Yeah, maybe."

In order not to let the mood sink even further, Thjodhild intervened with a smile. "As soon as Leif has rested, he will gladly tell about his journey. Now, go!" She banged her spoon on the tabletop. "Freydis, that goes for you, too. The men want to talk alone."

Outraged, the young woman threw back her braids. "Every time it gets exciting, you chase me away."

Erik raised his hand, and that was enough. Freydis strolled slowly through the hall. At the weapons rack, her fingers stroked some spear and ax shafts and plucked the feathers in the arrow quiver. And then, all of a sudden, she ran out of the room.

The silence stretched uncomfortably. At some point, Tyrkir offered to have a jug of Norwegian mead brought by the maids. "I'm sure a welcoming drink will do us all good."

"I've lost my thirst." Determined, Erik stood up. The stool toppled, but he didn't care. His back stiffened with every step, and by the time he'd settled on his high bench, cold dignity surrounded the lord of Steep Slope. "I am waiting."

One more look passed between uncle and godson, then they went together to the center of the living hall. Thjodhild rested her forehead in her hand; she wanted to follow the conversation from the table.

No, the two were not allowed to sit. "Whoever violates the sacred law of the family shall stand before the chief until the sentence is pronounced."

"Why do you judge before you hear us, Father?" Leif clenched his fists behind his back. "Or are we here at the gates of a court?"

"Were you expecting anything else, Son? This is a clan Thing. My position and the holy law allow me to condemn you and the German."

"You hide behind the law, you of all people, Erik the Red? I can't believe it. Was everything Uncle told me wrong? That trial against you in Iceland? It was then that the holy law tore our family apart." The attack had an effect, and Leif looked up. "Are you so old that you've forgotten the injustice against you? No, I can't believe it because I respect you, Father."

Erik looked up at the wind-eye for a long time. When he

returned his attention to his son, his voice had lost some of its coldness. "It was a hard time, boy, and I thought I'd left it behind me for good. Until you and Tyrkir showed me the cross . . ." He ran his fingers through his hair. "No, I will not pass judgment until I've listened. But how could this tragedy have happened?"

At the table, Thjodhild sighed in relief. It was a small step. Perhaps a way could be found after all.

"First, we were forced to the Hebrides. It took several weeks before we reached the southwest and could sail on." Leif did not reveal more about his stay there, and since his godfather didn't interrupt, he continued on. "We arrived in Norway at the end of August and anchored in Trondheim Harbor. Soon, King Olaf Tryggvasson summoned us. Father, it was as if we had entered another world. . . ."

"Save it for later. Right now, I just want to know how this god caught you."

"But the royal court's involved. Olaf Tryggvasson has converted to the Christian faith."

Leif didn't give his father any time to recover from the news. As he continued, Erik clawed his hand into his beard as if he had to hold on to it. Close to the king, there was no one left who had not been baptized. Olaf did his own missionary work and had set himself the goal of eradicating the old belief in the gods. With his bodyguard, he traveled from one district to the next. Anyone who resisted was forced by sword to be baptized, or else they would lose their lives most cruelly.

"Father, we had to watch how a man who disobeyed was tortured. He wouldn't let go of Odin and Thor. A stone was wedged between his teeth so that a snake could crawl into his mouth. Even the snake refused. By order of the king, the executioner tied a red-hot iron to the tail of the beast. And the serpent crawled into the mouth cavity and down the throat where it ate the man's soft parts."

Thjodhild froze. *What kind of god is that? If he forces people to believe in him with such cruelty?*

Erik leaned back. "Fear. Now I'm beginning to understand." He looked at his son and his friend. "You became Christians out of fear because Olaf would have killed you. Very clever. Don't worry. You're safe from him here, so you can take down that cross again."

Tyrkir pulled up a stool. Even without permission, he took a seat in front of Erik. "No, no. It's not that simple. The king's arm reaches far."

"What do I care about Norway. I'm the lord here."

Tyrkir rubbed his ear. "Let's talk about that later. So far, you only know one reason why it would be wise to convert to the Christian faith. Let's talk reason. I'm thinking about our business. We would not have been able to sell even one skin in Trondheim if Leif had not been baptized, or at least accepted the cross. Christians don't like to deal with heathens."

"Heathens?"

"Yes, that's what they call all those who still worship the gods in Valhalla. We must change our ways, my friend, and quickly, or soon no one will buy our goods. We'll lose our business connections, and with them our wealth."

"I don't think so. We can sell our woven fabrics, furs, and ivory anywhere."

"Father." Leif moved closer. Beseeching him, he raised his hands. "A new era has long since dawned, only we in Greenland have not noticed it."

Erik ran his fingers through his hair. "Since I can remember, I've lived with my Thor. I'll never give him up. I've taken every vow in his name and kept my word." He leaned toward Tyrkir. "And what about you? Did you throw your Tyr into the garbage with your baptism, just like that?"

"No." Tyrkir hesitated. He'd feared this answer for weeks. "I was not baptized in Norway."

"You want to tell me . . ." The giant rubbed his knuckles together violently. "There, there, my son and the crew run into trouble, and our Mr. Know-It-All stays out of it."

Thjodhild could no longer stay at the table; she came to the great fire and sat next to Erik. "I, too, thought that you and Leif had converted to the new faith." Her tone carried a bitter reproach.

"Not out of cowardice," Tyrkir assured her. "I didn't have to put on the white shirt because I was baptized right after I was born." He looked at her sternly. "I have always been a Christian."

Erik's hand went to his belt and drew out his knife. "Cheater!"

Thjodhild fell onto his arm. "Don't you dare! This is my house!"

"Let go, woman!" Erik pushed her aside, and instead of throwing the dagger at his friend, he threw it over the fire. The blade struck the bench of honor hard.

Thjodhild touched her aching shoulder. Frightened at his own reaction, Erik paused. "It's all right. Forgive me." He looked at Leif. "I did not want . . . I would never hit your mother." He narrowed his eyes at Tyrkir. "You're to blame, damn it! Why would you say that? We grew up together, shared our lives together. It was through you that I learned the stories of our gods. And now my best friend claims that he's been lying to me all these years."

"No, that's not true. Let me finish, and you'll understand." Cautiously Tyrkir tried to untie the knot. "Leif can testify that I was ready to be baptized in Norway."

But before that, the king's bishop, who himself had come from Germany, had had a conversation with him. When he'd heard about the village on the Rhine, he recalled that the people in that area had been Christians, even then. Tyrkir had been held over the baptismal font as a newborn child and a second time would be against God's will.

"So, I am a Christian, only I had forgotten it. I had also forgotten my Christian name, Thomas. Now and then, I remembered the church in our village, an image, nothing more." Tyrkir looked at his hands. "To make my slave life with the Vikings easier, my mother named me after God Tyr and gave me the firm trust in the Aesir in Valhalla. As well as I got along with the gods later, the true faith never let go of me. I know that now." He raised his head. "Even in this house, there is proof."

"Those crosses on your neck," growled Erik.

"You'll be surprised." A smile played at the corners of Tyrkir's mouth. He asked Thjodhild to get the soapstone lamp that Erik had given her out of joy over her first pregnancy. He showed them both the carved picture. "This woman is nursing her child. I didn't think about it then, but it is Mary who is holding Jesus in her arms. Christians pray to the Virgin Mary when they are in need."

Thjodhild carefully followed the lines. *So this is the mother of the son of God*, she thought. *How often have I looked at them with love?*

"Let me see!" Erik grabbed the lamp and growled. "I, of all people, have something like that in my house?" And he threw it into the embers.

"Father!" Leif jumped in, grabbed it with his bare hand, and returned the gift to his mother unharmed.

"Thank you." Thjodhild left the high seat. "Enough for today," she said. "Wounds don't heal in a day." She asked the voyagers to go to bed. Without a word, Tyrkir left the hall with Leif.

After some time had passed, Erik followed her into the chamber. Like a child, he sought shelter. Her touch freed him from the tightness and soon aroused his desire. "You're sure?"

"Yes, dearest. Today is your feast day, and I want to celebrate it with you."

She let him, without showing how little pleasure he gave her. *Maybe that must be my task*, she thought later as she listened to the quiet snoring next to her. *Perhaps I can keep the peace on Steep Slope.*

# THE BAPTISM

"A dead man!" It was four days later that the scream tore through the servants' house. A milkmaid ran into the living hall, interrupting the family's breakfast. "Master, a servant is lying behind the main b-barn," she stammered. "I came back from milking, and he was just lying there on his stomach."

"Calm down and get back to work!" Without delay, Erik emptied his cup of sour milk. "I'm sure he's just sleeping."

Freydis bent over the pot with a giggle and stirred the meat with a ladle. "You'd better have a look, Father."

She was scolded by Thjodhild. "This is men's business."

Erik got up. "Are you coming?" he asked his eldest. "Now that the ships have been unloaded, you should get used to your duties as a junior farmer again. And what about you, Know-It-All?"

Both men willingly followed Erik outside. On the way, he reported how many foals and calves had been born since they'd left. "We can be satisfied."

He had not mentioned their first evening, not even the priest, who was still living on the ship, and Tyrkir was grateful for that. *Let's fall back into the daily routine*, he thought. *Then, we'll gradually convince my Viking that the new faith will not poison his Greenland.*

Some slaves were waiting near the long hayloft. "What are you standing around for?" Erik asked. "Do you think the grass will cut itself? Off you go!"

They found the servant behind the barn, lying between scythes, rakes, and pitchforks; the frame on which the tools were usually hung had fallen over. Erik lightly poked the man with the tip of his foot. "Hey, wake up!" The man lay there motionless, his arms twisted; his nightshirt had slipped up to the back of his knees.

Leif crouched next to the still servant. "It's useless, Father. He's lying on a hay rake." He gently rolled the body around. The sharp wooden teeth were still stuck in the man's neck.

Without looking, Erik grumbled, "Close his eyes first!" Then he looked at the face distorted by shock and turned to his friend. "He was with you on the journey. Or am I wrong?"

"He was part of the crew."

"What was he doing hanging around the barn?"

Tyrkir shrugged and pointed up to the attic hatch. "Perhaps he lay down to sleep on the hay bundles up there, fell down, and, unfortunately, fell on the rack."

"That's what must have happened. Poor fellow. We'll miss him." Erik did not show more regret. The death of a slave meant the loss of a worker, and he needed everyone urgently for the hay harvest. "Providence has willed it so. When the workers return from the meadows, I'll have him buried in a slave grave down by the fjord." With that, the matter was settled for Erik. "Come on, let's go check on the horses."

"No, Father."

"What?"

Leif approached him calmly. "A Christian has the right to lie in consecrated ground, and this man has been baptized."

The vein of anger jumped onto the giant's forehead, but he fought it. "Good, good, Son. I swore to your mother I would do nothing against the priest. She also demanded that I let the Christians do as they would, and I must keep my word. Consecrated ground? Where is it?"

Surprised by the question, Leif was silent. Before he found an answer, Tyrkir realized what a chance this was. "It is a field of eternal peace. Something like a sacred farm where the living and the dead find protection. If it is not given to the Almighty God, he will hurl his curse on our pastures and houses. And believe me, my friend, the Lord God has more power than the Aesir in Valhalla put together. That's why we need a piece of land." Tyrkir rubbed his scar violently. "Why didn't I think of it right away? Father Ernestus must sanctify this field with prayers and holy water before it's too late."

"You know a great deal, Know-It-All. And your god doesn't strike me as particularly friendly." Erik was met with blank stares. "Very well. Choose a place for him, but far enough away from my home."

Leif lowered his head. "Thank you, Father."

"Tell your mother, not me. I . . ." With a nervous gesture, Erik pointed across the meadows. "I have to go up to my dam, check the wall." And he was already on his way. Over his shoulder, he called back, "The Christian body is your problem. Take it away!"

For a while, the two men watched Erik's back grow smaller. "Do you think he will be converted, Uncle?"

"It would be better for all of us, but I know that pigheaded man. We'll have to wait and see." Tyrkir pointed to the dead man. "As terrible a death as our crewman suffered, we should be grateful to him."

Leif did not understand, and Tyrkir gave him a small smile. "Without struggle, we got land from your father. The first piece of land for the Christians in Greenland! Untouchable! Do you understand now? And not just for the dead. Why shouldn't there be room for the living next to the cemetery?"

"Father Ernestus." Leif struck his forehead. "You're brilliant, Uncle. We can build a home for the pious man, and he can move there from the ship. No, I have a better idea. We could put his church right next to it."

"The harbor is still a long way off, boy," Tyrkir said, dampening his zeal. "A small house with a hearth and a weatherproof roof will do for now. May God forgive me for this little ruse. Your father is, and always will be, my best friend. I want to provoke him as little as possible, or he'll never find the faith." His gaze again drifted to the dead man. "But now we should hurry."

Tyrkir stopped and looked at the smock shirt more closely. It wasn't the bloodstained chest area that interested him. He pointed to a palm-sized patch deeper down. "The injury to his neck killed him. But where did this blood come from?"

Leif freed the corpse from the hay rake and pulled the gown up. Above the pubic hair, a broken arrow was stuck in the abdomen. "Damn," he whispered. "What now, Uncle?"

"I don't know yet, boy."

Was an enemy threatening them? The thought was frightening at first but was quickly dismissed. There was no feud with any neighbor. Still, the arrow wound could not be denied. Enemies, after all? But how had the servant fallen victim to them? Suppose he'd been upstairs sleeping in the hay. No archer, no matter how good, could have shot him in the guts. The servant must have been standing directly at the opening of the storehouse, making him an easy target. And if he was hit that way, he would have fallen onto the hay rake.

"No, impossible." Tyrkir smoothed the smock shirt. "There's no hole. The blood has soaked the fabric from the inside."

"So, he was naked?" Leif grinned. "He stuck his cock out of the hatch up there because he wanted to pee. That's what happened, Uncle."

His godfather searched the ground around the body. "Then the feather shaft would have to be here. No, the boatman was hurt, and before he fell, the arrow was broken off. No doubt he knew the person, or he wouldn't have exposed himself in front of her. There's no enemy, but there is a murderer!"

"You mean a maid? He met her in the hay? Then a fight?"

"Not here!" Tyrkir said sharply. "We must decide what to do, and we must decide now." If they waited for Erik to return, there would be a lengthy interrogation. A maid might even be convicted. A forbidden meeting with a Christian! "She will have taken an arrow from necessity and will surely escape without punishment. But this incident gives your father one more reason to see Christians in a bad light." Tyrkir nodded grimly. "The servant has fallen onto the hay rake. It should stay that way. We'll have to take our chance now and stake out that piece of land before Erik changes his mind."

Leif agreed but decided to keep an eye out for the murderer. They shared the tasks. While the godson fetched the priest from the ship, along with incense and holy water, Tyrkir wanted to go to the house and ask Thjodhild to choose the field for the cemetery and the pious man's home. Time was pressing.

"Et requiem capiat sempiternam. Per dominum nostrum." Only two stones' throws west of the embankment near the brook, Father Ernestus stood in the afternoon sun scattering dirt into the grave.

"Amen," muttered Leif and Tyrkir. Two of the Christian boatmen grabbed the shovel.

Thjodhild had watched the burial within earshot. The priest approached her, beaming. *How changed he looks now*, she thought. He had seemed so small and inconspicuous on the ship in his brown robe, but the white, billowing gown and his shawl transformed him.

"Though the occasion is a sad one ... I am happy to meet the wife of the Gode Erik Thorvaldsson." He gave her the back of his right hand. Thjodhild did not know what to do with this gesture, and because a handshake was not possible, she only briefly touched his fingertips.

"Welcome to Steep Slope, Father Ernestus."

"Welcome. This word is a gift to me. Blessed be the Lord for bringing me to this place of peace and devotion after a rough journey. How wonderful the view is from here across the waters of the fjord and up to the snowcapped mountains." Ernestus spread his arms. "Yes, praise and thanks be to the Lord!"

Thjodhild smiled. "I must confess, my husband did not do this of his own free will. It would be better if you stayed out of his way."

A shadow crossed the smooth, soft face. "Leif told me about the fight, and it grieves me, but I did not mean his father, but him, the Lord of heaven and earth. My first thanks go to the ruler of all destinies." He embraced her with a fervent gaze. "My second thanks go to you, and I hope to welcome you to our community soon."

Although Tyrkir stood nearby and wanted to intervene, he had not been able to prevent the last sentence. Angrily, he pulled the priest away from Thjodhild. "What's the hurry?" He pointed to the simple burial cross. "There stands the first sign of the Christians in Greenland. Isn't that enough for today?"

Father Ernestus nodded. "I got carried away. She is a truly impressive woman."

"I agree with you on that," Tyrkir said. Deep below, the water flashed and glittered. In the late afternoon, the sun cut a silver road from the west across the bay. "You should leave here as soon as possible if we do not want to endanger what we've achieved." He helped the priest collect the holy utensils and left him to his godson. "I think until we build a permanent place for our guest, he'll be safer aboard the *Falcon*."

On the way back to the house, Thjodhild strolled next to her friend. She felt lighter. *Maybe it's because you're near*, she thought. "Do you know why I chose this particular meadow by the stream for the sacred grove? After our arrival, this is where I rested for the first time."

"A good omen. And I am grateful to you for it."

She looked at him from the side. "Have you changed?"

Tyrkir stopped. Before he could answer, she added, "I do not mean you as a man. I only ask, has this other faith of yours changed anything in you?"

"No, I feel the same." Thoughtfully, he stroked his scar. "Only a few months ago, I begged my beloved Tyr or the other Aesir for help, and today it is Jesus and his mother Mary, or even the great God himself." He raised his shoulders and smiled. "So far, I've only changed their names, that's all. Admittedly, the Christian faith may be simpler. Instead of the many, now a single one has all the responsibility."

"And what of Thomas, your Christian name? Will you retake it?"

"No, I don't want the change to go that far. That would be betraying myself. Everything I am connects me to Tyrkir, and I'll hold fast to it."

Thjodhild waved her cloak. "The priest looked so festive. And his singing during the ceremony, I loved to listen to it."

"I only hope"—Tyrkir looked over at the farm buildings—"that our Viking will soon be able to bear this singing."

In an instant, the lightness of the moment fell away. "I try to make us happy." She didn't tell her friend how long the time felt every evening before Erik had finally fallen asleep next to her.

The lord of Steep Slope said nothing about the cross. When the Christian servants went over to the holy grove night after night after their day's work, he remained silent. But then one morning, it became clear that a house had been built there.

"Damn it! By Loki!" All the pent-up anger broke out of him. "Cursed by the Midgard Serpent! Let her eat the Christian vermin!" Erik roared in the hall, outside in the yard. One servant who didn't move fast enough was knocked down as Erik hurtled inside, screaming as he looked for his son.

He finally found him at the smelting furnace in front of the forge. "How dare you? I'm still the head of our family, and I tell you, I will never tolerate a priest near me."

"Ernestus needs a place to stay." Without looking up, Leif smashed a piece of slag and threw only the small lumps of iron back into the melt. "He has my hospitality."

The courage of his firstborn child took Erik's breath away. Dangerously quiet, he warned, "Order is shattered if a son dares to rebel against his own father!"

Leif flinched. He stopped working and turned around with his chin raised. "I'm not fighting you, Father." He threw the hammer aside to underscore his words. "I love and respect you."

"Then prove it. Send this hypocrite back!"

"No. The Christians on our farm need a priest. The roof will be ready tomorrow. And from then on, Ernestus will live by the cemetery."

"My land—"

"It no longer belongs to you," Leif interrupted him. "Mother gave me the meadow, and I made it available to the true faith."

"Oh, how brave," Erik sneered. "My son is hiding behind his mother's skirt. But that won't help you. Her word is worth nothing."

"Father! She is your wife!" Leif's lips trembled, and he struggled to remain calm. "Mother has as much right to the embankment as you do."

"Don't talk like that, boy." But Erik knew that he could do little about Thjodhild's decision, and that powerlessness brought sweat to his brow.

"Very well." His voice sank to a whisper. "For ten days, I've tried peace, but my generosity just gets taken advantage of by you all."

His voice became louder and grew cold. "From now on, son, I won't be so benevolent."

After that, Christian servants were no longer allowed to sit with the others at the front of the hall during mealtimes. Instead, they had to retreat to the stable corridor in the back. "Your prattling will only spoil the decent slaves. And you—you will sit with them. I don't want to see you at my table again."

Leif blanched. He nervously reached into his hair and wiped his mouth but couldn't form a response. It was inconceivable that the young farmer on Steep Slope, the heir, should share the soup with the servants! This meant humiliation, a loss of honor and standing. "Let's talk this over," he said. "Please, Father!"

"It's too late. And do not think your mother will change my mind. You must obey my order, and you know it." But though Erik had scored a victory, no triumph shone in his eyes as he left his son and stomped away with heavy steps.

Leif took the smelting pan from the embers—the iron could wait—and he hurried to his godfather's workshop. "The peace is broken," he began, and after a brief report, only one pressing question remained: "Can he inflict this dishonor on me?"

Tyrkir nodded. The woman ruled the house and the maids. She also owned half of the property. But in the education of the children, the parents had equal rights. "Your mother must not disobey the order. At best, she could persuade Erik to take his verdict back."

"If you'd seen the old man, you'd know it's no use. He's decided to fight." Leif threw himself onto a stool. "I only made the solemn oath to King Tryggvasson to introduce Christianity here to keep violence and torture away from Greenland. And what have I achieved? My father's at war with me."

"Easy, boy!"

"You're one to talk! Tonight, I sit with the servants."

"Damn it, stop whining!" Tyrkir gave Leif a sharp look. "These men stood by you in your worst hours in the Hebrides. It won't kill you to share their food now."

Leif pressed his fists against his temples. "Yes, yes. But what should we do next, Uncle?"

"Now you're thinking. 'Never retreat, but move forward!' That's your father's motto, not mine, but maybe it'll help us now." Tyrkir stared out through the doorway. A path—he could see it, but his fear swelled. *O God*, he begged silently, *you cannot let this family be torn apart because of you.*

He turned back to his godson. "I have a plan, lad. No, don't ask, and you won't be blamed if it fails. I expect you to obey your father's orders without complaining."

Leif jumped up. In his face, pride struggled with reason, but finally, he said, "I trust you, Uncle."

The servants didn't care where they ate. When they returned from the meadows, they were told about the order. There was no confusion in the hall. The non-Christians sat at the front of the hall, and the baptized sat in the passage to the stable. When the young farmer sat down among his boatmen, there were astonished glances, but as the young gentleman silently filled his bowl, no one dared to ask. Soon the servants left the hall, happy and full. Leif also retired shortly before the family came in.

At the table of the lordship, not a word was spoken. The two younger sons spooned their fish stew with their heads bowed; even Freydis didn't dare look up. It was as if a boulder hovered over them, threatening to fall at any moment. Tyrkir chewed every bite for a long time. Thjodhild had lost her appetite completely. Only the lord of Steep Slope ate with grim pleasure, the fat dripping into his gray-red beard. Finally, he emptied two ladles of sour milk one after the other and burped audibly before retreating to the high bench in front of the great fire.

Tyrkir accompanied Thjodhild to the kitchen. "Let's talk," he murmured, and left the building through the back door.

A little later, she followed him outside, but she did not stop, storming past him and out into the pasture. When she reached the middle of the freshly mowed grass, she turned around. "What have you done to me?" There were tears in her eyes. "My son is cast out. Our slaves sit apart. What good is the new faith if it destroys our peace?" She clenched her fists. "I-I tried. But now it's too late. I can't convince Erik. The priest must go and take his Christianity with him."

She piled up the mown grass with the tip of her shoe. This was clearly difficult for her. "If you give up the cross, Leif and the others will take it off, too. I don't know what to do anymore. Help me. Save our happiness."

Her grief pained Tyrkir, and he felt the urge to embrace her or at least stroke her shoulders. "There's no turning back," he began quietly. "Whoever's been baptized remains eternally in the hand of the only God, whether he wants to or not."

"I forbid it!" She stomped her heap of grass in two halves. "Is this to be our future? People divided. How long will it be before they turn on one another?"

"That's what I wanted to talk to you about." Tyrkir pointed over to the farm. "Yes, I made a big mistake hoping to convince Erik slowly. I, of all people, should have known better. Now, the reality is rolling over us like a tidal wave. Thjodhild, we must grab anything we can to avoid drowning." He kneeled before the two mounds of grass. "You're right. Two groups with such different beliefs cannot live peacefully under the same roof for long." Except for a small mound, he pushed the grass from the left pile back to the right. "Do you see? We have to face facts, and we have to do so soon. You're the only one who can prevent the fronts from hardening for good."

"Haven't I done enough? No, say no more. I'll do anything if it'll help keep peace on Steep Slope."

Tyrkir stood, his pale, scarred face clearly visible. "It will take courage and strength. But success? I dare not promise it."

They walked together farther into the twilight. An icy wind was coming down from the glacier, and Thjodhild tightened her cloak around her shoulders. She shivered but wasn't sure whether it was because of the chill or the plan her friend had laid out before her. There was no other way, she soon realized. She had to do it, and the longer Tyrkir spoke, the more her heart wanted his scheme to succeed. "Isn't this treason against Erik?"

Tyrkir shook his head. "God will help me win back my friend!"

At the first light of dawn, the servants shuffled one by one from the low sleeping shed, stretched their aching backs, and yawned. It was a new day. They looked at the sky—a good day for haying. But at the entrance to the main house, they rubbed their eyes. The table was not laid. No giggles and chatter drifted from the kitchen. The hall was deserted, and the ashes of the previous day still covered the embers in the firepit. The men only grasped the truth very slowly: no breakfast.

For the first time on Steep Slope, there was to be no warm meal before work. Only after a long search did the men find a few buckets of fresh milk near the cow barn and a wicker basket full of dried fish next to them. Well, at least their hunger could be sated. The slaves were not required to know the why and wherefore, and so they went out with rakes and forks to turn the grass.

When Erik stepped out of the bedroom, only Thorvald and Thorstein were sitting at the polished table. "Where is Freydis?" he growled. He did not miss his eldest. "What about the German? Is he still sleeping?"

The sons were silent. They preferred not to look at their father.

Erik took his place and called to the kitchen, "You can bring the soup now! And another piece of seal bacon. I'm hungry."

Nothing moved; no one obeyed the order.

He looked at his sons. "Your mother left her bed long before I did, didn't she? Why doesn't she send the maid?" He struck the tabletop with his flat hand. "Answer!"

The youngest son slipped his stool back a little. "No one is there," he whispered. "All the women are gone, even Mother." Then he jumped up. He was lucky—his father's arm didn't reach him—but the blow hit his brother in the side.

"What's that supposed to mean?"

"Thorstein is right, Father," Thorvald confessed. "The kitchen's empty. I've looked in the stables. Nothing. Not a maid to be found." He stood to put some distance between himself and his father.

"They can't have just disappeared!"

Thorvald motioned for his brother to answer. The eleven-year-old gathered all his courage. "Over by the brook where the cross is, and the priest's house. They're all there now."

But instead of rage, Erik's shoulders sank. "It's okay. We won't starve right away. Check the fence ... Oh, never mind, you're old enough to find your own jobs." He pushed himself up from the table and left the hall.

Like a sentry, Erik took up a position near the sheepfold next to a boulder. Farther west, he saw the priest's grass-covered house, and no movement of the enemy escaped him. The women had gathered on the bank of the stream. A little to the side, he also spotted the traitors, Leif and Tyrkir. The priest stood high in front of the group, and sometimes his singing drifted over. Later, the women took off their coats and put on white robes. The priest solemnly climbed into the water. With an inviting gesture, he called the first of the waiting women to baptism.

Erik sank to the stone. "Thjodhild." The attack had begun, and he had no weapon to repel it. "All my life, I fought only for you, for a home without enemies." Immediately, his anger rose again. His fists clawed into his beard as he stared at the sky. "Great Thor! You have never let me down. Why now? This Christian god is also a threat to all of you up there, don't you realize that? Damn it, why don't you smash him with your hammer? Or are you afraid of him?"

No answer or help came from Valhalla.

Around noon, the white-clad army returned from the stream. The maids approached cheerfully, led by their tall mistress, whose gaze thwarted any resistance. The victors just nodded to the guard in passing, and thus the farm was conquered. "To work, girls! We must make up for lost time."

Erik shook off his daze. "That's true!" he growled. "Order must be restored, and right away."

In the forecourt, he met Freydis. As soon as she saw her father, she gave a little twirl. "How do you like me in my white dress?"

"You, too, then?" He stared angrily at the daughter. "Take that off!"

"That's forbidden, Father." She wagged her index finger in front of her nose. "The priest has ordered that we are not to remove our christening robes for a week. Our God will be angry if we disobey."

"You little—!" He shook his fist. "It's about time I finally found you a husband."

Maids emerged from the bedroom, arms piled high with pillows and blankets. They scurried wordlessly past their master. When he reached the threshold, his wife was just pointing to a laundry chest. "You can take that over there, too."

"Hey, Wife?"

Thjodhild turned. "Almost done." She put another cloak and a strap dress on top of the chest and sent the two girls out with it.

"Are you leaving me?"

She grabbed her headscarf and felt her fingers tremble. *Stay calm*, she urged herself as she checked the fit of her pinned-up braid. "No, Erik. I will not leave you." Far too quickly, the hair was fixed. "I'm moving over to the women's shelter."

"Don't you dare! Your place is in my bed."

"You're wrong." His threat gave her strength. "I'm not a cow you can tie up in a barn." She put her hands on her hips. "No, Erik Thorvaldsson. You will not lie with me until you have accepted the faith. Get baptized, and I will return immediately to my marital bed." She'd said it! For a moment, Thjodhild was frightened by her hardness. *No, you mustn't give in now*, she warned herself. *Stay strong.* "The Christian faith can no longer be stopped, so it would be better for everyone if we yielded to it. Please choose peace."

She wanted to push past him, but he put his hand against the doorpost. "You think I can't find a replacement for you?"

"You don't understand!" Anger blazed in her eyes. "Well, do it then!" she shouted. "Take a maid for yourself, but remember, every ass, every thigh here on this hill belongs to a Christian." Thjodhild pushed his arm aside and ran out.

"Wait!" He ran after her across the courtyard. "I command you!" Frightened, the maidens forgot to close their mouths. Never before had a dispute been aired so openly by their master and mistress. "Stop!"

Before he had reached the women's shelter, the door slammed shut, and with a hard noise, the beam inside dropped. "Damned woman!" Erik had already pulled his foot back, but he didn't kick the wood. Instead, he turned around. Only now did he notice the white-clad witnesses of his outburst. "Don't stare, you geese, or I'll pluck your feathers out!" With that, he stormed on to the forge.

Leif didn't even have a chance to greet his father. "It's your fault!" The vein in Erik's forehead throbbed threateningly. "You will not only eat from a bowl with the servants. No, Son, from tonight on, you'll sleep with them in the shed."

"You wouldn't dare, Father!"

"Are you deaf? Until your mother comes back to me, there's no more bed for you in the house."

Every firm resolve broke. Leif jumped up in a flash, hurling away hammer and pliers. "I have pride like you! My honor is worth as much as yours! I'm leaving." He thrust his finger at his father. "And should you ever need your son again, you'll have to beg!" Leif rushed out of the forge. "I'm sick of it! So damn tired!"

The tears only came when Leif was already on the path down to the harbor.

The rest of the baptism day passed without Leif returning. In the following days, bitter silence weighed on the magnificent estate on Steep Slope. Duties and responsibilities forced the family into a respectful coexistence. Leif lived aboard his ship, and his mother had a slave girl secretly bring him his food.

"What is my son up to?" she asked the maid one morning.

"I don't know exactly, my lady. Egil, the neighbor's son, is with him. And Christian boatmen come every night to work on the knarr. It looks like the young masters want to go on a journey." When the maid saw Thjodhild's shocked expression, she quickly added, "But I don't know for certain."

Thjodhild took her shawl. Not seeing Tyrkir in the carving workshop made her uneasy. When she found him near the wine cellar pressing huckleberries, his bloodred hands startled her. *Stay calm,* she ordered her heart, *or the last remnant of my mind will drown, too.* "Our plan's failed." The wrinkles deepened in the corners of her mouth. "I've just learned that Leif is preparing to leave for the royal court."

Tyrkir dried his hands, but the red stayed on his fingers. "To Norway? Now, so late in August? There's no wind for that."

"What do I care about the wind? I don't want him to leave us, do you hear? And even if he leaves, not like this. Not when he's angry. Or he'll never return."

She looked so helpless.

"I'll ask him. Right now." How he would have liked to have promised her more. And yet all he could say was, "Maybe I can change his mind."

Leif jumped off the deck, ran toward his godfather, and grabbed his horse's bridle. "Get off, Uncle!" No sooner was Tyrkir out of the saddle than Leif enthusiastically clasped his hands together. "Thank God. I was afraid you wouldn't come. Now nothing can go wrong." He turned back to the water. "Hey, Egil. What do you think of that? I've brought you the best pilot in Greenland."

The heir to the neighboring farm was so happy, he hooted.

Tyrkir couldn't believe it. Life was choking away on Steep Slope, and these young men here were almost bubbling over. "Why pilot?" He pulled Leif aside. "Maybe my old age is playing a trick on me, so enlighten me, boy."

"Hasn't the news reached that dark den up there?" The god-father's shrug unsettled Leif. "And I thought you'd come here to see how far we've come with the preparations."

"Where are you going?"

"West!"

The longer Leif talked about the unknown land, the more enthu-siastic he became. He crouched and charted the course from the Eriksfjord to the open sea using a pebble in the sand. "From there, it's said to be only a few days farther west. And if we don't find the coast, I don't care. We sail the day after tomorrow." He jumped up. "You see, Uncle, I have to get out of here. Fresh wind. There's order onboard. There are rules for everyone, and maybe it'll help me get my mind straight."

Tyrkir ran his fingertip over his scar. "It's not a bad idea."

"So, you're coming? Say yes!"

The temptation was too great. "You have my word." No sooner had Tyrkir given it than he regretted it. No, he shouldn't flee, leaving Thjodhild with her worries. Unless . . .

Suddenly, almost painfully, the thought came to him. Just another idea, but was it also doomed to failure? No, this time he was going to bring about the longed-for solution, and Thjodhild would find peace and would be able to breathe more easily for a time. "On one condition."

At first, Leif cursed, running around like an unruly horse. Sentence by sentence, he pulled the bridle in, and finally the godson stood calm and collected in front of Tyrkir again. "Maybe you're right, Uncle. We brought the unrest. Running away now would be cowardly. Mother doesn't deserve that. Neither does Father." He hurled a pebble far across the water. "But you're my pilot. I won't release you from your word."

"I stand by it." Tyrkir sat up and demanded a full report from the skipper: provisions for several weeks, weapons. The crew was made up of twenty of their own boatmen, and Egil contributed ten from the neighboring farm. "Very good, boy! The day after tomorrow, your pilot will come aboard, and he'll bring a guest."

Thjodhild was waiting for Tyrkir at the edge of the meadow. He waved to her, trying to send her comfort before he reached the top of the steep path. But only his words gave her certainty.

"So, Leif just wants to get away. Thanks to Frigg." She smiled softly and stroked her white christening robe. "No, thank the Blessed Virgin Mary! I must get used to the names." The plan to seek a new land didn't even seem to worry her much. Her beloved son wasn't breaking with the family. That alone was important, the first good news all these miserable weeks. "Thank you, too." With a light step, she hurried back to the house.

Tyrkir watched her. *I mustn't upset her again*, he thought. *If my plan fails, she won't have much time to think. Maybe the rush will help. . . .* He shook his head. *Stop doubting!*

If the Almighty God really held his hand over the embankment, the new plan had to succeed.

The next morning, as he had every day since the baptism, Erik, armed with bow, arrow, spear, and battle-ax, rode up to his dam.

Tyrkir let another hour pass, then followed the giant. Except for his hunting dagger, he'd deliberately forgone any weapon. Instead, he put a leather tube of mead into his saddlebag.

He let the horse trot and absorbed the crisp scent of the air, passing fully loaded hay carts and servants waving and cracking their whips over the backs of the sturdy oxen.

In his mind, Tyrkir returned again to the first poor farm on Sharpcliff. *We had to drag what little grass we could scavenge in worn canvas on our heads. And here? How easily the harvest can be brought in. We have enough fodder for the cattle, no matter how long the next winter lasts.* "Happiness is here," he murmured. "It is only we who have forgotten how to see it."

During the ride, he admired the dam for the first time. It still withstood the water's pressure, and on its left side, a narrow waterfall tumbled down. No sooner had Tyrkir reached the high valley than he uttered a sigh. "Yes, my old Viking, I can easily see why you retreat to this place."

The lake lay before Tyrkir like a deep blue eye embedded in the green of the meadows. His gaze wandered over the water, and he discovered the giant a little above the stream inlet. Erik jumped back and forth, swung his arm, threw himself into the grass, and immediately rebounded. At first, Tyrkir feared that his friend was possessed by an evil spirit, but halfway along the way, he noticed the weapons in Erik's fists. "Hey! May I come closer?"

The giant looked up for a moment before fighting on. This invitation was enough for Tyrkir. In a light tölt, he drove his horse closer and let it graze next to Erik's pied stallion.

He watched in silence. Erik had a short bow in his fist. He let arrow after arrow fly. Soon, his quiver was half empty while a white-gray bouquet of feathers blossomed on the opposite hillside.

Tyrkir applauded cautiously. "You haven't forgotten a thing."

"Do you want to have a go?" Sweat ran from Erik's forehead. His eyes glittered mockingly. "A little practice won't hurt you."

Tyrkir took the bow, lowered it to the target, and the arrow struck only a little beside the bouquet.

"Not bad," Erik growled. "But not better than me."

"Do you think I would dare compete with you?"

"Just as well, Know-It-All." He had already grabbed the battle-ax and swung it back and forth a few times. Then, accompanied by a wild scream, he let it whirl through the air. The blade dug itself into the ground between Tyrkir's arrow and his own bouquet. "Though I am old, I can still take on any enemy."

"Where's he going to come from?" Tyrkir showed him his open palms. "I'm not your enemy. Nor is your son. Who do you want to fight? The little priest?" Tyrkir paused. When Erik did not reply, he went a step further. "No man fights women, even if they wear white christening robes."

"She's left my bed."

"So what? She'll get back in."

"What do you know? First, I'm supposed to let that hypocrite bathe me in the stream, too."

"So? Water can't hurt you." Immediately, Tyrkir knew it had been the wrong thing to say.

"Go away, Know-It-All."

"I'm sorry." Tyrkir retreated a few steps, then turned back. "Where did we go wrong? Friends that no one could separate?"

Erik's shoulders dropped. "I . . . I don't know, either." He wiped his sleeve across his face. "Damn it, I don't know."

"Let's find a new beginning. We need to talk."

"I can't do it while the hypocrite is down there."

"I won't mention him. You have my word." Tyrkir touched Erik's calloused hand, and Erik didn't pull it away. "I have a proposition for you. I think we should go away for a while!"

"What?"

"You and me and Leif."

Before Erik grew suspicious, Tyrkir quickly told him about the planned journey west, that Leif and Egil had prepared the *Falcon* for departure. "We don't need to worry about anything. We just need to board the ship tomorrow morning."

"Tomorrow?" Erik's eyes darkened again. "Did Leif put you up to this? Did he send you to ask me?"

Tyrkir recognized his friend's need, and never before had a lie come to him so easily. "Would I be here otherwise? He needs us old men, our experience. You at the helm and me at the front of the ship. Without us, the search for new land is too daunting for him after all. Your son needs your help."

Erik lifted his spear and pushed the sharpened tip deep into the ground. "Then all is not lost." Almost shyly, he put his arm around Tyrkir's shoulder, drawing him to his side. "I'm glad you're with me."

"And I, you." Tyrkir looked at him from the side. "Come on!"

Together they went to the grazing horses, and Tyrkir pulled the mead tube out of the saddlebag. "I've brought another good friend with me."

Later, on the ride home, they laughed a lot and were still laughing when they stumbled into the living hall. "Hungry!" Erik bellowed.

"Where's the food?" Tyrkir clapped his hands.

Thjodhild chased her sons and Freydis out and told a maid to bring bowls in. It took her a moment to realize that the men weren't fighting. All she heard from the babble of words was:

"... and who knows if there's anything there at all."

"Never mind, we'll find something."

"Even if there's no land."

"You're right, Know-It-All, as usual. And now I'm tired." Erik staggered toward the bed chamber, then suddenly stopped. "No, I don't want to sleep alone." He turned around, discovered his wife at the passage to the kitchen, and drew in a sharp breath. His eyes softened. "All right, so no farewell. But I won't forget my love. You needn't worry about that." And he shuffled into the bedroom with a yawn.

Immediately, Thjodhild was at Tyrkir's side. She pulled his arm hard. "What's going on?"

"How beautiful you are."

She immediately took a step back. "And you're drunk." She grabbed a fire bucket beside the great fire and poured its contents over his head. "Now I want clarity."

The shock brought back some sobriety. "We're leaving—Erik, Leif, and I. Together. Tomorrow morning." He brushed his fingers through his wet hair. "And don't think we were drunk. It's true, beautiful woman. And all will be peaceful for you here. Thank God, that's all I wanted."

When he threatened to tip over backward, Thjodhild held him up. "It's all happening so fast."

"We can't miss the boat tomorrow."

He managed to get back on his feet on his own. Raising his hand, he said, "And I will bring your son back to you. Because I—because

I always come back to you. That's the way it is." And with that, he walked stiffly through the hall, almost missing the doorway.

Thjodhild sank onto a stool. "You dear, good friend," she whispered. She felt new hope rising in her. "Yes, go ahead. I'll wait for you. For all three of you."

Where was Erik? Perplexed, Tyrkir stood next to the saddled horses. The slaves had already made their way down to the dock at the first light of dawn. In the meantime, Thjodhild had ridden ahead with the children. She wanted to have time to say goodbye to her eldest.

When the friend did not show up for the early meal, Tyrkir had tried to wake him, but his bed had been empty. Could he have changed his mind? A horn signal came up from the *Falcon*. "Yes, damn it! You wait!"

Just as he was about to send a servant to search for him, Erik approached with big steps from the direction of the barns. "Let's go, Know-It-All," he shouted, and obviously had trouble getting into the saddle.

"Where have you been?"

"Before the head of a family leaves his estate, there are important things to do."

They rode across the meadow and reached the steep path.

"Even though my head is bursting, Norwegian mead tastes better than your brew."

"Too bad." Tyrkir shook his head. "I was about to admit that you really did create a work of art up there with that dam, but now I wonder if you designed it all by yourself."

"What are you talking about?"

"Well, if you're going to talk nonsense, I'm entitled to doubt your wits."

"Must you always have the last word?"

They looked at each other from the corners of their eyes and both grinned.

*We'll have time on the ship*, Tyrkir thought. *I won't torment you with talk of Christianity, but who knows? You might even ask about it yourself.*

They'd reached the bottom of the escarpment. In single file, they rode through a hollow to the pebble beach. Suddenly, a wild goose fluttered up in front of Erik. His stallion rose, neighing and bucking. Erik's reins were too loose in his fist; he fell and hit his back hard on a boulder.

At first, Tyrkir shouted, "Can't you be more careful?" Then he heard the moaning, jumped off, and was by his friend's side. "Get up! No, don't move! Damn it, we don't have time for jokes. Say something!"

Despite his pain, the giant managed to grin. "I've had a bit of a fall, Know-It-All." He coughed, then vomited. "We're not going on this trip after all. And I'd been looking forward to it."

"Stay there." Tyrkir cried over to the ship, waving until his calls for help were heard. "Where does it hurt?"

Erik's right arm hung limp. "In the shoulder. And something stings when I catch my breath."

"You're going to be okay. I'll make sure of it."

"No, you go with the boy. One of us old folks has to be there. I know why I fell off my horse, and I'll pay for it."

Leif was the first to reach the scene of the accident. "Father!" He threw himself on his knees.

Erik felt for his son's cheek with his left hand. "Thank you, my son. I just wanted to say that. Now set the sail. Good luck!"

Pale, Thjodhild crouched beside her husband and wiped the vomit from his lips.

"You just can't get rid of me, woman." Ashamed, he looked into her eyes. "I buried our silver. Behind the main barn. This is what I get."

"All right. We'll get you back in the house, and then we'll get the money box back." She smiled at him. "And with my care, you'll be fine. It wouldn't be the first time."

Erik asked Leif and Tyrkir to help him up. "I want to know what else has been broken." His feet and legs obeyed, and he stood half bent before them. "I've discovered one country. That's enough for one man. Get out of here! The wind won't wait."

Tyrkir hesitated, then looked at Thjodhild.

"Go on, my friend!" Her voice grew stronger. "It's fine."

On the way to the ship, Tyrkir kept looking back, but Thjodhild was busy with Erik and didn't wave.

# VINLAND

The green hills stayed behind; rock faces approached from either side. For two days, the glacial wind had driven the *Falcon* through the Eriksfjord, and now the gloomy gate to the sea rose before them.

In spite of their good progress, Tyrkir ordered to have the sail reeled in.

Leif obeyed reluctantly and came with Egil to the fore. "Why, Uncle? It's only noon."

"By the time we get out there, it may be too late." Tyrkir pointed to his sketch, which he had carved into a wooden plank. "So, from the beginning once more: What route did old Herjulf's son take? Show me."

The young men exchanged furtive looks. This was the fifth time the pilot had questioned them, and almost indulgently, Leif gave him the information again. He drove with his finger from the south cape of Greenland southwest across the sea to the lowest of the three circles marked.

"After his wanderings in the fog, Bjarne saw the flat coast with the hills and forests about here. Then he sailed northward in clear weather two days. And here he saw land again. It was also flat, and there were a lot of forests. He sailed on before a good southwesterly." Leif tapped on the top circle. "After three days, he approached this island. There are mountains and glaciers, nothing more. Bjarne heaved to and made it across in four days from there to the southern tip of Greenland, where he reached the trading post." He flashed a boyish smile for his godfather. "We're taking the same route. Happy?"

"No. Bjarne never went ashore, right?"

"He wanted to return to his father before winter."

Tyrkir stared at the board. Since they'd left Steep Slope, and he had seriously committed himself to this daring project, he'd been tormented by restlessness. "What if these shores were only illusions?"

"Oh, Uncle."

This time, Tyrkir noticed the look between the skipper and the first boatman. "I don't care what you think," he grumbled. "There's no leisurely cruising on these seas. Never. I am the pilot and am responsible for the course. If you don't like it, then take me ashore in the dinghy and go on your own."

Egil turned pale. "Please don't, my lord!"

Leif also recanted. "Sorry, Uncle. We don't mean to interfere."

Satisfied, Tyrkir nodded. His sharp tone had served its purpose. Any recklessness had to be driven out of these young lads from the start.

"Listen carefully!" Since Bjarne reached the lowest circle only by chance but sailed from the third coast high in the north to Greenland by his own reckoning, there was only one option. "We follow his route, but in the opposite direction. We'll sail first to the land he saw last."

Without hesitation, Leif agreed and gave Egil the order to raise the sail again. As the wind pressed into the red-and-yellow-striped cloth, the skipper shouted to the crew from the helm: "New land is waiting! Ran, you cruel one, spare us!" He quickly corrected himself: "God Almighty, may God protect us!"

The pilot did not, as expected, chart a direct course to the northwest. Instead, he led the ship past the fjords of the western settlement and farther up along the Greenland coast.

On the evening of the second day, the *Falcon* anchored in a bay. Soon, a fire flickered on the beach, and the servants were chewing their dried meat. Nobody spoke, but the expressions on their faces clearly showed what everyone thought: This was the journey to new shores?

A little way from the camp, Tyrkir stood on a rock, his gaze fixed on the water. Finally, Leif couldn't stand it any longer. He stomped over and asked from below, "Why are you hesitating? The spirits of the crew are dropping by the hour."

"Tomorrow." Tyrkir nodded to himself. "Tomorrow, we go." He climbed down slowly.

"What's on your mind, Uncle?"

"The frontier, boy." After a long pause, he quietly added, "Heaven and earth are floating in empty space—I explained this to you when you were a child. And the world is surrounded by water. Venture too far across the sea, and you either reach the realm of the giants or you fall over the edge into the yawning abyss."

Leif looked at him, concerned. "But, Uncle, I thought since we are now Christians, there's no more world serpent and giant. God has driven them all away, hasn't he?"

"From Midgard, yes. Let's just hope he also took care of those across the water."

"I trust him, Uncle."

"There's not much more we can do. You asked, and now you know why I'm being so careful." Tyrkir forced himself to smile. "Tomorrow, we set sail. Let's see what's on the border."

Neither the daughters of Ran nor a lull of the wind stopped the *Falcon*. They chased over the wave crests in a steady northeast breeze, and after three days and nights, Tyrkir called from the bow, "Land! Land ahead!"

As they drew closer, their last worries fell away. They saw a flat stone desert. Beyond it, high glaciers reached into a cloudy sky.

They anchored off the coast, and Leif ordered the crew to stay on board. He only had himself, Egil, and his godfather rowed to the beach.

They were still sitting in the dinghy. Undecided, Leif scratched at his goatee. "What now, Uncle?"

"Your father never asked such stupid questions." Tyrkir waved his hand. "Come on! You wanted to discover new shores, so be the first to set foot on them!"

With a shout of joy, Leif jumped out of the boat. After he'd run a little way over the flat stone blocks, he waved. "Is that far enough?"

His joy was infectious, and Egil ran over. They slapped each other on the shoulders and romped around like young horses new from the winter stable. Tyrkir followed them more slowly.

They both stopped short. The godson smacked his forehead. "Why are we laughing?" He pointed at the beach wasteland. "Not a blade of grass. Every sheep would starve here in a few days. This place isn't even worth talking about. Come on. I want to find a country I can be proud of!"

He was already heading back to the boat, but Tyrkir stopped him. "Not so fast, you great explorer. No matter what it looks like, think of the sailors who may find their way here after us. You must give this island a name."

"All right." Leif bent down briefly and hit the hard floor with his hand. "Because you're so dull, you shall be called Helluland... Rockland!"

While the dinghy was rowed back to the ship, Leif touched his godfather's arm. "What was it like? Did Father parse out names, as well?"

"Erik?" Tyrkir quietly laughed to himself. "He wasn't as resourceful as you. No matter where we anchored or pitched our tent, he named every spot after himself. Except for Greenland. He came up with that idea just before we left."

Even though the first stop had been disappointing, the success lifted their spirits. With shining eyes, Leif stood at the tiller, and with a full canvas, he sailed south, often sending Egil forward to the dragon's head to check their course. Finally, after another two days, Tyrkir announced again, "Land!"

Although they walked on a white sandy beach and saw endless forests in the distance, nothing invited the explorer. "This land shall be called Markland... Woodland! It doesn't deserve a better name."

The haste with which Leif set sail again, not even giving the line guards enough rest, neither at night nor during the day, concerned Tyrkir. The expression on his godson's face reminded him of how he'd come aboard in the Hebrides in the morning. *No, no danger,* he thought, reassuring himself. *There are no lecherous sorceresses or giants here.*

From one hour to the next, Tyrkir felt a strange heat rising. Stealthily, he looked around. The crew were pulling at the collars of their seal coats. Then he realized, this was no disease that had attacked the ship—no, the air had become warmer. And at the next sunrise, a coast gleamed far off to starboard.

While the knarr aimed for it, the men gradually got rid of their thick-weather clothing. Spray splashed up the bow, but that was not the only reason Tyrkir kept wiping his eyes. A headland— green meadows and hills. And then the pilot saw that there was an island off the tip of the coast. He sent Egil to the quarterdeck with the request to drop anchor there first. Leif handed over the tiller to his helmsman and came forward himself. "We have found our land, Uncle."

"Nevertheless, I think we should approach it carefully."

Leif agreed. "If we need to get to safety, we need a base of operations. First, we explore the island."

The explorers reached the beach in the dinghy. At first, they hardly dared to breathe. Almost devoutly, they walked through high, untouched grass, seeing flowers without knowing their names. Leif stroked across the still-dewy stalks, then licked his fingers. "Uncle!" Again, he tasted some dew. "Uncle!"

Tyrkir moistened his hand and brought it to his mouth—a sweet taste. He tasted again. There was no doubt about it. "I don't know how it can be, but the dew tastes like honey."

From the highest point, they quickly realized that the island was untouched, and so they dared to sail between it and the headland. A wide bay beckoned with white, elongated sandbanks. The water quickly became shallower. In their wonderment, neither pilot nor skipper had expected the onset of low tide, and soon the *Falcon's* keel was stuck.

"I won't wait for the tide to turn while I'm this close to my goal!" Leif called out. He gave orders for ten armed men to follow him, and he and Egil jumped off the ship, not even waiting for his godfather.

"Welcome to my land," Leif said to Tyrkir a little later. He laughed and proudly spread his arms. "Here we will—" All of a sudden, he grabbed his throat as if an invisible force were choking him. His eyes became wide. "Uncle. I see . . . there is a child—" He staggered, then he fell.

In the living hall on Steep Slope, Thjodhild bent down and helped the little boy back onto his feet. "Did you hurt yourself?"

He looked at her with astonished eyes, and although his mouth smiled, tears rolled down his cheeks. "I . . . am . . . Thorgils," he said clearly, gasping for breath between each word.

"It's all right, little one. I know that now." She led him to the table. "Would you like some milk?" He reached for it twice, then held the cup with both hands.

*He has such long, thin fingers*, Thjodhild thought, dropping herself on a stool. "Oh, Holy Virgin Mary!" She stretched both legs, punching her heels into the peat soil. "What did I do to deserve this?" Wasn't it enough that Erik was injured and that she was now solely responsible for the farm and its workers? She smiled sadly to herself. "I have to take a deep breath before I can think straight again."

Just that morning, the fog had finally lifted, and the weather promised to be fine again. Around noon, the long-awaited freighter had dropped anchor down in the harbor bringing grain and goods from the trading post, the last shipment before winter. Thorvald had supervised the unloading; the second eldest son was helping her run the farm. The shipmaster had come to settle the payment. Up to that moment, the day had brought only good things.

But no sooner had Thjodhild agreed to trade with the taciturn man who smelled of sweat and oil than he grumbled, "There is still one more piece of cargo for your family"—he whistled—"and this one's already been paid for."

His slave came in with fur blankets on his arm. At first, Thjodhild believed he bore a gift from old Herjulf. But the servant did not put the bundle down, instead carefully placing it in front of her before beginning to strip the fur away. A round, waxy face, blue eyeballs with white rims, and a smiling mouth proclaimed thoughtfully, "I . . . am . . . Thorgils."

A little later, the child stood before her. A much-too-large head swayed above the long, thin body.

Only after some time did she find her voice again. "Who is this?"

"I took the kid on at the settlement. Herjulf says he came over from the Hebrides on a long-distance sailboat." Her expression prompted the skipper to push the limits of a speech that was already excessively long for him. "He was looked after by a maid all the way to Greenland. Must be your Leif's son. His mother sent him. She paid well in advance for his journey and care. He's a good three winters old. Well, that's all I know." Visibly strained by his efforts, the skipper had nodded goodbye and left.

Thjodhild rubbed her forehead. *No matter what adventure Leif had gotten himself into in the Hebrides, he should have told me. At least Tyrkir could have warned me. But just you wait, when they return, then I'll—*

She paused. Thorgils stood motionless before her, his head had sunk to his chest, and he was still holding the milk cup in his hands.

"Well, come." Thjodhild helped him to lift the cup. After he'd drunk his fill, he let himself be lifted onto her lap. He leaned his head against her chest. "Father ... is ... Leif," he said clearly, breathing between each word.

"I've heard as much, even if I don't want to believe it." She thought of the boy's mother, and her anger rose. The woman had taught her son two sentences as proof of origin and then sent him to his father like cargo, just like that! An infant! *Couldn't she at least have waited until he was grown? Or did she want...?* Thjodhild considered the boy's strange appearance. Deformed children were left to the mercy of wild animals. Is that what the mother expected from the father? "Oh, Leif, star of my heart, what a heartless woman you caught."

Thorgils was asleep. His mouth had not lost its smile. "You are here," Thjodhild whispered, and stroked his dark, curly locks. "So I'll take care of you. You won't starve with us."

Determined, she carried the boy to Leif's bedroom and covered him. "When your father returns," she muttered, "he'll decide about you. But before that, he'll have to consult me." At the door, she was seized by a sudden realization and almost tripped. "I am a grandmother. Oh, no."

*Every rebellion against providence*—Thjodhild caught herself—

*against the will of God only costs strength.* Looking forward was the only way in which happiness might one day be regained. She picked two older, experienced maids. "New blood has arrived. You two will take care of the child."

With no further explanation, she commanded that the sack with the children's clothes be brought from the storage shed, as well as bathtubs and soft cloths for drying and changing. "And look for the toy box!"

With the most urgent tasks assigned, Thjodhild tucked a strand of hair back under her bonnet and looked hesitantly toward the hall's doorway. *Not yet,* she decided. *Duty first. I'll see the priest tomorrow.*

Thjodhild opened the door to the infirmary. "Are you awake?"

A rattling moan came from the bed. Thjodhild lit a second oil lamp and checked the warmth of the bed stone under the blanket before she spread some grease on her husband's cracked lips. "You'll be all right. You just have to be patient."

Erik took the news of the new member of his family with indifference. Since the accident, he'd been confined to bed. His right arm was swollen and blue all the way to his fingers and could not be moved. Every deep breath went like a knife into his shoulder and back. Sweat ran down his face as soon as he even tried to move his body. "Show me the boy later." He coughed and closed his eyes in pain.

At dinner, Thjodhild informed her children. "So be considerate. I'm counting on you."

A short time later, she led the freshly bathed boy, dressed in Leif's gown, into the hall. He toddled along beside her on bony legs.

At the sight of him, the others' jaws dropped.

"My little one, this is your aunt Freydis, and these are your uncles Thorvald and Thorstein. Tell them your name!"

The spherical head wobbled alarmingly. "I ... am ... Thorgils. Father ... is ... Leif."

No sooner had he spoken than Thorvald turned away. "Where did you get this, Mother?"

Thorstein snorted, "He looks like a troll."

"Shame on you!" Thjodhild's admonishment did not help much; both fled to the great fire where they continued to laugh.

Freydis crouched before her nephew. "You have a beautiful head," she purred. "Like a cheese ball. You must be careful it doesn't roll away. And what fine toes and fingers I see there. Which spider did you pull them off?" Lured by the soft singsong, Thorgils stroked her nose. "So you like this, you little ugly bastard."

"Enough!" Annoyed, Thjodhild pulled Freydis up by her collar. "I'm glad if you want to make friends with him, but don't speak that way to him. He can understand you."

Thorgils pressed himself against Freydis's skirt and wrapped his arms around her hips. "You see, Mother, he doesn't understand, but he knows where a man likes it."

"Oh, girl." Thjodhild shook her head. *I agree with your father on one thing*, she thought. *We must find you a husband as soon as possible.*

"This is Leif's son," Thjodhild pleaded. "You'd be helping him and me if you looked after him from time to time."

In Freydis's brown eyes the strange light flickered, just for a moment, then it went out again. "Of course. Don't worry." She briefly touched her mother's hand. "And thank you for trusting me. It doesn't happen often."

Thjodhild nodded and went to her sons. Behind her, she heard Freydis say to her nephew, "You'll probably never get rid of that grin. Oh-ho, what a taste in women, my proud brother must have, to result in such a splendid creature. But we'll feed you for a while. Otherwise, nobody's going to want to eat you later."

The next morning Freydis carried her nephew over to the cemetery with her mother. The priest had rolled up his robe sleeves and was sealing the northern wall of his new house with sod. "Welcome in the name of the Lord," he called out to the women.

"Thank you, Father."

Ernestus reached out his hand to Thjodhild, then to Freydis, hesitated briefly, and stroked the boy's curls. "Who do you bring me, my daughters?"

*Daughter or daughters!* At first, this address had offended Thjodhild's pride, but now she accepted it as one of the priest's quirks. "This is my grandson."

"Not from me," Freydis added quickly. "This was my brother's magic."

"This boy shall be accepted into the Christian congregation." Ernestus beamed. "This pleases the Lord God."

Thjodhild stepped up to him. "Thorgils is baptized. He wears a chain with a cross around his neck. Father, I wanted to ask, how does God deal with children like this? The ones who ... Oh, you see for yourself, this mite can never become a full man."

Immediately sobered, the priest wiped his earth-smeared hands on the robe. "I see." He escorted Thjodhild into the house. Freydis wasn't curious to hear the conversation; she wanted to play with Thorgils at the grave.

"Sit down," the priest suggested. "Please wait a moment!" He kneeled in front of the wooden cross on the wall.

Thjodhild looked around. There was a bed with a hay sack, a table and stools, the fireplace. She'd entered the sparse room only once before, and that was only because Sunday mass had to be celebrated inside due to bad weather. Even though the congregation crowded together, there wasn't enough room for the Christians from Steep Slope and the newly baptized from the neighboring farm. The priest had been forced to repeat the mass four times.

Ernestus returned from his silent prayer, put on a stole, and since there was no other stool, he leaned against the wall. "I will not deny how deeply moved I am by your visit. So far, I've baptized, I've celebrated mass, and considering how short a time I've been here, it's already been a blessing. Today, however, you come and ask your first question of faith, and with that, I may truly begin my service here in the name of the Lord, for he answers through my mouth."

Impressed by the solemnity in his voice, Thjodhild asked quietly, "And what does God say about such crippled beings?"

"Blessed are the meek, for theirs is the kingdom of heaven. Do you understand? Thorgils is also a creature of God. He loves him."

Thjodhild pressed on. "So, he must not be left out in the wilderness."

"God forbids it."

"That's good." She'd always despised the custom, and now the new faith agreed with her. She felt strengthened and wanted to show her gratitude. "When I think of our long winter..." she began. "And looking at this confinement here, wouldn't it be better for our God and his family to have their own dwelling place?"

"You mean a church?" It took Ernestus's breath away. "My daughter!"

Thjodhild stood. "It will be done. You have my word. It'll be built against your house, with a door in between so you can warm up the worship room before mass. Those who are cold won't be able to listen to you for long."

"My daughter."

"I'm not—" She paused and smiled. "It's all right. Tonight, I'll send some servants to you. They're to mark out the outlines immediately. We'll have to hurry before the first snow."

The priest hesitated. "And you think your husband will not object?"

Thjodhild raised her chin. "*I* am the mistress. Until Erik is well again, I run the farm. I alone."

Her back straight, Thjodhild left the dwelling. Outside, her daughter played with the boy, rolling him back and forth in the grass, and he bleated happily like a lamb.

"Imagine, Uncle, if only we'd brought four ewes and a strong ram on our journey!" Leif pointed over the green hills of the headland and the mouth of the river in the bay. "I'm sure within three years, a large herd would be bleating here."

Tyrkir found it challenging to follow his steps. "You're like your father," he teased. "As soon as we'd built our first house in Greenland, he was running around, and though there was nothing but wilderness, he saw sheep and goats grazing, horses jumping, and cows bellowing in the barn. No, boy, let's be thankful we've found this blessed land and that we can already rejoice in a solid roof over our heads." Out of the corner of his eye, he watched his godson. *Above all, I am relieved to see you so full of energy.*

Leif's sudden cramp and shortness of breath lasted the rest of the day and into the night. By the next morning, it had subsided. As after a binge, he'd struggled out of his fur blankets with a heavy head. Tyrkir had sensed the power that had reached for Leif and was sure his godson knew it, too, but neither of them dared to mention Thorgunna for fear she could be summoned just by speaking her name.

"We should be satisfied," he murmured. "Winter can come now."

"I don't think it's going to be cold." Leif combed through his bright red mane. "Have you noticed how long the days are here? How much strength the sun has? And it's already the middle of September! I bet there's hardly any snow in winter. And no frost at all." He stretched his back and let his muscles ease. "Life lasts longer in my country, Uncle."

"It's not that miraculous," Tyrkir said drily.

On the way back, they met some of their boatmen who'd caught salmon farther up the river. Full of pride, they showed off their catch. "Nobody back home will believe this, my lord!" Even the smallest fish was bigger than the thickest salmon in Eriksfjord.

Tyrkir pointed to a particularly silvery one with shimmering blue-green scales. "Such was the salmon that Loki, the devious one, must have turned into when he fled from the gods."

"And you say there are no miracles in my country." Leif smirked. "Look closely. There's another one! Every day we'll find another one."

The area had to be thoroughly explored, so Leif divided his team in two. He led one group himself and put Tyrkir and Egil in charge of the other. Every day, one band set off. The order applied to all: "Stay within shouting distance at all times. Never go so far away that you can't return before dusk!"

But on the evening of the third day, when Egil and his group reached the house on the hill, exhausted and breathless, Tyrkir was missing!

In a wild rage, Leif shouted, "Where is my uncle?"

"I don't know. I don't understand it either."

"You idiot!" Leif pushed Egil in the chest. "You fucking idiot!" Driven by worry, he hurled the fellow explorer back and forth until Egil fell to the ground. "Why didn't you watch out for him?" Leif yelled. "No one is worth more to me than my uncle." He stared into the horrified faces of his men. "I don't need any of you!"

With the next breath, he paused and regained his composure. "No, I'm sorry. I don't mean it. I'm just worried about Tyrkir." He reached out to Egil. "I'm sorry, friend!"

"Already forgotten."

"Can you remember approximately where you last saw the German?"

They'd penetrated deeper to the south, crossed a deciduous forest, and had reached a long valley basin covered with bushes and shrubs. "The air was so stuffy, we could hardly breathe, and because everyone was sweating, we were looking for some shade." Egil shook his head. "When we left after a rest, the pilot was gone." They'd called, waited, screamed, and searched in vain. "I just can't understand it."

Leif looked at the sky. The sun was already leaning to the west. "There are still a few hours of light." Determined, he chose twelve men from his own group, then turned to Egil. "You lead us."

Running, they soon reached the edge of the forest. The search party spread out into a chain. Meanwhile, the shouting and noise only scared the birds out of the treetops. They'd almost reached the middle of the forest when Egil stopped. "Do you hear that?"

Leif nodded. There was a strange singsong coming from somewhere nearby. The two men silently signaled to each other, pulled the axes out of their belts, and crept on, crouching, always making sure one of them stayed covered while the other scurried to the next tree trunk. In that fashion, the men worked their way to the edge of a small, mossy clearing. The singing could now be heard clearly. Dry branches cracked loudly. Ready to attack, they gripped their ax shafts tighter.

Beyond the clearing, branches were swept aside, and from the bushes, Tyrkir stepped into view, wobbling slightly. "No more need until the morn, no more thirst until dawn." He backed up the beat with large flaps of his arms. "No more need until the morn, no more thirst..."

"Uncle!"

Tyrkir interrupted his chant. When Leif rushed toward him, he grinned and ran his sleeve over his sweaty face. "Youare—you arereallyclever. I'mnotjustsayingthat." Though he tried hard, he couldn't manage the pauses between the words, and so one merged into the next. "Everydaybringsamiracle. That'sright. AndIhave foundthegreatestmiracle."

"Where the fuck have you been?" Leif wavered between amazement and anger. "Why did you leave the men?"

"Because I had too much of the miracle. But now my head is clear." He carefully opened the linen pouch on his belt and brought out a handful of yellow-red berries. Some were chapped or wrinkled, but most were round and plump. His finger stroked the shiny skin. "These make our journey truly worthwhile. Taste, my boy, taste!"

Leif chewed a berry. "Not bad." He took another one. "Sweet and slightly ticklish on the tongue as if fermented..."

"Not bad?" Tyrkir gave Egil a taste, but the man's enthusiasm wasn't sufficient, either. "You numbskulls. In every berry, there's a bit of wine, you understand? They don't grow on vines, but on bushes. But they are grapes. All I have to do is squeeze them, and I have wine. That's it!"

Leif clapped his hands. "Now I know what my country will be called. Because Thorgunna paralyzed me, I did not get the chance. In honor of you and your wine, Uncle, I christen it Vinland!"

"Really?" Touched, Tyrkir stuffed the rest of the delicacies into his mouth. "You're a good boy."

"And happy to have you back." Leif hugged him. "We will dig up these bushes so you can grow wine at home. Uncle, you have no idea—" The laughter died away. Leif grabbed his throat, gasping for breath. "The blue silk," he gasped, and pointed to the edge of the clearing. "There. There is her canopy bed..." Tyrkir managed to hold his godson up for a while, but eventually, they both dropped into the moss.

The summer in Iceland had been wet. Despite all the prayers to the new God, the longed-for dry season came very late, and the landowners on the shore of the Breidafjord could only begin the hay harvest in September. Every hand was needed.

Thurid, the small, chubby housewife of the farmer at Frodisach, had not slept for three nights. It wasn't the wet grass, but jewelry, clothes, and shoes that robbed her of her sleep. The treasures belonged to the noblewoman Thorgunna. She'd arrived from the Hebrides on an Irish merchant sailboat, and she'd been waiting impatiently in the harbor for days to continue her journey to Greenland.

Thurid had only been allowed to take a brief look at the treasures. She'd wrestled with the urge, but her curiosity and craving were stronger, and today she climbed aboard determinedly. "There will be no favorable wind before next spring," she began cautiously.

"Believe me, I know."

With her eyes fixed on the large, iron-fitted chest, she made her offer. "Why don't you come and live with us at Frodisach for the long winter?"

"It's not my habit to fraternize with peasants." Thorgunna paced back and forth before the housewife, her hips swaying. "Nevertheless, I agree out of necessity. However poor your dwelling may be, it's certainly more comfortable than this dirty tent here on this ship."

"Does that mean you'll stay?"

"I will."

The servants had picked up the luggage, and Thurid had shown Thorgunna to her chamber. Now she stood at the threshold with her mouth half open, her heart beating. Finally, the locks clicked, and Thorgunna slowly opened the wooden lid. First, she took a white cloth embroidered at the edges from the chest and spread it over the hay-stuffed mattress.

"May I feel, please?" Devoutly, Thurid let her hands run over the sheet. "So wonderful."

"This is the finest English linen, my dear."

Silk cushions appeared and elicited ecstatic cries from the farmer's wife.

"I need four ropes and four long sticks." No sooner were the words said than the requested objects were at hand. "Fasten one of the ropes to each corner of the chamber ceiling." The mysterious tone in her voice raised the tension. Solemnly, Thorgunna pulled a miracle of blue silk from her treasure chest.

At first, Thurid did not understand. She threaded the loose ends of the rope through the eyelets according to the lady's instructions. When at last the stretched fabric floated above the bed, Thurid hardly dared breathe. "What is this?"

"Don't be so impatient!"

Thorgunna stretched out her arms, grabbed the bulging edges, and as if by magic, the curtains fell.

"Never," the farmer's wife murmured. "Never have I seen anything so precious."

"I would be amazed, too, my dear. This is a bed canopy under which I like to rest."

"'Under which I like to rest...' Oh, what pretty words you have. I envy you"—Thurid swallowed violently—"for your language." But she could not hold back. "Because you own this canopy, these pillows, and this shawl." Over and over, she licked her lips. "How much? I mean, sell me everything. I must have the whole bed."

Thorgunna's eyes darkened, and laughter gurgled from her throat. "Where are your wits, you vain little peasant? There's a divide between us. I will not leave heaven to you and sleep on a hard litter myself."

"I don't understand. Tell me your price. We can offset it against the cost of your board."

Thorgunna stared at her coldly. "You forced your hospitality on me, so I will pay for lodging at my discretion." The gold ring on her finger flashed. "Don't even think about my canopy!"

Just one moment, then Thurid had swallowed the insult. "Good, good. But maybe you could sell me some of your jewelry?"

Thorgunna's fingers stroked over her bosom, playing with the gold fibulae of the strap dress, touching the pearl necklace, and finally checking the silver combs in her pinned-up hair. "I think you'd better just look, my dear, for it takes a well-shaped body to make them really shine."

"Please, don't say such things. I'm a respected, well-regarded woman. We have forty servants, and I have more than twenty maids under me."

"Oh, I'm sorry." Thorgunna gave her a radiant smile. "How could I be so rude?"

Immediately reconciled, Thurid pointed to the scarlet cloak. "But I'm sure you'll lend me this wonderful piece for church on Sunday."

"I'm so sorry." Thorgunna pressed her full lips into the wool fabric. "It was a gift from the lord of my heart. I will not desecrate it."

Tears came to the housewife's eyes. "But there must be something you can give me."

"Don't be impatient, my dear!"

No sooner had the farmer returned from the meadows that evening than his wife ran to him. "Wash yourself, Thorrod. Put on a fresh shirt, even your Sunday jerkin. We have a distinguished guest. A lady. She'll be staying with us through the fall and winter."

"How much will the woman pay for room and board?"

"I don't know. Thorgunna wants to set the price herself."

The master of Frodisach narrowed his eyes. "I don't like the sound of that."

His wife raised her finger threateningly. "Don't be unkind to her. Now wash."

Before dinner, Thorrod greeted their guest flatly: "Welcome to my house." He was about to turn away, but Thorgunna held fast to his hand.

"At first, I was dubious." Her gaze slid pleasantly from his sharply cut, light-bearded face to his broad shoulders, touched briefly on his sinewy body, and returned to his eyes. "But now," she cooed, "I'm glad to have the protection of such a strong man during the long winter months."

"What?" Almost startled, the farmer pulled his hand back to safety. "Yes, I'm glad, too," he muttered. He did not offer Thorgunna the seat of honor next to him but assigned her the stool on the other side of the table.

Thorrod did not take part in the women's chitchat about English fashion. When nothing but the head and bones of the fish were left, he cleared his throat. "We should come to terms at once. The food and drink are—"

"How right you are," Thorgunna interrupted, smiling over to him under her eyelashes. "I know a lot about spices. If your wife allows, I'd be happy to give you a sample soon. My recipes for mead and beer are especially esteemed by all the gentlemen."

Thorrod tugged at his shirt collar. "That's not at all what I mean."

After a sharp look, Thurid intervened. "My husband is satisfied."

Now the farmer stretched out his chin. "Our year was terrible, so be frank. How much will you pay us for lodgings?"

"If I'm being honest, I have to be very frugal with my travel funds." Before the peasants could say anything more, she added, "I was hoping to earn board and lodging through work." Like little snakes, she let her fingers play. "These hands can work wonders. If you're not completely satisfied with me, I'll compensate you out of my fortune."

The fact that she had any chopped silver at all reassured the farmer. He took his time with his answer, and finally his mouth twitched in scorn. "Agreed. We'll try it for a few days. You can go to the meadows with the woman and the maids. The grass needs to be turned."

"Into the hay? Me? Are you trying to offend me?" Thorgunna soon recovered her composure. "Oh, I see. You want to keep an eye on me at all times. Very well. I'll prove to you wherever you go that I'm better than you expect me to be."

On the third morning, a clear, deep blue sky stretched over the Breidafjord. The morning sun made the top of the Snow Rock Glacier glow. There was no mist mantle; not even a hazy veil lay on the shoulders of the capricious mountain. Like a guard, he seemed to stare down into the valley of Frodisach.

The peasants set out early. Thorrod gave his instructions, ordering the servants to bring in the dried hay. The women were to turn the still-wet grass. He led Thorgunna to the large meadow near the farm and divided the area into three strips. "You take the middle section. I wonder how long your hands will be able to hold the rake."

Like the other women, she wore a loose, gray smock shirt, her plait of hair hidden under a cloth. "You mock me," she snapped. "I am your maid now, but it won't help you—I always win in the end. Before spring comes, you'll be on your knees."

"Don't be so sure." He clenched his fist. "You think I don't know what you're up to? You can't make me restless. By God Almighty, I have a wife, and that's enough for me." He quickly crossed himself and ordered, "Work well and you'll eat well!" And with that, he went to check on the other women.

"The devil may take you," Thorgunna said through clenched teeth. She rammed her rake into the grass, whirled it up, and struck the blade into the grass again.

Around noon, she declined her break, continuing to work, and even refused water. Shaking her head, Thurid and her maids watched Thorgunna from the edge of the meadow. "She does the work of three of you."

In the late afternoon, a dark cloud appeared over the fjord, clenching above Frodisach like a massive fist.

"It's going to rain," Thorrod yelled to the women. "Pile the grass so at least some of it stays dry, then run to the house!"

They hurried to gather haystacks. The cloud sank deeper and deeper, blanketing Frodisach in darkness. Now, the edge of the meadow was barely visible.

"Enough! Make sure you don't get wet!"

Maids and servants left carts and tools behind, running for shelter under the canopy of the barn.

"Where is Thorgunna?" Thurid asked.

Thorrod pointed over to the meadow. "That cursed woman!"

Despite the impending storm, she'd stayed outside, had not piled up any hay, and continued to swing the rake tirelessly. "The woman is willful."

Darkness was spreading. All that remained was a gray silhouette of the lonely figure in the meadow.

The cloud opened, releasing a torrent, silent yet so fierce that the farmers huddled together afraid. And then the storm broke off. The cloud became a fist again, rising and drifting away toward the snowy glacier. The day became brighter. The farmer stepped outside and stared at the cloud, watching as it shrank until it disintegrated into nothing and the sun shone brightly over Frodisach again.

"Th-Thorrod! There! A m-miracle," stammered the housewife

as she pointed to the meadow in horror. "Oh Holy Mary, protect us!"

Blood—a deep red puddle—had spread on the field. And in the middle of it, Thorgunna was working, bloodstained from head-scarf to feet. She struck the rake, threw up the sticky hay, and struck the rake again.

"Never mind her," Thorrod whispered. "Go back with the maids and tear up the piles so our hay won't spoil!"

After an hour, the blood was gone, and the smell of the harvest spread, but the middle part of the meadow did not dry. Thorgunna waded ankle-deep in bloody hay, raising and lowering the rake. Red sweat ran down her dirt-grimed face.

Cautiously, Thurid ventured toward her. "Do you know...? I don't know... The miracle? What does it mean?"

Without pausing, Thorgunna said calmly, "The blood rain is for one of us. Death is near."

As evening approached, she walked to the courtyard, washed at the well, stripped off her headscarf and gown, and lay down under the blue-silk bed canopy. Soon, a shudder went through her body. She gasped for breath, reaching for her neck as if strangled by an invisible force. The fight continued, and only toward morning did Thorgunna find rest on her pillows.

The master of Frodisach entered the chamber. He placed his rake against the wall, still wet with blood. "Maid, it is time. The hay is waiting!"

She shook her head.

"Are you trying to avoid work? First, this sickness, then the next, and so on?"

"Rest assured, except for this one, I will have no other disease." Thorgunna tried to smile. "A woman knows when she has lost. Listen, Thorrod, you with the chaste heart. Because you're so incorruptible, I want to entrust you with my last will before my strength fades. Are you prepared to dispose of my estate and myself as I wish?"

"If it really comes to that?" Thorrod wiped his mistrust aside, and assured her, "I am a man of my word."

"As soon as I draw my last breath, you will take me to Church Hill. Let the priest sing a requiem mass over my body, and there I will lie in consecrated ground. I know that in this place, many Christians will gather for prayer one day. Now, for my possessions."

Thorrod stepped closer to the canopy bed. She reached for her neck again, struggled, and only after a while did she manage to speak "Give the scarlet cloak to your wife—she will be content with it. She must have nothing else, only the cloak. Take enough of the silver to pay for my board and my funeral."

She kissed the gold ring on her finger. "This memento shall accompany me to the churchyard. But the rest, you must burn."

"Are you sure?" The farmer did not understand her instructions. "With your wealth, you can do many good things, here on Frodi-sach, or leave it to the church."

She raised the ring, looked at it, and her eyes began to flicker. "You do not know me, proud Thorrod. My money, the jewelry, the belt of ivory, my clothes, and above all, this canopy, into the fire!" Her voice grew stronger. "My possessions will bring happiness to no human, do you hear? If even a piece of it is not burned, terror and sorrow will haunt your farm."

The blood had drained from Thorrod's face. "No, not that. I swear I'll settle everything as you wish. Everything."

Thorgunna stared into the silky blue canopy. "One more thing." She soundlessly moved her lips.

"I cannot understand you."

She waved her finger at him, and he kneeled next to her bed. "What else do you want to tell me?"

Then she turned her head to him. In her face lay triumph. "You little peasant," she said coldly. "Didn't I promise you? Before spring comes, you will be on your knees before me. Now I have you there. Because, in the end, Thorgunna always wins." With a short laugh, the sparkle in her eyes went out.

The spray foamed before the bow, shimmering across the stern; Tyrkir stood with his legs apart and tasted the salt on his lips and tongue. Behind him, the men leaned into the lines and offered full sail to the southwesterly wind. For an hour, he had hoped for it, but now there was no doubt. "Land! Land!" The pilot waved to the helm and pointed forward again. On the horizon lay a dark coastal strip, and above it rose the majestic ice ridge with its countless snow-covered peaks. "Greenland!"

The call lifted every heart. Soon the crew cried out as if from one throat: "Greenland! Home!"

Immediately, Leif let Egil relieve him at the tiller. He jumped from the afterdeck, dove under the yardarm, ran across the cargo of timber, and swung himself onto the planks by the dragon's head. "Uncle! We made it." He grabbed Tyrkir around his hips, whirled him around, and put him back on his feet. "Only he who returns can claim to have discovered a new land."

"Very clever, boy." Tyrkir laughed and let himself be carried by the high spirits. "But more than that, you've extended the edge of the world a little farther west."

"Yes, and there are no giants there, but huge trees. Uncle, the logs we're carrying are enough to build three ships. Even with the rest, we can still make a profit." He stopped. "Yes, it would be wise to—"

"Don't you dare!" Tyrkir growled. "I've had enough. First to Norway. Four years! Then straight to Vinland. Almost a year again. Put that thought right out of your mind. Not with me. I want to go back to my bed."

"And plant your shrubs, I know. In every berry is a sip of wine."
He crowed. "I can still see you stepping out of the bushes into the
clearing, singing. Oh, Uncle. And I was right—there was hardly
any frost. We cut wood all winter long." He went up to the dragon's
head and looked over to the rocky coast. After some time had
passed, he sighed. "Yes, we had a good time in my country. And
now? What awaits us at home?"

Tyrkir stayed silent, running his fingertips thoughtfully along
his scar from his mouth to his ear and back. Since the attack last
September, the invisible power had never again reached for his
godson. Ingva, Egil's sister, had been mentioned now and then
during the evenings by the fire, and Leif had openly admitted that
he liked the young woman.

Yes, they had even both uttered the name Thorgunna without
consequences. Had the sorceress let him go? Tyrkir thought so, but
the final proof was still missing. *Whether her curse is indeed broken,
we may soon find out. Until then . . .*

"Uncle!" Leif shielded his eyes, then pointed to port. "There on
the skerry, isn't that a knarr?"

Immediately, the pilot was beside him. "All I see is the reef," he
murmured. Both stared intently at the wave crests. Only when
the *Falcon* was carried up from a wave valley did they recognize
not only a ship but also people waving over to them from the
skerry.

"Those people are in trouble!" Leif ran to the helm, took over
the tiller again, shouting the order to tack against the wind. He
dropped anchor as close to the rock as possible.

The knarr was stuck with a broken mast and torn hull between
high, angular boulders. Fifteen shipwrecked men stretched out
their hands, laughing and crying at their rescuers.

"Who is your leader?" roared Tyrkir through the funnel of his
hands.

A stocky man broke away from the crowd. "I, Thorir, envoy of the Norwegian royal court! Who commands your ship?"

"Leif, son of Erik Thorvaldsson! Get ready! We'll bring you aboard."

The dinghy was launched. The surf in front of the dangerous reef demanded bravery and daring. Soon, strong arms were pulling the last of the weary sailors over the *Falcon's* gunwale.

"God is great," the envoy said on a sigh. He stretched out his hand to the young skipper. "My mission is to visit the gode of Greenland, and now his son rescues me from the sea." The man fell to his knees. "God is great."

Leif cast a fearful look at his uncle, and then asked, "What does the king want with my father?"

Tired, Thorir waved him off. "I have to find out how Christianity is faring in Greenland. But that's not important right now."

"You're lucky," Leif said. "I mean, that you ran into me first."

The envoy didn't understand the implication; he was almost asleep. "Yes, fortune. You are my savior," he murmured. "You are Leif the Lucky." And the man's lids fell shut.

"Did you hear that, Uncle? He's coming to check on us. If he finds that Father rejects the new faith, what then? Knowing King Olaf, he will send his berserker hordes."

"Wait and see! But I agree with him on one thing." Tyrkir smiled. "Whoever discovers a country, whoever fishes people out of the water, has earned this name. Yes, Leif the Lucky is returning to Greenland. And may God grant us the mercy of bringing happiness to Steep Slope."

The envoy only woke when the *Falcon* had long since sailed through the narrows of the towering coastal cliffs into the interior of the fjord. Gentle hills and birch woods welcomed them. While Egil cared for the other castaways, Leif brought dried fish and water to the envoy.

"Thank you!" Thorir ate, drank, and could not get enough of the landscape. "I would never have expected to find this blooming splendor behind the hostile stone crust out there on our skerry."

"You haven't been to Vinland." With a forced smile, Leif sat with him. He painted pictures of extensive deciduous forests and salmon-rich silver rivers. "There are wheat fields there that no man has sown. Honeyed dew drips from the blades of grass. And even in autumn, the sun burns the skin." He had saved the best until the end. "We found berries, and in each one was a sip of wine."

Thorir sighed. "You rave as if you had discovered paradise."

"A fitting name for my Vinland." Leif sat straighter. "To your task. Last spring, I made a promise to King Olaf to spread Christianity here. Isn't it too soon to be checking on my progress—"

"Olaf Tryggvasson is dead," the envoy interrupted. Before Leif could process the news, Thorir added, "Now Erik Jarl and Sven Jarl rule over Norway. Two kings. They seem to me to be even more intolerant than Olaf was. Right after their coronation, they sent me here. I'm to appear at the June Thing." His gaze became probing. "You've kept your oath, yes?"

"Certainly." Leif let the silence stretch between them. "There was some resistance, as was to be expected, but the success was already evident before I left for my trip."

"That reassures me. Yes, the new faith is unstoppable. I'm looking forward to meeting the famous Erik Thorvaldsson."

"No! Anything but that," Leif blurted out. "My father has . . . well, he is . . . To tell you the truth, shortly before my departure, he fell and injured himself badly."

"I'm very sorry to hear that."

"Yes, I'm very worried." Leif's voice became surer again. "Since I don't know how he's recovered, I must first check on Steep Slope alone. I suggest you stay on the next farm for the time being. It belongs to the father of my friend Egil."

The envoy nodded. "I'm sure we can find a way before the Thing. I can't wait too long."

"Certainly," Leif agreed, "and now I have to relieve my friend at the tiller. You should enjoy the journey after all the fear you've endured."

He climbed to the afterdeck, explained the circumstances to Egil, and when the neighbor's son nodded, he embraced him.

# ERIK

A light easterly blew from the glacier down into the fjord. The sail had to be furled. The farmhands pushed the long oar blades through the portholes in the gunwales, and the knarr glided across the water. People stood on the shore waving, and as soon as they heard about the discovered land, they cheered Leif. Half an hour from home, the *Falcon* anchored below the neighboring farm.

Ingolf Arnesson proudly greeted his eldest, and mother Solveig wept. Ingolf offered both hands to the skipper and the pilot. "I gave you a boy, and you bring me back a man."

"And a rich man to boot." Leif beamed. "A third of our cargo is his." He skillfully combined this generosity with the request to provide food and shelter for the envoy and his flock.

"You are most welcome," Ingolf said, but a deep wrinkle furrowed his forehead. "I, too, think it would be appropriate for you to return home without guests for the time being."

"How's Father?"

Ingolf shook his head and finally sighed. "Maybe he'll come alive again when he sees you and his old friend."

"He has to get better." Leif clenched his fist. "He will be fine." The freedom of the past months was now tinged with bitterness.

The distribution and unloading of the cargo could wait, Tyrkir suggested. "Let's go right away!"

He'd noticed that Ingva had been missing at the welcome. Leif hadn't asked about her, either. They were both all the more surprised to see the young woman waiting on the beach. She stood there in a deep green skirt, wrestling with her silver brooches, hastily straightening her comb.

Tyrkir smiled. *How in love she is. She quickly threw herself into her Sunday best.* But he feared Thorgunna's power. *What will happen to Leif? Should he intervene?*

Too late. With a bright red face, Ingva took a few steps toward Erik's son, then stopped again. He beamed at her. "I have thought of you sometimes."

"Me too. Very often."

"You've become even more beautiful."

"You really think so?"

"Oh, yes. You're beautiful, Ingva."

Her blush deepened. "My father thinks I should leave the house soon. I wanted to tell you that."

Leif grabbed his throat. Tyrkir's breath faltered, but his godson only scratched his chin beard. "That's good to know. I'll see you soon, Ingva."

Then she sighed and ran over to her family.

The spell seemed to be broken. Tyrkir was so relieved that he barely managed to climb over the side of the ship on his own. Leif had to drag him up on deck. "Are you all right, Uncle?"

"Yes, it's nothing." Tyrkir cast his eye over his godson. "Wipe that grin off your face, boy! Be grateful, for only now are you truly Leif the Lucky!"

Horn calls, low and long, then chopped off, and long again. They sounded across the bay and made their way up to the farm. Everyday life dropped out of its routine. Erik's younger sons stormed toward the skipper and his pilot. "Have you found the land?"

"What does it look like?"

"Is there enough grass?"

"What about water?"

At the edge of the meadow, Thjodhild stroked her son's forehead. "I prayed for you."

And he put his arm around her slender shoulders like a boy. "Your prayers worked, Mother."

She broke away and stepped toward Tyrkir. "I feel as if I had to wait years for you this time, but it was only months—long months."

"Your son is back," he said, noticing how the worries of the past months had carved themselves into her face. "Forgive me for not coming back sooner."

"It was my will." She raised her chin. "And on Steep Slope, the mistress found little time to brood. Come. You must meet Erik in the hall."

Freydis greeted the returnees in the farmyard, giving Tyrkir only the briefest of welcomes.

She beamed at Leif. "At last . . . Our womanizer is back. Brother." She threw herself at his chest. "How I've missed you. And I can't wait to see the look in your eyes."

Leif hugged his sister. "Has a miracle come over you?"

"Yes, right! I've fed it for you—"

"Silence!" Thjodhild sharply said to her daughter. "Not another word! Go to your brothers."

Right at the entrance, she stopped and pointed to the center of the hall. "He knows you're back."

The flames crackled in the great fire. Light twitched on the wood-paneled walls. It smelled of freshly laid birch logs. The returnees approached the high bench with firm steps. There, Erik crouched bent over, his left hand clasping a long pole.

"Father."

Erik raised his head. Joy lit the amber of his eyes, and a smile greeted his son and his friend. Slowly, he put one foot on the step, pushed himself forward, felt for the stamped ground with his other foot, gasped, and with great effort, left the seat. At last, the giant stood half-erect in front of them, a tree, broken in half by the storm, its mighty crown supported by a stick, its right branch hanging limply down as if it no longer belonged to him.

Since Erik said nothing, Tyrkir nudged the young skipper in the side.

Leif stood taller and reported as custom demanded. "Our journey was accompanied by good fortune. We lost no men. Your son returns from the edge of the world and brings you a new, fertile land. It will bring honor and glory to our family."

"Welcome, Son, in the name of..." Erik coughed and continued hesitantly, "Yes, in the name of the great god Thor. Welcome under the roof of your father." The cough became stronger, pain and joy fighting in the gray-bearded face, but finally the smile prevailed. "I am proud of you because, like your father, you have discovered a new shore. Tell me its name!"

"We landed on three foreign shores, but only one of them is worth mentioning. I christened the area Vinland."

"Very resourceful." Erik glanced at his friend. "I'm sure you helped with the idea, Know-It-All."

"Your son was not as vain as you," Tyrkir replied. "Across the sea, there is not one Leif Hill and no Leiffjord." *At least we can still jest,* he thought sadly, realizing that for the first time, he didn't have to look up when they talked to each other. "Besides, you'll soon taste why this country deserves the name."

"Now I know you're back." Erik closed his eyes and when he opened them again, his gaze was tired and lost. "I've been waiting, Know-It-All," he murmured. "Waiting for you."

His tone increased in strength. "Leif, your return relieves me of a great worry. No gode can speak in this state before a gathering of freemen. Therefore, you shall lead the Thing of my Greenland for me in June."

"Father, you will—"

"No, don't say anything. I've had long enough to think about this. It is my firm will." Another cough shook him. "And now I must rest." With that, Erik turned and walked carefully step by step to the sleeping chamber.

Leif had tears in his eyes. Tyrkir wiped his face with the back of his hand. "My proud, strong friend," he whispered.

Thjodhild had come to their side. "Even if the sight frightens you, you must not pity Erik. He despises all pity. And he's not as bad as he was. I give him a daily dose of willow bark dissolved in herbal tea for the pain."

"But, Mother, I see him suffering!"

She touched the arm of her eldest. "I'm not blind. When your father has come to terms with his mind, his body will be restored. Believe me, there's nothing I long for more, for him and for those who have to live here with him. But to free him from his inner prison, for that there is no potion. He must find that strength himself. He's achieved so much in his life. Now he could sit happily in front of the house and play with the little one—" She broke off and laughed. "Oh, what am I saying?"

Freydis giggled and only stopped when her mother shot her a pleading look.

"There will be a feast in your honor this evening," Thjodhild said, turning back to the men. "Until then, you should rid yourselves of the stench of travel. I'd also be glad if no lumps of dirt or vermin from your hair and beard fell into the bowl. From now on, all your food will be seasoned only in my kitchen."

Grinning, the voyagers went outside. Freydis made to follow them, but her mother held her back. "You'll stay by my side. I'll decide the time. Now, do as I say."

Oil lamps bathed the hall in a warm yellow glow. Erik couldn't be convinced to join the celebration. He didn't want to disturb the joy with his appearance and had stayed in bed. Thjodhild ordered her eldest to sit at the head of the table and asked Tyrkir to sit by her side.

Leif lifted his cup. He was about to open the meal when Thjodhild knocked on the edge of the table with her spoon.

"Patience!" She put her hands together, as did Freydis and the brothers, and now finally the men understood and followed their example. In a low voice, she thanked God, the Lord, inviting him to the table as a guest. The amen was spoken by all. Thjodhild winked at her friend and said, "It seems to me that you may not have followed the customs of our Christian faith during your journey."

"Yes, I did," he assured her, but couldn't suppress a smile.

"To our homecoming!" Although it was only sour milk, Leif emptied his cup in one go.

With the chicken broth, the men told of the crossing and the discovery of Rockland. With the fragrant seal roast, Leif served his mother and siblings the white sandy wastes of Woodland. With the fresh salad of leaves and stems of angelica, Leif and Tyrkir took turns approaching the shores of Vinland. And as soon as they'd entered it, they tumbled over each other's words.

Only after many questions and interjections did the family manage to get an idea of the paradise they'd discovered. During dessert, Thorvald stuck his spoon into his brother's berry-sweetened soft cheese.

"Me too!"

Stunned, Leif cut off his tale.

"I want to go to Vinland." The excitement gleamed in Thorvald's eyes. "You could lend me your knarr."

"That's all we need. How far do you think you'll get?" mocked the explorer. "Before you even leave the fjord, you'll have my *Falcon* lying at the bottom with a broken mast."

"You think I couldn't run a ship? I've been at the tiller as far as the trading post." Thorvald grabbed his spoon and waved it threateningly. "If you won't give me your knarr, I'll ask Father."

"And then I get to fish you out of the water as I did with the envoy from the king's court."

"Enough!" Thjodhild snapped. "We'll talk about it later. Today..." She paused, frowning at the great fire.

Tyrkir and Leif also turned.

Freydis stood there, gracious as an angel. She held the child by the hand. The boy's big head wobbled above his shoulders. He was dressed in a white smock, and he was smiling.

"Come on, you gorgeous creature!"

"Aunt." The spider feet set themselves in motion.

"That's a good boy." Freydis led him to the table.

As they approached Leif, he moved his stool back a little. "Who are you bringing?"

Freydis briefly pulled at the boy's curly locks. "Go on!"

The smiling mouth opened, and between each word, he gasped for breath. "I ... am ... Thorgils."

Again, she tugged his hair. "Go on, little one!"

"Father ... is ... Leif."

Leif grabbed at his throat as his sister purred on mercilessly. "Doesn't the sweet one look like a miracle? You have put a fine thing in our nest. Yes, this freak is yours."

Leif gasped for breath, jumped up, and backed away to the wall. He turned and pressed his forehead against the wood paneling.

At first, Tyrkir wanted to follow him, but then he realized that it was not Thorgunna's invisible power again. He looked at Thjodhild helplessly.

She came to him. "Although I'd hoped for a gentler encounter, you know what transpired. I must know the truth. No details, please, only clear answers. Did Leif meet a woman in the Hebrides?"

"I couldn't stop it."

"Did he get her with child?"

Tyrkir felt his scar redden. "Against this Thorgunna—" He saw Thjodhild's stern look. "Yes. That's what happened. She said that she'd send the child to Greenland."

"So, my son is the father. Why did you keep silent? I would have liked to have been prepared to become a grandmother."

Tyrkir wanted to answer, but Thjodhild shook her head. "Later. For the moment, I'm asking for your help. No, I demand it of you. Leif must accept this child, if only out of Christian duty."

Tyrkir immediately agreed, and both crossed the room to him. The conversation lasted only a short time—it required little persuasion—and Thjodhild's brow smoothed. "I'm glad that you've discovered a country, but that you want to grant your protection to this poor mite fills me with pride."

*Maybe he's taken on something of me after all,* Tyrkir thought.

Leif returned to the table, both hands extended to Thorgils. "Come!"

The boy stumbled confidently into his arms. "Father ... is ... Leif."

"Yes, you've found him." He lifted the little body and held him high above his head. "By baptism, you are already a member of our Christian faith. But today, you shall also be accepted according to the customs of our fathers: Thorgils, I recognize you as my flesh and blood. Great God, I swear before you that this son will be a full member of our family from now on."

Thorgils wagged his thin arms; he liked the game and laughed like a bleating lamb.

No sooner had his father put him down than Freydis tore her brother around. "You idiot!" Her lips trembled. "What have you done? Is it not enough that this freak has been polluting our air for months? Do you think I fed him so he'd stay with us forever?"

Thjodhild wanted to intervene, but Tyrkir held her back.

Leif looked calmly into his sister's face. "Get used to it, Sister. This child will be safe with us."

The strange light flickered in her eyes, then quickly disappeared again, and she smiled softly. "As you command, big brother." Without another word, she turned around and danced past the great fire. Her fingers ran over the ax shafts next to the exit, played with the feather tufts of the arrows, and then she was gone.

"She'll calm down," Thjodhild sighed and asked a maid to take little Thorgils back to the women's shelter.

The good mood had been spoiled. Thorvald withdrew, humiliated because his big brother had spoken disparagingly of his skills as a skipper, and Thorstein followed him.

"You should give him a chance," Thjodhild scolded. "He's long since reached manhood, and such a mysterious country whets the appetite for adventure."

"Thorvald has to be patient." Leif took his father's place again. "First, we must use the *Falcon* to recover the cargo from the damaged knarr out on the skerry. I owe it to the envoy."

Full of admiration for her eldest, Thjodhild listened as her son described the rescue. "Leif the Lucky," she repeated quietly. "Let this name clothe you like a festive robe, my boy."

Meanwhile, her concern grew when she heard about the envoy's assignment. "Father Ernestus is very popular. Almost all the families on the fjord have now been baptized. Our church can barely hold the faithful on Sundays. The king's messenger can leave with good news. If only Greenland's supreme gode would not refuse to accept Christianity."

She looked at her friend. "That pigheaded man. His back may be crooked, but when it comes to the gods in Valhalla, he stands tall and firm like a rock in a raging torrent."

"And I hardly blame him." Tyrkir rubbed his scar. "The world has changed around him, then the fall broke not only his body but his soul. Perhaps insisting on the old values still gives Erik some strength. Should we take that from him?" He smiled thinly.

"But as for the spy of the Norwegian kings, I think we have nothing to fear on that front. Without knowing it, Erik himself has found the solution. Leif will open the Thing of the freemen, and the envoy will see the progress of the Christian faith." He pulled an oil light closer and shielded it with his hand. "And in the meantime, we hide our beloved heathen from the man."

As on every morning, Thjodhild's first concern was for her grandchild, but today his bed was empty. She asked one of the two old slaves she'd chosen to care for the little one where he was.

"Your daughter woke him at sunrise," replied the maid. The weather was fine, Freydis had said, and she wanted to ride with Thorgils into the countryside.

"Ride?"

"That's what I understood. Freydis fed the boy and told him about colorful flowers. He stroked her nose, which he always does when he's happy, and then they went over to the stable. Have I done something wrong, Mistress?"

"No, no. It's fine." Thjodhild left the shelter. Freydis had often taken Thorgils with her to play in the meadow. But why hadn't she waited until after their breakfast? And why hadn't she stayed nearby? Thjodhild accelerated her steps. When she reached the stable, she asked one of the hands if he'd seen them.

"That's right. I saddled a bay for the young mistress."

"What else? Tell me exactly what happened."

He scratched his bald head. "She placed the little one in front of her. Oh, yes, then she asked where the willow slope was where we built the walls for the reindeer trap. I described it to her, and she went off with the boy. The young lady was so cheerful. I've never seen her like that. And the boy seemed to be enjoying himself, too."

Thjodhild's heart seized. "How long has it been?"

"A good hour." Thjodhild hurried to the house. Leif lay buried deep under a blanket of fur. She shook him awake. "Get up. Hurry!"

Drowsy, he staggered from his bed.

"Your sister has taken Thorgils out."

"So? After last night, she wants to prove her good intentions."

"I don't think so. Usually, Freydis doesn't take a horse. She plays with Thorgils in the meadow. But today of all days, she rides with him to your reindeer trap? I may be wrong, but you have to go after them. Please!"

Leif gaped at his mother. "That steep slope is no playground." Now he was awake. Just the boots—there was no time for trousers and a belt. As he stormed out, he slipped on a smock shirt, grabbed it over his knees, and jumped onto an unsaddled horse. In a wild tölt he dashed through the blooming meadows, soon reached the juniper bushes, and rushed up into the eastern hills.

The sun stood high. Above the hillside, Freydis squatted next to the child at the edge of the birch forest. "Now raise your arms, you ugly thing," she whispered, and pushed Thorgils's soft woolen doublet up to his neck. Because his head was so huge, she rolled the wool gently over his face. "Your cheese ball has gotten even bigger."

He made a grab for her nose. "Auntie... is... lovely."

"You learned that very well." Freydis loosened the wraps on his stomach and pulled them through his legs. She hesitated for a moment, then smiled patronizingly. "Keep your sandals on, or you'll get poked in your spider feet. Auntie doesn't want to cause you pain."

She reached into the pleated pocket of her dress and revealed an arrow. "Well, there you are. I've brought us a nice toy." She stroked his laughing mouth with the feather shaft and held the arrow high above his forehead.

Thorgils followed it, bending his head to his neck, but the weight made him fall back into the grass, and his big eyes filled with fright.

Freydis tickled him with the feathers on his neck until he kicked with pleasure again. She stroked his sunken chest.

Several times, she made the shaft bounce on his round belly. "Yes, we have fattened you up nicely. No telling how fat you may still get, you goblin. And who knows, you might live forever. If your flabby father gives you an inheritance, you'll get a wife. Oh, yes, the money will make you beautiful. But you mustn't continue on your legacy. You're four winters old now, and I think that's enough. What do you think?"

Thorgils rolled back and forth. "Auntie . . . is . . . lovely."

"Well, there you go. We agree."

Humming a tune, Freydis took the naked boy in her arms and carried him down the sloping pasture. As the stones narrowed the trap on either side, the meadow came to a point. She set Thorgils down and pointed forward to the gap in the stones. "Over there, heaven awaits you."

The strange light flickered in her eyes, and this time it did not fade away. She tickled his back and Thorgils eagerly stalked in front of her on his spider legs, laughing like a bleating lamb and rowing with his arms. Slowly, but steadily, they approached the narrow opening. When he fell down, Freydis picked him up again, praising how beautifully he walked, and continued to tickle the boy toward the edge of death.

Then Leif appeared on the stone wall. He spied the pair below him, and with one leap he was in the trap, charging down. "Freydis!"

She spun around, then she pushed the boy forward. Thorgils fell, rolled over his head, and rolled on pushed by her.

"Freydis! Freydis! No, don't!"

"Get out of here!"

Leif pushed her aside and threw himself over the naked rolling bundle. He grabbed Thorgils in his arms and stormed back up the slope with him.

Freydis chased after her brother. "You bastard!" she screamed. "You miserable dog! Give me back the brat!"

At the edge of the forest, Leif lay his whimpering son in the grass. With clenched fists, he waited for his sister. She was panting, her face twisted, and no sooner had she reached him than she kicked him between his legs. Her boot caught in his long gown.

Leif grabbed her heel, tore it higher, and Freydis slammed backward into the grass. Immediately, she was back on her feet, hissing and grasping the shaft of the arrow like a dagger.

"Sister." He held out his hands defensively. But that's all he managed to say.

With a wild curse, she rushed forward and stabbed at his abdomen. At the last moment, he managed to grab the sharp point, deflecting the thrust, and snatched the weapon from her.

She didn't give up, attacking again. Leif punched her hard in the stomach.

Doubled over, Freydis fell to her knees, groaned, gasping for breath, and vomited.

Stunned, Leif stared down at her.

"S-so you hit women after all," she stammered between choking and coughing. Freydis raised her head. There was no trace of anger or hate. Only reproach was written in her brown eyes, and her chin trembled. "You shouldn't treat a woman like that. You know that."

Leif crouched by her.

"Don't hit me again," she begged.

"No, calm down." He stroked the hair from her forehead. "You're sick."

"Bullshit." With her sleeve, she wiped her chin. "You didn't hit me that hard."

"That's not what I mean. Why did you want to kill Thorgils?"

"Oh, my brother." She rolled onto her side, leaning her head on her hand. "Because I must help. No, not just you—our family. Until yesterday, I believed you would get rid of that troll right away. All winter long, I was kind to him for Mother's sake. It's not his fault that he's worthless. And it was fun with him, too. But I was only fattening him up for the animals."

Thorgils came crawling toward them. "Aunt."

"Yes, yes, you bug." With her finger, Freydis caressed his curls and sighed. "Look at the brat. I know that Mother's consulted the priest, and he persuaded her that God forbids it, but what does he know about our customs?" Freydis sat up and wrapped her arms around her knees. "Such a creature is a disgrace to us. And since Father won't say anything and you're backing down, I'm the only one left. Our clan must be full of strong, healthy people. If we're not careful, we'll soon have a whole horde of cheese balls like this."

Horrified, Leif shook his head. "Only a man can decide whether a child should be expelled. It is the custom. And I have decided." He waved the arrow at her. "This boy will live with us as my son. He may be weak, but it is God alone who will determine his fate, not you. Do you understand me?"

Freydis raised her eyebrows and grinned.

Angrily, Leif broke the arrow over his knee. He hadn't noticed until that moment, but he'd nicked his hand on the sharp tip of the arrow while defending himself earlier. Now he watched the blood drip, and he looked at his sister, stunned. "When we returned from Norway last year, a servant was lying behind the barn the following morning. He'd fallen onto a hay rake, but he also had a broken arrowhead in his belly. Do you know anything about that?"

"That horny goat." As the memory returned, the tip of her

tongue quickly slid over her lower lip. "It was quite easy. He came out of the shed to pee. All I had to do was wink, and he followed me into the barn. Upstairs, I showed him my tits, and he wanted to prove himself. I stabbed him for that. He didn't scream. Just looked stupid. I put two fingers against his forehead, and he was gone." Freydis giggled.

"Why, damn it? Tell me!"

"Because I wanted to do Father a favor." She batted her eyelashes disarmingly. "You had arrived with the priest, and he was so sad, so I gave him a Christian."

Leif tugged at his hair with both hands. "You killed a man."

"It was just a slave."

He jumped up, stomped to the edge of the forest, and kicked at a bush, sending leaves and branches flying. Behind him, Freydis made the boy laugh with her cooing voice.

Finally, Leif returned. He was no longer just her brother; his face showed that he was the heir to the clan of Erik Thorvaldsson. "Listen carefully. When a woman kills a man with vile intention, she, too, is subject to the law. She will be decapitated or stoned. This sentence can be passed by the Thing court."

His cold tone sucked the blood from Freydis's cheeks.

"You're a vicious murderer, and I'll be the chief justice at the Thing instead of Father."

"You wouldn't dare. I'm your sister."

"Don't count on it, half sister. You are 'only the daughter of a slave.' The fact that you were adopted by my father may just move me to keep your deed from the assembly. But then I must hold a House Thing. You may be cast out of our family, or at the very least, lose your claim to a dowry." He smiled. "And I can already see our proud Freydis living with a poor peasant and giving birth to her children in a smoke-filled hut."

"No, no!" she cried, and struck her own face in horror. Her eyes filled with tears. "Please!" On her knees, she slipped in front of her brother. "You can't do this to me. Please, brother!"

"Unless . . ." He let the silence stretch.

She immediately reached for the straw. "Ask it. Ask for whatever you want. I'll do it!"

Leif took his naked son and pressed him into the sister's arms. "From now on, you are responsible for Thorgils. Until a man marries you, you will guard the boy like your own life, for if something happens to him or if he dies by some accident, you will not receive a bride-price. I swear it."

Freydis could only nod. She pressed the boy to her, caressed him, and kissed the laughing mouth. "Come on, let's get dressed." Carefully, she slipped the wool jerkin over his head.

"Auntie . . . is . . . nice."

Meek as a lamb, she asked the brother, "Shall I carry Thorgils to your horse?"

"Why?" The sudden change in his sister surprised Leif, and despite everything, a smile twitched at the corners of his mouth. "Don't jump over your heart, Sister! You won't last long, anyway. But we have a firm understanding with each other."

She dared to bat her eyes. "And you won't say a word to Mother or Uncle, not even to Father?"

"Not as long as Thorgils is doing well, no." He hurled the arrowhead and feather shaft far away. "I'll ride ahead. You better pick some flowers before you follow, or else no one will believe you went on an outing with your darling."

A drinking horn filled with the best Norwegian mead, maybe two. Erik had asked for it, and Tyrkir had climbed into his storage cellar. He'd sat by the sick man's bed all night engaged in long, intimate conversations in which the mead was their only companion until the first light of dawn.

"And you will help me?" Erik asked. The amber in his eyes gleamed.

"I won't leave you alone."

"What are we waiting for?" Erik smiled, knocked the blanket aside, and slowly put his feet on the floor. He stretched his left arm out to Tyrkir. "Now prove that your strength isn't just in your head and pull me up!"

After a few vain attempts, Tyrkir managed to help the stooped giant to a secure footing. "You'd better take it easy," Erik chided, coughing. After he'd regained his breath, he added, "Call two servants to dress me."

When Erik entered the living hall in a fur-trimmed cape, belted with his sword, and demanding a hearty breakfast, Thjodhild looked at Tyrkir in surprise. "Did the mead not agree with you?"

"It was worth every sip," he assured her in a low voice.

The master of Steep Slope ate sparingly, and with great pleasure. His wife had to cut the bacon into bite-size pieces. Again and again, he asked for a newly filled cup of sour milk.

The strange cheerfulness between the friends worried Thjodhild. "What are you going to do?"

"I haven't been up there for a long time." With his left hand, Erik pushed the cutting board into the middle of the brightly scrubbed tabletop. "It's high time. It's time I checked my dam."

"No! I forbid it," she said quickly, but his reproachful look made her relent. "Forgive me. It's your decision. But in your condition, how will you get up there?"

"Know-It-All will lead the horse." Erik frowned. "Wake my son! He must come with us."

"Even for two men, it will still be hard, especially on the way back."

"We'll see about that."

Outside, in front of the living hall, the saddled horses stood ready. The sun had risen over the glacier, and its rays laid a golden ribbon across the bay. Leaning on his cane, Erik looked at the scene. He crossed to Thjodhild, and with his face close to hers said, "I have not said it for a long time, but thank you. You nursed me. You've always been good to me. Even recently. I simply wanted to say it."

"My proud Erik." She smiled. "I don't want to complain. Not anymore."

"That's good."

With the help of a bench, and pushed by Leif and Tyrkir, Erik got into the saddle. Despite the pain, he cried out, "Today will be a good day!" Then he quickly touched the flanks of his pied stallion and rode ahead, bent over the mane. Leif stayed close to his father's side.

When Tyrkir mounted, Thjodhild reached for the halter of his horse. "Is there something you're not telling me?"

His head shook slightly. "Erik wants to find his happiness."

"So, farewell?"

There was nothing more he could say. Slowly, Tyrkir began to move.

"Wait a little longer. Come back!"

But without turning around, he allowed the horse to fall into a light trot until he'd caught up with his friend.

"What do you think, Know-It-All?" Erik didn't wait for an answer. He spoke to his son of the fresh sprouting grass, thought aloud how wet or dry the summer might be. And in between, he kept saying, "What do you think, Know-It-All?" It's as if he wanted to savor the sentence.

At noon, they'd crossed the vast pastures. In front of them stretched the hills and high up between the rocks stood the dam wall. On its left side, the waterfall sprayed down to the valley. "My work is done!" Erik laughed, though it turned into a fit of coughing. "Know-It-All, I completed my task before you managed even one drinkable swill of wine."

"Wine is not pressed from stones," Tyrkir retorted. "But the berries from the new land..."

"Oh, leave it. We don't want to get into that again." Erik turned to his son. "Before I forget, boy, you shall be my successor. You will lead our family."

"There's still time."

"Don't you dare interrupt your old father," Erik joked, then grew serious again. "I gave your godfather precise instructions last night. Ask him if you don't know what to do. As for the farm, you'll have to come to an agreement with your mother, and we know how strong-willed she is. Be on good terms with her. She'll decide when you can come into your inheritance. Do you understand me?"

"No, Father!" Leif quickly steered his horse closer. He bent deep over the mane and tried to take in Erik's bearded face. "Please look at me. Please look at me."

With great calm, Erik turned his head toward his son. "There's nothing more to discuss. We don't have much time left, so let's enjoy what little there is."

Leif's lips trembled. He turned to Tyrkir for guidance. "Uncle, where are we going?"

"Up to the dam."

Before Tyrkir could continue, Erik said, "So it is, my son. And when we reach the top, I will soon ascend to the very top and be pampered in the hall of the gods with sweet mead and meat from the boiled boar."

"No, Father! No!" Desperate, Leif gave his horse his heels and flew away.

Erik sighed. "What joy I have today. My wife has forgiven me. My son loves me. I can be happy. What do you think, my friend?"

Tyrkir didn't answer.

Below the hills, Leif waited. His cheeks were still wet, but his tears had stopped. "Must you do it?"

"Yes, as long as I still have the strength for it myself, for only if I die a manly death can I go to Valhalla and will not need to go down to the realm of Hel. Now ask no more questions!"

They tied his body tightly onto the stallion's back, pulled and dragged the animal up the steep path, and finally, they had reached the height.

Moaning, the giant lifted his face out of the mane. "Untie me!" With his left arm, he pointed underneath him to the narrow canal for the beam lock. "Every spring, the boulders have to be removed. Otherwise, the ditches in the pastures become blocked. Make sure you do it." His gaze slid over the deep blue lake and remained fixed on the other side of the stream inlet and the stony meadow slopes. "Know-It-All, you know where I want to go."

While Tyrkir led the horse, Leif stayed by his father's side. Erik tried to look at the sky more than once.

"What are you looking for?"

"The white falcon. I had hoped Goddess Freya would come for me. A pity. But never mind, I'll meet her soon."

On the ledge above the lake, they reached the end of the path. Here, Erik had practiced with his weapons when he'd wanted to steel himself for the overpowering enemy who threatened his old world with the cross.

Leif cowered on his hands and knees. Tyrkir gently helped his friend push one leg back over the stallion's croup; carried on Leif's back, Erik finally got out of the saddle. "How good that I don't have to go back up," he joked.

"Stay on your knees, Son! Your father is not as tall as he used to be." Without his stick, Erik's left hand felt over Leif's hair and touched his forehead. "Even though you brought this hypocrite into my land, boy, you are my beloved firstborn, my Leif the Lucky.

May my gods and your god protect you. No, don't look at me. Sit by the lake. There, you'll see our sky in the mirror."

For the last time, the son obeyed the father. As he went down to the water, two ravens sluggishly lifted themselves up and jumped onto the next boulder.

Tyrkir tried to stay cheerful. "If Freya does not come, at least Odin has sent his scouts Hugin and Munin to you, so don't complain." With this, he handed the staff to Erik.

"One more thing, Know-It-All. Please, at least today, let me have the last word!"

Tyrkir silently pulled the sword from the giant's belt loop. He drilled the handle into the ground and secured it with three stones.

They had already said goodbye in the night. Supported by the stick, Erik moved closer until the sharp point flashed under his bent chest. "I am glad, my friend, that you were at my side. Now take care of our Thjodhild! That's all."

For a moment, their eyes locked, and then Tyrkir turned away. It was as if the wind had stopped and only started again after a deep sigh. When the two ravens fluttered up, he thought, *Yes, carry the news and announce to Odin the arrival of the bravest fighter.*

With his upper body lowered, Erik was still held up by the blade; no other support was needed. He'd closed his eyes.

Tyrkir fetched Leif from the shore. "It's all right," he murmured. "Your father wants you to know that."

They lay him on the earth and put the sword on his chest. Tyrkir tore out tufts of grass to seal the orifices of his body according to ancient custom, then thoughtfully refrained from doing so. "Perhaps his soul will find its way to the other heaven."

Together, they piled the burial mound from stone boulders and gave it the shape of a ship. Their tears only dried when the grave was complete, pointing toward the deep blue eye of the lake. Tomorrow, Tyrkir wanted to chisel a rune stone as a memento.

For a long time, Leif stared ahead. At some point, he asked, "What now? I am the lord of Steep Slope. But what now, Uncle?"

Quietly, Tyrkir looked at him. "Marry."

"What?"

He smiled slightly. "I said, you must get married, boy! So it can go on."

"Ingva," Leif murmured. "Her father wants her out of the house." He smiled. "Yes, Ingva is a good woman."

On the way back through the pastures, Tyrkir looked steadfastly at the riderless stallion in front of him. *I never told my friend about my dream*, he thought at one point, saddened by the lucky stone that had fallen into the black sea. He immediately wiped the memory away. How many times had they jumped after it over the edge of the rock and yet had not drowned with it? Perhaps not drowning meant happiness?

They reached the farmhouse in the late afternoon. Tyrkir got out of the saddle. "You take the horses to the stable," he said, and his voice barely obeyed him. "Let me go to your mother alone."

Thjodhild sat in front of the house. Below her, the sun shone from the west, creating a silvery road across the bay. She raised her eyes, but only briefly. "I've been waiting since morning."

Silently, Tyrkir sat down beside her and put his hand on hers. After a while, Thjodhild whispered, "Yes, hold me, please. For a long time."

# INDEX OF NAMES

| | |
|---|---|
| **INGVA** | Daughter of Ingolf and Solveig |
| **KATLA** | Slave of Erik, mother of Freydis |
| **KETIL** | Erik's slave |
| **LEIF ERIKSSON** | Later called Leif the Lucky; eldest son of Erik and Thjodhild |
| **ODD THORGESTSSON** | Son of Thorgest of Breida Farm |
| **SIGRID** | Daughter of Ingolf and Solveig |
| **SOLVEIG** | Wife of Ingolf Arnesson |
| **STYR** | Landlord on the south side of the snowy peninsula; ally of Erik |
| **THJODHILD** | Erik's wife |
| **THORBJÖRG** | Thjodhild's mother |
| **THORBJÖRN** | Thjodhild's stepfather |
| **THORBJÖRN VIFILSSON** | Gode (judge) from the south side of the Snow Rock peninsula; squire of Warm Spring Slope |
| **THORGEST** | Landlord of the Breida Farm by the Breidafjord |
| **THORGILS** | Leif's son with the sorceress Thorgunna |
| **THORGUNNA** | Sorceress (völva) in Drimore in the Hebrides; a Christian |
| **THORROD** | Farmer at Frodisach on the Breidafjord |
| **THORSTEIN ERIKSSON** | Third son of Erik and Thjodhild |
| **THORVALD ERIKSSON** | Second son of Erik and Thjodhild |
| **THURID** | Wife of Thorrod of Frodisach |

| | |
|---|---|
| **TOKE THORGESTSSON** | Son of Thorgest of Breida Farm |
| **TRUDE** | Sorceress (völva) in Drimore in the Hebrides; pagan and adversary of Thorgunna |
| **TYRKIR** | Called Know-It-All; German slave of Erik's, and his best friend. His Christian name is Thomas. |
| **ULF EINARSSON** | Gode (judge) of the valleys by the western Hvammsfjord |
| **VALTJOF** | Lord of Valtjof Farm in Hawk Valley |